ABOUT THE AUTHOR

David Sunderland is British, almost French, and Brazilian by osmosis. His day job entails occasional bureaucratic absurdities but also the privilege of working for a bigger cause, which frequently provides a catalyst for creativity. His literary output over the last 20 years has been eclectic, including poetry (as yet unpublished); satirical plays, songs and sketches (each with unique performances); and Angeland (his first novel). He lives just over the border from Geneva with his impatient and adorable Franco-Brazilian wife and 30-odd plants.

www.david-s.site

'Don't read this book: for the true story see "Angel Catastrophe Now!", on sale in the Mall within a Mall within a Mall.'

Archangel Yuri

'This book is out of date, full of metaphors and it's a work of fiction. Far better to read about me in The Bible or Qur'an.'

Archangel Gabriel

ANGELAND

David Sunderland

Matador
9 Priory Business Park,
Wistow Road, Kibworth Beauchamp,
Leicestershire. LE8 0RX
Tel: 0116 279 2299
Email: books@troubador.co.uk
Web: www.troubador.co.uk/matador
Twitter: @matadorbooks

ISBN 978 1789018 226

British Library Cataloguing in Publication Data.
A catalogue record for this book is available from the British Library.

Printed and bound by CPI Group (UK) Ltd, Croydon, CR0 4YY
Typeset in 11pt Sabon MT by Troubador Publishing Ltd, Leicester, UK

Matador is an imprint of Troubador Publishing Ltd

'Obsession takes you a long way, but you need to make sure you're pointing in the right direction.'

à mon ange

BLUE

PROLOGUE

We angels come to the same places again, and again, but each time the players and we are different, and the positions new. Of course I've seen it all: Archangels making melodramatic landings on aeroplane wings. Souls falling in and out of love. Tiny mishaps to astronomical catastrophes. What seems small might turn out to be big, and vice versa: the real significance is often only revealed with time. Attributing things to fate, or making the most out of the hand you're dealt with – it's all a question of perspective.

But I'm getting ahead of myself. Let us turn to Tony, our human protagonist, who has just become part-angel. He is about to embark on an unusual tour of the realms of angels, and is promising to shake things up for the first time in a long while. The game's afoot...

—— * ——

Tony stepped out of the toilet cubicle into the interior of a plane that was unlike anything he had ever seen in his life.

Although he did not know it, he would be experiencing this reaction rather a lot in his coming adventures.

An elderly man in white robes, a little shorter than Tony but with a face that seemed vaguely familiar, was gingerly approaching him. There were embarrassed hisses of 'Go on, Albert' and 'You've got to tell him' behind the old man as he walked towards Tony.

'Hello, Tony, it's nice to meet you. Well, in fact you don't know me, but I know you rather well. Well, um, what can I say? There's been a terrible and highly improbable mistake and I'm sorry to say that nobody's quite sure of what to do. But I forget myself; it's most rude of me not to introduce myself. I am Albert, your guardian angel.'

During this strange introduction, Tony had had a chance to take in the scene before him, which was just as peculiar. He blinked, thinking for a moment that he was staring at a zebra crossing. Looking back down the plane, it was twice as long and twice as wide as it had been before, with twice as many seats. Everything was illuminated by a strong white light. There was something strange about many of the people. Those in the front row, and those in every alternate row right to the back of the plane, were all motionless as if they were in a photograph. They were frozen in the act of doing all of the regular things people do on a plane, like talking, staring out of the window or simply staring. Not far from the front a flight attendant was pouring out a hot drink to a passenger, but both of them were motionless, and the liquid was suspended in mid-air, defying gravity.

The frozen people were wearing the normal assortment of clothes you would expect on any flight, but in the rows between them there were other people who looked quite different. They all looked rather old and were dressed uniformly in the same white robes as Albert. There was a line of them in the second row, another in the fourth, and another in every

4

other row behind, creating distinctive stripes. And they were moving. Some of them were murmuring to their neighbours, while others were blinking and gently moving their heads like normal passengers. All of them were staring at Tony in a way that made him feel he was about to be interviewed.

Seeing that Tony was in no physical or psychological state to do much more than continue to digest the scene in front of him, Albert continued, 'This will all be rather a shock for you, I should imagine. You will no doubt have many questions, but I need to check how damaged you were during the process of transmutation. How many fingers am I holding up?'

'Three,' said Tony.

'Thank goodness, your basic language skills and perception are functioning,' said Albert. Then he suddenly lunged forward and poked Tony sharply in the chest.

'Ow!' Tony flinched and backed away a step.

'Excellent, excellent, your reactions seem perfect,' Albert gleefully observed.

He was about to open his mouth again when Tony spoke up. 'Now look here, I don't know what's going on here, but this is all too strange for my liking. Is it some funny virtual reality thing?' His hands went up to his eyes as if to pull off a headset, but he was left patting his head as Albert looked on sympathetically.

'It must be a dream then,' Tony went on. 'I should wake up any second now.'

But he did not wake up. Albert hesitated for a second, then said, 'Tony, I need to ask you just one more question and then I promise I will start to answer yours. Just tell me what you remember.'

Tony stopped. He remembered the pain, the light, and spending what seemed like an eternity staggering down the aisle. Then it started to come back to him.

'I remember there was... an angel with big wings.'

5

'OK, we're on the right track!' exclaimed Albert. 'What else?'

'He was standing on the wing. As if he was singing, although as he was outside I couldn't hear anything. But it's starting to get a bit hazy.'

'Fine, fine, you don't need to worry, carry on.'

'Well, I was quite close to the doors in the centre of the plane, so I had a fine view. I remember there was quite a commotion inside as the door opened, and then... the angel stepped through. He was very handsome. He smiled at everyone and...'

'Yes, go on, go on.' Albert had begun to quiver slightly.

Tony hesitated. 'You know, I'm having trouble getting the rest.'

'Oh, well, when one is under a divine presence one's memory can be lost,' Albert interposed. He seemed quite relieved.

'I just don't know...' Tony went on.

'Excellent, excellent,' purred Albert, who was beginning to smile. He rubbed Tony's arm.

'No, I just don't know why he then turned out to be so nasty,' said Tony.

'Oh dear,' said Albert, and his mouth dropped.

CHAPTER 1

The drummer had set up her kit and was now seated facing the rest of the band and waiting. They were making typical mundane small talk before playing, speculating about the upcoming football match, reflecting on how they remembered gaining their 'wings,' or simply enjoying the view from 10,000 metres. Putting a big band on the top of an aircraft entailed certain challenges, including the limited width and the slopes, and the logistics of arranging one's own wings. Fortunately the potentially trickiest aspect of facing a 700-kilometre-per-hour wind was not in question, as the angels were sensibly impervious to air resistance.

When they saw a single white speck appear on the horizon, the band stopped talking, set their instruments, and prepared to start playing. The speck rapidly grew into a very bright and beautifully-manicured angel, who circled the aircraft a few times with impeccable finesse before gently descending onto the tip of the starboard wing. The Archangel Gabriel had arrived. Having adjusted his posture for the most majestic effect, he nodded up at the drummer, who played three quick beats on the cymbals, then one medium one.

Tony was in his seat reading. He overheard someone say, 'Mummy, there's an angel on the wing,' followed by several sharp exclamations and shrieks which sounded unlike those you would hear on a common-or-garden flight.

Tony gazed out from his window seat, just behind the wing. There was indeed an angel, singing rather melodramatically – although inaudible from the inside of the aircraft – and walking slowly from the wing tip towards the main body of the plane. He was certainly quite the stereotypical angel: all in white, with big and powerful wings, and terribly handsome. This was no hysterical mass illusion; the passengers' curious glances had turned to jaw-dropping stares. Very quickly, almost everyone on the plane saw that this apparition defying the normal laws of physics was, without any doubt, an angel. The plane was suddenly filled with expletives and exclamations of faith, while some reacted with open-mouthed incredulity.

The fervour began to shift towards genuine terror for many and, for some, greater religious elation, as it became clear that the angel was steadily approaching the starboard centre doors and looking very much as if he was going to open them. Without giving anyone much time for reflection upon the matter, the door handles slid open. Instead of a blast of explosive decompression, however, the air pressure did not change at all. Instead, a mellifluous baritone voice wafted into the aeroplane, singing something about New York being 'A, Number One'. Few people on an aircraft at 39,000 feet would expect to see an angel walk in through the door singing a Frank Sinatra hit. However, the series of events that followed were to prove even more improbable.

—— * ——

The Archangel Gabriel entered the cabin with an immaculately smooth and adroit turn of his body, gracefully sliding past the backs of the seats, the tray tables with their clustered masses of plastic, food and hot drinks, not to mention the people crammed up together on the seats. There was no doubt that the Archangel had the dexterity to surpass the very best cabin crew in the world – or even, should he put his mind to it, to pass a dromedary through the eye of a needle.

There was no doubt either that even Frank Sinatra would have wept on hearing how beautifully he intoned *New York, New York*. However, it was highly improbable that an eyelash should detach itself from Gabriel's face just before his feet landed silently upon the floor of the aisle, his wings arranged behind him in all their gleaming splendour. It was even more unlikely that the eyelash, once detached, should happen to drift in the air circulation within the cabin and weave and spin, up and down and around, in just the direction it chose. And it defied all probability that Tony's mouth was open just as the eyelash reached it.

Of all the times to do it, it was precisely at that moment that Tony gave an involuntary hiccup. As he inhaled, mouth open, in floated the eyelash, down his windpipe, down until it reached the level of his heart, where it pierced the inner lining of his left lung, the substance of an angel within the body of a mere mortal.

It would have been impossible for the angels to foresee any of this.

Gabriel finished his song. Having landed in the middle of the aisle he continued without missing a beat, and began purposefully moving down towards the back of the plane. At this point, the expressions on the faces of the passengers were all modulated into a similar stunned look as the performance continued. The wails and screams were now replaced by a gaping silence.

The end of the song was fast approaching, and when Gabriel reached the third row from the back, he turned towards the front. At the end of the phrase 'It's up to *you*,' he raised his right hand and laid it upon the shoulder of the passenger on the aisle seat, then looked down at him as he rendered the last two 'New Yorks' in a crescendo.

The passenger was a small, rather obese woman who had very thin, poorly-arranged hair. She had a rather dirty-looking and ill-fitting cream dress. She looked up and calmly addressed the imposing figure above her.

'Always one for a flashy entrance, Gaby. You should be careful, with all these daring theatrics. One day you might upset that beautiful coiffure of yours.'

Gabriel roared with laughter. 'My dear Fifi, you deliver such beautiful yet twisted words, but you are the last angel who is competent to make judgements on hairstyles.'

Fifi smiled, 'I'm touched that even a lowly and renegade angel such as myself deserves an archangel and his band to arrest me when a single lower-grade angel would have been enough.'

'Don't give yourself airs, my little traitor.' Gabriel looked coldly at Fifi. 'The Archangel Gabriel will not be mocked.'

Fifi continued to look rather amused. 'Well, the Archangel should take me out the side doors for everyone to see. Although rather than have the chance to show off, maybe he simply yearns for the roles to be reversed and to be taken captive himself from the back entrance.'

A vein twitched on the side of Gabriel's forehead as he looked down at Fifi. From out of thin air, a roll of white duct tape suddenly appeared in his hand, and he quickly stretched a strip across her mouth to stop her in mid-sentence. He continued to wind it around her wrists and around the upper part of her torso.

Gabriel looked pleased at his handiwork. He glared at Fifi. 'Now, where were we? The side door. Yes, a spectacular departure. Perhaps I should accidentally drop you off the wing and see how you cope stuck in the body of a human. As we know, you are so good at *accidents* yourself.'

Gabriel began to drag Fifi down towards the centre of the aircraft. The passengers had simply been following the verbal exchange from their seats, but as they approached a tearful woman sitting on the aisle suddenly stood up.

'My lord angel, merciful saviour, I am your servant and humbly ask you to bless me,' she said. The woman reached out to touch the angel, but rather than the beatific look she was obviously expecting, he glared at her. Then he shot out the hand that was not attached to Fifi, clasped her face and pushed her back into her seat.

'My dear lady,' he said, stooping to bend down and position his face above hers, 'You can shut the fuck up and start praying that you die quickly when I walk out of the door and the stale air and contents of this flying fibreglass cucumber start to shake and disintegrate.'

A wave of shock and gasps replaced what had hitherto been silence from the passengers. Gabriel stood up straight with a little smirk. Tony saw a man in glasses stand up just in front of Gabriel. The man gasped, 'Look, I... I... don't know who or what you are but I'm not afraid of you and...'

Gabriel smirked at him. 'Ah, my dear little hero, but you should be very afraid of me. And I think you too can go fuck yourself.'

The man suddenly jerked backwards, as if he was having a fit, falling so that he was seated on the aisle before Gabriel. It was difficult to make out his movements from Tony's seat, but it was impossible not to hear the man's shaking and screaming. The man's body started to bend involuntarily forward. Tony could hear him crying out, and then the shrieks of horror from the passengers around him and the sounds of bones cracking and squelching.

'So, little hero, does that feel good?' said Gabriel, looking down. 'You should be pleased. Not many people have the distinction of being able to put their heads up their own arses.'

The clamour that then began from some of the passengers was worse than before Gabriel's entrance into the cabin. But then all of a sudden it stopped. Gabriel put his finger to his lips and looked around calmly. Tony noticed that a man across the aisle who had been yelling no longer had a mouth. His lips had disappeared, leaving only his nose and his terrified eyes.

'So,' Gabriel began again, 'you can see that your more talkative compatriots have been silenced or have anally pleasured themselves. Anyone else wishing to comment? Now, give me your full attention please.'

There was silence, punctuated by weeping and whimpering. Tony did not dare to look away from Gabriel. He felt a warm, familiar hand slide over and grasp his own.

'My dear, dear humans,' Gabriel continued, 'I have so much fun pitying your feeble mortal condition. Each time I drop by Earth I find you so amusing. Do you remember when you were children, looking at ants, probably smashing your heel down on them or perhaps lifting a stone and pouring boiling water onto their nests? It's just one way I can describe how I look at your pathetic and predictable lives – and what I could do to them. Or perhaps it's easier to think, as you reflect at the end of your life on all the important moments, of the meaning that you might place on the life of a single fly that suddenly smashed into your windscreen on one of the countless times you took a trip in a motorized vehicle.'

His audience was not about to move, and he was beginning to warm to his speech, which was beautifully intoned and underlined with gestures.

'And what fun it is to smash your pathetic stereotypes of ME. Of course, what you see in front of you is the finest specimen of angel in existence, and, yes! I've done all of those great things you've heard about. Normally I let people in first class with a bit more space prostrate themselves before me, but as you're all so cheap that you're on a flight with only economy class, you don't deserve it.'

Gabriel was looking around and some passengers were flinching slightly, but he did not break his flow. 'And then you poor non-believers, particularly those atheists among you. I've amused myself so much with humans like you in the past. But why? Why am I not the 'nice' angel that you might imagine me to be? Well, you can't imagine eternity, but having virtually nothing to do for over one of your millennia gets just a little bit tedious. So, shall we say I'm just letting my hair down every now and then to help pass the centuries? But I think I've had my fill of fun with you and I'm wasting a lot of time when I could be in Angeland. Now, if the little hero will roll out of my way' – he kicked the contorted human ball in front of him – 'I seem to recall that you might appreciate some fresh air.' He waved his hand, and the three people in the seats by the wing door suddenly slid upwards and backwards like puppets, and ended up separated from their seats and flattened against the roof above the seats behind, so that Tony had to duck slightly to avoid the unfortunate woman who had been in the seat directly in front of him.

All this time, Fifi had been motionless, still grasped by Gabriel. He led the little woman towards the side door, through the now-vacant row of seats, and proclaimed 'Adieu, cretins!' Then he dived gracefully through the door while yanking Fifi with him, so that she left the plane horizontally. She raised her head, and in the brief second before she was pulled out of view, she winked at Tony. Immediately afterwards there was an explosion of noise, wind and pain, and everything went black.

CHAPTER 2

'Then I recall staggering into the toilet cubicle... then out again, to here. I think there were only two gaps in my recall of how it unfolded. But that's nothing compared to a gap that's somehow... somehow much bigger. I can't recall anything... anything... in my entire life before that child saying there was an angel on the wing.'

Albert and the other guardian angels had been listening carefully to Tony as he related everything he remembered. Towards the middle of his monologue, several had started approaching him more closely. Albert had urged him to continue even when they started lightly touching his back and chest, and Tony rather hesitantly finished his tale despite these peculiar intrusions. It was perhaps more unnerving to see the same angels who had poked and prodded him whisper and nod to each other, accentuated by the fact that they were very old.

There was a silence after Tony had finished, which Albert filled. 'Well Tony, let me start by excusing Archangel Gabriel. He – ahem – is known for getting a little carried away sometimes.'

'But what about those people? He killed a man in the aisle, closed up people's mouths. It was like something straight out of a horror movie. Are we all... dead?'

'No no!' Albert weakly raised his voice. 'Look all around you, everyone on the plane is here, just as if nothing happened. You are simply looking at things from the perspective of an angel now. Everything has been reset to the moment just before the Archangel arrived to perform his duty, and no one will remember a thing. Well, except you.'

Tony had been looking up and down the plane between the rows of angels, searching among the frozen faces for passengers he remembered from before the carnage. The man who had been screaming was there, with mouth intact – in fact everyone on the plane seemed to have normal mouths now. The man with glasses who had stood up to the Archangel was also there, although his face and ears were red and there were faintly perceptible brown smudges on his glasses.

'So,' Tony turned to face Albert, 'how am I not dead then, if I'm talking with a bunch of angels in this goofy plane full of frozen people?'

'We understand a lot more clearly what, erm, went wrong.' Albert gently laid a hand on Tony's shoulder. 'After inspecting you it seems to be clear that something – we don't have any idea what – of the Archangel got stuck inside you. It's difficult to believe, even for us lowly G-class angels, but the fact that we are having this conversation shows that you have part-transmuted into the state of an angel. There are precedents for this, but it hasn't happened for a very long time.'

Tony searched around the cabin. He saw the empty space where Fifi had been sitting, and glanced at his own empty seat. He started to look more closely at the angels, who were – like the group who had been poking him – almost uniformly old, well beyond retirement age but nevertheless looking quite sprightly. Then he started noticing some individual angels who were much younger, including one who couldn't have been more than six years old. The person in the seat in front of the boy angel was also a boy... and it was suddenly clear. He realised why Albert reminded him of someone.

'Albert, you're me! But you're older, so much older. And yet this little boy here looks almost identical to the angel behind him.'

The angels had been continuing to look at Tony all along, and were nodding and looking very wise – even, disturbingly, the boy angel.

'My dear Tony, you're quite right, and that's something I can easily explain. Each person's guardian angel is always right behind them to follow everything they do. I'm not sure why we look exactly like the person for whom we vouchsafe, but it certainly helps with rapid identification in cases such as rock concerts, in metro carriages, or after a particularly stressful Black Friday. The visible age of a guardian angel is quite simple. It represents how long the person will live for. But I can give you more explanations later. You and I need to get moving at once.'

Tony looked at the young boy and his slightly older guardian angel. There was something, someone in fact, very important that he wanted to remember. But this memory and everything before the moment he had become aware of Archangel Gabriel on the wing, though teasingly close, was lost. It was like having not a word, but an encyclopaedia or perhaps something larger, like the contents of the Internet, on the tip of your tongue and simply being unable to express it. *Someone... someone's fingers...*

'Sorry Tony, it's time to go.' Albert tugged Tony out of his reverie and pulled him up the aisle, past the flight attendant with the coffee, past the alternate rows of frozen passengers and rows of wise, nodding white-clad angels, and up to the front toilet cubicle in the plane. Tony's head was spinning again, and with a wince he recalled the pounding pain of the last time he had been at this door. He took a final look down the aisle, searching for the gap where his seat was, glancing to the side and seeing the top of a head with familiar brown hair...

'Tony, the next CRAP is due to take place imminently and I've heard that it will put this incident at the top of the agenda,' said Albert, pulling Tony's attention back to the angel and the cubicle door.

'CRAP?' said Tony, forgetting everything he had previously been thinking about.

'Sorry, it stands for the *Conseil Religieux des Archanges Ponctuel*. You'll see that we have quite a lot of acronyms, but you'll get used to them quickly, don't worry.'

'Isn't that a rather inappropriate acronym?'

'You might find it amusing as a human because it sounds like defecate to you, but as angels don't need to eat or drink or have associated bodily functions it doesn't carry the same connotation. But we are wasting time, let's get inside.' Albert opened the door of the toilet cubicle, slid in and drew Tony in beside him.

Most toilet cubicles look, smell and feel much the same, but the state of the one Tony found himself in was towards the less appealing end. There was toilet paper, some apparently used, strewn over the damp floor. The sink was nearly full, and a paper towel was swimming in the grey, soapy water. And it stank.

'Never judge a book by its cover,' said Albert gaily as they squeezed into the tiny space together. He pushed the door closed and slid the lock shut with a neat *clack*.

'Could you please explain to me,' said Tony, 'what we are doing in this place?'

'We are now ready to use the HARP,' replied Albert, suddenly looking a lot less flustered.

'What's a harp got to do with anything? I don't remember being able to play that, but I imagine you're an expert.'

'I'm forgetting myself,' replied Albert, 'not harp, HARP. It stands for Human Angel Rescue Portal.' He looked quite pleased with himself. 'For all angels, every aircraft toilet at a plane's cruising altitude is connected to HARP. It's a multi-dimensional emergency portal to Angeland, for stranded angels. It's also the only way for humans to get there.'

'So people have travelled using this before? How are we going anywhere?' said Tony, beginning to feel distinctly crushed.

'Well, no, in fact you'll be the first human, so the E4 who invented the system will be very excitedly following how things go. There's been plenty of testing using human, er, matter, but we've never had a real-life incident of this nature before. I can tell you I'm really rather honoured to be here with you to inaugurate the first full human passage.'

Albert was getting uncomfortably eager as far as Tony was concerned, but he bowled on, 'It's before your lifetime, I know, but you can't imagine the sensation that the invention of air travel for humans made in Angeland. Once planes had enough space to add toilets and enclose them, it was easy for our angel technicians to secretly tap into the base of the cubicle to configure them to HARP to channel the divine wind.'

Tony had been looking around the cubicle, and his attention was drawn to the toilet cover, which he lifted to see the grey bowl lightly flecked and streaked with water, with lines of brown just above the hole.

'I think I've seen enough strange things already to deduce that what you're saying is that we are going to leave through there when the toilet flushes?'

'Why of course,' replied Albert. 'Isn't that the obvious way out? Just imagine the distinction you'll have. It's not always you can say you're the first to do something.'

Tony didn't have much space to manoeuvre, but he had begun to squirm. He exclaimed, 'Actually, can we go back? I'm beginning to have second thoughts about this. It was quite comfortable on the plane…'

Albert, however, who had now become quite manic, put his hand across the door. 'No, no, no, we can't risk going back now, and you have an important date with the CRAP.'

Tony began to try to extract himself, but the angel, despite his age, was remarkably strong. 'Don't panic, that's the last thing to do,' Albert said in a slightly piqued voice, gazing around and then seeming to remember. 'That's it. You've already kindly lifted the lid. Hold your breath. And – something very important but I can't recall why – you might feel a bit queasy after we arrive, but if you're going to be sick, please do it on the floor or on your chest and not in the toilet bowl. Here we go!' He reached down and pushed the blue flush button.

Tony, pinned back and still in a state of disorientation following those previous events in his lifetime which he could actually remember, was not really in any state to protest further. There was a clunk and then a whooshing, sucking noise from the toilet. Tony looked down into the bowl, which was rushing up to meet him. He felt stretched and twisted, and for the third time that day his consciousness was suddenly whisked off.

When it was all over, Tony found himself in exactly the same position that he had been in just before Albert had pushed the flush button. He was promptly sick into the toilet bowl.

'Oh dear,' said Albert, who was calmer than before and still crushed opposite Tony. 'There will be repercussions, and I'll be blamed. But onwards and upwards.' He had released Tony at this point and looked at him, saying quietly, 'Tony, we're going to enter Angeland now.'

Tony had added queasiness to his state of continued disorientation, so he simply nodded weakly at Albert as he continued. For the first time, the old man looked his age, and there was sadness in his voice.

'It means that I will not always be with you as I have up to now in your life. We may walk side by side for some of the time, but in Angeland my link to you is broken. You will be entering a place where you will find everything is different and familiar at the same time. But remember that however difficult the situations are, you must have faith in your own ability.'

Tony noticed that it was now silent in the cubicle; the background hum of the air conditioning had stopped. Albert briefly wiped one eye, then swung back into what Tony now recognised as his typically upbeat manner.

Albert smiled. 'Are you ready?'

'It sounds as though I'll have even more questions than I do at the moment,' Tony said, smiling back weakly.

'Welcome to Angeland.'

The door slid open.

CHAPTER 3

Gabriel

I hate having a CRAP. But it's always worse if there's an item on the agenda under my responsibility where something's gone wrong. And downright embarrassing to be hauled away from my important duties for something I don't completely understand.

They say part of me got lodged in a human during my mission retrieving that weasel Fifi. But I'm good at what I do – the best. No other messenger comes close. Oh yes, there are some jealous angels who insinuate that I shouldn't be visiting Earth so often, but they don't have anything like my experience there. No other angel has gone through so much hurly burly, had such direct interactions with Mary and Mohammed, or is as handsome as me. With the pedigree and honours I've racked up, I've always taken great care to keep my wings, body and mind in tip-top condition.

It makes me think of A1. He would appreciate me now. It's been such a long time, but the other A2s had insisted on waiting, keeping on going without Him. Waiting. That was an understatement. I remember the CRAP quite clearly when A1 had last been seen, in the meeting with all of the A2s, the eight seats of the council room filled for the last time.

'I'm just going to nip out for a little while,' He had said all of a sudden during a pause in the discussions. It was a funny thing, and we were all surprised when He strode out of the council room with His great white beard, hair and robes trailing behind Him. A1 had been apt to come up sometimes with surprising things, which I didn't always agree with, but He had been fair. And I remember the last words He threw out as he left: 'just keep things going while I'm away.'

Anyhow, that's all a long time in the past now, and my thoughts focused on the present as the lift climbed the last few floors of the ARC building. As I'd expected, the conversation in the lift had been all about the football match that had just finished, with the Angeland angels finding it hard to control their elation. I felt sorry for Sandeepa, as her guardians had played really well, only being robbed at the end, but one has to admire the skill of Rita in smashing the records that had withstood for so long, even if she is a bit annoying. My Poste team may be playing Angeland if we get through to the last four, and our team preparations will need to be undertaken very carefully to counter the threat that she poses.

The lift arrived at the top floor, and I came into the Jardim do Céu, the location of the council room, and walked round the table to take my seat. I'd been there many times. It was a beautiful place to work: the austerity of the room, with eight comfortable white leather chairs around a round table, and the huge expanse of glass giving spectacular views over the city. The wide Semaht River was glittering below, the major landmark, with the lights of many other tall towers beginning to twinkle as the sun began to set.

The conversation about the match among the other archangels fell away as I entered, and as I sat down the peace of the room was shattered by the hoot of none other than Natasha's laugh. This was one of those occasions when it did not feel so infectious, although when she started her loud and sudden squeals I admit that it was normally very difficult not to raise a grin or succumb to it.

'My dear Gaby,' Natasha began, having silenced the room, 'you surpass the best of us again. It was amusing to learn about your, er, conduct on the plane, but to learn that you shoved such a precious part of yourself into some innocent human has sparked the greatest excitement in Angeland, second only to His departure and the final of the Angel Cup. But the biggest treat for me was the sheer bafflement on your face as you tried to grasp what on earth had happened.'

Natasha had glanced at the empty chair to my right when referring to Him, and I decided to hold my tongue and let this barrage pass by, scrutinizing her scornfully with my usual elegance and discipline. She was pathetic really, with her strawberry blond hair and contrived accent; any human with any sense or taste would have laughed at her garish teenage Barbie doll image. Although I have to admit that she throws great parties.

At least we don't sit next to each other on the council table, as we have Michelle between us. Michelle has always been a fellow staunch soldier whose innocent image cunningly belies her experience, and whose charm and panache melt the hardest of human and angel hearts. Moreover, her innocent appearance hides the full fury and power of persuasion that only a toddler can unleash. She was in her cot and gurgling at me, but I was not quite in the mood to start playing with her yet.

In jumped Yuri at this point, always impatient for things to move on. His ginger hair and light moustache quivered. 'So let's get this straight,' he said, speaking quickly and deliberately, 'I don't know about you, but I've got business to do, and now we're all here I think it's time to work out what's happened and what our strategy is, fast.'

Then, true to form, Sandeepa comes in with her usual conciliatory tone. 'Yuri,' she said, stretching out her hand to touch his arm. She hadn't changed one bit since she first became an angel: her long single jet-black plait almost down to her waist, a simple white sari and a garland of white flowers, and those sandals that always flapped as she lankily paraded around.

'My dear Yuri,' she continued, looking sympathetically at me, 'I don't think we should be rushing off jumping to conclusions, or pointing a finger of blame too quickly. We know that the human Tony became semi-angelic after his encounter on the plane with Gaby, and there must be a simple way to put things right. We just need to put our heads together and work out a solution.'

Yuri lightly thumbed his trouser braces, rocking backwards and forwards. Any human would have mistaken him for a chubby adolescent, rather than the leader of the realm that keeps zillions of angels commercially in thrall, and he was impatient to get back to business. I smiled quietly to myself as he turned the situation round, making Sandeepa look quite deflated.

'Yes, dear Sandeepa, and rather than have the sense to keep Tony on the plane to give us time to find a quick solution, your G4 Albert panics and decides to bring him to Angeland. Where Tony then vomits on the HARP and is caught between worlds, creating a stasis for ten Earth minutes.'

I thought this line of questioning was going well, but of course it's the cue for Ray to jump in. I don't understand why he insists on wearing that tired-looking waistcoat and bow tie, which sit so at odds with all his experience. But having sent so many souls on their way, you have to respect his insights into the human as well as the angelic condition. But his place at the table, with Natasha on his right and Sandeepa on his left, does provide a little pragmatic balance.

'What's done is done, Yuri,' said Ray. 'And we give angels autonomy to make operational decisions in the field, isn't that right? So Tony is in Angeland, and we have ten Earth minutes to find a way to make him completely human again. It will certainly make for a bit of a change round here, and old Ray is ready to help out where he can.' He finished by looking round at all of us with a gentle smile, but I was thinking simply that the sprinkling of salt-and-pepper hair above his ears and below his broad bald patch could do with a trim.

I was about to suggest a rapid and practical solution for dealing with Tony, one which I knew would not meet with the approval of the majority of the angels but would at least have helped to move the discussion along, but then of course Mehi, our resident clever-clogs, jumps in and not only embarrasses me but demonstrates how badly the operational decisions of Sandeepa's G4 magnified something that could have been easily dealt with at the time.

Mehi had been scrutinizing me for a fair time. Irritating as he is sometimes, at least he dresses the part: a neat suit with his black hair slicked back.

He addressed the room and focused on me. 'The shock of the situation is clearly straining our powers of perception. 'Gaby, do you realise that you are missing an eyelash?' he announced.

In the ensuing pause I reached up. Incredibly, seemingly impossibly, an eyelash was gone from my perfect face. The nagging sense of loss that I had experienced after knowing that something had been transferred to the human Tony suddenly exploded. Although I kept my cool externally, internally I felt a burst of shame and catastrophe. I had deliberately said nothing at the start of the meeting but now, although I would be the last to admit it, I was temporarily unable to communicate for the first time in my existence.

Of course Natasha was the first to break the silence, with one of her quips. 'Mehi, you are a clever one,' she said. Then she turned to me. 'But, dear Gaby, perhaps this means that before we know it you will be as bald as Ray.' She hooted with laughter.

I appreciated Mehi's imperturbable professionalism. Without a flicker he continued in his monotone, 'It has probably lodged in Tony's lung. We have lost the window of opportunity to conduct surgery while he was in the plane.'

Good, I thought, that's another jab at Sandeepa's poor management and really, given the very unfortunate and distressing accident, the obvious place to point the blame in the circumstances. Nevertheless, given my self-consciousness with the eyes of the others upon me, the best course of action seemed to be to pick up Michelle and start bouncing her up and down on my knee. I did so, and she started to babble and coo.

Meanwhile, however, Natasha was looking a little anxious. She asked Mehi, 'So what does this mean in practice for Tony?'

Mehi continued, 'As you are aware, we know the destiny of all things on Earth, while in Angeland and its divine realms, everything, particularly the Angel Cup championship, is uncertain. Tony, however, has become part-angel as well as entering Angeland. His destiny now, like those of angels, is currently impossible to predict.'

I and all the other angels, including Michelle, were looking intently at Mehi as he forged on.

'However, there are some parameters that are certain. If the eyelash is removed from Tony's person, after about an hour or two of angel time, he will then experience human time and become effectively frozen. In this catatonic state he can simply be propped up by the HARP and be flushed through after it opens, upon which he will regain his memory of his human life and forget everything he has experienced in Angeland.'

Yuri cut in. 'So the sooner we extract the eyelash, the less we all have to deal with.'

Mehi nodded. 'However, if the eyelash is still not removed when the emergency portal opens, the imbalance between Angeland and Earth will create a vacuum that will not just tear Tony apart cell by cell in what will feel like eons of excruciating pain for him, but also threaten the very fabric of Angeland.'

At this point Michelle suddenly let out a shriek and started bawling, and didn't stop despite my best efforts to rock her around and bounce her up and down. I looked at all the other angels and appealed to them with a clever idea.

'This is not my fault, I'll have you know. I was just doing my duty. Can't we just cut Tony in half and take out my poor eyelash?'

'No, as angels that's the last thing that we can do,' said Sandeepa, looking rather severely at me, as I had expected. 'Some of us might get away with certain things on Earth but there'll be none of that here.'

I felt that was a bit of a low blow, but by this stage everyone but Mehi seemed a little nervous.

Yuri cut the silence and got to the point. 'OK, OK, so how much time exactly do we have until the emergency portal opens? Is there another solution?'

Mehi gave a rare smile. 'The portal will open approximately 24 minutes into the first half of the Angel Cup final.'

It was good to come back to a really serious topic. My several millennia of experience in the field of various near-apocalyptic events meant that I was able to maintain my calm and full powers of observation while Michelle was having a tantrum on my knee.

I had been observing Natasha's fidgeting since Mehi's earlier forecast of doom, and I smiled inwardly to myself to see her reaction to the timing of the portal opening. She had never won the Angel Cup, but this year she did have a strong team which looked as though she had a real chance, even without some of the backstage manoeuvring that was no doubt up her sleeve. I glanced again at His chair and mulled at how His team, the Angeland team, had also never won the Angel Cup since He had disappeared.

Natasha, however, was the next to speak. She clicked her fingers and looked at Ray. 'Heaven,' she said. 'We simply send him to Heaven.'

We all turned to Ray, and Michelle paused in her tantrum with her mouth open expectantly.

'Slamming the pearly gates irrevocably shut on Tony as he became a denizen of Heaven would create a protective barrier,' nodded Mehi. 'Angeland would be safe.'

'Sure,' said Ray, 'I can give Tony a one-way ticket at the end of his scheduled time in Angeland, which is a bit radical before his time on Earth is due. But we could even exceptionally give him a two-way ticket, as a bit of relaxation and angel hospitality might do wonders to tease out the eyelash. Before we try the one-way ticket, we need to do everything else we can to free the eyelash.'

I would have seconded Natasha's suggestion that we should send Tony straight to Heaven on a one-way ticket, but I decided to hold my tongue. The relief was palpable all round and despite my earlier annoyance I began to reflect that with this fail-safe option, some interesting benefits could well arise from the situation.

Yuri stood up as if to leave. 'Excellent, so we can all continue to prepare for the Angel Cup then. Call on me if you need me to help, but you must excuse me now as I have things to do.'

'Please wait,' said Sandeepa, standing up and towering above Yuri, encouraging him to sit back down again. 'I have just heard that Albert and Tony have now left Angelgate Station and will be joining our meeting in a few minutes. We need to think about how we first go about freeing the eyelash.'

CHAPTER 4

Gathering his breath after hurrying from the station as the lift in the centre of the building climbed towards the top floor, Tony reflected on his initial experiences of Angeland. Overall, getting from the HARP to ARC had been somewhat eventful, but straightforward. Albert had explained that ARC stood for Angeland Republic Centre, carefully noting that the C in the acronym was pronounced softly, and adding that Tony would soon get used to the pronunciation of Angelese and its quirky linguistics.

Tony's mind drifted back to his first experiences of Angeland. Stepping out of the aircraft toilet, the surroundings had neither been a normal plane nor an expanded-guardian-angel-one. Tony was perturbed when he and Albert emerged into the end of a rather dingy corridor, dimly lit by a bare and dusty light bulb. The walls were dirty concrete, here and there with scrawls of what looked like algebra.

'Don't worry about the state of all this,' Albert said, seeing Tony's gaze. 'You have to remember that this is the back entrance and it isn't used very much.' He stopped and looked proudly at the writing on the wall. 'Ah yes, such brilliance in these calculations. They helped build the HARP. There are not many angels who have been fortunate enough to see these workings, and that's another first for you as a human. But we must be getting on. Follow me!'

Albert strode down the corridor, closely followed by Tony, and soon arrived at the foot of a spiral staircase covered in a light scattering of debris. 'Up we go,' Albert said gaily, and they went up about a hundred steps, with more dusty single light bulbs at intervals, just close enough to each other to provide the illumination the pair needed to climb without falling over. Then the steps abruptly stopped, with a panel blocking any further progress.

'Just needs a little push,' said Albert, nonchalantly applying one hand. The panel did not move, so Albert pushed a little harder. He then tried with two hands, without any sign of movement from the panel. 'Nothing to worry about,' he said, although he had begun to perspire. He smiled at Tony. 'If you'd just be so kind as to descend the staircase a few steps, it will allow me to make a run-up and get a bit of momentum.'

The manoeuvre, however, led to the same result, and after a few minutes of ever-more insistent and violent barraging a rather discomposed and forlorn Albert sat down at the foot of the panel, which had resolutely remained in its original place.

'I hope they haven't walled up behind it,' said Tony, 'but perhaps I can lend a hand or, rather, another shoulder?'

Albert looked a little worried at the first suggestion but quickly returned to his optimistic self, and nodded. 'Yes, you're right Tony. I'm glad I didn't come here on my own.'

Albert and Tony arranged themselves side by side and with gestures to synchronize their efforts, they shoulder-charged the panel. There was a light but perceptible movement inwards, and traces of dust around the panel drifted down.

'Here we go!' exulted Albert. The two took a few steps backwards again and did the same again. There was more give and more dust.

'Third time lucky!' Albert grinned, although Tony reflected that bearing in mind the old man's initial efforts, thirtieth time was nearer the mark.

They prepared themselves once again and launched a third assault upon the panel. This time the outcome was startlingly different. Albert and Tony did not realise that the panel would have fallen inwards with the mere soupçon of extra force, and man, angel and panel all flew sharply forwards before landing and skidding for several metres across a smooth white marble floor.

The first things Tony noticed as he sprawled horizontally on the panel were the sudden increase in luminosity and the delightfully sweet air, which contrasted so much with the dim and musty staircase. He stood up, helped Albert to regain his feet and brushed himself down. Then he gazed incredulously at the structure around him.

They were on a wide marble floor that formed the base of a huge white dome. The "floor" was in fact more of a wide walkway or ledge than a base, for it surrounded a gaping open hole some 200 metres in diameter below the dome. There were hundreds of angels, again all dressed in white, moving purposefully in all directions on the walkway. They were all coming from or going to seven double escalators, situated at even intervals around the walkway and going into the hole, and their movement resembled the hustle and bustle of a busy train station.

A low wall, which had stopped Tony, Albert and the panel from sliding into the void, reassuringly provided a border between the hole and the walkway, which Tony now peered over. The seven double escalators were suspended without any support, carrying angels upwards and downwards and spiralling elegantly around each other for about 100 metres before ending in mid-air. About halfway down an escalator, each descending angel sprouted wings, while those coming up folded their wings away out of sight at the same level. Below the feet of the escalators, there was an expanse of open sky, with the tops of clouds in the distance. Thousands of airborne angels were leaving or joining the bottoms of the escalators, floating like choreographed dandelion seeds.

'Golly,' said Tony.

'It is rather impressive, and using it is a little more salubrious than using the HARP to get to and from Earth,' replied Albert. He had picked up the panel and fitted it back into the hole in the wall from which they had arrived.

Tony saw that there was an exquisitely painted picture of a harp on the side of the panel facing the inside of the dome, one of a series of frescos depicting cherubs, angels and accompanying heavenly paraphernalia on the wall around the foot of the dome.

Exits led out of the dome opposite each of the helical escalators, while midway between each of the exits and escalator points huge television screens interrupted the other-worldly frescos. A large number of angels were peering at them intently.

Despite the unusual entrance that Tony and Albert had made into the dome walkway, the various angels passing by had not paid them much attention, although some did stare at Tony and whisper and nod to each other. With the HARP panel back in place, Albert invited Tony to walk to the nearest screen, where something rather gripping was going on. The roar of a crowd emerging from the television grew as they approached, and on the screen Tony was surprised to see two teams of women, one in white football strip and the other in blue, playing a football match that looked much more human than angelic. The commentary of the match became more and more distinct as they approached.

'Rita dribbles past Fatima... does a great one-two with Jennifer... oh! she's beaten both remaining defenders with a deft little wiggle. There's only Nora in goal to beat. Could this be the moment... she turns... oh and it's a fantastic little chip... Goooooooooaaaaaaaal... Gooooooaallllasssou! Rita gets her ninth hat trick of the season, sensationally breaking the record held by Ruth for the last 14,964 years. And the referee blows her whistle and it's all over! Angeland 4, Guardians 3 the final score, and Angeland not only move into third in the league but are guaranteed a place in the semi-finals of the Angel Cup, a privilege they'll finally enjoy for the first time in 3,424 years.'

As the commentary and the drama unfurled, Tony tried to digest the scene. All angel eyes around the screen were glued to it. Some angels jumped up and down and yelled and hugged each other with delight as the goal was scored. Others, Albert included, were muttering and shaking their heads, looked disconsolate and somewhat annoyed as the Angeland supporters started chanting, 'Reeta, Reeta, Reeta... there's only one Ree-ee-ta!'

Tony was confused as he looked at the screen, with the players, crowd and everyone else looking distinctly human. The pitch and players were muddy; the crowd were dressed not in white but like you would expect on any Saturday afternoon during a football match on Earth, and behaving in a rowdy but good-natured way. The only thing that was different was the distinct references to the Angel Cup and Angeland.

The angels around the television were beginning to drift away as the post-match analysis and interviews were now taking place. Rita appeared on screen and Tony became a little more attentive to the transmission as she started speaking and humbly thanking her team-mates. She was wearing a white top and her short brown hair was tied back in a rather endearing ponytail.

'Well, guardians still might qualify, but we'll need to win all of the last three matches in the league,' said Albert, leaning over Tony's shoulder. 'Time to go, I'm afraid, I'd love to stay and watch but the CRAP is calling us.' Tony nodded and they set off towards the nearest exits at the rim of the dome.

Once outside, Tony realised that the dome was slightly elevated above the landscape, where a forest of deciduous trees stretched in most directions. He and Albert walked a little way around the dome, where everything was in immaculate white marble, before leaving it and reaching a grand flight of tree-flanked steps. Here they descended towards a lower street. Thousands of angels were walking up and down the steps outside the dome, talking among themselves, while those nearest to Tony were glancing curiously at him. He became suddenly self-conscious among the white-clad wave of statuesque angelicness that swept past him, and he noticed the contrast with his own clothes, a pair of blue jeans and a yellow football shirt.

'We are at the end of the line here but there's a direct train that will take us close to ARC. If we're lucky we'll get the fast one that arrives in just less than an hour,' Albert explained as they descended the steps.

The steps ended at a tarmac road that led underneath a railway bridge, turned to the right and went past a mini roundabout. On the right was a grey brick one-storey building with the station concourse visible behind. A sign stood prominently outside the station, with a red circle and horizontal blue bar through the middle on which 'ANGELHAM' was written in white text.

During this short walk, Tony focused less on the two columns of angels heading towards and away from the dome and more on the surroundings. A series of rather quaint two- or three-storey brick buildings surrounded the road to the station, and he began to feel slightly disorientated. 'This all seems awfully familiar,' he said to Albert as they approached the station.

'Oh, I'm sure it's just a coincidence,' replied Albert, and they passed the mass of angels inside the station. Albert was pleased to discover that the fast train was standing on the platform and they boarded it, taking two seats in a long row on the inside of the carriage that faced a similar row on the opposite side.

'It's always good to leave from the terminus and be guaranteed a seat,' Albert said contentedly, adding, 'We'll now have plenty of time on the journey when I can start to explain anything you don't understand.'

There was the sound of a siren, and a few angels jumped on the train just before the doors slid shut and it pulled out of the station.

CHAPTER 5

The train accelerated out of the station and then maintained a gentle swaying and clattering rhythm as it continued on its way. The view out of the window had predominantly been of trees, but these quickly thinned and were replaced by a steady procession of brick buildings only two or three storeys high. One could have easily confused it with a typical suburban panorama on Earth, apart from the vehicles and figures going about their business, all dressed in white.

Tony was digesting the changing scene and looking up at a plan of the train line above the seats opposite him. The names of the stations were marked and he was able to read some of the names of the nearest ones: Landwirtschaftsbetrieb, Pinheirinho and Preosttunweg. Albert observed him and saw his confusion. 'I dare say these all seem a bit strange to you,' he said. 'The Subsolo has 270 stations and 11 lines and is quite complex. But the rules for avoiding congestion and ensuring a pleasant trip are quite simple: you just try to avoid eye contact or having a conversation with any other angel. Thankfully we've got these to help us.' He pulled out what appeared to be two smartphones. 'But where was I? Oh yes, after a football match the rules tend to slip somewhat. In fact you should prepare yourself for an almighty crush and all manner of rule-breaking when we get to Waldgebietpark.'

This sudden surge of new information was disconcerting Tony, although he had noticed that the same characteristic red, blue and white sign which he had seen at Angelham was repeated on the passing trains and stations, frequently with SUBSOLO on it. He turned to see Albert, who was engrossed with his two gadgets-cum-smartphones, one with a big 'R' on the back and the other with 'A' on it. He was apparently tapping some text into one of them, but they were both angled carefully so that Tony could not see the screens.

Albert had become so engrossed with his devices that he did not at first respond to Tony. Tony called Albert's name a few times before leaning over to try to see what was on the screens, at which point the angel looked up and hastily put the devices away.

'What are those?' said Tony.

'Oh, please excuse me. I was miles away. It was better in the old days when there were two angels doing the job, but with modern technology and the growth in human population, they can't be spared any more,' replied Albert.

'I'm not any clearer,' Tony pursued, and Albert looked a little surprised, but then nodded understandingly.

'Well, as your guardian angel, I need to record your actions, thoughts and feelings through life. It's normally easy, given how slowly human time passes in comparison to angel time, and as I mentioned, every guardian angel had a couple of scribes to help them in the past. I was just catching up writing it down. Here on one of my two oticels. It'll look like a smartphone to you.'

'Can I see what you've written?' asked Tony.

'It would be quite against protocol for you to see it,' responded Albert. 'It's... well... a sort of book of life which contains many divine and mysterious things that you're not supposed to know about. I hope you understand.'

Tony was a little rueful but he continued his questioning, now that he had Albert's attention, and there was little else to do but see the same and rather monotonous suburban sprawl pass by. The other angels on the train were generally observing the rule of not talking with or looking at each other, but Tony figured that as he wasn't an angel there wasn't any problem continuing to talk.

'The first thing I'd really like to know,' said Tony, ' is how you apparently have elevators, smartphone-oticel things, televisions, football leagues and aircraft toilets that are all, well, inventions of the modern human world. You're all wearing what look like Roman togas, which is true to stereotype, but I would have expected you to be sitting on clouds and strumming harps. Furthermore, rather than fly around you don't have any wings here, apart from under that big dome we saw, and you have cars and this metro.'

'Angels move with the times,' said Albert, smiling at Tony. 'Although what you see here is based on where and when you have come from and the innate logic and metaphors that go with this. If you had been living in the Middle Ages we would be travelling in a horse and cart. If you've read some old religious books, that gives you an idea about how life was then and how it changes with time – although in some cases humans can get a bit stuck in old books for their vision of the world rather than seeing the modern reality.'

'So you're saying this is all a figment of my imagination?'

'Oh no, no,' said Albert, 'Every thought and experience you have here is simply the way you are able to translate the reality around you, much like on Earth. Thoughts, words, deeds – all are waiting for their meaning, even though that meaning might not be obvious immediately. Perhaps you'll get to have a chat with the Archangel Mehi sometime, he can explain it all better than me.'

'Talking of which,' said Tony, who was getting rather lost in this metaphysical talk and was pleased to have the chance to start on another subject, 'can you tell me about these archangels? The one I've seen wasn't the nicest angel I've met, and as we are going to their CRAP, or whatever, I'd appreciate a bit of background.'

'Yes, you're right,' said Albert. 'You're probably aware that there are seven archangels who currently represent the most senior level of angeldom. They are at the A2 level, but their supervisor, the only angel at A1 level, left in mysterious circumstances over a human millennium ago and He hasn't been seen since.'

Albert ended the sentence with a dramatic flourish and continued, 'And I'm sure you're wondering what grade I am. I can proudly say that I'm a G4.'

Tony's face remained rather blank, and this did not elicit the reaction Albert expected, so the angel continued.

'On Earth there are many misconceptions about angels, and I hope your stay here will help to address these. It's true that there are orders of hierarchies of angels, but we don't call them silly things like dominos, kerugmas, opranims or principalities. It's much simpler to use the letters A to I for the nine hierarchies, with each hierarchy having seven levels. So I'm senior to a G5, but obviously lower than an F7. Each angel has seven reporting to him or her at the level below.'

Tony was trying to imagine this while Albert paused for effect. He finished, 'In total, that's an awful lot of angels. More than could fit on a pinhead, in any case.'

Albert looked up. 'Well, we're nearly at Waldgebietpark,' he announced. 'I'd better tell you about the realms of angels, and more specifically football, which I think will also be helpful.'

Tony nodded, seeing a stadium on the horizon. It was all white but with a vast arc above it spanning its entire surface.

Albert continued, 'Each of the A2s – sorry, the archangels – resides over a realm of existence which is essential to the functioning of the whole of the multiverse of angels. Angeland is an additional central realm and acts as the Secretariat for all essential angel business, and is normally overseen by Him – I mean the A1. The most important event bringing the realms together is, naturally, the Angel Cup, which is held once every four angel years. The impressive building you see in front of you is the renowned Waldgebiet Stadium and it hosts many of the most important football games, including the Angel Cup Final.'

The Stadium was now in plain view, about 400 metres away as the train pulled slowly into Waldgebietpark Station. Hundreds of angels thronged the platforms, dressed in white apart from the odd blue scarf standing out, while those with white scarfs looked very animated and a little threatening.

A wave of noise built as they approached. As the train doors slid open, a wall of bawdy sound preceded the rowdy crowd of angels bundling into the carriage. All of the seats on the train were already taken, with the result that Tony's view of the windows and angels sitting opposite him was replaced by a crush of standing bodies trying to fit into every possible niche.

Tony noticed that the rather subdued angels with blue scarves had assembled together at the end of the carriage, looking rather sorry for themselves. Albert had nodded at a few of them who had caught his eye, and was now looking rather downcast himself. Conversely, there was a constant stream of chanting and cheering from the Angeland fans, bantering with everyone on the train and taunting the Guardian supporters. 'Aain-ge-land, Aain-ge-land, Aain-ge-land!' was chanted in a beautiful but peculiarly raucous harmony, along with 'we're gonna win the Cup, we're gonna win the Cup!' and 'Ree-ta, Ree-ta, there's only one Ree-ta!'

There were two angels standing directly in front of Tony. One was a tall thin woman, and the other an imposing woman with slightly untidy hair and a red face. The latter had boarded the train looking a fair bit more jovial and animated than the others, slapping the other angels on the back, taking a series of selfies with other supporters with her oticel, and squeezing the buttocks of a significant proportion of the male angels she passed while shrieking raunchy comments. The reaction of the male angels to this treatment was somewhat mixed, with some reacting playfully and others looking rather awkward.

'Oh Gertrude,' said the thin woman, giggling, 'You're irrepressible. You'll get yourself into trouble if you continue like that.'

Encouraged rather than chastised by this comment, Gertrude grasped the buttocks of the male angel just in front of her with both hands, letting out a loud 'Phwwooaaarrrr!' He turned and looked rather bashful, nodding timidly in agreement as she looked at the thin lady, and then at him, exclaiming 'You see Helen, my dear, I'm irrepressible.'

Tony grinned awkwardly and Albert looked as though he would prefer to hide under his seat. Gertrude looked down and noticed Tony for the first time.

'Ey up, Helen, look what we've got here. The human who came through the HARP. My my, it's my lucky day. Who'd have thought I'd lay my hands on a human in Angeland?'

Gertrude leaned over Tony, placed her hand on his thigh and moved it inexorably up between his legs, licking her lips. At this unusual turn of events, and given the apparently unstoppable and imposing figure above him, he was quite frozen.

'Now Gertrude,' said Helen, pulling her friend back at the last moment. 'I think you know very well that you're touching something which is absolutely off limits.'

Gertrude rolled her eyes at Helen, and smiled and puckered a kiss at Tony, sobering up somewhat but huskily addressing him. 'Oh, what everyday pleasures we poor angels miss in the metropolis,' she said suggestively.

'You'll have to excuse Gertrude,' Helen said, speaking to Tony and Albert. 'She only got back from a trip to Hull a couple of days ago and you know, with the excitement of the football she hasn't quite got back to everyday life.'

At this point, the train – which had not left the station, as angels were still trying to squeeze in – began to shake back and forth. The Angeland supporters, both inside the train and on the platform, were jumping up and down as they chanted their repetitive 'Ain-ge-land' slowly, in unison and then with increasing tempo as they tried to create enough momentum to collectively jolt and sway the train. Tony was relieved that the attention of Helen and Gertrude was directed elsewhere, and he looked at Albert, who smiled wanly. It was impossible to talk above the din.

Tony took the time to look around at the angels in their disorder, and reflected on the surprising advances of Gertrude and all of the strange but not completely out of the ordinary other things that had transpired. He heard the siren for the doors closing; after several attempts, they somehow slid shut. The standing angels were squashed together and continued to sing, shriek and jump, but as the train advanced the pressure was relieved at each successive station due to the departing angels, and the boisterous behaviour gradually diminished.

The train entered a long continuous tunnel, and a little while later the crowd in the corridor cleared sufficiently at the next station so that Tony could finally read the name of the sign: Estrada Padeiro. The angels had become more and more composed with each passing station: the scarves had all been put away, each (including Gertrude, who was looking quite transformed) had ordered their hair and garments perfectly, and everyone was looking away from each other in silence.

'So that was all rather strange but, at the same time, very familiar,' said Tony to Albert. 'All that behaviour around the football stadium is what I'd expect to see humans do on Earth.'

'As I was about to say before we arrived at Waldgebietpark,' responded Albert, 'football – the beautiful game, of course – is one of many things that angels have copied from humans. You see, even though angels are immortal, it gets very dull with nothing fun and unpredictable to look forward to. Humans, on the other hand, tend to be much better at inventing things than us, for better and for worse, and we angels simply use the best human ideas.'

'There's something else,' enquired Tony, 'something a bit back-to-front with the gender relations here. Don't male angels play football, for example?'

'Well, a little bit,' replied Albert, 'but in minor leagues with no significance. Actually, we angels find it very peculiar that on Earth men's football is so prominent. But at least there is some equivalence of angel normality in most human choirs. Actually, you might even get to see the best angel choir of all the realms, which is based in the Bright Hall, on the other side of the city. The conductor is my archangel, the one in charge of all of the guardian angels, Sandeepa. She's ever so nice and you'll meet her at the CRAP.'

The conversation came to a lull and Tony sat thoughtfully as the train rattled along. All of a sudden, Albert shook him. 'We're arriving at Angelgate,' he said.

Before he knew it, Tony had left the carriage, been whisked up a couple of flights of stairs through the station, and found himself in a road with a cityscape rising up around him. Albert hailed one of the many rather chunky white taxis, and they headed towards a curious skyscraper down the road that swelled towards the top. Again he felt he'd seen everything before, but he was tantalizingly unable to recall just what, how, why or when.

They arrived quickly at the foot of the skyscraper, which Albert said was the home of ARC, nicknamed the Dumavoltape-Fofoca, or D-F for short, but it was also known simply by its address – 20 Rua Brigreja. They passed through reception and into the lift.

'Welcome Tony,' said the tall and kind-looking lady waiting by the lift doors as they opened at the top of the building. Behind her, he saw the six other archangels, including a scowling Gabriel.

CHAPTER 6

Sandeepa

As soon as I saw him I was reminded of my eldest son. I didn't need to be Mehi to realise that Tony was a very distant ancestor. Something in the soft, innocent eyes, perhaps something in his nose. I was struck by a feeling I had not experienced for a long time, since before I was in Angeland. When I was human.

Gabriel was still as bombastic as ever when he came and lifted my crumpled body from the ground. But he was tenderer then and less grumpy; how the millennia following His absence have changed that. I remember so clearly as he cradled me in his arms how all of the pain was replaced by ecstasy as he flew upwards, higher and ever higher for what seemed like an eternity, until I realised we were at the top of the Ladder.

Over three human millennia ago, I had been living and breathing on the Earth, a simple villager in what is now eastern Andhra Pradesh who loved her family with all her heart. I recall that as my human body died and I became an angel, I was listening to the angels who marvelled at the extraordinary lengths of mistreatment and abuse I had suffered to save my family. I had no idea that it would eventually lead to my appointment as an archangel, from being a guardian with unconditional love for my family to taking the responsibility of overseeing the guardians for humankind.

I remember Him telling me that Mehi also was originally human (and he of course became my favourite angel, given that he was the only one with whom I could properly reminiscence). I also appreciated His kind words and guidance in entering the extraordinary universe of angels. But I also quickly found out His ulterior motive: oh no, it wasn't just the Sandeepa selfless paragon story (which still really makes me feel rather embarrassed). No, I remember Him slipping it in as an 'afterthought' during a long conversation when He just 'wondered if I might possibly be interested in just having a little look at the choir when I was passing by one day.' I should have realised that the whole thing was a set-up, and I still wonder to this day the degree to which managing the guardian angels may actually be incidental compared to leading the choir.

Of course when I did 'pass by' the choir, how could I, the conductor in my village (with a passion for music which over time exceeded that for my husband), refuse the offer 'just to stand in and be an assistant conductor for one session.' But I'm not complaining. After the first trial session, before I knew it I had become Artistic Director. As long as the other angels find that I'm the one for them, I'll joyfully continue and help build their repertoire and give a little bit of ex-human vim that they like.

Anyhow, I digress. I quickly introduced myself and the rest of the archangels to Tony and thanked Albert, who was understandably nervous, for bringing him. I could see that both of them were a bit overawed at both the company and the view from the Jardim do Céu, so I joked a little about the football match, even though I was still thoroughly annoyed at that Rita for scoring in the last minutes of the game.

I tried to be as diplomatic as possible for both Albert and Gabriel's sake when explaining about the eyelash. Gabriel looked as though he was about to have a hissy fit, but, thank goodness, he still had Michelle in his arms and she was doing her best to gurgle at him soothingly and soften him up. Albert looked terribly downcast when I saw he realised it would have been better to keep Tony on Earth rather than come through the HARP, but I pride myself in giving my guardians the right to act autonomously and take decisions on their own.

Tony was very courteous and self-effacing and I was pleased that I would presently be spending more time with him. I outlined how the CRAP had discussed and established – with more than a little persuasion on my part – that the first efforts to dislodge the eyelash from his lung would involve the good old-fashion controlled use of one's respiration, in other words a good old sing-song.

Without further ado the other archangels filtered out of the council room. Michelle cheerfully waved and smiled delightfully at Tony, which was rather a contrast to Gabriel. If he hadn't been holding Michelle as he left I dare say he would have issued some obnoxious threat, but instead he rather coldly told Tony that the sooner he was reunited with his eyelash the better, and that everyone would be a lot happier, so Tony could quickly be back on Earth and forget about all of this.

Yuri was next and he positively bounded up to Tony, vigorously shaking his hand and saying that if the choir didn't do the trick then he should come down and visit PirogRus as he'd be a sensation and help to boost sales no end. As usual you could see that Yuri's business mind was ticking over and coming up with all sorts of ideas, and his rather weak and hesitant suggestion at the end that this would be the next best possible way to dislodge the eyelash wasn't entirely convincing.

In his more gentle and considered way, Ray was next and he looked Tony in the eye and simply wished him well and said that he'd be there waiting for Tony and was looking forward to spending some time with him when the time came, whether during his visit to Angeland or after that.

Then Mehi stepped up and told Tony that it had been a very long time since he'd seen a human in Angeland, giving me a short but meaningful look. He invited Tony to come and visit the Cube if he had a moment, as he wanted to learn more about how things worked on Earth. Oh yes it would be interesting to have the unusual case of a human without a destiny, and how entering the HARP wouldn't be the same as leaving it. I still marvel at how he pulls off all of this in a mysterious way, but even I could see how he was enjoying being a bit tongue-in-cheek as he was more deliberate and solemnly theatrical than usual.

During all of these discussions, in the corner of my eye I could see Natasha. It astonishes me how she gets away with being so very brazen sometimes, and indeed looking at her I occasionally forget how experienced she is. With deliberate and sensual strides she approached Tony, who had already shot several sideways glances at her as she expertly ogled him while the other archangels said their goodbyes. She simply said 'well,' taking and rubbing his hand with both of hers, then gave a pregnant pause, and oozed out that he should "come down and see her sometime." Then she walked away. His eyes were popping out of his head and his mouth was open like an infatuated teenager.

I only hope that the choir works some magic, or another wholesome method does, to spare any chance of them meeting again, so that any ambitions of hers can be scotched before they have a chance to develop.

Anyhow, that left just Tony, Albert and me in the council room. I told Albert that I would take charge from now, at which he naturally looked very sad, but he was slightly happier when I told him that he might be needed another time soon and that he should stay in the city until further notice. It was quite touching to see the two of them say goodbye – a unique couple for Angeland, a human and his guardian together. They shook hands and then Tony hugged Albert to thank him for everything. Albert left after reminding Tony of the importance of love, and it was all thoroughly unmasculine. I beamed benevolently at it all from a polite distance, in complete agreement.

I liked Tony. I told him that if we left now we could arrive just in time for the rehearsal at the Bright Hall, so down we went in the lift. There was still time to walk to Angelgate station, as I love seeing the city around me, and then an easy thirteen stops on the Linha Redonda in the Subsolo to Avenida do Povo Cynsige.

Poor Tony was struggling with his memory loss, but I explained that it was quite impossible for me to tell him anything about his past before the eyelash incident as it could jeopardize the balance of his existence in Angeland. I did however tell him that he might naturally start remembering some things, and in any case I could see that he was struggling with a certain subconscious familiarity with the city.

He was certainly curious about things and I did happily explain my story, and how I came to be an archangel. He was quite relieved to know that I had been human and I told him that it was nice, after 3,000 years, to talk with a human directly, as I was only able to manage the guardian angels from a distance, given my responsibilities with the choir.

We arrived at Avenida do Povo Cynsige and as it was a bit of a trek to the Bright Hall, I explained during the walk a little bit about the choir and assessed his musical ability. He seemed to have a good ear and sang bass, which was good as it meant he'd be in a bigger group, as we only have a few tenors. We approached the familiar rotund structure of the Hall and went in.

CHAPTER 7

Tony found Sandeepa to be a pleasant, albeit rather talkative, angel. He had understood more after meeting the archangels, and the view from the Jardim do Céu was rather splendid, although very evocative of something or other he couldn't quite put his finger on. The business of the eyelash was actually rather funny, and he had to stifle a guffaw when he saw Gabriel again after the Archangel's pompous promenade in the aeroplane; this time the Archangel was both angry and a shade emasculated, holding that sweet toddler and evidently self-conscious with an eyelash missing.

Tony found all in all that the archangels were rather a strange bunch, not least the toddler who was the Archangel Michelle. Sandeepa had insisted that the toddler did actually have this status, noting that while Michelle and Gabriel were probably the most experienced and strongest archangels, Michelle was probably the most revered and the wisest. Michelle was also the protector of children, and Sandeepa explained this in such a matter-of-fact way that Tony decided not to probe further in asking for any more details.

It had been sad to say goodbye to Albert as Tony had been rather getting to like him, but it was more of an 'au revoir' than an 'adieu' when they parted. Then Sandeepa had explained her story how she had originally been a human and Tony felt a little bit more at ease. She certainly had an amazing, if rather sad, story to tell, about how she had given everything to protect her family, and finally after much suffering and pain she had been brought to Angeland.

As she was relating her story, they had got onto the Subsolo and she had talked about her 'little' choir. She felt Tony would enjoy it, besides it being a potential solution to the eyelash problem, and got him to sing some scales to find out his voice register.

But Tony's mind wandered, aided by the fact that Sandeepa didn't give him much time to say anything before continuing her own story and regaling him with anecdotes about the choir and the various things they had worked on over the last 3,000 human years. Of all the things he had laid eyes upon in Angeland, the one he kept on remembering during the Subsolo trip was the beautiful Natasha, who had been unlike any of the other archangels. She was young and sparky and he had felt as if a thunderbolt had struck him when he laid eyes upon her. An irrepressible and irrational passion had seized him as she approached him in the Jardim do Céu, and when she seductively took his hand she sent a frisson surging through his body. As he gazed into her deep blue, almost violet, eyes, he was struck dumb.

Tony was desperately trying to tune into the conversation with Sandeepa and take in the surroundings of the Subsolo as he walked with her in the streets full of white cars and the white buses. But like a broken record, Tony's mind took itself back to Natasha. He began to fantasize about what it would be like to be with her, and tantalizing images entered unbidden into his thoughts.

'Come down and see me sometime,' she was saying, and her smile revealed perfect teeth while her tongue licked her luscious lips. There was a strange, almost unearthly light as he sat on a sofa facing her. She was on a large round bed with red silk sheets, in a round room with large panoramic windows on all sides looking out onto an exotic city nightscape, with elaborate and fantastic buildings and a large circular boulevard full of cars. She was wearing the same revealing white dress as she had in the Jardim do Céu, and she slipped down the white strings that held the dress onto her shoulders, revealing a black lace top. She widened her legs and continued to look at him, then began to lower the top. Her bright red lipstick was the same colour as the sheets. She beckoned him closer with a finger and almost sang 'I'd love to turn you on'…

'Welcome to the Bright Hall,' said Sandeepa, pulling Tony sharply out of his reverie. He looked up and saw an imposing oval building that was older than the buildings he had seen in the city from the Jardim do Céu. Constructed principally in red brick bounded by white stone, it rose five storeys high with windows snaking around it on the first and second floors. All around him, angels were streaming into the building, with those passing Sandeepa exchanging short cordial greetings.

As Tony and Sandeepa waited at the main entrance, she explained that she was waiting to catch a couple of basses that he could join in with during the rehearsal.

Sandeepa spotted a couple of men and hailed them. 'Hello Graham, hello Alphonso. Would you be so kind as to accompany Tony here?'

'Oh, someone new!' said Graham, a jovial middle-aged angel with a well-manicured beard and moustache. 'We haven't had anyone join the choir for quite a while. Of course, you're most welcome.'

Alphonso was an older-looking angel, with slicked-back black and grey hair, and he also warmly greeted Tony.

'Well, I'd better be off,' said Sandeepa, 'see you at the warm-up in 10 minutes.' She disappeared into the innards of the building.

'We've got a few minutes before we start,' said Alphonso. 'Come and join us – we were going to have a look at the photo exhibition in the corridor before we take our places in the choir.'

They went inside, coming into a corridor with doors on either side that followed the curve of the building. On the walls were pictures of football players in action, the sort of images you might see gracing the sports pages of a newspaper. Tony recognised a few of them in the blue strip that he had seen on the television earlier.

'I see there are some Guardian players here,' he said to Alphonso and Graham.

'That's right,' said Graham, 'although most of the Guardians are keeping their heads down after the match earlier today.'

'This time of year,' said Alphonso, 'this exhibition shows the best players in the Angel Cup – the 30 most highly rated, in fact. For the first time, the highest number are from the *Alles Schwarz*.'

As they milled down the corridor, mingling with other angels, Tony noticed that quite a number of the pictures showed angels in black strip. Alphonso commented on the pictures as they walked by.

'Here's Cristiana, having just done a brilliant little chip against the Hexahedrons,' he said. Tony saw the player in black pumping her fists, while her opponents in purple strip looked on disconsolately.

'And Rupa, the goalkeeper for the *Alles Schwarz*, has the record for the longest clean sheet in the tournament,' Alphonso continued. The picture showed the goalkeeper diving acrobatically to nudge the ball away from the net.

'Yes, the odds are on for the *Alles Schwarz* to get the Cup this time,' said Graham. 'My own team, the Bills, are already eliminated, although Bella and Harper have been by far the best midfielders in the competition.' He pointed to a larger picture showing the two players in a green strip.

'I've seen her before,' said Tony, pointing to what appeared to be the only player in white strip. 'She's Rita, isn't she?' The photograph showed her holding her hands to her mouth with several team-mates leaping with joy behind her.

'That is the great Rita, who played such a decisive role in today's game,' said Alphonso. 'In this picture she'd just scored from behind the half-way line, and she's the only Angeland player in the hall of fame here. She's such a rare talent that she may even have the ability to single-handedly take her team to the finals.'

Graham, however, shook his head, 'not likely, dear Alphonso. I know there is eternal hope in Angeland, but even coming from PirogRus I wouldn't be willing to make a wager on it.'

CHAPTER 8

'Oh look, a man!' exclaimed a number of female angels as Tony made his way up a flight of stairs with Alphonso and Graham. Tony had noticed that the female angels in the building, who he realised were in a substantial majority, had been smiling and looking him up and down with a certain curiosity.

They continued to climb, and suddenly there were only male angels around Tony. Then, all of a sudden, he entered a huge auditorium, which was oval but almost round, and paused for breath. Thousands of red chairs were arranged around the interior, staggered downwards from the top circle area where he stood, and underneath this, another tier of chairs stood above two rows of boxes. At ground level, chairs were lined up in straight rows, with all chairs facing a stage at the end of the oval on which a classical orchestra was warming up. Behind the stage, rows of chairs rose diagonally on either side of an enormous organ. The hubbub of several thousand angels settling themselves into their seats and chatting with their neighbours merged into a gentle turmoil of sound.

'That's the *Stimme von staurn*,' said Graham enthusiastically, pointing to the organ. '150 tonnes with 10,000 pipes that would be nearly 15 kilometres if you laid them end-to-end. The biggest weighs nearly a tonne and the smallest has the width of a drinking straw.'

'I see,' said Tony, who was still taking in the scene in front of him. About 90 per cent of the angels were women, arranged in all of the seats below the level of the circle that he was on, with only male angels on the upper level where he was situated.

Alphonso was following his gaze. He explained, 'So you've got the sopranos on that side and the altos on the other. The tenors and the basses get relegated up here.'

While Tony was reacting to the auditorium, he realised that the auditorium was reacting to him, particularly the lower part. The volume of the buzz of conversation descended perceptibly from all around, as did the peeping and twirling sounds of orchestra, and he sensed a murmur from afar and saw angels reacting to his presence with glances, nods and nudges.

'Good evening everyone,' said Sandeepa, who had entered and positioned herself in the middle of the stage. 'We are very lucky to have a new member of the choir this evening, because he's a human who might teach us a few things. He's just here for this evening, but I know you'll take just as good care of him as if you were his guardian.'

Tony continued to feel rather self-conscious, but thankfully Sandeepa called on another angel, Pippa, to report back on the previous concert, and he was no longer the centre of attention.

'Hello everyone,' said Pippa, an angel with round glasses who was stern but droll at the same time. 'I think we did very well at the open-air concert in Esconder Park, but a few of the sopranos were a little flat during *Summertime*. I noticed creases in some of your wings, so do please take the time to make sure they are well ironed beforehand. That goes for some of the basses too. During the Gloria of the *Misa Criolla* they started dragging everyone else down. And I know we all like having fun with *Si Ya Hamba*, but one archangel – excluding beloved present company – remarked that we looked like a cloud of drunken moths during the rendition, so a lot of improvement is needed next time. As a consequence we will be spending twice as long practising choreography over the River Semaht after we've finished in the Bright Hall, to ensure our flypast is perfect for the upcoming Trooping the White event.'

A light wave of annoyance rippled around the building when this announcement was made. Tony reflected that apart from the time when he had arrived in Angeland and seen all the angels flying at the bases of escalators under the big dome, he hadn't come across a single angel with wings, including here. The angels were however all still wearing white, generally the same toga-like outfits he had seen the guardian angels wear on the plane (he noted the archangels were set apart by a somewhat more pronounced individual style).

Graham and Alphonso were either side of Tony. Seeming to notice his initial thoughts, Graham explained, 'It's true that in Angeland itself, we angels don't tend to have our wings out, but they're jolly useful to provide a suitably acrobatic display for the choir's performances. We also show our wings when we want to let our hair down and, even before our choreography lesson, just for the fun of it. You might hear a call to run through a few numbers of the Last Night of the Fluts which could lead to the emergence of some Flutterers.'

Tony was a little mystified by this, but he realised that Graham had been the only one talking in the entire amphitheatre, and he became distinctly aware of the gaze of Sandeepa, seemingly far away but suddenly rather close.

'Good,' she said, 'Now that I've got everyone's attention we'll do some warming up. Let's start with some stretching.'

She proceeded to lead the angels in the hall through a series of physical warm-up exercises, including some forward bends that produced a certain amount of groaning. At this Tony and a number of the angels had a good giggle.

Then Sandeepa started humming a scale. Soon the whole hall was buzzing to the same sound, ascending and descending the scales, with the sopranos and tenors going higher and the altos and basses going lower. She explained that you didn't need to move your chin or even your tongue to articulate notes, getting everyone at first to hold their chin and sing scales, and then do the same holding their tongue with their hand, which proved both a rather curious spectacle and a strange experience. The warm-up got even more physical as members of the choir were told to pair up, back to back, and sing to feel how the muscles of the back were engaged during singing.

Tony couldn't remember ever singing in a choir before, so all of this was rather novel, and quite fun too. As he leant against Graham's back, he was facing Alphonso, who explained that since Sandeepa had started leading the choir, the angels had loved the freshness and enjoyment of her unique approach, so much so that they all categorically refused to go back to 'professional' rehearsals, which had proved to be a lot more serious and dull.

'Time for an Indian,' chuckled Sandeepa, and proceeded to get the choir to sing 'chicken tikka' then 'saffron rice' and finally 'poppadum' up and down the scales at high speed, leaving Tony spluttering with difficulty as he tried to articulate – although Sandeepa was berating the whole choir for not pronouncing the consonants, so he didn't feel so bad.

However, he did feel suddenly self-conscious at the end of the exercise when Sandeepa announced, 'This next one's an old favourite, but one that you might find particularly useful, Tony. I think it might be the solution for all of Angeland's worries.'

Tony picked up an almost imperceptible edge to her voice and a gleam in her eyes, and became aware of the interested gaze of several thousand angels upon him.

'Just follow me,' said Sandeepa. 'A deep breath out, then hold a few seconds without breathing in. Then a controlled inhalation.'

Sandeepa repeated her instructions and as the hall resounded to the sounds of puffing out and sucking in, her pitch heightened. She drew yet more attention to Tony by specifying his name: 'Out, a big push out, Tony! And hold... then controlled in. OUT, TONY. Hold. In. OUT, TONY, OUT. Hold. In.'

The tempo seemed to build and Tony began to feel more and more overwhelmed at the combination of Sandeepa's insistent instructions and the intense gaze of so many faces, their cheeks puffing in and out like a crazed consortium of trumpet players. Feeling somewhat dizzy, he reached out a hand to one side and as Graham supported him, he felt the instructions penetrating deeper and deeper inside him as his breathing became more and more staccato. His head was spinning and he was beginning to hyperventilate as he began to mix his ins and outs; he lost tempo on an enormous 'OUT', sensing at this stage that the whole hall was commanding his breathing. Suddenly he involuntarily took in a huge breath and felt a searing pain in his chest. With a helpless sense of déjà vu, he passed out.

When he came to, Graham and Alphonso were still there, standing either side of him. Alphonso told him he had only fainted for a few minutes. Peering down at him, with her hand to her mouth and looking extremely sheepish, was Sandeepa, who had come up from the stage.

'What's happened?' asked Tony.

'I'm terribly sorry,' said Sandeepa. 'But that doesn't seem to have helped. Quite the opposite, in fact. The eyelash has lodged even deeper in your lung.'

CHAPTER 9

As Tony pulled himself together and stood up with the help of Alphonso and Graham, Sandeepa remained in front of him, looking rather flustered. The background murmuring increased gradually in volume, but all of a sudden she turned to address the auditorium, announcing in a booming voice, 'That's enough excitement! The show must go on. Let's get on with our programme for the evening. Pippa! Please start us on *Si Ya Hamba* as I get back down to the stage.'

Sandeepa disappeared down the stairs, while Pippa stepped onto the stage and addressed the choir,

'Now, everyone knows this by heart – Tony, this is simple so you'll soon pick it up – and we'll just practise swaying together now, as we are wingless.'

The choir started singing together in a lilting melody, following Pippa who conducted, and Tony felt immediately lifted by the energy all around. It seemed to reverberate through his whole body.

Graham had suggested to Tony that he should just listen initially, and so he did. Gradually, he absorbed the sounds of the bass singers while realising that the tenor, alto and sopranos had different but complementary parts that harmonized rather wonderfully. Round and round the song went, with the same *si ya hamb'e* lyrics, emitting a gentle catchy rhythm and including the *oo-oooo* of the Sopranos. Tony plucked up courage and began with a *si ya*, but stopped when he realised that the angels were singing in a different language with the same melody.

The singing continued to twirl and harmonize agreeably, and Tony became more conscious of the sideways swaying of the angels rippling across the hall in perfect choreography. He swayed the same way and then the language changed into something he recognised, *Marching in the Light of God*. The swaying and the song took on a new significance as he felt the choir was striding purposefully onwards together; he smiled at Alphonso and Graham, as he felt he was part of a wave.

'This is a favourite marching song for angels when they're trying to get their wings,' said Alphonso, and Tony nodded, although he didn't quite understand and wasn't in a position to ask a question.

The language changed again and many angels suddenly erupted in clapping to express delight, many shrieking and whistling with joy.

'We always finish with the language of Angeland,' said Alphonso, 'although things are likely to get even more high-spirited towards the end of the rehearsal.'

The choir went through two rounds of *Caminhando* and the whole finished with a crescendo as the angels raised their hands in the air and waved them around.

'Lovely!' said Sandeepa, who had returned down below, centre stage. She thanked Pippa and applauded the angels around her. 'That's got us all nicely into the spirit, although if you're that wild during the choreography practice with your wings you'll be more like hyperactive butterflies than drunken moths, so just remember to keep your balance and not be too over-enthusiastic.'

Sandeepa then turned to look up at the organ and Tony realised that in front of it a screen was slowly descending from the ceiling.

'This is for you, Tony,' she said. 'We haven't had a new member of the choir for a few hundred years, so we're pleased to test this new technology for the first time. Rather than give you individual music scores, you'll simply be able to follow the music and words on the projection. Just think Karaoke but a bit more upmarket.'

The screen had descended by this time and a projector behind lit it up with the song *Lerchengesang*. Tony recalled seeing music before, but hadn't a clue about what all the dots going up and down the horizontal lines meant. He knew that the funny squiggle at the beginning was a treble clef and could see the four sets of ruled lines, Soprano, Alto, Tenor, Bass. Alphonso seemed to sense his plight as Sandeepa motioned to the sopranos and altos to start, and away the music went, whirling with another rather frenetic and joyous melody that he recognised.

'Don't worry,' said Alphonso as this was going on. 'Just listen for the moment and you'll see our first entry comes just after the ladies finish.'

Tony did as he was told, and saw how the basses and tenors came in and then overlapped, this time in a somewhat different rhythm from the previous song, making him feel quite uplifted.

They started again, and this time Tony plucked up enough courage to join in with the basses. He was rather tentative but was reassured by the confident, booming voices of Alphonso and Graham either side, compared to which his more tenuous efforts were comfortably muted.

Sandeepa was pleased at the difference produced by the choir and congratulated Tony for joining in. She then focused her attention on the sopranos and their pronunciation, taking them through their part on their own, stating rather sternly at the outset, 'Now I know all of you can out-sing the greatest diva on Earth, but in a choir I have to keep on reminding you to stop trying to be the prima donna and listen to each other in order to sing as a choir, not as individuals.'

As the sopranos went through their paces, Graham explained that you had to forgive the enthusiasm of the other angels, as the song was about a lark flying and singing as it ascended through the clouds towards the sun.

'When you get a few angels together, you might well hear us singing. In fact, singing this particular song has become a tradition for angels competing in the final stage of the trials for their wings.'

Tony had been looking around the hall. Above him were some big round saucers hanging from the ceiling that looked like upside-down mushrooms. However, rather than ask about them, he asked, 'What does that mean for an angel, getting one's wings?'

Alphonso and Graham smiled at one another. Alphonso replied, 'It's a curious but rigorous test, a bit like an MoT for a car I guess. Angels are picked at random to do it every 500 angel years to prove that they are worthy to undertake missions on Earth.'

Graham jumped in enthusiastically. 'Up, down, around and through the White Mountain and then finally the eye of the needle, all before the cock crows on the third morning. On average less than half of all angels manage to pass each time they try, much less during a year when the weather is bad.'

As usual in Tony's experience of Angeland, these responses generated even more questions and confusion, but just then Sandeepa brought all of the choir into *Lerchengesang*, running through the whole piece twice before taking them through a range of other songs (including *Yonder Come Day*, *Flying Free* and *Yexwe*). This all seemed to happen at such a pace that Tony did not have time to ask any questions, and indeed he forgot them and almost everything else as he began to throw himself heart and soul into the songs, following the karaoke screen with growing voice and gusto. The music embraced, exhilarated and exulted him, raising his spirit and leading him to feel part of a special shared sensation that he had never encountered before.

All the while, Sandeepa had been leading the choir, magically modulating the singers with a gesture or a glance. Despite the thousands of other angels in the hall, Tony felt that Sandeepa was conducting for him alone. During those moments when the basses sung louder, there appeared to be a hint of anxiety in her glance towards him, but she was otherwise practically always smiling.

Then, all of a sudden, there was a pause and Sandeepa announced that it was time to focus on *Messias*. The orchestra, which had up until this point been silent, given that the singing had been a cappella, now all reached for their scores and looked up at her in anticipation.

'Given that Tony is here, just for a change, let's do the English version of the *Coro Aleluia*,' said Sandeepa.

As the orchestra searched through their scores, Graham explained. 'We perform *Messias* every year as part of our duty as the *Sociedade coral real*, and this piece is a real favourite.'

'And I think at this rate we'll definitely do a number or two from the Last Night of the Fluts,' Alphonso added enthusiastically. 'You'll get a real flavour of why they affectionately call this place Angeland's village hall.'

At a sign from Sandeepa, the orchestra began to play. Though she faced the orchestra, her image was also beamed onto the screen alongside the music so the choir could follow her. Tony saw 'Hallelujah Chorus' up on the screen and looked at Alphonso and Graham. 'I really do know this!' he said enthusiastically.

Before they had a chance to respond, all of the choir sang, and the hall resonated with '*Hallelujah! Hallelujah! Hallelujah! Hallelujah! Hallelujah!*' Tony was pleased that they were finally singing something he knew, the music at least, although it was an education to see and sing the words on the screen for the rest of the piece, given that all he could remember was 'Hallelujah'.

'Well,' said Tony when they came to an end, 'That was enjoyable. We definitely have that on Earth.'

'Yes,' responded Alphonso, 'we borrow a lot of things from Earth.'

'Although the words of this are a little ironic,' said Graham virtually inaudibly. 'All this business of being around forever and ever is rather paradoxical given His disappearance for so long.'

Alphonso nodded but raised his finger to his lips, as if to warn this was rather forbidden territory.

'And now at last,' Sandeepa addressed the choir, 'I think that given all those choreography lessons we'll be working on, the best way to loosen some of you up is to have some fun and do a number from The Last Night of the Fluts. You might recognise this one.'

Sandeepa turned to the orchestra and they started playing, which brought a huge roar of delight from the angels around the hall. Once more Tony stood mouth open in recognition. 'I definitely know this one too,' he said, and suddenly a surge of memories of Earth seemed to tumble back to him, including a hall which was a lot like this one with a concert filled with a hotch-potch of colour, and slightly crazy-looking people waving and swaying to the very music he was now listening to.

The angels in the choir began to bob up and down in time with the stirring march that filled the hall. Then, little by little, spots of colour appeared as individual angels pulled out scarves and hats in black, blue, green, pink, purple, yellow and a chequered black and white pattern. Graham put on a green scarf with 'Bills' written on it and Alphonso put on a white hat. They both grinned at Tony.

In marked contrast to the previous atmosphere, a much more relaxed feeling now flooded the hall. Graham gestured at the open expanse in the middle of the hall and announced to Tony, 'Sorry, I can't hold myself back anymore. Nice to have met you if I don't see you again this evening.'

With that, Graham slithered past the angels on his row, ran down the stairs to the front edge of the circle and vaulted over, launching himself into the abyss. Tony grasped Alphonso's arm in terror, but the angel only giggled and pointed as Graham, whose wings had now appeared, spread in full splendour, as he rose up, waving back at Tony and flying to the centre of the open space in the hall. Angels from all parts of the hall were doing the same whether leaping from the circle, or the middle tier or rising from the ground floor, and each was sprouting wings in the same way that Tony had seen under the big dome when he had first arrived in Angeland. There were perhaps a thousand angels in total, circling each other in a beautiful bobbing choreography to the music, moving in a similar way to the seated angels, although the latter for the most part did not have wings. Coloured flags of all sizes began to emerge. There were a few enormous black ones requiring to be handled by two angels and small ones like the white one that Alphonso was waving.

After a particularly energetic burst from the trumpets and strings, the march suddenly came to a pause. The penetrating squeak as a balloon which had been released into the amphitheatre deflated made everyone laugh – in a strangely identical way to something that Tony remembered. The orchestra then played a gentle tune and the angels and Tony hummed along to it. There was a clash of cymbals at the end and the tune was repeated. Tony was about to start with 'Land…' but then heard the lilting language that was distinctly that of Angeland. It wasn't quite as punchy as the version Tony was used to, but the angels sang with great enthusiasm, waving flags, scarves and hats all the while. The same instrumental march was played, and by this time Tony was enjoying himself so much that he even tried to join in the verse as it was repeated again with even greater volume.

When it finally ended, it was followed by a huge reverberation of cheers and whistles. A steady bumping began as the angels began to thump their feet on the ground and clap in unison, chanting 'Mais um' over and over again in time.

Sandeepa turned to face the hall and gestured for silence. 'I think we shouldn't get too carried away. We'll save the repeat for the real thing,' she said. Sighs of dismay and a few boos followed this announcement.

'However,' she continued as this died down, 'there is just enough time, before we need to move on to the choreography, for a quickie to send you all into paroxysms of sentimentality.'

She turned back to the orchestra and a rousing but solemn tune began, one that Tony also remembered. But this time he simply turned to look at the angels.

Alphonso had begun to cry, and Tony realised all the angels were singing with intense passion. Suddenly, for an instant he had a vision of Earth, before the incident on the plane; he had been working with numbers all day and had cycled home past many buildings in glorious evening sunshine which seemed like Angeland, in a city that was called Bundan or something similar. He came up a back alley into a homely flat and a cat purred at his feet and rubbed his ankles. He needed to prepare a meal for someone coming later, and there was a photo of his grandparents, Fanny and Quentin, on the wall.

As the song came to an end Tony was shaken out of his reverie, but, frustratingly, nothing else was revealed. Alphonso put his hand around his shoulder. There was applause again, but it came quite quickly to an end as Sandeepa announced that they were late for the choreography practice and everyone should get a move on to reach the Semaht river. Tony noticed that the airborne angels were gently descending in the direction of the ground floor exits and retracting their wings, while all the flags, scarves and hats were being stowed away to reveal again the uniform white dress the angels had worn at the start of the rehearsal.

Alphonso accompanied Tony down the stairs along with other descending angels, and complimented him on his singing.

'I hope we can see you again soon,' Alphonso said. 'It's been jolly fun to have someone new, to be honest. And, as for the Angel Cup, I hope you'll support Angeland.'

They reached the exit of the Bright Hall and Tony recognised the Archangel Ray, with his distinctive bow tie and waistcoat, waiting for him outside.

'Hello Tony,' he said. 'Well, you may have had fun during your singing, but it seems to have aggravated rather than solve our little conundrum. So now it's down to your servant Ray here to try a more radical approach. You're going to Heaven.'

CHAPTER 10

Ray

My job has variety, and I've seen a lot of things in my time, but sending someone on a temporary rather than a permanent visit to Heaven is a first for me. I've seen all sorts on the way in – actually I've seen every person – and interviewed them, firstly to get them used to the idea of where they'd like to go, and then to work out all the details. Well, of course it's not *every* person – there's a fair number that I don't see en route to the other place but, praise be, they're in the minority.

Anyhow, when Tony comes out of the Bright Hall I tell him where he's going and he looks understandably perplexed, but then he looks over the road, staring into space at nothing but a wall with a lost and rather lustful look. After a few seconds I jolt him out of this, but I can easily imagine that crafty old Natasha has started to bewitch him a bit with her charms, although it's not my place to comment or speculate.

There are angels streaming out of the Bright Hall, so I hail a taxi to get away quickly and avoid the Subsolo, which will be filling up with all the singers and make it hard to get seats.

I prefer the traditional white cabs rather than those Rebu-cars that you can call up with an oticel. Call me old fashioned, but even with all this new-fangled GPS stuff I still believe a white cab driver will get you there faster.

Once we're off I put the situation straight to Tony: as the singing didn't solve our little conundrum, a little relaxing sojourn and a change of air in Heaven might be just the thing to help dislodge the eyelash and get him back to Earth where he should be. And suddenly the irony of the situation strikes me as awfully funny; here he is getting a return ticket to Heaven after I've been handing out one-ways for so long.

But there's a catch, I remind him. If you get the one-way ticket you define where you'd like to go, but as I'm kind of granting him a temporary visa, he can only go on a visit. So of course I ask him whom he'd like to visit. 'Just pick a relative of yours who's passed away,' I say, 'someone with whom you'd like to catch up with and spend an extended and relaxed holiday'.

As we pass by Esquina Parque Gleba, I can see Tony's having a bit of difficulty with all this. Well, I don't blame him. The range of reactions I get when people walk into my shop and I tell them I'm here to work out the direction shows the full range of humanity. Tears, laughs, screams, hallelujahs, plus a lot of incredulity, right up to the moment when I give them their costume and send them on their way. At least Tony didn't leap out of the taxi. Some people run out of the shop into the street in a panic, a scene my neighbours are well used to by now.

I think for many the mundanity of it all contributes to their disbelief. When people die they expect dramatic pearly gates, to sit on a cloud, to start up as someone or something different, or even to have a bevy of young ladies waiting to perform all sorts of sexual services for them. Instead all they get is me and my little old shop. I guess I'm a bit like a souped-up counsellor, there to talk through all those questions about where people come from and what their destination is, someone who can really make their dreams come true, although of course Heaven isn't all that different from Earth, just a comfortable place to spend an eternal retirement.

'So Tony,' I say, 'You've perhaps seen enough now of Angeland not to be too astonished by all of this, but you can think of me as being a bit like the doorman who directs people to the part of Heaven that they'd be most comfortable in. It will be incredible for you to imagine this, but I've seen everyone who comes in. So just tell me who you'd like to visit.'

'My grandmother,' he says, after thinking a bit. 'Yes, Grandma Fanny. She was in the old people's home close to my parents' house before she died. With this funny amnesia I seem to be experiencing, I can remember at least that much about the place, but I can't forget her and how dear to me she was. Her wicked sense of humour, and how sad I was when she passed away. Yes, Grandma Fanny. I never imagined I would have the chance to get to see her again.'

Naturally I remember Fanny, as I do everyone who's passed my shop. I never forget a face or personality. She was quite a religious woman, very calm and pragmatic when I explained who I was, and we established quickly where she wanted to go. Of course, the choice for her was easy and she was terribly excited at the thought of being reunited with her husband Quentin. Like most people she was sad to think that she would probably never see the rest of her family remaining on Earth, including her beloved grandson Tony, but she was very devout and stoic. It's heart-wrenching to hear the Heaven-bound sometimes, particularly those with regrets about not giving enough expressions of love and, often, forgiveness for those left on Earth. It's like a reverse bereavement for those close to them that they left behind.

Fanny however was full of love and had few regrets. She had lived to a ripe old age, and the discussion we had filled my shop with joy and laughter. She was one of those people who reminded me how much I enjoy my job; a real tonic to counteract all of the difficult cases I have, suicides and people who for one reason or another reject or struggle against death. Oh yes, I've had a few late nights talking for hours with some of them. When someone isn't happy on Earth it can be quite difficult to place them in Heaven.

We passed Festive Road with all its nicely-coloured terraced houses, and then down into the back lane where my shop was tucked away. 'Come in,' I said to Tony, and he walked in past the front window with the red knight costume. Well, he was certainly impressed with all the costumes lined up: the clown, the chef, the American Indian with feathered head dress, the diving suit, the spaceman, oh yes I've got them all – all sorts of interesting things to wear. He liked my rug with fish on it in the centre of the room, which I stood on proudly as he looked around. Of course I also pointed out the picture of me in my younger days punting on some river, where I must say I looked really quite dapper.

CHAPTER 11

Tony had started to forget the alluring image of Natasha, but as he left the Bright Hall he swore that he caught a glance of her again, in her black sexy lingerie, waving at him across the street. He wondered if it was a mirage, because when he blinked the vision vanished, and he was brought back to an equally strange reality as the Archangel Ray broke his reverie and informed him that he would be going to Heaven.

Ray was an amiable old fellow, if a bit slow and absent-minded. It seemed strange to Tony that he would be going to Heaven from a rather moth-eaten fancy dress shop down a back alley, but he had seen enough of angels now not to ask too many questions and instead to go with the flow. So he had sat back and enjoyed the taxi ride to Ray's shop.

Once there, Tony was happy to follow Ray's advice on what to wear, because he had no idea where and how he would find his Grandma Fanny on his visit. Ray seemed very much in his element as he went around the shop and picked for him a fedora hat, a dress shirt, some dandy two-tone shoes and a striped suit.

'You'll fit in a treat,' Ray said. He opened the door at the back of the shop leading to a changing room. 'Well,' he continued, 'it's time you went on your way.' He smiled at Tony, who looked a little confused as he continued, 'All you need to do is put on your clothes and walk through the other door in the changing room. It'll take you to where your Grandma Fanny is.'

'But what will I find and what will I do?' said Tony. 'When will I know when to come back?'

'Don't worry one little bit,' said Ray, 'It's all very simple, and there'll be no need to come back. Sandeepa explained to you about the eyelash trapped in your lung, and I'm sure that within a few days you'll be enjoying yourself so much and feeling so relaxed that you'll expel it naturally. An hour or so after that, you'll start to feel a bit drowsy and drop off to sleep, and then bingo, you'll wake up on Earth and won't remember a thing about us angels, and everything will be fine. You'll have the distinction of being the only human in the history of the world to have visited Heaven before their due time, and when you come through my shop a second time we'll have lots to catch up on together.'

Tony was a bit dubious, as he was after all in Angeland due to a mistake, and he wasn't convinced that more mistakes weren't possible.

'But you did say I'm a rather unique case with my two-way trip and all that. There's no scope for a further mistake or any trouble?'

'Trouble!' exclaimed Ray, 'My dear Tony, I've seen billions pass that door you're about to walk through without a single unhappy soul. You've nothing to worry about at all.'

He instructed Tony to enter the changing room, which had orange walls. Tony took one glance back at Ray, who was beaming benevolently, then he closed the door and changed into his clothes. There was a mirror where he was able to admire himself; the suit fitted a treat, although it was rather wide cut, making Tony feel a bit like a gangster.

'Well I never,' he said to himself and he turned and walked through the second doorway. On the other side, he found himself in a long dark tunnel. He felt that he was walking on crushed stones and could make out what appeared to be railway tracks stretching into the distance. He walked towards the bright light at the end of the tunnel, with the darkness gradually fading away as he advanced.

At the end of the tunnel, there was a railway station with a single wide platform that had one seat and five or six lamp-posts along its length. There was no one to be seen; a single sign, 'Pwllhimmel,' announced the location. Climbing on to the platform, Tony could smell the sea, and then he saw it, about 100 metres away. There was a bay with houses scattered around its shoreline and a few small sailing boats moored up. The landscape was very green.

Tony turned and found the station's exit. He walked out onto the forecourt.

'Hallo!' a deep male voice called, 'Tony?'

Tony turned to see a rather extraordinary-looking man, tall and dark, with a wide forehead, in his late 20s. A shiny blue Rolls-Royce Phantom II car stood behind him. The man approached and grabbed Tony's hand, shaking it vigorously. 'You don't remember me, I expect,' he said. 'I was old and doddery and rather bent over when we last had the pleasure of meeting.'

Suddenly things clicked for Tony, and he was astonished.

'Of course. You're Grandpa Quentin! I remember we never really spoke much and you had a very fierce frown. But you were in your 70s when I knew you, when you, er, died, and I was very small, and you look so different. Why, you're younger than me!'

'Well, old chap, I've been in Hefyn a good few years now and you can see what all the fresh air has done for me,' smiled

Quentin. 'Come on, let's get into the car and back to the cottage. Fanny can't wait to see you.'

Quentin turned the ignition and the Rolls purred up the road away from the sea. 'Our cottage is just a few miles over the other side of the peninsula,' he explained as they coasted along, waving at the occasional passing car.

The sun was shining. There were dappled clouds in the sky and on either side of the road there were fields in which people were tilling the land and working. When they saw the car, they would wave and smile.

'Everyone seems very happy here,' said Tony, 'and I saw that most of the people working in the fields are dressed in white. Are they... angels?'

'Of course my dear fellow, you'll see plenty of them. There are some humans who like to till and look after the land, but the angels do the majority of the farming around here, as well as helping to do things that no human here fancies lending their hand to. It's a perfect coexistence.'

Occasional trees, some with beautiful spring blossom, bordered the road.

'Spring blossom and midsummer every day,' said Quentin, looking at Tony. 'Wonderful, isn't it?'

Tony agreed that the landscape and the set-up seemed quite idyllic. The freshness of the environment and the welcome that he had felt was quite intoxicating. As they careered along, he eased himself back into the comfortable leather seat of the car. But not for long. He jerked himself upright in sheer horror when Quentin turned and manoeuvred himself over into the back of the speeding car, adopting a prostrate position whilst keeping his heels on the driving wheel.

'You look as though you've seen a ghost old boy,' giggled Quentin after regaining his seat. 'I know Fanny wouldn't be too happy if I did that when we were driving together, but there's absolutely nothing to worry about. Nothing can go wrong here. In any case, I found what I was looking for, something Fanny wanted me to give you.'

Tony, not quite believing what he had seen, took what he found to be a framed photograph from Quentin. There was a picture of old Grandma Fanny together with Tony in his early teens, looking rather maladroit. Tears came to Tony's eyes as he looked at it and snatches of lost memories of his Grandmother suddenly came flooding back.

'This was taken in the month before she died,' said Tony, 'almost exactly ten years after you died, Grandpa Quentin. And now here you are, and I'm going to see her again.'

The tears continued to flow and Quentin, happily for Tony, stayed in his seat and looked ahead. He patted his grandson with empathy.

'You know, Tony, I think your visit is the most unexpected and exciting thing that has happened to us here. It's impossible to complain about our existence here, but I think all of our friends and neighbours are hugely jealous that we have such a special visitor.'

Tony smiled at Quentin, feeling a deep and strange sense of gratitude that he was here. He reflected that in the few minutes they had been together, he had got to know his grandfather far better than when he was alive. The separation of two generations seemed not to exist, and with the unexpectedness and gloriousness of it all Tony started to laugh with sheer joy.

Quentin started to guffaw as well, but at the same time Tony realised that the car was whizzing up towards the brow of a hill, with another car parked just before the summit. His laughter abruptly stopped. 'You don't mean to overtake that car,' he said, as he gripped the base of his seat.

But Quentin only continued to laugh as he steered the Rolls to the other side of the road, leaving only a few metres of the road ahead in view.

'My dear fellow,' Quentin said, as they passed the stationary car and then the brow of the hill before plummeting into a descent the other side, 'as I said, there's absolutely nothing to worry about – but you'll quickly get used to that. Here we are in Hefyn!'

Quentin gave a magnanimous sweep of his hand to indicate the sea again a few miles away, the green landscape gently undulating down to meet it. Tony was hoping there would be no more awkward motoring moments.

'This is Moreno Bay, where our cottage is, just a short distance from Hefyn,' said Quentin as they approached the sea. A rocky little island guarded the entrance to the bay. 'There are quite a few tales about Moreno Island but we'll have plenty of time to tell you all about those. I'll take you out there soon.'

They arrived at the cottage, which was situated on a low cliff overlooking the bay. It looked quite old and was not really a cottage, more of a big house, built of old stone. Roses clambered over the front of it and the garden was full of flowers.

Fanny had heard the car coming and ran out of the house to greet them. 'My darling Tony!' she cried. Tony leapt down from the car and they embraced.

'Well, haven't you grown!' she said. Tony replied, 'Well, haven't you got younger!' They laughed, and gazed at each other in amazement. Tony could hardly believe how youthful and in the prime of life she looked, compared to the photograph of the two of them that Quentin had given him.

'I thought you'd like the photo. I was much more beautiful, and you had so much more maturity,' she joked. 'But do come in, I've prepared dinner for us, although I'll show you your room first. Where do we start catching up?'

They walked arm in arm into the cottage, and all of Tony's earlier worries about the car evaporated. He was given a bedroom that overlooked the bay at the top of the house, with a sloping ceiling. He realised with a shock that he hadn't stopped or slept since arriving in Angeland.

Fanny proudly gave him a tour of the cottage, which was very tasteful, the décor reminding Tony of the house she had lived in before she'd gone to the retirement home. A large sitting room occupied the centre of the house, with bookshelves lining nearly all the walls, and there was a cosy little fire in the corner. On a large table were displayed photographs of Fanny and Quentin – the youthful versions – in front of various souvenirs of monuments from around the world: the Taj Mahal, the Pyramids, and one of Quentin with a rifle standing beside a dead elephant. Many of the photos included a young girl, perhaps eleven years old, some with the couple and some alone, and Fanny picked one of these up.

'This is Georgina, the girl we adopted after moving to Hefyn. She's in boarding school now so I'm not sure if you'll get to see her, but she's quite a tomboy!'

They settled down to dinner, Fanny having prepared fish pie, Tony's favourite, followed by some delicious strawberries and cream. Upon arriving in Hefyn, Tony had realised with a start that in Angeland the digestive process, both in and out, had ceased to function. It was rather a welcome relief to rediscover these bodily functions and many of the pleasures associated with them.

'Well, I feel quite human again,' he beamed, leaning back in his chair after the meal and puffing on the cigar that Quentin had offered him.

Fanny explained, 'Of course, when your man Albert came to visit this afternoon I thought he was going to invite us to help with the harvest or deliver the post, as you might expect an angel to do. When he explained that you were going to come this evening I nearly fell off my chair. Anyhow, the news of your visit will have gone all round Hefyn by now – we might even get a queue of people at the front door wanting to see you! But I understand that you've had a shock which has given you terrible memory loss. We hope that staying with us will help you to get better and return home to where you belong. In the meantime, we're so lucky to have you here.'

Fanny and Quentin talked very matter-of-factly about coming to Hefyn. Quentin had come first, and found the cottage and furnished it ready for Fanny, who had arrived ten years later. They said that most people in the area were roughly the same age as them – physical age, of course. There were many couples who, like them, had been together on Earth. Although they had not known anyone else initially, they had quickly got to know other people and made many friends. Quentin said, 'You can't be friends with all the people all the time,' to which Fanny added, 'Different people like different things, but we all get on together fine.'

'We don't reflect on things too much,' continued Quentin, 'For whatever reason, without making a conscious decision but clearly suiting our heart's desire, we've ended up here, as we are, and we couldn't ask for more. We're very blessed.'

They went on to explain that after a few years, an angel had knocked on the door and asked them if they would like to adopt Georgina. She had died on earth as a child, and was looking for a family in Hefyn to adopt her. They met Georgina, and hit it off immediately, so it was easy to make the decision for her to join the family – indeed she filled a gap that they hadn't until then realised was there. A few years before, she had had quite an adventure when three cousins had visited. They had discovered gold ingots under the ruin of the castle on Moreno Island, which had been thrillingly exciting.

As he continued puffing on his cigar as Fanny and Quentin told him about their regular travels, Tony commented that they must have been in Hefyn for at least 20 years, although he realised how angel time was distorted.

'Well, it feels like we've been here an awful lot longer,' said Fanny, 'and of course I haven't aged a single day. But that's the wonderful thing in Hefyn, we don't change – we simply have one perfect day after another, like one long unending holiday.'

Tony smiled. It was clear that Fanny and Quentin were still blissfully enamoured of each other. After all, what more would you want in life or death than to be with the love of your life in the place on Earth you liked the most, doing everything on Earth you might have possibly wanted to do, for ever?

He said goodnight and climbed the stairs to his room, leaving the window open to hear the gentle sound of the sea. He was very happy to be where he was. A niggling worry about something crossed his mind briefly, but as soon as he laid his head on the pillow it disappeared, and he fell into a deep and satisfying sleep.

CHAPTER 12

Tony opened his eyes and looked around the room, and for a second he was unable to work out where he was. But then he heard the sea, and sighed in satisfaction as he lay in bed and wriggled his toes, feeling wonderfully refreshed after an uninterrupted night's sleep. Sunshine glowed around the edges of the curtains, and he leapt out of bed and threw them open. The bay was beautiful, with a couple of small boats bobbing on the sea accompanied by the cries of the seagulls.

He looked down into the garden, where Fanny was tending some runner beans, and she waved up at him.

'Hello Tony! I hope you slept well. If you look in the wardrobe you'll find some clothes that Ray bought for you soon after Albert passed by yesterday. Pick a suit, we'll be going to church after breakfast.'

In the big wardrobe in the corner of the bedroom, Tony found a range of neatly-folded and arranged clothes, with a short note – 'A few things to help you fit in around here. Enjoy! Best, Ray.' He put on a grey suit, a little less wide than the one he had been given in the fancy dress shop, and walked downstairs towards the smell of bacon.

'Delicious, absolutely delicious! Quentin, you are a lucky man to have a wife who's such a great cook.' He tucked into a perfect cooked breakfast. 'Do you ever cook?' he asked.

'Well, things may have moved on in your day old chap, but we're both jolly happy to fit into the gender stereotypes of our age, aren't we love?' said Quentin, beaming at Fanny.

'Yes, and even in Hefyn I can still use my feminine wiles to get my way, even if I'm always the one cooking around here,' Fanny said in a mock-serious way.

Tony smiled, feeling very happy and bathed in both energy and relaxation. The niggly knee, the slightly dodgy lower back and the patch of psoriasis which had been minor but recurring irritants in his life on Earth had diminished somewhat after entering Angeland, but he now realised that they had disappeared overnight in Hefyn.

As it was a Sunday, during breakfast they had agreed to begin the day with church, followed by a picnic on the beach. Fanny was a keen golfer and, although Tony had never played, she insisted that he should come along in the afternoon, as the course was splendid. Then in the evening they would go into town for a dance.

'Well that seems a full schedule,' said Tony. Even though, like golf, church had never been his thing, it would have been rude not to go. He felt as if he was starting a long holiday. He wandered around the garden while waiting for Quentin and Fanny to get ready for church, breathing in the fresh air and admiring the variety of vegetables as well as the splendid view.

'Tally ho,' said Fanny when they were all installed in the Rolls-Royce. They drove for a short while before arriving at the church, a quaint building with a tower that had rounded parapets.

'I trust you didn't frighten Tony with your antics when you were driving up from the station,' she said to Quentin. She glanced back at Tony in the rear seat, but he was so happy now that he had no problem conniving innocence.

Several other classic cars were parked at the entrance to the church, and Fanny introduced him to a number of the people who were making up the small throng heading into the church. 'This is Margaret and John, with Jeremy and Anna, and James...'

'You can't imagine how excited we are to meet you,' said Margaret. 'We love life here, but I'm so curious to hear how things are on Earth.'

'Now Margaret,' interjected Fanny, 'I told you that Tony has had a nasty shock and we're not to ask difficult questions about his past life.' She steered them towards the priest, who was greeting people at the door.

'Reverend, I'd like to introduce you to my grandson, Tony,' said Fanny, 'and Tony, this is the Reverend John Prester, our parish priest.'

They shook hands.

'I've heard quite a bit about you already,' said the Reverend, 'and it's an honour to have you here. You are most welcome to our service. In fact, we don't often have visitors but today we have two, including you.' He indicated inside the church, with its simple but attractive wooden beams and pews, to where a short woman with a veil was sitting at the back.

They entered the church and Quentin started talking about cars to some of the men, while Fanny started talking about golf to some of the women, so Tony edged his way away from of the group. He felt drawn in a funny way to the woman in the veil, and wandered down the aisle and sat next to her.

'Hello poppet,' she said, drawing back her veil and smiling at him. The other people were all perfectly tailored, coiffured and well proportioned, but this woman was rather fat and her cream dress was old, grey and poorly fitting, while her thin hair was arranged in two untidy pigtails tied up with cheap elastic bands.

'Of course you remember me,' she said. Tony reeled back in disgust at the unexpectedly strong body odour and halitosis that wafted towards him.

Then he did remember.

'Fifi! That's it, Fifi. You were in the plane with me. The Archangel Gabriel took you. You winked at me as you got dragged out.'

'Excellent, excellent, ten out of ten, you'll be the Brain of Britain before you know it.' She nodded theatrically. 'Indeed, Fifi they call me, and Fifi I am, sixty-third grade angel, lowest of the low and officially renegade. But keep mum, my dear, and now it's time to keep quiet, to pay homage to the highest of the high.' She indicated that the service was starting, and Tony looked forward to see Fanny looking back to check everything was fine.

They sang 'Amazing Grace' and 'All Things Bright And Beautiful,' and then Margaret, to whom Tony had been introduced, read 1: Corinthians 13. Tony noticed that Fifi had been a little agitated throughout the ceremony and when the bit in the verse about the mirror came up she rocked gently back and forth, mumbling 'mirrors, oh glasses darkly.'

Then they sang 'O Come All Ye Faithful'. Tony saw that Fifi looked rather pained whenever angels were mentioned, ejaculating, 'Angels! Dirty filthy angels!' A few people frowned at them.

'We are gathered this beautiful Sunday to give thanks,' said the priest as he began his sermon. 'We give thanks to how we are blessed in Hefyn and for our community of love. We thank the angels' – at which point Fifi coughed and began rocking back and forth – 'for their tireless efforts to support us.'

The Reverend then said something about welcoming visitors and healing, but Tony didn't really pay much attention as Fifi was still rocking back and forth, looking not only distracted but somewhat rabid, as a light trace of foam began to escape from her mouth. The Reverend stopped his sermon and asked if she was quite well, and the half of the church that had not turned to look back at her with Tony beside her now did so.

'Thank you Reverend, I'm absolutely fine,' Fifi said, quite transformed, upright and composed in an instant. 'Please continue your moving sermon.'

The Reverend continued to the end and then invited members of the congregation to take communion or receive a blessing if they wished. The organ played soothing music and people in the church stood and moved towards the front of the church in an orderly way to partake of the bread and wine.

For some reason Tony felt he did not want to join the queue of people kneeling before the priest, but he was surprised to see Fifi rise. He whispered to her, 'But you're an angel, why are you going?'

She tapped his nose, and replied 'Poppety Einstein, do you see any other angels here? I'm just blending in, unlike you.' She strode haughtily down the aisle to join the back of the queue, glancing back at him a couple of times.

The gentle organ music continued and Tony remained seated. As people filed back to their seats he noticed that one or two of them looked at him a little curiously. Fifi returned and smiled at him and patted him on the knee, and then they rose for the final hymn, 'Abide With Me.' Rather surprisingly, as the hymn was sung, Fifi stood perfectly still in a sombre and reflective attitude.

'Some things you have to respect because of football, of course,' Fifi said as she started to leave rather abruptly after the end of the hymn. 'Now poppet, remember that I'm a renegade angel, so don't go telling on me. In fact you might need a bit of help. You look like just the sort who might get into trouble around here, so if you need to find me, watch out for the cream-coloured beach hut.'

She started down the aisle, then looked back. 'Oh, and I'm sure you might want to hear more about what these archangels really have in store for you.'

With that, she pushed her way swiftly to the front of the church, shook the hand of the Reverend, and disappeared from view.

Tony got up, suddenly becoming conscious again of the enveloping miasma of body odour and halitosis Fifi had left behind. He admired the simple interior of the church for a few moments before making his way to the front of the church. The Reverend seemed to be a very reasonable and liberal man, and Tony couldn't resist asking, 'Reverend, how is it that you continue to worship even though you're in Heaven now? It doesn't make sense to me.'

The Reverend smiled. 'You might be surprised to hear that not everyone in Hefyn pays much attention to God, Tony, even though His existence, and that of angels, is indisputable. Yet in Hefyn and on Earth, the church-going flock is much the same. Everyone in Hefyn has lived and lived decently, but the individual conventions that we have on Earth continue, which may mean we do different things. But we all coexist perfectly.'

Tony thanked the Reverend and moved towards the entrance of the church, pausing a moment to look at some posters advertising an upcoming jam-tasting evening and a proposed visit to the Holy Land. At the same time, some voices from outside wafted his way and he recognised those of Margaret and Anna.

'...rather shocking that he didn't take communion.'

'...and chatting during the service with that odd-looking woman, never seen her before.'

He paused for a moment before walking out of the church and seeing the two women who were talking with Fanny. They all looked up and Fanny looked very pleased to see Tony, while the other two looked a little sheepish.

'Tony, Margaret and Anna were just saying how much they'd like to see you again. Perhaps they can come round for a drink this week?'

'Oh that would be lovely,' said Margaret, brightening up. Anna nodded for rather longer than one would expect.

'Time for a picnic!' announced Quentin, rounding them up, and they bundled into the blue Rolls-Royce.

CHAPTER 13

Down on the beach overlooking Moreno Island, Fanny laid out a large red and white checked tablecloth and Quentin and Tony brought the picnic hamper. They kicked off their shoes and socks and cracked open some bottles of ginger beer. Cold tongue and salad, loaves of bread, plum pie and custard and then cheese were all laid out and given due attention before they all reclined contentedly.

Tony mentioned the trip to the Holy Land he'd seen advertised in the church, and Quentin and Fanny said they had been a few times. Once a year they would take a long break from Hefyn, often leaving the British Isles by plane, flying boat, steamer or airship.

'They give a consistently impeccable service,' said Quentin, 'as it's generally angels that crew the ships and help show you around. They really do fulfil every need you could imagine.'

The conversation gradually petered out as the three watched the sea in quiet and satisfied contemplation. Quentin and Fanny dozed off in each other's arms, so Tony got up and wandered to the edge of the water, rolling up his trousers and paddling gently along the shore. He understood how pleasant it must be to stay here, although he felt strangely old compared to most other people, who appeared to be so young.

It had been very odd, however, to meet that stinky and strange angel, Fifi. He thought that the Archangel Gabriel had captured her and yet, only a little while later, she had appeared apparently at liberty. He didn't really understand how he could get in trouble here, but her insinuation about the archangels' hidden purpose was distinctly worrying. Sandeepa and Ray had seemed both earnest and kind, and the others, apart from Gabriel, seemed decent enough. He realised that he certainly wanted to get to know Natasha better, although since he had arrived in Hefyn he hadn't been troubled by any visitations from her.

He was jolted out of his thoughts by a couple of 'Hellos' from the sea, and saw that a white boat with a white sail was anchored not far from shore. Two women were in the sea, and they swam towards him and then walked out of the sea to approach him. As they approached, Tony saw that they both wore white swimsuits and had an overpowering freshness, beauty and sensuality. One was blonde and the other brunette.

'You must be Tony,' the brown-haired one said. 'We've heard a lot about you and how you came through the HARP. It's a great honour and pleasure to meet you.'

She thrust out her hand for him to shake and the blonde girl followed suit, giggling.

'She's always forgetting her manners,' said the brown-haired one. 'She's Eva and I'm Lorraine.'

'Er... you must be angels, I guess,' said Tony, and they both nodded and 'mmmed' in agreement.

Tony continued, 'I thought you tilled the fields and delivered the post and that sort of thing, rather than swimming around in the sea?'

'We do all sorts of tasks and things to help,' said Lorraine.

'I'll have you know I grew those strawberries you ate last night,' said Eva proudly, and the two nodded to each other.

'In fact,' said Lorraine, 'we like to help people in Hefyn enjoy their stay as best as possible.'

'As best as possible,' echoed Eva.

'And if you think of anything one of us could do for you, you know where we are,' said Lorraine.

'Or maybe both of us at the same time could provide a useful service,' said Eva. 'We know all sorts of ways to release tension, to make you happy and joyful.'

Quite apart from the suggestive language and the way it was spoken, Tony felt rather ill at ease, but he was also strangely rather turned on, as Eva and Lorraine's body language seemed to point in a very clear direction.

'Tony!' Fanny called, coming down the beach.

'Hello,' said Eva and Lorraine rather deferentially to Fanny, who looked uncharacteristically pugnacious.

'Well, we'll be off,' said Eva, 'strawberries to tend, you know. Nice to meet you, Tony.' They plunged back into the sea, turning to wave goodbye.

Fanny smiled and explained to Tony that he needed to be a little careful around the angels as they could be a little enthusiastic, and he might want to settle in for a few days before getting to know them.

'Well,' said Quentin, who had been watching from afar as they arrived back at the picnic spot, 'we are in Hefyn after all, and I'm not sure either you or I are ones for moralising about the angels.'

He shared a knowing smile with Fanny and winked at Tony, playfully boxing him in the chest. He started humming 'Cheek to Cheek' as they climbed back up the beach towards the car.

'All right dear boy, it's time to hit the links,' said Fanny to Tony after they had returned to the cottage and got ready to go to play golf. Tony had found a set of golf knickerbockers and hose, and adjusted his tie as they got into the car together.

'Cheerio Quentin,' called Fanny. Her husband had decided to stay home and work on his book for the afternoon. With that, she steered the Rolls down the drive. The clubhouse was just over a mile away and Tony immediately appreciated his grandmother's driving style, which was more gentle and cautious than that of his grandfather.

The clubhouse was a rather unremarkable building, although the course commanded fantastic views of the sea. Among the crowd of twenty or so people on the clubhouse terrace, Tony recognised on the terrace a few of the people who had been in church. They made small talk for a while with him and Fanny before he changed into his Oxford shoes with spikes.

'Let's find ourselves some caddies,' said Fanny, and they went over to a group of a dozen or so angels who were sitting in a corner of the terrace in fine but practical white clothes.

'Now, Geoffrey, I think as usual you can come with me,' she said to a dark-haired angel who had two buttons undone at the top of his shirt, with prodigious chest hair emerging.

'I'm sure you girls and you, Christopher, would love to caddy for Tony, but I think today Clement would be ideal,' she continued. The excluded group had been looking Tony up and down in rather the same way as the two bathers earlier, and seemed downcast at his grandmother's decision.

Clement had curly brown hair and was impeccably buttoned up. He and Geoffrey shook Tony's hand, saying how much of an honour it was to be accompanying him on this round of golf. Like all the angels and humans that Tony had seen so far in Hefyn, they appeared to be miraculously young. The glances and metaphorical stroking he received made him feel like a film star slightly past his prime wandering among his fans.

The two angels each fetched a bag of clubs and they went together onto the putting green.

'I can manage this,' said Tony, and memories of being a dab hand at crazy golf as a child with his grandmother came back to him. 'But I don't think I've ever swung a golf club to lift the ball off the ground,' he continued, rather concerned.

'Dear Tony, just give it a try and after a few seasons you'll be playing like a pro,' Fanny said. 'With some expert angel tuition you'll have a single-figure handicap before you know it. Why, Clement can give you a quick lesson now if you want.'

Tony and Clement went to a practice area with signs marking intervals of 50 yards stretching into the distance. Clement explained a few of the fine points of the game, demonstrated the swing and helped Tony get the hang of it. Before he knew it he had hit a ball in a beautiful arc more than 150 yards.

'Thank you very much,' Tony said to Clement, who was very agreeable. However, Tony was a little distracted when he turned every now and then and saw his grandmother talking with Geoffrey in a rather more friendly way that you would expect between a married woman and her caddy, and he even caught a glimpse of her twirling his chest hair.

Tony and Clement rejoined them. By now they had adopted a more platonic demeanour. They walked up to the first tee, with the fairway stretching away in front of them and the 18th fairway parallel on the left.

'I say,' said Tony, 'did I see that man in the distance on the 18th tee kissing his angel caddy?'

'Well, maybe you did, my innocent little grandson,' said Fanny and laughed out loud, 'in any case, a kiss is just a kiss.'

Tony smiled. He felt a little awkward, but he recomposed himself quickly and fell back into the carefree spirit of everything in Hefyn. Clement and Geoffrey were looking at him amiably.

'Don't worry one bit,' said Geoffrey, gazing at Fanny. 'in Hefyn all is pleasure and when you realise nothing can ever, ever go wrong, the sky's the limit.'

'You see, Tony, I only pick poetic angels to be my caddy,' said Fanny.

Tony didn't feel that what had been said had been particularly poetic, but he didn't want to spoil the moment. 'So Grandma, I think it's age before beauty, and the honour is yours,' he said, gesturing for her to take the women's tee.

'You see, Geoffrey, he's charming and cheeky, as I've always told you,' she said, tapping the angel in the chest with her driver. She placed her ball, and with a graceful swing sent it down the middle of the fairway. Tony and the two angels applauded.

Tony felt a little nervous as he approached the men's tee, which was a good 40 yards behind the women's tee. Fanny's ball seemed a long way in the distance. Clement had suggested that he take a 3-iron rather than a wood, gently reminding him of the technique. Tony was a bit confused that the little bit of wood used to support the ball had the same name as the place where he was standing, but he put his tee on the first tee and lined himself up a little stiffly. Back he swung, but on the forward stroke the club sailed low into the ground and the ball ballooned upwards, bounced a few times, and ended up about halfway between the men's and the ladies' tees.

'Oh Tony,' Fanny said, looking rather amused. Clement and Geoffrey were looking more sympathetic.

'I think you'd better start again – after all, you are a beginner,' she said kindly.

Clement had retrieved his ball and brought it back to Tony, who looked back at the clubhouse and saw several sets of eyes looking at him. They rapidly turned away when he caught sight of them.

'I'm just getting warmed up,' Tony said, 'I want to make sure you have a chance, Grandma.'

However, he still felt slightly tense and as he lined up his ball on the tee again, he was aware that he was the centre of attention. He swung backwards with more deliberation, but again came down stiffly and this time he topped the ball, making it skim rather ineffectually along the ground before resting on the women's tee.

At this point, Fanny hooted with laughter and Clement and Geoffrey were infected and started to smirk. 'Why, it's an incredible improvement as you're shooting twice as long,' said Fanny, and she collapsed on the ground in paroxysms of giggling. 'I am sorry, dear boy,' she gasped, 'but you really are a wonderfully rare treat to have here.'

Tony couldn't help but smile back, although he had begun to feel a stab of frustration. All the people and angels in the clubhouse were now looking quizzically in their direction.

'OK, third time lucky,' said Tony, determined to send the silly little ball into the distance this time. Clement approached him and got him to do a few more practice swings, breathing methodically so he began to feel calmer.

Tony lined up his ball on the tee once more, having retrieved it from the women's tee once again, and tried to relax and remember what Clement had told him. He was conscious that many eyes were upon him. He swung backwards and through, and the ball shot away from him in a satisfying way.

'Well done Tony,' said Clement.

'Oh, I think he's hooked it,' said Geoffrey.

'My my, it's heading towards Henry on the 18th,' said Fanny. 'It can't be carrying that far. Gosh, I've forgotten what to... Fore! FORE!!!' she bellowed.

The man who Tony had seen coming up the 18th fairway had approached to within about 150 yards, side by side with his female caddy. They looked up a second after Fanny had bellowed, and an instant afterwards Tony's ball landed squarely in the middle of the man's forehead, and he crumpled to the ground.

'Oh my God!' said Fanny.

'That's impossible,' said Geoffrey.

Clement fainted and collapsed to the ground.

Tony heard shrieks coming from the clubhouse, looked back and saw the humans in a high state of agitation. The angels hesitated in confusion for an instant, but then they all started running out towards the 18th fairway.

Tony had assessed the situation rather more quickly. 'Come on,' he said, gesturing to Geoffrey and Fanny to join him as he ran to the prostrate golfer.

Arriving at the scene, Tony found the female angel caddy cradling Henry in her arms and bawling her eyes out. The others arrived and stood around agog, with Geoffrey repeating, 'impossible, simply impossible!' over and over again.

'This type of thing is unimaginable in Hefyn,' said Fanny. 'Oh, poor Henry, what can we do?'

'Well, aren't any of you going to do anything?' asked Tony. The growing crowd looked from one to another with glazed and shocked expressions.

'Someone get some crushed ice in a bag at least,' said Tony, 'And perhaps I can put him in the recovery position.'

At this point Henry moaned and opened his eyes.

'Oh, my head is killing me,' cried the prostrate man. 'I never thought I'd feel pain like that again after coming to Hefyn.'

'My poor Henry,' the female angel caddy said, hugging him.

Several of the crowd were crying now, human and angel alike, and everyone was stunned.

'It's not possible,' Geoffrey continued, now sitting down and shaking his head. 'It's simply not possible.'

Within a few minutes, however, everyone was in a much happier mood. Tony helped Henry up, an ice pack arrived, and the injured man was able to hold it to his head and even make a joke or two. Clement recovered consciousness and looked very embarrassed. They all walked back to the clubhouse, and Tony told Henry to expect a big bump and warned him about concussion.

'We've all virtually forgotten about these things in Hefyn,' Fanny said in a rather subdued way, holding onto Tony and inclining her head onto his shoulder.

'Oh Teetee, I'm so happy you're here,' said Henry emotionally to the female angel caddy, who was hanging on to him as if for dear life.

'Oh Heehee, I'm going to adore you twice as much for each round of golf we have together,' replied the wide-eyed Teetee.

CHAPTER 14

＊

'Well, it's certainly quite remarkable,' said Quentin as he thoughtfully puffed on a pipe in the sitting room after Fanny and Tony had told him the story. 'As you've seen, Tony, after you've been around in Hefyn a very short while, you become accustomed to the fact that nothing goes wrong. Almost anything you would have considered a risk on Earth becomes immaterial here.'

'Yes,' said Fanny, looking rather stern, 'like driving a car with your feet on the wheel while digging something out of the boot.'

'Indeed,' said Quentin, 'but that perhaps is one of my worst excesses. There are a certain number of people here who have taken up cliff diving, skydiving, mountain climbing and so forth, which on Earth would lead to a certain number of casualties. But I have never heard of any problems – and certainly not a bump on the head.'

'But don't you think people who end up in Hefyn are all responsible and sensible people?' said Fanny.

'Yes, yes,' agreed Quentin, 'and nothing untoward has ever happened all the time we've been here. We have had a blissful existence. In fact, when we arrived here we noticed that a few people arrived after us, but then no one else did. I remember Ray in his costume shop telling me that the choice of Hefyn was just right for me and you, and some others too, but it would be different for some others.'

'I can testify to that,' said Tony, 'It's obvious to me that this place is your youthful idyll, but it's a nostalgic period piece to me. My memory of my past life might be bad, but I can't imagine I'd choose this place to spend eternity.'

The grandfather clock in the hall ticked and then chimed three o'clock. Fanny and Tony had come back very soon after the accident, deciding that any further golf was off the agenda that day.

'But clearly I'm responsible,' said Tony, 'I hit that golf ball. I've got a unique two-way ticket here and I don't really fit in.'

'Hold on,' said Fanny. 'I can tell you another thing that disconcerted me earlier in the day. I've never heard Margaret and Anna criticise a visitor to our church like they did. I was quite upset.'

'There you are, I think that confirms on a number of levels that I'm a walking disaster zone here in Hefyn,' said Tony.

'Oh Tony, don't be so silly,' replied Fanny. 'We mustn't go jumping to conclusions. We must have faith in the wonderful angels. I was about to mention that there was another new thing that has stood out much more than you today. We get visitors in the church every now and then, but I've never seen, let alone smelt, anything like that strange lady you were sitting with at the back of the church. She was talking quite a lot to you, and apparently to herself too, but I didn't feel at all comfortable with her there, with her dirty dress and the funny veil.'

Tony hesitated, weighing up the possibility that Fifi was malevolent, particularly as she had rather proudly described herself as a 'renegade angel'. But he also remembered her entreaty not to share any of the information she had divulged.

'Yes, she was a bit odd,' he said. 'She said she'd come down from London, and kept on mentioning football.'

'Ah well,' said Fanny, 'that might explain it a bit. Every now and then we get these people from the capital who are a bit peculiar. But I think she won the award for being the most peculiar.'

Quentin proposed that they should row out and see Moreno Island. 'Assuming we don't all drown because of Tony,' he added. Fanny didn't really like the joke, saying she was tired and preferred to have a nap.

The two men walked down to the beach and pulled a rowing boat down to the sea. Soon Quentin was taking them towards the island with powerful strokes.

'Coo-eee!' came a call, and they looked up to see that the white sailing boat that had been moored off the beach with Lorraine and Eva on board was 50 yards or so away and approaching.

'Hello girls,' called Quentin. 'I've been told you need to go easy on Tony for a few days at least.'

'We're waiting patiently,' Lorraine said.

'Ready to be boarded,' Eva added. They waved seductively as the boat sailed by and cut across their trajectory.

'Energetic young things,' smiled Quentin, but Tony was not in too much of a mood to react or respond, as he had been wondering about Fifi's real intentions.

They quickly approached the island, with Tony having a turn at rowing even though Quentin was much stronger. Quentin manoeuvred the boat between the rocks and into an inlet, and the boat nestled easily on some sand.

'Let me show you round,' Quentin said, and they walked up to the ruined castle. There were a lot of rabbits, which were very tame.

'It's in the dungeons of this castle that I was telling you where my adopted daughter and nephews and niece found some gold ingots,' explained Quentin.

They could see the cottage in the distance; Fanny was in the garden and they waved to each other. Tony had enjoyed the trip and had begun to feel a lot better after the shock at the golf course; this and the worries about Fifi seemed to be slipping from his mind. He and Quentin had a swim off the other side of the island, and then rowed back. By the time they arrived back at the cottage the sun was getting lower in the sky.

'Time for dancing!' Quentin announced as they entered the cottage. Fanny was already looking slim and glamorous in a long floral dress. 'Sunday night is dancing night,' she explained. 'You'll love the dance hall in town.'

After a light supper, the two men took quick baths. Tony found a tweed vest and dancing shoes in the bedroom wardrobe, and they set off once again in the Rolls-Royce. Tony saw Hefyn Bay for the first time as a beautiful dusky sunset spread over the sea. There were only a dozen or so buildings around the bay, all with lights twinkling prettily. A row of beach huts stood just above the beach, and Tony looked for a cream one, but he could only see brightly-coloured ones.

'Welcome to Hefyn Shangri-La,' said Quentin, as they approached a large building at the corner of the bay. There were at least 100 cars parked outside and their elegantly-attired occupants were either admiring the sunset or had already started to climb up a wide staircase to enter the building.

'It might not be the Savoy, but it's certainly got glamour and class,' said Fanny as they entered the lobby, where Tony could admire the cut-glass chandelier and marble staircase.

'Tonight we're very excited to have the famous singer Frederica Arder from across the Atlantic,' said Quentin, pointing to a poster advertising the evening which showed an exotic-looking lady. They climbed the marble staircase and entered a large room decorated in pink and adorned with many mirrors. Tables and chairs were positioned all along the sides of the room and at the end was a stage, where a Big

Band all decked out in white were playing gentle jazz as they entered. Some of the band members had been playing on the top of the 737 airliner at the start of Tony's adventure. They were excited to see him in the flesh, although this small-world coincidence was sadly lost on Tony as he had only heard and not seen them.

A separate group of angels dressed in white waistcoats paraded into the room and proceeded to hand out glasses of champagne to all the guests.

'You'll see it's a bit formulaic,' said Fanny, 'but it's ever so much fun. We're going to be starting with the Big Apple, and you should join in whenever you feel like it.'

The music changed and the guests rose and started twirling, swinging and turning counter-clockwise, throwing up their arms and legs and going in and out to their own version of the hokey-cokey. Tony just watched at first, a little nervously, as he had never seen the dance before and had a nagging doubt that he might cause some kind of accident. Everyone seemed very polished in their dancing, but they were obviously having a lot of fun. Fanny, Quentin and many others encouraged him to join in and before he knew it, he was up and dancing with them. He found it relatively easy to follow, and although he was wrong-stepped a number of times and bumped into quite a few people, it was all good-natured and full of merriment.

They went through a few rounds before stopping. Tony was quite out of breath and perspiring, but he felt a lot more alive that he had done in quite a while.

'Marvellous!' was the only word that escaped his lips as he sat sipping more champagne with Quentin and Fanny.

During the pause, Quentin and Fanny introduced Tony to a woman called Beatrice, who seemed a little shy but very pleasant. They talked about Tony's opinions of Hefyn and she was sympathetic about his memory loss. She looked at him a little oddly and then excused herself to prepare for the next dance.

'I'll be quite straight with you, Tony,' said Fanny, 'we've been trying to find Beatrice a partner, human or angel, since soon after we arrived. She's lovely. She gets a bit lost in her thoughts, although she seems happy like the rest of us here.'

The next dance was a foxtrot, and Fanny advised Tony to sit this one out. 'We've been practising the routine for years and years,' she said. 'I hope you like it.'

With that, the couples took their places and for 15 minutes they performed a choreographed set of moves both as couples and in groups. Tony enjoyed watching them and as the dance ended and they left the dance floor, he gave them enthusiastic applause, the champagne servers following his lead.

More champagne was proffered and Tony started feeling a little light-headed. Fanny once again suggested that he should sit out the next dance, the jitterbug, as she said the moves were a little technical, and he was again pleased to just watch. This time the dancers reached acrobatic prowess, with the men regularly sweeping the women through their legs or rolling them over their shoulders.

At the end of the dance, the visiting singer Frederica Arder was introduced and greeted with warm applause. 'Let me start with an old favourite,' she said into the microphone, and Fanny rushed over to Beatrice, half-dragging her towards Tony.

'This time you can dance, Tony,' Fanny said. 'Beatrice has kindly agreed to be your partner.'

Beatrice looked rather reticent and embarrassed, but she smiled gamely at Fanny.

'Come on then Tony,' Beatrice said, 'Do you know how to waltz?'

Tony didn't know how to waltz, and Beatrice laughed.

'Well, Tony, you're going to be the woman in this dance,' she said. 'Just follow my lead.'

The music started and Frederica Arder began singing. The music was very familiar, but the words were new.

Hefyn, I'm in Hefyn, and my soul throbs so that I can hardly think…

It seemed a little strange to be the only man dancing backwards. Some of the couples looked at Tony with kind amusement, but Beatrice was so strongly effective in guiding him around that he soon got the hang of it. The cares that had hung around him earlier in the day seemed to vanish as he gazed at Beatrice. She looked serious most of the time, but occasionally she shot him a smile which was alluring and strangely conspiratorial.

Federica stopped singing while the band continued the melody, and Tony thanked Beatrice as they continued to glide around the dance floor.

'I really enjoyed that. And I'm enjoying being with you. Thank you.'

'You're welcome, Tony. No doubt Fanny has explained that I'm a spinster well past her prime who's just gagging for a handsome and innocent man like you to sink my claws into.'

'Not quite like that,' said Tony, 'but yes.' He paused as Beatrice manoeuvred him past a group of angel servers who waved at them, then resumed, 'Although I get the impression that whatever approach you use it's a lot more subtle than the angels around here.'

'The dear angels, yes yes,' said Beatrice. 'You know Tony, they may be very affectionate but I've never seen one express real love, at least not towards me. It's like… well, almost as if they are afraid. In any case, however much they provide eye candy, or any other type of candy, there's no point in getting too attached. They come and then go after a few years at most, and I almost get the impression that it's a bit of a holiday for them here.'

'So you prefer humans then?'

'Well, unfortunately there are not many suitable candidates around,' said Beatrice. 'You, however, are a rare and rather interesting possibility.'

The music stopped and she put her arms around him and gently slid her hands up to his head. Her face was a little flushed and he blushed, but felt very at ease.

'But I know that regrettably that will never work out,' said Beatrice, running her hands through his hair. Her tone had become a little downcast.

'Why – why's that?' said Tony, who had become rather attracted to her.

'Because, dear Tony, I've been around long enough to read people quite well, and I also heard about your story. It's because it's obvious to me that you are deeply in love with someone else, even if you don't know it or you choose to deny it.'

With that, she looked deeply into Tony's eyes, kissed him on the cheek, slipped her fingers slowly out of his and returned to her seat.

Left alone on the dance floor, he suddenly remembered being on the plane, holding the hand of someone, some familiar brown hair… and nothing else, just a gap that made him profoundly sad. Next, the perfect, sexy image of Natasha abruptly intruded into his thoughts. He made his way to a nearby seat and stared distantly at the happy throng of people in the room, somewhat confused, and a tear came to his eye.

CHAPTER 15

'Oh, I'm so excited,' said Fanny as they drove back to the cottage. 'I've never seen Beatrice act the way she did tonight. A peck on the cheek! And after just one dance. And you seemed to enjoy it Tony, if I may say so.'

Tony had got back into the spirit of the dance soon after he had separated from Beatrice, and had rejoined the rounds of dancing, quaffing champagne, listening to music and making small talk which lasted until early in the morning. He had propped himself up, tired but contented, on the back seat of the car and did not want to disabuse his grandmother, so he simply responded by saying he was looking forward to next week's dance and to getting to know Beatrice better. Beatrice, however, had left the dance hall soon after her dance with Tony, and they had not had a further chance to interact.

Perhaps it was the rather tranquillising consequence of being in Hefyn, but in any case the effect of the alcohol, the exercise, the social pleasure and the agreeable nice-time breeze made Tony feel as though he had no cares in the world at all. He hardly batted an eye as Quentin drove the Rolls-Royce at top speed through a crossroads with steep and semi-blind turns on either side of the road. They reached home, said their goodnights and Tony hummed 'Perfect Day' to himself as he walked upstairs and collapsed into bed.

'How about spending the morning on the beach?' suggested Quentin as they had breakfast the next morning. Tony and Fanny both thought this a wonderful idea. After breakfast, Tony discovered a dark blue one-piece tank top and shorts in the bedroom wardrobe, which he tried on in front of Fanny and Quentin.

'Very stylish,' said Fanny, 'although a shade passé these days as it doesn't show the torso. We might be able to get hold of some trunks for you down on the beach.'

They took a parasol and hamper with a packed lunch, and drove back along the same route to Hefyn Bay that they had taken the evening before.

'There's sure to be some visitors, but there's always plenty of space,' said Quentin, and as they arrived Tony saw a couple of charabancs, with big open-air compartments for people to sit in. One had just arrived as they pulled up and people were getting down with their own picnics, balls and other beach equipment. Men, women and children all looked very cheerful.

'Well, isn't this gay,' said Fanny, as they walked along the path that bordered the beach. There were railings on one side to guard against the drop to the beach, and on the other side there were brightly coloured beach huts. About a third of the huts were in use, with people sitting outside or going back and forth. Tony still couldn't see a cream-coloured hut, but he didn't really mind as he was more focused on the chance to settle down on the beach and have a swim.

An ice-cream cart was parked at the top of the ramp leading to the sand, and as they walked down Tony took a closer look at the jetty on the other side of the beach, from which several people were fishing. The beach sloped gently down with the parked vehicles on one corner, the path in the middle, and a jetty marking the other corner. The sea stretched out before them and there were some quite choppy waves which a few surfers were expertly negotiating, while others swam and paddled nearer shore.

'It's gorgeous,' said Tony.

They put down a rug in the centre of the beach and raced into the water. It was deliciously fresh, and they frolicked on the surf before swimming out into calmer waters away from the beach. Tony looked back and saw the bay and the green landscape that embraced it. On the beach, a few games of volleyball were in progress and some people had made sandcastles.

'This is perfect. Simply perfect,' said Tony, and he felt that he could happily spend eternity in this location. He had loved being reunited with his grandparents, and everything seemed so splendid. He also realised that he had begun to take an interest in a few attractive-looking angels here and there on the beach, noting as he entered the water who he planned to approach later that morning for a chat. His memories of Fifi and Beatrice's revelation seemed unimportant and distant as he lay on his back in the water, closed his eyes, and floated comfortably with the sun and the undulation of the water lapping his skin.

When Tony, Fanny and Quentin emerged from the sea Fanny realised that she was missing a towel.

'It's not the end of the world,' she joked. 'Tony, you see the angel with the stand in the corner there? He has a heap of beach towels, you can grab one there.'

Tony walked up the beach, noticing that several people were lying on big white beach towels; he was given an identical one from the stand. He dried himself quickly, and wandered up the ramp to the path bordering the beach to get a better look. He smiled at the one-piece tank top and shorts that he wore and peeled down the top so his torso was exposed to the sun before wrapping the towel around his waist and leaning on the rail to enjoy the view.

'Hello there,' said a voice, breaking into his meditation.

Tony turned to see a man with blond hair wearing swimming trunks and smiling at him.

'I don't think I've seen you around,' said the man. 'I'm Harold'. They shook hands. Tony introduced himself and told Harold that he had arrived from outside of Hefyn a few days before, and found the place fantastic.

'Well, you're very different to the crowd here in a number of ways,' said Harold. 'It's quite exciting being with an older man.'

Tony noticed that Harold had moved in a bit closer to him than he would normally feel comfortable with, but as he was still intoxicated by the beach atmosphere he brushed it off.

'It's so wonderful having angels come so fresh and ready to meet our every need,' said Harold. He put his arm around Tony's shoulder.

Tony had been looking at one of the female angels that had caught his eye earlier, and although he felt Harold was now being a little over-friendly, he nodded.

'Yes, they're very enthusiastic. I can't wait.'

At this point, Harold turned Tony to face him, exclaiming in a husky voice, 'Oh Tony, my beach hut is just over there, I can't wait either!' He grasped the back of Tony's head with one hand and kissed him, his other hand reaching down beneath Tony's towel to find his crotch.

Tony recoiled, appalled. His towel had been slightly dislodged by Harold's ardour, revealing Tony's dark blue swimsuit.

Harold froze, and stared at Tony with a horrified look. 'But... but... that's not possible. I thought you were an angel. It's impossible in Hefyn. I've never... never... ooooooh...,' and he began hyperventilating. 'Oooooohh, oooooh, oooh my head, my feet, my chest!'

Tony had tried to intervene as Harold's paroxysms intensified, but they had the opposite effect and sent the man into a more intense state of distress. Harold flailed around and did not see another man who had come up to help, who accidentally received an almighty punch in the face. The other man recoiled backwards towards the railing, the force causing him to topple over it headfirst onto the beach below. Cries and shouts of distress surged upwards from the beach and a woman on the path began to scream. She had backed away from the scene and bumped into the ice-cream cart that had been parked at the top of the ramp leading down to the beach. With a jolt, the cart moved towards the ramp and with growing momentum it trundled straight down, the people on the ramp yelling and jumping out of the way.

Tony heard another commotion and turned to see a charabanc also begin to roll down towards the centre of the beach. It was full of people, but had no driver.

'The handbrake, oh the handbrake!' Tony heard the driver say, as he ineffectually tried to mount the vehicle. He had abandoned it to get a better view of the fracas around Harold and in doing so had forgotten to secure the handbrake.

The heavy charabanc careered across the beach, creating a trail of havoc, while some of the passengers chose to throw themselves out of it. The vehicle crossed the central slope of the beach before climbing upwards, slowing slightly before smashing with a considerable thud into the jetty. As it approached the jetty, the fishermen on the structure jumped off in all directions, or were thrown off, to find themselves tangled up in the lines of one flustered fisherman's rods.

Tony could not believe the scene of devastation before him. As the domino effect of the carnage continued, he saw people thrust ice-cream cones in other people's faces, sandcastles smashed and the volleyball net torn down, while people standing by the water were getting knocked down by a big wave that they had failed to see as they gaped in horror at the beach massacre. Wails and screams replaced the serene atmosphere of only minutes before, with humans and angels alike in much distress.

Then, out of the corner of his eye, slightly set back at the end of the beach huts, Tony saw a rather ramshackle and unkempt cream-coloured hut.

CHAPTER 16

'Come in poppet,' called Fifi as Tony knocked on the door of the cream-coloured beach hut, having negotiated the war zone of cries and shellshock that the beach and its surroundings had become. 'Just close the door and take a seat, I think you can help me.' She was chewing furiously on the end of a pencil with a crossword in front of her. 'Six letters, begins with 'B,' fourth letter 'G,' and the clue is 'Mistake like the twisted sound of a large bee.' It took me ages to guess the other lines that it passes through, they were so esoteric – I means who's ever heard of St Brendan's Island, two, eight, six, and MacConglinne, twelve?'

As Tony sat down and looked around the interior of the beach hut, the familiar wave of BO and halitosis washed over him. The hut was shockingly dirty compared to the manicured environment in the rest of Hefyn, with a couple of empty, dusty shelves and two wooden chairs and a greasy table, all half-rotten and with flaking paint. Even though Tony had closed the door, the plaintive cries from outside were hardly lessened.

'I think I've made a terrible bungle,' said Tony, who hadn't really registered Fifi's question as he came in.

'Poppet, you are a genius!' she exclaimed and carefully wrote in the last four letters of her puzzle. She closed her book, which was entitled 'The Bumper Book of Crossword Puzzles,' with a satisfied look and replaced it on one of the shelves. 'I think that merits tea and flapjack, don't you think?' She turned on a gas stove on which there was a little black kettle.

'The bungle, my dear, was out of your hands,' said Fifi, 'but it's getting a whole lot worse now. I can picture those archangels convening another emergency meeting just to discuss you and realising how much higher the stakes are rising. They'll be absolutely petrified.'

'I'd like to know more about this,' said Tony, who had finally begun to gather his wits about him after the beach drama. 'As you said, the archangels had things in store for me. You seem to know an awful lot about what's happening. In fact, to be perfectly frank, I find that you're one of the most repugnant angels that I've ever met and I'm quite suspicious that your motives are not the best.'

Fifi stared at him for a second and then leaned back and cackled with laughter. 'Moi?' she said. 'Poppet, how could you suspect little old me, the lowest of the low?'

'And my name is Tony, not poppet,' Tony countered, quite cross by now.

'I think what we need is a nice cup of tea, poppet,' she said, and pulled out two filthy-looking cracked mugs, putting a used and mouldy-looking teabag into each and pouring water over them. 'Best to let it brew a few minutes.' She pushed one towards Tony and pulled out a greasy paper bag from which emerged a flapjack. Tony had the distinct impression that some of the black spots on the flapjack had legs, so he declined Fifi's offer to tear it in two and give him half.

'As you wish, but you're missing out on a good thing' she said, taking a bite and making crunching noises. 'Now I hope you haven't been going and telling on me.' She gave him a grin and fluttered her eyelashes.

Tony didn't respond and twiddled the handle of his mug.

'Of course, you must be confused when I told you that I'm a renegade angel,' she went on. 'There's quite a difference between fallen angels and renegade angels, you know.'

'So what did you do to become renegade?' said Tony. 'Every other angel seems impeccably well behaved and in their place.'

'Let's say that from the lowest rank of angels, I've seen a fair bit of sloppiness and complacency. A general decline. A lowering of standards. So I took it upon myself to point these things out. Nicely, at first, but the hierarchy doesn't take kindly to angels talking out of place. Oh yes, my dear, I've suffered tremendously in my time, but after you've been locked up or abused for the hundredth time you become acclimatized to it.'

Tony was not completely convinced. He warily lifted the mug to his lips and sipped, but the liquid was foul and he had to spit it out and couldn't help spluttering.

'And it's a bit below the belt to call a beautiful angel disgusting,' said Fifi, looking rather miffed, 'so you fully deserve the wrath and punishment associated with sipping tea that's too hot.'

Tony recovered, and continued with a question. 'So what's this about angels having sex with humans in Heaven?'

'Decadence and wholesale abuse of power,' said Fifi, 'a privilege that only started after He left us. It's only open to angels of D-grade and above, not to the lower hierarchies. Even then, of course, there's a long waiting list, but there's terrible bragging between angels who come to Heaven about the number of conquests and the fun they have. In any case, they all reason to themselves that what's the logic of having a human form without being able to use your genitals?'

'Tell me more about this,' said Tony, who was feeling slightly more comfortable. 'Let me see, this reminds me of a place called Hull.'

He remembered being frozen on the Subsolo as the angel Gertrude made a pass at him. The cries outside had diminished somewhat and he even lifted the mug up and took a cautious sniff, but quickly put it down again.

'Good, good, perhaps you've heard about the White Mountain as well,' said Fifi. 'Put them together and you've learnt a lot about angel cycles. Get screwed first, then have a fling, but the most privileged have a shag.'

'I beg your pardon?' said Tony. 'That seems uncharacteristically crude.'

'Well, what do you expect angels to do when they're not engaged in divine assistance, strum harps all day on clouds?' said Fifi. 'You owe me a great deal for the education I'm giving you, young man. In fact there are three realms where angels become part or completely human. The first is the Realm of the White Mountain, which every angel has to pass through in order to complete a rigorous series of physical tests as a human with all the associated weaknesses and risks. Every angel has a chance of being called to participate in this every five hundred angel years to prove their worthiness and literally regain their wings.'

Tony listened and sipped his tea, which was bitter but, he decided, not too bad after all, and Fifi carried on.

'Once an angel gains his or her wings, those of the D hierarchy and above have the – ahem – honour of serving humans in Heaven, although generally without their physical wings, of course. Finally, angels with wings from whatever hierarchy can go to Hull, where they don't generally get to see many humans but end up having angel orgies and casual sex together, although it's not exactly heavenly.'

Fifi leaned back and then refilled Tony's mug, which he had emptied.

'I've got a corner of flapjack if that still tempts you,' she said. Abandoning his earlier scruples, he took it. 'But what's this got to do with me?' he said. 'I shouldn't be here at all.'

'Ah, but no, it's what's inside you that matters,' said Fifi, poking Tony in the chest. She folded her arms and leant forward. 'I don't know if you realise it, poppet, but as well as being the most exciting thing that has ever arrived in Angeland and its realms, you are now the most dangerous thing.' Tony was taken aback. 'By having that eyelash inside you, and then through a very innocent and very silly error which brought you to Angeland, you are now the number one potential source of complete angel catastrophe.'

'I haven't done anything wrong,' said Tony. 'Well, apart from that mis-hit golf shot.'

'Did you know, my dear,' said Fifi calmly, 'that if the HARP – that portal you came through from the plane – opens again and you still have Gabriel's eyelash inside you then there will be, well, a big bang that will spell the end of Angeland.'

Tony looked horrified, and Fifi smiled.

'Let's continue our story. Sandeepa, bless her sandals, thought she could get you to expel the eyelash by singing, but you ended up embedding it even further. Ray, on the other hand, another lovely angel by the way, had thought happiness and fun in Heaven would get the eyelash to pop out. On the contrary, your presence here has disrupted the equilibrium and the longer you are here, the worse it will be.'

Tony reached for more tea and flapjack crumbs on the table.

'I've saved the best for last, Poppet,' continued Fifi. 'If you still have the eyelash inside you, the archangels had a splendid Plan B.'

'Which was?' asked Tony.

'Which was to send you to Heaven. There's one eensy weensy problem, however. Because of the route you've taken already, you'll have to come by the same route into Hefyn again, and each day you spend here you will create more and more disruption. Disruption and chaos, indeed, which would end up reverberating around every corner and every part of Heaven.'

There was a long pause, and Tony looked up.

'I shouldn't be here. But how do I know that this isn't a big lie? I mean, things started going wrong when you arrived.'

Fifi reached across the table and started to jab her fingers between the table and her mouth to pick up and then lick off the crumbs. 'It's up to you what you want to believe,' she said after some slurping.

'Tony! Tony! Where are you Tony?' It was Quentin's voice outside.

'I'd better go,' said Tony, remembering where he was and the carnage he had left outside.

'Very good, poppet. I hope you've enjoyed my tea and the flapjack,' said Fifi. Tony got up to leave. 'Oh, by the way, I think you can expect to go somewhere cold quite soon. Such a pity, as I imagine you've just got used to the weather here. Good luck, and I'm sure our paths will cross again.'

'Goodbye and – thank you,' said Tony, who felt he had experienced quite enough of catastrophe and revelation for the moment. He opened the door and stepped outside. No one had apparently seen him emerge onto the Hefyn promenade. He saw Quentin and went up to him.

'Thank goodness you're safe,' Quentin said. 'There are a lot of people who have cuts and bruises, and nearly everyone is suffering from shock. Like Fanny, for example. Look, she's sitting over there, she's quite beside herself.'

Tony could see Fanny with her head in her hands. Many others were in a similar state, some of them sitting, others lying down, many hugging each other.

'I say, old chap,' said Quentin, 'I prepared a first aid kit back at the cottage some time ago just as a precaution, but it would really be useful now. I need to stay with Fanny, but you could drive there and back in ten minutes. You do drive, I imagine?'

'Well yes, although…' replied Tony, but before he knew it he was handed the keys to the Rolls and gently directed towards the car park.

Tony didn't feel very comfortable, particularly after what Fifi had said, but at Quentin's insistence he got into the blue Phantom and started it up. The route was easy to remember and he drove carefully. After a couple of minutes, he saw the crossroads with the blind turns and slowed down to see if there was any other traffic. He was about to set off again, but the car stalled. He tried several times, turning the ignition, but it wouldn't fire. Then he remembered that he had seen a hand crank in the boot, so he got out to find it.

As Tony got out of the Rolls, he heard a low rumbling in the distance and what seemed like rowdy singing and laughing. Before he knew it, a charabanc rounded one of the blind bends just before the crossroads. It was going at some speed, certainly at a speed that would be inadvisable, except of course on a normal day in Hefyn. This was not, however, a normal day in Hefyn. The charabanc ploughed into the centre of the blue car and smashed it across to the other side of the road before turning on its side and ejecting many of the passengers onto the tarmac. Then it rolled a couple of times and finally came to rest.

The Rolls had been whipped away inches in front of Tony, who stood unscathed as he surveyed the scene of smashed metal, glass, blood and broken bodies in front of him. He looked up and saw, coming in the other direction, a red car. However, he did not see the face of the driver, only his heels on the steering wheel, as he was obviously reaching for something in the boot. Tony yelled, and the astonished driver turned to get back into his seat, but it was too late. The red car skidded, twisted and smashed at high speed into the melee of torsos and chassis. It spun, across the crossroads and towards Tony, catching him just before it had slowed to a stop and throwing him to the side of the road.

The impact rendered him semi-conscious. He was dimly aware that his leg was hurting, and he tried to look up, but was unable to. Within the space of a couple of minutes, there seemed to be several more smashes, each followed by an increase in the moaning and screaming around him. Finally he faded into unconsciousness. The last thing he remembered seeing and hearing was a pair of great white wings.

Tony woke up in the bedroom with the sloping ceiling to see the morning sunlight filtering playfully through the curtains. He looked up and saw a figure sitting at the bottom of the bed.

'Hello Albert,' Tony said, recognising the old man.

Albert smiled wistfully.

'Hello Tony, I hope you're feeling better. Your leg took quite a nasty knock and you've been kept asleep for a while.'

Tony felt his leg, which seemed fine.

'Should be good as new,' Albert said, 'although several of the others will have some nasty scars. Ambulances and hospitals aren't generally found in Heaven, so there were some quite surprised guardian angels who were called out of retirement.'

'Oh dear,' said Tony, 'It's my fault that there are all these mistakes.'

'No, no,' said Albert, shaking his head. 'Dear Tony, the fault is mine. I should never have brought you to Angeland.' The old man faltered and looked close to tears.

'Well I think you're the best guardian angel a person could ever have,' said Tony, patting the old angel on the shoulder. Albert smiled thankfully at Tony, then composed himself and paused for a few seconds, contemplating him.

'I'm afraid you won't be pleased at the next thing I'm going to tell you,' Albert said carefully. 'I've been instructed to ensure that you leave Hefyn as soon as possible. I'm afraid that means you need to leave this instant, without even being able to see your grandmother and grandfather.'

Tony was speechless. Despite all the commotion at the beach and the accident on the road, it was the last thing he expected or wanted. He had adored being with Fanny and Quentin, and his heart suffered a stabbing sensation as memories of them earlier in his life suddenly flooded back to him. He would not have a chance to say goodbye now, just as he had not been there when either of them had passed away back on Earth.

Albert helped Tony out of bed and opened the wardrobe, picking out a very modern-looking ski coat, warm trousers and snow boots, all coloured grey and looking very out of place.

'But I'll boil if I put these on,' said Tony.

'I'm sorry Tony, but they're for where you're going next,' replied Albert. Tony put them on. They hugged and Albert directed him to the wardrobe. 'Just keep on pushing your way through to the back,' the old man said.

Tony hesitated for a moment, half trying to get his bearings and half wondering whether to rush out of the room and down the stairs. But Albert looked insistent and Tony, who getting used to doing odd things like walking into wardrobes or dressing rooms to travel somewhere else, nodded trustingly at him. He stepped into the wardrobe, pushing through a rack of golf clothes and then a second rack carrying big grey ski jackets. He went further in and found a further row of jackets hanging behind the first row, and as it was quite dark he stretched his hand out in front of him. All of a sudden he noticed something crunching underfoot, and stooping down he felt something powdery and chilly. The temperature fell sharply. Moving ahead, Tony suddenly realised that he was outside; it was dark and he was in a wood amid heavy snow. In a clearing up ahead he spied a modern lamppost illuminating the snow around it, and next to it stood a tall man dressed in grey and a toddler. They were holding hands.

CHAPTER 17

Michelle, in an approximate translation of the Archangel's divine thinking.

White room again.
Natasha and Gaby play
Talk talk
Trying
Tony on track
Uh-oh
Tony do big mess
Tony fall off
Ray sad sad
Gaby big talk
Want bunny. Want my bunny. Bunny now!
Gaby do big talk
Go way!
Climb chair. I go climb it play with Natasha.
Gaby big talk all done.
What?

This is snow way
This very dangerous
No other ones?
Because I have a tell you
Very dangerous
This a way
Putting it
Snow way cold and black
Because it has no bandaids on it
Uhuh
More talk talk
Taking Tony
Snow way all done
Sad it
This is the track
I got Tony on it
I make Tony needs track
Faster as me
Tony go plane
Plane with bunny.
What I do to it? Bunny. Bunny climb chair.
All gone white room go go
Gaby me go fly. Like flying! Flying to snow.

WHITE

CHAPTER 18

'Pathetic! I've never seen such a miserable little excuse for a two-legged being,' said Sue, looking down at Tony, who was lying gibbering in a pool of his own vomit.

'This is it,' Tony groaned to himself. 'I can't go any lower. It must be the end.'

He was so weak and dehydrated that he was unable to offer any response to the insults. He could only gaze up at the slightly stocky but perfectly toned figure leering down at him. Light flecks of mud on her calves and shoes were the only indication that she had just run the equivalent of more than three and a half marathons.

Tony had also covered the same distance since the afternoon of the day before, but he was in a rather different state. His ripped clothes and most of his exposed body were streaked with mud and blood as a result of several earlier falls on the trail, and he was shaking uncontrollably. His digestive system had finally given up after months of rigorous training and a dose of e-coli, and had come to a final point where all efforts to take on some form of nutrition or hydration had seen it rebelling and shooting out liquid from one end or the other, or both. This did at least give him something to focus on other than the pain of his blisters, the incessant sandpaper-like rub-rub-rub of his running trousers on his crotch, the agony of his split nipples, or the sunburn he'd picked up earlier in the day on that part of his neck on which he'd been unable to apply sun protection, or his slightly dodgy knee, or that patch of psoriasis, or that dull ache at the base of his back.

Now the light was going and he had no torch. The last fall he had endured had been too much, and all he had been able to do was pull himself into a muddy ditch on the side of the track which offered limited protection against the elements. Visibility in the mountains now that the clouds were low was only a few hundred metres, and as the light fell and rain turned to snow he had begun to weep great sobs and dribble in self-pity at his condition, the loss of his best friend, the ridiculous trials he had engaged in around the White Mountain, and nostalgia for pleasanter days and for his far-off hazy memories of Earth.

It was in this state that Sue found him as she brought up the rear of the group. She had been Tony's personal trainer (he thought drill sergeant was more apt) since he had arrived in the Realm of the White Mountain eight months before. Her facetiousness seemed to increase inversely to his physical state, so on this new low her countenance gleamed with apparent exultation at his emasculated condition.

'With this lovely weather you'll be delighted to know that we can't get a helicopter to pick you up,' she clucked at him, adjusting his bedraggled clothes and wrapping a couple of jackets and a fleece around him to provide better protection. Propping him up against a rock, she put a head torch on him in the dying light.

'Just twelve kilometres to go,' she said, 'but first there's a special treat for you.'

She pulled out of her backpack a pot that contained a grey, glutinous substance and scooped some up in a spoon.

'Time to play aeroplanes – or perhaps wingsuits would be more appropriate.'

She whirled the spoon around with a 'neaarrrooom' and poked Tony, who wearily opened his mouth.

'Don't gobble it down all at once, hold it nicely in the mouth like a good boy,' said Sue. Tony anticipated throwing it immediately back up, but with a little water he kept it down and began to feel a little better and somewhat warmer. To his relief his nausea diminished somewhat.

'We'd better be off then,' said Sue a few minutes later, now with Tony leaning against her. 'Steady on champion, you'll break the record if you continue at this rate.'

His repositioning had made various other aches reappear, but he gently tried to start moving. Slowly, steadily, they advanced, with Tony hobbling and then gradually picking up a bit of speed and feeling a little less dreadful. It was almost pitch dark now, and their headlamps illuminated the trail ahead. Then the snow gradually eased off and the cloud lifted, revealing a panoply of stars. Up in the distance, some ten kilometres off, they saw the twinkling lights of the town of Gostosa.

It was beautifully calm and Tony stopped, indicating to Sue that he was ready to continue without her by his side in case he slipped. She prepared to make a remark, but Tony put his hand on her shoulder and said simply, 'Thank you, Sue. Thank you for saving my life.'

For the first time since he had met her, for an instant her face changed in a way he had not seen before. The sides of her mouth flickered and her face revealed a glimpse of something that seemed like loss and longing. Then she blinked and returned to her normal controlling, detached manner.

'Well, last one back gets to do burpees all day tomorrow,' she smirked and started off in front, at a pace that seemed just a little too fast to follow.

CHAPTER 19

Thirty-five weeks earlier, under the lamp post by the back entrance to the Realm of the White Mountain, the Archangel Michelle had been extremely preoccupied with her floppy rabbit toy, and did not seem at all perturbed by the cold and heavily-falling snow. Wearing a white parka jacket cum jump suit ensemble, she had taken a few moments away from her fluffy toy, waving cheerily at Tony. When he approached, she pawed affectionately at him.

The Archangel Gabriel, holding on to Michelle's hand, looked scornfully at Tony. Rather than white, he was wearing a stylish grey ski ensemble, the same colour as Tony's.

'You've created a great deal of mischief,' Gabriel said without greeting Tony. 'Given the gravity of the situation, the other archangels have finally agreed to my suggestion, in an extraordinary vote of four to three.'

Gabriel looked sideways at Michelle, who waved her soft toy at him and added for emphasis with some seriousness, 'Snow, fly snow Tony with bunny.'

'The Archangel Michelle is for some reason delighted to welcome you to her realm,' Gabriel said. 'Somehow she thinks you will succeed in the trials ahead of you, although I think her expectations are rather over-optimistic. Given your pathetic physical condition I'll give you a few months at most before you're broken and finished.'

'No Gaby, Gaby naughty, bunny bunny,' said Michelle, poking her rabbit into Gabriel.

In the distance other figures were approaching slowly, the beams of their head torches visible through the flurries of snow.

Gabriel looked up at them. 'About time too,' he said.

Tony used the pause to interject, 'Listen, I thought all of this was a big mistake. I'm sorry but none of this is my choice. I've got nothing against you and I just want to go home.'

'Oh no,' said Gabriel, with sudden extra cruelty. 'You – a mere human – have humiliated me, but now it's my opportunity to come down to your level and see you suffer miserably, physically and mentally, so much that you will painfully retch out my eyelash, and perhaps several internal organs at the same time.'

'Bunny no bad, bunny,' said Michelle, biffing Gaby on the side with it.

'I'll give you a few months, maybe only weeks or days,' said Gabriel, glaring at Tony. Sweeping up Michelle in his arms, he turned and walked swiftly into the wood.

'Hello,' a rather more cheery voice said behind Tony. He saw that the three approaching figures were, like him and Gaby, dressed in grey snow gear and snowshoes in addition to head torches.

'I'm George,' said the man who had greeted Tony, who had a brown and straggly beard. He thrust out his hand to shake in welcome, then introduced his companions Fiona and Gustavo. Fiona was tall with a long face, and Gustavo had olive skin and jet-black hair.

'We're honoured and delighted to welcome you,' said Fiona, and they all beamed at him amicably, in sharp contrast to Gaby.

'Come on, let's get these snowshoes on you and then back to the car,' said Gustavo. After attaching them to Tony's feet, and giving him a head torch, they turned back all four of them the way that they had come.

After they had walked for about 20 minutes, Tony was beginning to feel a bit cold and was pleased to see a solid-looking white car, an Ange Rover, waiting for them. They brushed the snow off their clothes and boots as much as possible before bundling in. Fiona started the engine and the car soon heated up comfortably as they set off, with George accompanying Fiona in the front and Gustavo sitting next to Tony behind.

'Terrible weather for this time of year,' said George. 'Snow at this altitude is very rare in late summer. You know only 20 per cent of participants managed to complete the UEWM last week, the lowest for a long time.'

'Sorry, what's the uoohmm?' said Tony.

'Oh, silly me, I forgot that there's a lot you don't know,' replied George. 'the UEWM, pronounced uoohmm, stands for the Ultra Event of the White Mountain. Every year angels who haven't done the event for more than 500 years are selected at random across all grades to complete the event, to regain their wings, before they are once again eligible to enter into the other angel realms and Earth.'

'Ah yes,' said Tony, remembering the conversation in the Bright Hall that he had had with Alphonso and Graham, 'the MoT for angels.'

'That's it,' said Gustavo. 'You've just missed the last UEWM, which you'll have gathered was very tough. Those angels who failed to pass this time hang around to help organize and support the next event before being able to try again. The event only takes place once a year.'

The Ange Rover had been descending a winding road and the intensity of the falling snow had lessened. The road became clearer and Fiona continued driving.

'All angels who are trying for their wings and the UEWM temporarily become human and mortal,' Gustavo went on. 'We all wear grey to show our status.'

Tony had noticed that he had been feeling slightly different since leaving Hefyn. There, apart from his accident, he had enjoyed a sensation of full health and no niggles with his body. Now, he realised, they had crept back.

'So, this isn't like Hefyn?'

'Well, some of us will never get there,' said George, briefly catching the eyes of Fiona and Gustavo, 'but here in the Realm of the White Mountain we all come to the same level, in human form, to help us experience and appreciate what you go through.'

'Even death, sometimes,' said Gustavo, and there was silence in the car for a few moments.

'But we're delighted that you're joining us new UEWM novitiates,' smiled Fiona. 'It's easy to forget how it is to be human if you only do your wings once every half-millennium or so, and to have the unique opportunity of having a real human with us on this occasion will be great. We're looking forward to training together.'

'Wait a minute,' interjected Tony, thinking of Gabriel's invective about him being 'broken and finished' while being poked by Michelle's bunny. 'You mean to say I need to do the UEWM? What is it exactly?'

The three novitiate angels looked at each other.

'Well, even archangels have to participate, and this year the Archangel Gabriel will be doing it,' said George. 'I hear he's aiming to finish it in less than 24 hours to break the course record.'

'No novitiate will get close to his level of fitness and determination, of course, but in a typical year 50 per cent will complete in the 48-hour limit,' added Fiona. 'But conditions this year are particularly bad, though they're likely to be better next year.'

'But what do you do in the UEWM?' insisted Tony, as the car continued its descent, light rain tapping against the windows.

Gustavo looked a bit sheepish. He responded, 'We imagine you've already got plenty of experience as a human in many of these competences. You might be a bit behind in some, but I'm sure you'll be very comfortable in the catch-up courses that we and the other novitiates do.'

'You're not really answering my question,' said Tony. The three novitiates were exuding a sense of forced gaiety.

'Well,' said George, taking a deep breath, 'you start off by climbing the White Mountain, then ski down it, run 160 km around it, then 12km underneath it in the tunnel, and finally you jump out of a helicopter to wingsuit under the bridge across the Agulha do Meio-dia. Doesn't that seem simple to you?' He gave a rather strained smile.

'I've never climbed or skied, I don't generally do more than a light jog for 5km when I run, and I've never jumped out of a plane,' said Tony.

'Oh,' said the three others simultaneously, looking at each other. The tap-tap of the rain and swish-swish of the windscreen wipers continued.

'We thought you might have had a little more experience and a bit more advanced training,' said Gustavo.

The four novitiates, one of whom was feeling a growing sense of foreboding at the task ahead, did not talk much more about the trials of the UEWM as they drove down the valley. Fiona changed the subject to the weather forecast, which was good for the next few days, and as the rain stopped they glimpsed a town ahead of them.

'Welcome to Mayeurgericht,' said Gustavo. 'This is the main town south of the White Mountain and the trail for

UEWM runs through it. We're staying in the Willkommenhaus chalet a few kilometres away.'

Tony noticed an increase in the number of white and grey cars going back and forth on the road, while lights from the town illuminated the houses, side streets and occasional trees. There was no snow here, but looking up towards the mountains through patches in the clouds he spied a white dusting some hundred metres up. The car left the town and they passed occasional houses and chalets on the side of the road. They took a left turn off the main road and climbed for a few minutes before parking outside a large chalet with 'WILLKOMMENHAUS' above the door.

'It's after most people's bedtime, but let's see if we can grab you something to eat,' said George, as they stepped into an entrance hall with a welcoming log fire burning in the hearth. A couple of other novitiates, wearing comfortable grey clothing, were reading by the fire, and they looked up as the group entered. The sound of a piano accompanied by a solemn solo female voice drifted hauntingly from one of the corridors.

'Let's go to the cafeteria,' said Fiona, and they headed down some stairs and emerged into a large open room with long tables and benches. She went through some swing doors into the kitchens and came out with a tray of cold meat, cheese, bread and fruit.

'Tomorrow you'll meet Sue to establish your training programme and you'll get a view of the White Mountain for the first time,' Gustavo said to Tony.

They tucked in heartily to the food. Tony was feeling very hungry, and he reflected that the last time he had eaten had been breakfast in Hefyn before the imbroglio on the beach and then the accident. Apart from the unsavoury appearance of the Archangel Gabriel, he had begun to feel quite at home in the Realm of the White Mountain, and had felt welcomed by everyone he had met.

Tony was feeling a little sleepy towards the end of the meal, and George took him down some corridors to a room bearing the number 30 on the door. There were other doors with numbers and the wooden corridors were rather spartan.

'Here's your room,' he said, handing him a card that opened the door electronically. 'Get some good sleep – you'll need it. Training at 8am.' He patted Tony on the shoulder, wishing him goodnight and then left him.

The room was simple, with a single bed and desk either side of the window and a bathroom en suite. He hung up his clothes in the wardrobe, which he noticed was filled with other grey garments. He brushed his teeth using the toothbrush and toothpaste laid out in the bathroom, put on the grey pyjamas that were neatly laid out on the pillow, and collapsed onto the bed, falling asleep almost immediately.

CHAPTER 20

On top of the mountain, Tony gazed at the silver peaks and the scattered glinting bodies of water illuminated by moonlight. The same moonlight was bathing the snow slopes with an eerie sheen. Wispy clouds drifted in the valleys far below and as he gently breathed, a black shadow crept softly over the moon, engulfing it before turning it red.

Now his grandmother Fanny was somehow beside him. 'Go on, my darling boy,' she was saying, urging him to carry on up to the peak. He walked through the snow as instructed, the white powder feeling like sand under his bare feet, the landscape now shrouded in a scarlet haze. On the other side of the peak, lying on the ground, writhing and moaning sensually, he saw a shapely woman in black lingerie, her face hidden by a black veil. The woman beckoned to him and her hands played over her body as she spread her legs, making him feel sharply aroused. He approached and knelt before her, unbuttoning his pyjama top, leaning towards her and pulling away the black veil to reveal voluptuous red lips. He lifted it further…

'Poppet! Poppet! Poppet!' a voice rapped in his ears and then turned into a sharp knock-knock at his bedroom door. He pulled away the sheet covering his face and the mountain scene dissolved.

'Tony, are you in there? Wake up! You've only got 15 minutes to have breakfast and get to the roll call,' said the voice of Gustavo through the door.

'Umm, coming, thank you,' said Tony, feeling a little disorientated after the dream. He leapt out of bed and slipped on a grey tracksuit. Drawing the curtains to one side, he was dazzled by the bright sun. Towering in front of him under the blue sky was an enormous white mountain largely covered by snow.

Without much time to take in the view, he made his way to the cafeteria with Gustavo, who explained to him that you couldn't see the peak of the White Mountain from this side. About 30 figures in grey tracksuits were finishing their breakfast, and they turned and looked at him and smiled. Tony picked up some muesli, scrambled eggs and tea and wolfed it down as all the other novitiates filed out.

'Come on now, no time to waste,' said Gustavo, leading Tony down some stairs and out behind the chalet into a large flat space which had a panoramic view of the White Mountain that Tony had seen from his bedroom window. A full-size running track filled the space, with buildings on either side with large windows, containing all manner of exercise machines. On the side of the running track, about 100 novitiates lined up in five rows, with two spaces in the front row which Gustavo and Tony filled.

'Good morning everyone,' said a crisp female voice, and Tony saw a short woman with a ponytail walk in front of the group. 'I know we're all delighted to welcome a human among our ranks and can't wait to get to know him.'

She walked in front of Tony and scrutinized him, and he felt a little small. 'I'm Sue,' she said, sticking out her hand.

He grasped it and then winced as she delivered a crushing handshake.

'We're all eagerly waiting to see the vigour and quality of your abilities at the various UEWM disciplines, so we can learn something,' she continued, maintaining her grasp and winking at him. Mercifully releasing his hand, she continued, 'I am the training coordinator and I'm accompanying all novitiates in this chalet up to and including the UEWM. My job is to stretch, push and pull you over the coming year so you've got the best chance to get over the finishing line. There may be moments when you might feel a little uncomfortable but, with all my care and attention, you will learn to adore me by the end.'

Tony already did not feel very comfortable, particularly at the idea of being stretched, pulled and pushed by this diminutive but formidable figure.

'But let's start with a little light warm up,' Sue continued. She turned to Tony. 'We don't want you to show off your prowess all at once. 'Right everyone, let's have 50 press-ups, 50 squats, a lap of the track, then 50 burpees!'

With perfect synchronicity, and before he could digest what had been said, the group of novitiates around Tony glided down and started doing press-ups. Tony saw that he and Sue were the only ones standing. She folded her arms and nodded at him to start, and he did so without daring to stop to ask what a burpee was.

Adopting a press-up position and about to start, the novitiate bodies around him bobbed up and down with energy. He didn't recall having done push-ups for quite some time and as he approached the twentieth one he began to feel distinctly weak and slowed down somewhat. Looking up helplessly, he met the inscrutable gaze of Sue and meekly continued. After about five more push-ups, the other novitiates started to pop up and do squats. By the time he had finally and agonizingly got to 50 press-ups, he realised that the majority of the other novitiates had finished their squats and left to run around the track.

The squats were less awkward than the push-ups, but before he had finished, many of the novitiates returning from their 400-metre run were coming back to their places and doing what he realised were the burpees: they leant forward, did a quick squat thrust, and then bounced up in a motion that Tony found exhausting just to watch.

Tony set off alone on the track, passing the last set of novitiates returning to do their burpees, who looked at him rather curiously and with pity. He was more than warmed up now: he was well primed to regurgitate his breakfast, which he had already had to keep down on more than one occasion during the push-ups and squats. At least on the track, while being embarrassingly alone, he could admire the mountains all around, but he nevertheless pushed himself onward and on the bend he turned and headed back to the group of 100 novitiates. Most had finished or were in the process of doing so, but as he arrived he slumped into his spot next to Gustavo.

'Please,' he gasped at Sue, 'no burpees.'

'Not today for you,' said Sue, 'But you have been blessed in that you need to spend a lot of time with me. You will learn the meaning of the word sacrifice through a great deal of hard work.'

Thus Tony's introduction to the training sessions with Sue and the other novitiates began. He quickly realised that in stark contrast to the easy life in Hefyn, he had ended up in a year-long boot camp to prepare him for a near-impossible feat of endurance.

'Don't worry,' Fiona had said during the lunch break after Tony's first experience with Sue. 'In fact you're lucky, as you'll be able to see enormous progress and learn ever so much.'

She, Gustavo and George were sympathetic, but along with the other novitiates they could not hide a sense of disappointment in Tony, after so much had been promised about his potential abilities. Tony quickly realised the immensity of the task ahead of him over the next year: not only did he need to develop phenomenal athletic and endurance abilities, he would also need to become a highly proficient skier and learn how to operate a wingsuit.

'It's very straightforward,' Sue reassured him concerning the latter. 'Just a small matter of getting the experience of doing 200 skydiving jumps first and then you can start training.'

On that first morning in the training ground, as the other novitiates were gliding around the running track or engaging in complex exercise machines, Sue took Tony to an office in one of the buildings.

'You're really lucky to be filling your day with all different types of physical training,' she cooed as she poked at a computer, entering his fitness level and experience. 'While your body is recuperating we'll fit in all the skiing and skydiving jumps, and all of the theory and background.'

She finished printing a document which was about as thick as a telephone directory, and handed it to him.

'This is a detailed schedule for every day of the coming year. So today after lunch – and you'll need to carefully follow the menu plan of every meal – you've got your first skiing lesson at 1400, cardiovascular training at 1600, weights at 1700 and swimming at 1800. After dinner at 1900 you'll have two hours of study on physical technique and the White Mountain.'

Tony flicked through the heavy document and realised that almost every hour of the day for the next year had been filled with activities. There did not seem to be much blank space.

'Given all the work you need to do, you've been scheduled activities for most Sundays as well. I bet loads of humans would be envious at the opportunity you are being given,' continued Sue. Tony had very little to say in response.

She then pulled out what seemed like a mobile phone and gave it to Tony.

'This is a specially adapted oticel for you, for training purposes, and it's a good deal easier to carry around that the reference document which you can keep in your bedroom. It will show you your schedule and automatically update if we need to change anything due to the weather or if you injure yourself during training.'

So Tony entered an intensive and soon monotonous schedule that began at 0700 with breakfast, with meal breaks at 1230 and 1800 acting as the main structure for his existence. He had thought he would interact more with the other novitiates, but most were studious in their preparation for the UEWM and beyond offering a few pleasantries were not particularly interesting company. Even Fiona, Gustavo and George, with whom Tony felt he had a slightly stronger relationship, were as dedicated and focused as the other novitiates, and quickly retreated into their own routines after he had settled in. The days passed with monastic observance; evenings were spent reading and studying books about the massif of the White Mountain and sports technique. Occasionally, some novitiates organized music, but this tended to be rather sober and serious, and nothing like as much fun as he had experienced in the Bright Hall with Sandeepa.

Skiing lessons were conducted a little way up the valley. The ski instructors, after getting over the shock on hearing that they would have to teach someone from scratch rather than take them on a hazardous off-piste adventure, delivered their lessons in a rather half-interested way and Tony was shocked to see that, unlike the serious novitiates he lived with, they rather self-consciously preened themselves and seemed overly interested in their appearance and poise.

'They've failed the UEWM several times and they've started to adopt bad human traits,' explained Sue. 'They are in fact not novitiates but novices, offering help to this year's novitiates. They have clothes in a different shade of grey.' She told Tony that the Willkommenhaus chalet was the most serious training chalet for novitiates, particularly compared to those north of the White Mountain.

'I didn't see any difference in the grey they were wearing,' said Tony.

'Well, to be honest neither did I,' said Sue, unusually embarrassed, 'but you'll see the difference clearly enough during the practice and race days.'

Despite the somewhat detached manner of the instructors, Tony quickly picked up the basics of skiing and started enjoying its pleasures. After a few lessons, he was able to snow plough, stop and turn, gently going down the mountain on green and a few blue slopes, breathing in the lovely fresh air and even starting to enjoy the view.

'Good flexion and extension,' said Lara the novice. He didn't really understand that, but he was pleased, as it was one of the first compliments he had received.

One morning on the slopes, Tony met with Lara, who indicated that she had a surprise for him and would meet him at the chairlift. Just before they got on he saw that Lara was carrying the Archangel Michelle, who stood out, thanks to her little white parka, the fact that she was a toddler and that she was waving a bunny at him. They mounted the chairlift and Michelle reached out to him.

'Tony go snow snow. Bunny very happy indeed!' she said excitedly, playfully tapping Tony with the floppy rabbit.

'The Archangel Michelle is very happy to hear about your skiing progress so far,' Lara informed him, 'and wants to personally see how you are getting on.'

Tony initially felt a slight sense of panic, but he knew that on a green slope he should be able to hold his own. Michelle was really quite cute and as she kept on telling him 'bunny Tony snow go go,' with smiley gestures, he quickly relaxed.

'Here we are,' said Lara, as they arrived at the top of the chairlift that led down to the starting points for the green, blue and red slopes. Tony hadn't quite got the hang of getting off chairlifts, accelerating a bit too sharply and falling once or twice. However, as he concentrated and prepared to leave the chair, Lara whipped away his ski poles with one hand and with a 'here she is,' placed Michelle on his chest. Michelle clung to Tony's neck and beamed up at him as Lara gave Tony a shove off the chairlift.

Tony was speechless, with Michelle screeching excitedly around his neck, 'Bunny Tony snow go go!' They plunged down the slope, wobbling crazily, and, as he looked up, he saw to his horror that he had passed the starting point for the green and then the blue slopes and was heading for the red slope. He passed a group of novitiates who were lining up to go down the slope, and they gazed in surprise as the strange swaying grey skier with a little archangel dressed in white whizzed past them wobbling precariously. At this point Tony found his voice, although with very little coherence, and he yelled gutturally as he gathered speed.

Tony remembered Fiona's comment when he had arrived in the Realm of the White Mountain that everyone there was mortal, and the next five minutes passed in what seemed an eternity. He desperately tried to keep upright as he picked up more and more speed on the fiendishly steep slope. Back and forth he leaned, sometimes leaving the piste temporarily to narrowly miss hitting a tree or falling off a precipice. Michelle pawed with her hands and thrust her fluffy toy in his face, blinding him on occasion. All the while, novitiates skied by while Michelle waved at them.

By some miracle he did not fall, and finally the ordeal was over. He approached the end of the piste and saw Lara waiting at the bottom, and as the slope eased he came to a halt. Lara took Michelle from him, and he promptly fell over, drenched in sweat, and started to vomit.

'The Archangel Michelle thanks you for the ride,' said Lara, 'and I think you could do with a hot drink.'

CHAPTER 21

Tony soon realised that the two archangels in the Realm of the White Mountain commanded awe and respect from the novitiates. He learnt that it was not unusual to find Michelle overseeing the preparations for the UEWM in all sorts of places. Gabriel, on the other hand, was training with the novitiates and played up his reputation for being the ultimate athlete. When Tony spotted him in the distance on the few occasions that he had seen him, Gabriel was always accompanied by a dozen or more novitiates and novices, acolytes bowing and scraping around him. On one occasion, when Gabriel finished a training run, a full orchestra and a 50-strong choir assembled around the finish line to pompously sing 'See, the Conqu'ring Hero Comes' and place a wreath on him.

Tony had witnessed this while preparing to train on the same course, and had rather enjoyed the music. Despite the pretentiousness, it was nice to hear something a bit more lively than the dull monastic chants and weird atonal numbers he heard in the Willkommenhaus chalet some evenings, and he fondly remembered his evening in the Bright Hall.

Then, one evening, everything changed. Tony noticed on his oticel that unusually, his schedule was clear. The demeanour of the novitiates in Willkommenhaus shifted suddenly from ascetic to unrestrained as a number of them put on yellow or black football kit. Television had been completely absent, but now the cafeteria, as the largest room in the chalet, was transformed and a projector beamed images onto one wall. At the opposite side, the serving area became a bar that served beverages, including alcohol.

'Alles Schwarz might have already topped the table, but Poste could come second,' enthused Fiona, wearing a yellow top, to Tony.

'No chance,' replied Gustavo, who was decked out completely in black. 'We're going to whap your ass!'

George was still wearing grey, like most of the other novitiates, and he explained to Tony that the teams Poste, Hexahedrons and Guardians were within a point of each other and third, fourth and fifth in the league.

'A win for Poste would take them into the semi-final, but a loss or a draw would leave things open going into the least two games of the league,' he told Tony, sipping a beer. 'And of course, as Poste is Archangel Gabriel's team, if they win you'll see mighty celebrations around Musikalische Kraft, his chalet here in the realm.'

Looking at the group of novitiates watching the match, Tony couldn't help but feel again, as he had when he had come out of the HARP and seen the end of the previous match, that the whole thing reminded him very much of watching a game of footie on Earth.

'We copy the best things on Earth so we can enjoy them for ourselves,' said Gustavo, 'and of course better understand humans so we can serve them as well as possible.'

The screen flicked to a ginger-haired chubby young man with a light moustache, who looked intently out of the screen and announced in measured tones, 'Take a chance at five-to-one on Alles Schwartz beating Poste by more than three goals.' Text appeared beside him and Tony realised that it was the Archangel Yuri, whom he had met in the Jardim do Céu.

'Don't you think this is great?' said Gustavo to a confused Tony. 'I love the commercial break.'

The screen then proceeded to show a series of slick adverts: Ange Rovers whizzing around empty streets; Angel White and Angel Red beer consumed by female footballers wearing yellow and black stripes and doing acrobatic keepie-up manoeuvres; and an Angel Slimming product advertised by a waif-like male angel. Tony looked searchingly at Fiona.

'This is just for those angels visiting the realm of PirogRus,' she said, and pointed at the screen, which showed Yuri beaming and opening his arms inside an enormous shopping centre.

'Essential for angel research and training,' said Gustavo.

At last the commercial break ended and the screen switched to the inside of a football stadium bedecked with yellow and black and filled with the sound of the rising and falling roar of the crowd. Tony recognised two of the Alles Schwartz players from the exhibition he had seen in the Bright Hall.

'That's the striker Cristiana and the goal keeper Rupa,' he said.

'Excellent that you know them,' said Gustavo, moving onto another beer. 'They're a formidable team, and I think they'll finally go all the way to winning the final for the first time ever.'

'Hold on,' said Tony, 'what are those big black things?'

'Oh, they're Lapindee and Lapindum, the giant rabbit mascots for Alles Schwartz,' explained Gustavo in an offhand way, and Tony saw that they were indeed black rabbits the size of elephants, rearing up on their hind legs in perfect synchronization and padding their front paws to whip up the Alles Schwartz crowd into a frenzy of excitement.

Rather quickly the game became a rout. Cristiana scored two goals in the first 20 minutes, and then Penelope got another for Alles Schwartz in the final minutes of the first half.

'It's a disaster,' said an upset Fiona. Gustavo grinned at her and tapped his backside.

There were more adverts during half time and Yuri came on again to suggest yet another bet on more Alles Schwartz goals. The novitiates in yellow were dispirited, but the drinking continued and the noise and general rowdiness in the room increased. Tony noticed that a number of the novitiates had uncharacteristically started to flirt with each other, in complete contrast to their day-to-day chaste and monk-like or nun-like behaviour. However, at the back of the room there was Sue in the corner, somewhat distant from the others and looking rather stern. She was sipping what looked like tea and she nodded acknowledgement at him with a wan smile.

'Match days are an opportunity to let our hair down,' said George, who had consumed so many beers that Tony had lost count, and was well on his way to being very drunk.

Tony was also feeling the rare experience of a couple of beers getting to his head as the second half kicked off. Once again, Alles Schwartz dominated, and on the few occasions Poste players got to the goal, the goalkeeper Rupa made some outstanding saves. Penelope scored another goal and the triumphant black-clad novitiates in the room jumped up and down and yelled delightedly, while Fiona and other Poste supporters looked very glum. All the while, Lapindee and Lapindum could be occasionally seen in the background, waggling their ears, thumping their back legs and using their front paws like conductors' batons to the merriment of the Alles Schwartz fans. Tony found them very strange and rather sinister.

After the match, the celebrations intensified, with Alles Schwartz supporters and some neutrals doing a conga round the building. Fiona retreated meekly into the corner with another Poste supporter, Martin, and to Tony's surprise, after a few minutes they started snogging. By this stage George was becoming to be very verbose, crude and somewhat incoherent, blabbering about the glory days of the Sabres (Archangel Michelle's pink-clad White Mountain team, which had no chance of getting to the semi-finals) and the importance of indulging in human pursuits to do a fucking good job as an angel.

He was in the middle of a long exposition about how they should all run up the White Mountain naked when he looked up out of the window.

'By gum! It's the Archangel Natasha,' he announced.

'Cooo-eeeee!' floated up from outside and Tony got up and saw a group of black-clad Alles Schwartz supporters surrounding Natasha. She was wearing a skimpy black dress and a veil-like scarf around her shoulders, and she was waving to him. George opened the window and they and several other novitiates gazed down at the new arrivals.

'I've been thinking of you often, Tony,' Natasha said to him. 'You must be so lonely and I can't wait to get to know you better. Why not come down and join our little celebrations?'

Tony felt suddenly bashful and did not respond. He remembered how she had so seductively introduced herself at the Jardim do Ceu and the various lustful visitations from her. He also recalled his first night in the chalet and his dream, which had come for the first and only time, in which he had found himself on top of the mountain with a woman with a black veil.

'Time to go to bed now,' said Sue, who had suddenly stepped in front of the window, and half-guiding, half-pulling, she led Tony away from the room while surprised novitiates looked on.

'Tony, Tony!' Natasha's voice wafted after him, and despite Tony's weak protestations, Sue managed to lead him to his room. 'You'll need these,' she said, handing him some earplugs. 'It's now well beyond your bedtime and with your training routine we can't afford you losing any sleep with all this rowdiness.'

Tony meekly entered his room and in his tipsy state he reflected on the strange turn of events that evening. He had put in the earplugs in front of Sue, but once he was in his room he took them out again and could hear a hubbub of drunken festivities outside as well as Natasha's voice in the background still calling him. He decided to wait for five minutes and then gently opened his door onto the corridor and stepped out.

'If you keep your earplugs in you'll get a good night's kip,' Sue barked at him. She was sitting on a chair on the other side of his door. She looked at him very sternly, adding with finality, 'sleep well now.'

Tony retreated back into his room, nodding mutely, feeling obliged to obey the formidable figure. Looking through the peephole in the door he could see her seated outside like an immovable object. Reluctantly he slipped the earplugs in, prepared for bed, and fell asleep almost immediately.

'When a football team wins you sometimes get the victorious archangel doing a tour of the Realm of the White Mountain, but we were lucky to see the Archangel Natasha come to our chalet,' said George as they ate breakfast the morning after. 'I daresay she went to the Archangel Gabriel's chalet afterwards to have a good gloat.'

'It's the closest I've been to the Archangel Natasha,' enthused Gustavo. 'I was so excited.' Looking at Fiona, he added in an ironic tone, 'I really sympathize with our Poste novitiates.' Fiona looked miffed and turned away.

Apart from these little exchanges, and the fact that most of the novitiates were, in various degrees, hung over, everything had returned to puritanical normality in the chalet. There was a primness once again in the air and all were once more clad in grey. Tony wondered if the previous evening had all been a dream.

'Glad to see at least some people can do their burpees,' said Sue during the warm-up session, as Tony realised he was coping considerably better than many others who were slightly the worse for wear. To his shock, Tony realised it was the third month that he had been in the Realm of the White Mountain. In addition to now being able to take on most red ski runs, he had increased his maximum running distance to 25 kilometres. Despite cumulative tiredness, blisters and many times on the trail when he was fed up and felt he didn't want to continue, he realised how much the capacity of his body had changed. George in particular had been a major support, taking time out of his routine to cajole him through the first runs and offering moral support in many other ways.

'Sue was acting in your best interests,' he said out of the blue as they climbed a path up through a wood that morning. 'You should be very careful around the Archangel Natasha,' and then made no more comment.

Tony had also got used to, and indeed enjoyed, the skydiving training that he did several times a week, which gave him respite from the skiing and physical training. Each time he did it, he had to go by car to the city of Zimbro, which had a runway, and this took about 90 minutes. He went through the White Mountain tunnel, nearly two-and-a-half kilometres below the summit and 12 kilometres long.

'Running through the tunnel is the penultimate and for many the hardest task of the UEWM,' explained George, who was driving as they went through it the first time. 'We're safe being exposed for the ten to fifteen minutes it takes by car, but any longer and you're subject to the influence of the dark heart of the mountain.'

George shuddered and said quietly, 'Nothing can prepare you for what you experience here. Many novitiates fail at this point and some never come out.'

The tunnel seemed to be perfectly ordinary and dull, and rather long, but Tony was nevertheless always happy to pass through quickly. The role it played in the UEWM was little talked about afterwards, and going through by car was almost always done in silence.

Zimbro was the biggest town in the region, picturesque but lacking excitement. It was positioned at the end of a long lake that was either Lake Zimbro or Lake Amada, depending on who you spoke to. As Tony passed through the centre on the White Mountain bridge, he saw grey-clad figures busily going back and forth, and at times a huge fountain on one side of the lake, renowned as the Brunnen. From the bridge, it was possible to see the White Mountain at times, although there was a joke that visitors sometimes confused the closer and smaller mountain, simply known as A Toupeira, with the White Mountain.

The runway was just a few kilometres from the bridge, between the border of Zimbro and the village of Voltagem-Samambaial. A few small buildings and some hangars were situated off the centre of the runway, and it was here where Tony started studying the theory of jumping out of a plane.

When Tony took off for the first time, Monica, who was to take him down in tandem, remarked that he seemed very calm.

'I feel completely secure,' said Tony, 'because the Archangel Michelle isn't in the plane waiting to jump into my arms at the last minute.' He related his skiing story, which amused Monica no end.

It was nevertheless with some trepidation that Tony prepared to leap out of the side door of the plane at 5,000 metres, but the view of the landscape, from Zimbro to A Toupeira to the White Mountain and the range of mountains surrounding it was breathtaking. He had been told to expect the rush and noise of air as he fell, but it was still a shock the first time as he and Monica fell at nearly 200 kilometres per hour for a minute. He gave the thumbs up and then before he knew it they were drifting under the parachute.

In fact Tony's parachute training for the first few months had been almost entirely without incident. For the next jump he was on his own, with two instructors jumping beside him to make sure he opened his parachute, and before long he was tracking, turning and spinning in freefall with aplomb. Whenever he had a number of 'rest' days from physical and ski training, he would look forward to going to Zimbro and putting in several jumps a day. Before he knew it he had completed 50 jumps, including several group freefall jumps. George was frequently with him.

'Skydiving is exhilarating, but it's even better with a pair of wings,' George said, 'and once you get into a wingsuit you'll get pretty close to the sensation of having them.'

So Tony settled into the routine of physical training, skiing, skydiving, and learning about the region and the various paths around the massif of the White Mountain that might form part of the UEWM. Visiting Gostosa, the main town north-east of the White Mountain and the classical starting-off point, he walked and climbed on and around the White Mountain, reaching the peak a couple of times after staying in a number of the excellent network of 'refuges' – mountain huts – on the way up and down. The other novitiates commented encouragingly on his progress, and even Sue said that he might at least make it to the UEWM starting line.

Nevertheless, his increasingly strenuous and lengthy runs in all types of weather left him regularly feeling stiff and nursing various scrapes and rubs, with a few toenails lost due to the continual punishment endured by his feet. It was only the variety of other activities that kept him going. Before he knew it he had unquestioningly fitted into the monastic regime undertaken by the other novitiates. His memories of Earth and other experiences in Angeland and Hefyn dimmed as he became more and more obsessed with the goal of completing the UEWM, and he sank exhausted every night at 9pm into a deep, unbroken and dreamless sleep.

CHAPTER 22

'Today is your first marathon,' said George to Tony, as they lined up on the starting line, 'and I want to give you something.'

He lifted a necklace from around his neck, and Tony saw that it had a small silver wing with 'HOPE' inscribed on one side.

'I got it the last time I gained my wings, and I think you need it now,' George explained.

Tony was deeply touched, as he had felt quite dispirited by the training in recent days. 'I can't take this,' he said, but George insisted. 'It may help you in times of darkness,' George said, and they set off together with a 42-kilometre trek over the mountains ahead of them.

'Careful with your footing later in the course,' said George, 'it can be quite treacherous after this rainy weather, particularly when you're above the cliffs.'

When they started the weather was beautifully sunny, but it was damp underfoot, and after about 10 kilometres Tony was beginning to slow slightly. George offered to stay with him, but Tony insisted that he should go on ahead. Now alone and towards the back of the group, Tony pushed up a steep path that wound up an escarpment. At the top he turned to take in the view and saw a strange figure in a cream-coloured dress sitting on a rock by the path.

'Poppet!' said Fifi as she turned to see Tony. He had become used to the zealous hygiene, dress and earnestness of the novitiates, and he unconsciously flinched at her neglected state.

'I see my pulchritudinous appearance pleases you,' she said. 'Why, you've lost weight since I last saw you. You've also have turned quite supercilious.'

Tony remembered the last time he had seen Fifi in her cream beach hut in Hefyn, and her fondness for crosswords. He wanted to get on and continue his run, but he remembered Fifi's warning of how dangerous he was to Angeland.

'Much as Gabriel would like to think you'll agonizingly expunge his eyelash somewhere around the White Mountain, I suspect something a lot stronger than any physical effort or torture is needed,' Fifi continued, seemingly picking up on his thoughts. She turned back to the view.

'Look here,' said Tony, going to join her on the rock on which she was seated, 'I've learnt a lot here and I feel a sense of purpose. I'm not so sure I'm happy to see you, you seem to pop up whenever something is going wrong.'

'Well, the mountains are indeed dangerous. As is a human with an archangel's eyelash lodged in his lung. But be careful, my dear. Obsession takes you a long way, but you need to make sure you're pointing in the right direction. Which, by the way, is along the path over there,' and she pointed to where the run continued, gesturing for him to start again. Tony hesitated, but Fifi was still pointing. He turned and ran a few steps, and when he turned back she had disappeared.

The run was hard work and it started to rain. Although Tony knew he had the capacity to do it, he felt sore, dispirited and a little perplexed at the sudden visitation of Fifi. Before long he came to a part where the path narrowed by the cliff with a precipice of several hundred metres' drop. He remembered George's warning and took his time to negotiate the slippery rocks underfoot.

Rounding a corner, he was surprised to see a group of novitiates gathered on the path ahead. Down in the valley at the foot of the cliff, a helicopter had landed and brightly-coloured rescue personnel were moving around. He joined the group of novitiates, who were visibly upset.

'Oh Tony,' said Fiona, tears streaming down her face, 'It's George. He fell. I'm afraid he's... he's dead.'

Tony remembered that when he had arrived in the Realm of the White Mountain, Fiona had told him that all angels became human and mortal during their training. A barrage of emotions swept across him. He looked at the 'HOPE' engraved in the silver wing given to him by George earlier that day, and he hugged Fiona and wept.

The novitiates decided to run the rest of the marathon, as they felt George would have wanted them to continue. It began to pass in a blur for Tony. As they trudged on together, Fiona began to sing *We are Marching in the Light of God*. One by one the other novitiates joined in, as did he, as he recognised the song from the Bright Hall. They sang other verses, in other languages, and he began to feel lifted. He knew then that he would make his very best effort to complete the UEWM. He clutched the silver wing in his hand. He would do it for George.

So it was that Tony lost his best friend in the Realm of the White Mountain, and dedicated himself to training during the following months with a new intensity that surprised all of the other novitiates, including Sue when he asked for additional sessions to fill almost all of his free time. He even missed the Hexahedrons–Guardians football match which all the other novitiates watched, just to get more running practice in the pouring rain. Hexahedrons won by one goal to nil, consigning Guardians to fifth place in the league, meaning Alles Schwartz, Angeland, Poste and Hexahedrons were guaranteed semi-finalists. When he was told the result, Tony thought for a moment how sad Albert would be that his team had lost, but he ignored the merriment and debauchery after the match and, with his earplugs in, went straight to bed.

He progressed quickly in all of the disciplines, rapidly going from red to black slopes to off-piste skiing, carving perfectly and learning to jump and tackle all types of surfaces. On the days that he did skydiving, he jumped tens of times, undertaking complex manoeuvres and precision landings, as well as night jumps. He quickly passed 200 jumps and began wingsuit jumping, with Sue – renowned as one of the best wingsuit jumpers – training him.

'You're single minded enough, but I fear you're not taking enough time between jumps to process everything you've learnt,' she said. In a surprising undertone of something that seemed almost like affection, she added, 'Like you're in danger of burning out before you know it, or having a nasty accident.'

But Tony pushed on, perfecting his technique while running on every type of mountain surface in all weathers. He had been up the White Mountain dozens of times now, as well as having climbed many of the peaks around it. He was running an average of over 100 hours a week, including sessions once a week when he would spend the whole night running up and down and back up the mountains close to Willkommenhaus with nothing but a small bottle of water and a head torch. On and on he went with grim determination, devouring each new race with a fervour that generated further admiration from the other novitiates. He even started arriving sufficiently near the front after short races to witness Gabriel's assorted bands play pieces of stirring music. These ranged from 'Simply the Best' to the William Tell Overture and 'Eye of the Tiger,' although for some reason he couldn't quite define, Tony couldn't help laughing when Gabriel proudly passed his adoring followers with the Liberty Bell march or the Entry of the Gladiators.

'Time for the 160-kilometre race,' announced Sue to the novitiates early in the morning as they were preparing one day. 'Remember to pace yourselves!'

Spring and summer had long passed, providing the best conditions to train, and this race in late autumn represented the first and only chance for Tony to go all the way around the White Mountain massif before the following spring. He had now grown in experience and confidence: he had capably done a couple of 100-kilometre races and one of 140 kilometres, and he felt well prepared. The weather in the mountains, which could treat you to four different seasons in one day, seemed to be set to overcast and quite still, with cool constant temperatures, perfect for running. The group of all 500-strong novitiates from all the chalets gathered at the starting line. Tony saw Gabriel, who did his best to ignore him, but in any case he was surrounded by his acolytes from his Poste realm, including Fiona, with several carrying small musical instruments to salute him on his way.

'Many are novices, can't you see?' said Gustavo, 'They're just running in the first half of the race alongside Gabriel to serenade and pace him.'

'They're the ones with clothes a different shade of grey?' said Tony, a little sarcastically.

'Yes, yes, that's right,' said Gustavo, with complete seriousness.

'Can you point out which are which?' said Tony. Remembering the time when Sue said she couldn't distinguish them, he added, 'and Fiona or other Willkommenhaus co-novitiates are in the lighter grey?'

'Er... well actually I can't, said Gustavo, who seemed to blush. 'They are quite difficult to tell apart in this light actually.'

'I see,' said Tony, again unconvinced by the explanation of the shades of grey that he had heard from distinguished novices and novitiates.

At the starting line, Michelle was held on a podium and delightedly waved her floppy rabbit at everyone as she set off the siren to start the race. The novitiates were off.

Tony mentally checked the key contents of his small rucksack: head torch, spare batteries, gloves, sunglasses, sunscreen, spare socks, hat, jacket, wipes, the ever-essential sports tape (particularly to protect his nipples), a variety of high-energy snacks, his two water bottles...

The runners had started in the early afternoon, which in theory would only require them to run one night, and they all ran without incident up to the evening and through till morning. The weather brightened and as he rounded a bend Tony saw that a stream had burst its banks. He waded across, taking off his socks first, but after putting them back on they quickly became damp. After running a few more kilometres, he changed into his second set and immediately felt better. But the next section of the path was muddy, and he misplaced his feet and plunged knee-deep into a quagmire that soaked that set of socks too.

Knowing that wet feet caused blisters, Tony slowed and hitched his wettest socks onto the top of his backpack to dry. Despite Tony's training, as the other novitiates had several millennia more training than him, he was close to the back of the pack.

He then realised that he was approaching the cliff path where George had slipped to his death, so he was prudent and slowed down. Meanwhile, the clouds had begun to part and the temperature warmed. As he descended the rock path by the cliff edge, he momentarily lost concentration. He suddenly became aware of a blister that was beginning to form, and slipped on a sharp rock and fell headlong towards the cliff.

Panicking, he turned and managed to avoid launching himself into the void, but only through a contortion that saw him fall heavily on rocks and badly cut his leg and graze his arm and hand. At the same time, another rock sliced through his bag, and with a clatter the contents tumbled out and bounced over the cliff.

Tony picked himself up. He was bleeding badly, but he had no other option than to tear part of his shirt as a makeshift bandage. He was fine, but realised that without his provisions he could find himself in serious danger. Alone, with no other option but to continue, he pushed on. The sun came out and beamed warmly, but it was not a welcome change, as he had lost his hat, suntan lotion and water bottles.

After a little while hey began to feel dehydrated and acutely unprotected as he lightly hobbled along feeling his wounds. He knew that there should be a number of streams from which he could drink, as long as he was careful. Yet along the trail, he found no water sources. To his disconcertion he sensed rubbing and realised the tape covering his nipples had fallen off some time ago, so both these sensitive areas, as well as his thighs, were unprotected without lubrication or protection. On he jogged, under the now fierce sun, and when he relieved himself he saw that his urine had become very dark.

Tony felt really worried now, but suddenly as the path dipped and climbed he heard the welcome babble of a stream, and spotted it ahead running down the side of the path. He continued upstream for about ten metres to check nothing was polluting the water source, stopping at a dark red flower, then returned and gulped great mouthfuls, immediately feeling better. There was no time to waste, as black clouds had suddenly started to build and cover the sun, and he felt a chill breeze pick up.

Tony headed back upstream and stopped once more at the red flower, offering a silent prayer of thanks. He was weakened and had had a shock, but he felt if he continued steadily he could still finish. Climbing just a few metres further, he came to a small pool in the stream, in which there was a stinking dark carcass surrounded by flies. The half-decomposed head of a sheep looked macabrely at Tony as it gently bobbed up and down.

CHAPTER 23

A few hours later as the day faded, Sue found Tony at the end of his tether. She saved him and sent him on his way to complete the 160-kilometre challenge. He arrived at the finish line frazzled but wiser from his exploits, yet he couldn't forget that funny look on Sue's face when he had thanked her for saving his life. Something changed in their relationship from that moment when she had unguardedly revealed a tender side for a second. She had a new, uncharacteristic and almost indiscernible awkwardness with him in all their subsequent interactions.

—— * ——

Tony was eight months into his training and was not going to let his mishaps put him off – he was in fact encouraged to have finished, and to have done so despite the adversity he had encountered. Exceptionally he was consigned to a couple of days in bed and Fiona, Gustavo and many other novitiates passed by to wish him well. Even Sue came, reminding him she was owed a long series of burpees. However, staying in bed was a lot harder to bear than his regular training, and so in secret Tony paced up and down his room and stared out of the window for long periods of time.

The second afternoon, when everyone else in Willkommenhaus was out training, Tony saw a woman who'd seen him from her car and had now spotted him peering out of his room. She waved.

'Hi Tony!' she called, 'I'm Gill from the Hartes Arbeitshaus chalet down the valley.'

Tony was happy to have someone to chat to and Gill told him she was on her way to the town of Saint Wünschenswert down the valley to go in the public spa. She asked Tony if he'd like to come too. The Willkommenhaus chalet spa was very well equipped, and great for relaxation and revitalization, but the Saint Wünschenswert one sounded better and bigger. During all of his training, Tony had been free to wander, but he had chosen to follow his programme religiously and not wander far from the Willkommenhaus aegis. A mix of peer pressure, collegiality and pride – Willkommenhaus was considered the most disciplined chalet – had meant that Tony knew very little beyond his immediate surroundings, apart from going to the various external training venues, and during the big race days when all the novitiates in the region came together.

'Come on,' said Gill, and as Tony was approaching the second day of his recuperation, and feeling a bit pent up and frustrated after the trials and his success in the 160km race, he didn't see any reason not to go. He hadn't heard about the Saint Wünschenswert spa before and was curious to see it.

'No need to bring anything, everything's provided in the spa,' said Gill cheerfully. Strange to say, Tony immediately felt she was a lot more 'human' than his chalet colleagues. He got into Gill's silver Seraph car, which he duly admired.

'It's terrific to whizz round these mountain roads in,' Gill said, rapidly accelerating down the hill and onto the main round to Saint Wünschenswert. 'You're quite a celebrity. I warn you, you're going to receive quite a lot of attention.'

As they pulled into the car park by Saint Wünschenswert, there were lots of novitiates milling around in the entrance and things seemed a little disorganized. However, the receptionists quickly noticed Tony and came up excitedly and asked for his autograph. Apparently allowing him to jump the queue, they handed him a white bathrobe, towel, sandals and swimming trunks. He passed through the men's changing rooms and then through a café, which was full of many novitiates all wearing white bathrobes.

'You rather lose the semblance of being novitiates,' said Tony to Gill, 'this is like a gaggle of angels with everyone in white.'

'Appearances can be deceptive,' replied Gill. 'I suspect you've been rather too conditioned in Willkommenhaus.'

A tall novitiate approached Gill and kissed her.

'This is my boyfriend Pradeep,' said Gill, and he and Tony shook hands. 'Boyfriend?' said Tony aside to Gill as they headed down together to the main pool. In the corner of his eye, Tony saw some other novitiates canoodling and there was even a group where some were smoking.

They installed themselves in the main pool, which was deliciously warm and giving off steam in the cool outside air. The spa had all manner of individual jets to massage different parts of the body. The jets where Tony was seated were rather fierce, but there were no other spaces free so he rather awkwardly twisted his body to avoid being pulverized for too long in the same spot. All around him, a number of attractive novitiates looked appraisingly and rather flirtingly at him, and he nodded and gave them a strained smile.

'You see, bhai,' Pradeep explained, 'we're all thoroughly impressed at how you've managed to prepare for the UEWM, especially given – or perhaps because of – your placement in Willkommenhaus.'

Pradeep put his arm around Gill and kissed her again, then continued, 'In the other chalets, we train hard but we take the opportunity of being human seriously, doing research to ensure we understand the full extent of the human condition to help us serve you better when we're angels.'

Meanwhile Gill had got hold of some cigarettes, which she offered to Tony who declined. She and Pradeep started puffing away, the smoke mingling with the steam.

As Tony looked around he felt that everyone here was indeed acting a whole lot more, well, human, than his Willkommenhaus compatriots. It had only been on the evening of the football match, when everyone had got drunk and less inhibited, that he had seen this type of behaviour before. A number of the other novitiates came up and introduced themselves to congratulate Tony, with many literally clinging on to his hand when shaking it and looking at him with longing and a distinctly sexual edge.

'Poor Tony,' said Gill, after a particularly attractive blonde novitiate had made a distinctly lustful pass. 'You see you are a luscious but untouchable novelty, thoroughly out of bounds.'

'Out of bounds?' said Tony, 'I get the feeling that I'm like a forbidden apple or something.'

'Not entirely untrue,' said Pradeep, 'although I should be careful what I say. Let's say that you're... erm... reserved by a higher power.'

Gill interrupted, 'Now, now darling, we mustn't confuse Tony, better perhaps to point out the cardinal rule that angels mustn't fall in love with humans. Angel, novitiate, novice, earth or angel realm, that's completely off limits.'

Gill and Pradeep's exposition intrigued Tony, but he was not able to elicit much more detail from either of them or from the other novitiates he spoke to, who were unusually reticent on the subject. He pointed out that in Hefyn he had seen instances where angels were apparently in relationships with humans, but was told that that was a special case because there angels served humans, and love didn't come into the equation.

'Just bear in mind that you're the first real human I think anyone has ever seen in the Realm of the White Mountain, with the obvious and famous exceptions of Sandeepa and Mehi before they became archangels' said Gill. 'That makes you a complete novelty and also a terrible temptation given our current mortal states. Fortunately we have discipline drilled into us as angels all the time.'

All in all, however, Tony enjoyed his visit to the Saint Wünschenswert spa, and although his Willkommenhaus colleagues (particularly Sue) seemed a little disdainful and hurt at his choice to go to another chalet, no one objected. So Tony continued to visit the spa once or twice a week. After a while he stopped being the centre of attention, although he continued to receive admiring glances, and he started to enjoy the escape from the rigidity of Willkommenhaus.

Meanwhile, Tony continued to train intensely, although a little less obsessively than before, with Sue making a number of indirect swipes at the pernicious influence of the Saint Wünschenswert spa.

Winter came quickly, which meant a little less physical training outdoors and more use of the treadmills and other gym apparatus. There was more skiing and within a few weeks on clear days Tony was practising skiing down a good part of the White Mountain, after being dropped by helicopter. He also made more wingsuit jumps, including a couple of high-risk wingsuit flights from the helicopter under the bridge of the Agulha do Meio-dia, which was strung beneath the two pointy rocky outcrops at an altitude of about four kilometres, only a kilometre short of the White Mountain itself.

'Even in perfect conditions this is a tricky manoeuvre, and any error will lead to certain death,' said a deadpan Sue. 'You have to pass through a space approximately ten by ten metres. Regrettably a number of novitiates fail at this point, the final and perhaps most exacting UEWM test, because they are so exhausted from having completed all of the previous stages. It gets a bit messier when the weather's bad.'

'What about the White Mountain tunnel?' enquired Tony of Sue, Gill, Pradeep, and a number of others. He remembered George relating that the passage through this was one of the most terrible stages of the UEWM.

'It is a voyage through terrible shadows,' said one.

'It forces you to confront one of the worst sides of human existence,' added another. 'It takes you close to death and, for some who cannot resist, leads them to embrace it.'

The responses were all rather metaphorical and spoken in unusually fearful and hushed tones.

'Ironically, that's why being novitiates every half-millennium or so is so important for angels,' said Gill in a reflective moment. 'Becoming mortal here, we have to face both life and death in a way we can't when we're immortal. It's an intense, beautiful and sometimes confusing experience for us each time we do it. Yet despite all the millennia we have existed, having got to know you here, Tony, I understand now that in these eternal questions we angels are like children compared to real humans.'

The week before the UEWM, there was the last football match before the knockout stages of the Angel Cup. The game was academic, Angeland against Sabres. Sabres were Michelle's team, playing in bright pink, and had no chance of qualifying now. Tony saw the game in the Willkommenhaus cafeteria, and it started in a rather muted atmosphere, not only because the result had no consequence, but because it was unwise to let one's hair down too close to the UEWM. Furthermore, Tony and the other novitiates were acutely aware that Sabres had been George's team, so there was a general sense of sadness as the lively chants of 'Aain-ge-land!' and 'Ree-ta, Ree-ta!' could be heard from the crowd.

As the match unfurled, Tony saw that Rita, the star of the Angeland team, lived up to her reputation and began to demolish the Sabre defence, with perfectly-timed passes and dribbles. Before too long, she scored with a missile-like shot from distance.

'Angeland will be playing Poste in the semi-finals,' said Fiona, 'and if Rita is playing this well we won't have a chance. She's the standout player in the competition by a long way. Some people think she's even better than the legendary Ruth. However, by means fair or foul I daresay that some of the archangels in the remaining four teams would do almost anything to gain an advantage. Of course that would never include my Archangel Gabriel,' she said, winking at Tony.

Meanwhile Tony, who was enjoying sipping a beer, followed Rita as she spun and danced around the pitch, scoring a second and then a third goal during the match.

'A tenth hat trick of the season,' said Gustavo, 'it will be like an unstoppable force hitting an immovable objective if she and Rupa from Alles Schwartz meet in the final. Absolutely epic.'

He couldn't put his finger on it, but there was something about Rita that stirred memories in Tony. It passed fleetingly as Sue, incongruously animated for her team Angeland, had begun to get more and more excitedly vociferous and triumphant as the match unfolded. She embraced all the novitiates at the end of the match, consoling Fiona and other Poste angels, and then when it came to Tony she hesitated for a moment before giving him a warm hug.

'They say there's a possibility He might come back if Angeland wins the final,' she said somewhat breathlessly. 'Ever since He left we've been waiting so He can put all these errant archangels in their place.'

CHAPTER 24

At last it was the day of the start of the UEWM. The forecast was unusually good for the coming two days. Tony stood in the group of novitiates lining up in the road in Gostosa and waiting for the dawn to signal the start. The mood was one of anticipation, brooding and celebration. Those novices not taking part lined the streets and cheered, waving all manner of paraphernalia: banners, flags, whistles and the like.

Tony knew the course by heart. He turned it over in his mind: climb the White Mountain, ski down it, run 160 km around it, then run 12km through the bottom of it and finally wingsuit under the bridge across the Agulha do Meio-dia. He remembered Graham's description just over a year ago in the Bright Hall: 'Up, down, around and through the White Mountain and then finally the eye of the needle, all before the cock crows on the third morning.'

There was a great spirit of solidarity as the novitiates embraced everyone around them. Michelle was bouncing up and down delightedly on the starting platform, next to a big cockerel that was about to be used as a starting pistol. Gabriel was surrounded by his Poste angels at the front of the group, many with musical instruments. The only time he and Tony briefly had eye contact, Gabriel shot him a withering look. Sue was standing with the spectators, who were obviously novices, although they were still wearing what Tony found to be the same shade of grey as the novitiates.

She addressed Tony. 'Remember now, mummy won't be bringing up the rear for this race. If by some miracle you get as far as through the tunnel, you might see me in the helicopter making sure you're wearing a wingsuit before you jump out.'

Tony reflected that he hadn't painfully retched out the eyelash and inner organs as Gabriel had predicted when he had entered the Realm of the White Mountain, although perhaps there was still time. The last year had flown by and Tony's experiences in Angeland and Hefyn seemed quite distant now, but as he stared at the mountains he had the sense of dancing with Beatrice in the Shangri-La club in Hefyn, shuffling his position so as to stand next to a half-naked female form on the top of the mountain.

'You're miles away,' said Gustavo, patting Tony on the back and bringing his attention back to the group of novitiates.

The cock crowed, and with a sense of relief and great excitement the novitiates set off up the mountain. The time had finally come to gain their wings.

The dawn sunlight touched the Agulha do Meio-dia at the very moment that the cock crowed; it was a perfect midsummer morning. The novitiates climbed the mountain, some like Tony with skis on their back for part of the descent. While Gabriel had shot ahead and would probably do the ascent and descent in less than five hours, the other novitiates were happy to come in at under double that. With freshness and purpose, many indeed behaving in rather a pompous manner, they strode up the lower forested slopes, drinking in the cool air of the morning and calmly exhaling, jumping over the streams occasionally cutting across the path, and settling into a meditative routine, putting one foot and pole in front of the other as they gained in altitude.

After about three hours, Tony arrived at the snowline, and soon afterwards he saw Gabriel coming the other way on skis, accompanied by a brass band of Poste novices. They were clearly not doing the race this year, but had climbed the White Mountain earlier to ski down with the Archangel, playing their instruments with triumphant gusto. Gabriel slid to a sharp halt just aside Tony, spraying him with snow.

'Break a leg,' Gabriel snarled as the band paused, and then he was off again, bombing down the mountain.

The climb then passed uneventfully, as the other novitiates following Gabriel, descending by skis or on foot, gave much more cheery salutes. At the top of the mountain, Michelle was alone on the summit, and she delightedly high-fived Tony.

'Tony go go with bunny!' the toddler shrieked delightedly, and then for a few seconds looked oddly serious.

For a second Tony thought she was suggesting that he pick her up and ski down, which would have been difficult, even with the experience he had subsequently gained since their last encounter, but instead she handed him her floppy bunny.

'That would be an honour, Michelle,' said Tony, stowing the white fluffy toy carefully into his backpack. He took a quick look around, then took out his skis and fixed them on, waved at Michelle, and headed down the mountain.

Tony knew he was at the back of the pack now, but he kept Sue's advice in mind: slow and steady gets to the finish line. He took care with his skiing, following the tracks left by the other novitiates, but nevertheless feeling exhilarated by the descent. After a while, as the snow began to thin, the most well-worn tracks pointed to the best route to take, gaining him valuable time. When it was impossible to ski any further, he jettisoned his skis, handing them to a novice who was there to collect all discarded skis, and began running down the mountain again.

Gostosa came into view and as he arrived Tony checked his watch: nine hours and forty-five minutes. All was well and on time. He looked back up at the summit of the White Mountain, far in the distance, realising that the 160-kilometre trail around it was just starting. In the centre of Gostosa, he was welcomed and uplifted by a band of about fifty novices playing a range of drums at a fast pace. He entered a refreshments tent and helped himself to a late lunch of pasta and tomato sauce, which was a welcome change to the energy bars that he had been munching on during the first part of the day.

Fiona was sitting disconsolately outside the tent. 'Oh Tony, I've peaked far too early by going with the Archangel Gabriel's vanguard,' she said.

'Come with me,' Tony said. 'We'll run together from the back as the Willkommenhaus wonder team and one by one we'll pass them and get to the front.'

Fiona was cheered by Tony's enthusiasm and support, and they set off together in the mid-afternoon, happy to spur each other on. Before too long they came across other novitiates, passing about 50 fatigued competitors by early evening. As they climbed up and down the contours of the White Mountain massif, they saw tiny pinhead figures engaged in a slow strenuous dance across the landscape.

'Like me, they haven't paced themselves well,' said Fiona. Although Tony remembered that if 50 per cent of novitiates made it to the end it was a good year, he was quietly encouraged to pass the novitiates, who had seemed so fit and confident during the year.

'We are like children to you…' Gill's voice echoed in his ears. Many of the novitiates he passed were panting and struggling with the effort.

Dusk fell gradually, accompanied by a rising full moon and a beautiful red sunset. Tony and Fiona took out their headlamps, and soon after they reached a refreshment tent where they stopped as briefly as possible; many of the novitiates were receiving attention from novice masseurs and already looking as though their UEWM was over.

The path rose, zig-zagging up an escarpment for several kilometres, and in the clear night air it was possible to see tens, perhaps a hundred, novitiate headlamps ascending like a string of pearls. Then they heard the sound of voices being softly carried towards them: '*Si ya hamb'e kukhanyeni kwekhos...*'

Tony reached out to hold Fiona's hand briefly and in unison they joined in, with voices behind them in the darkness coming to accompany them as well, urging the weary runners forward with verse after verse in different languages:

Caminhando com a luz do Senhor
Wir marschieren im Lichte Gottes
We are marching in the light of God.

CHAPTER 25

At the dawn of the second day, news quickly spread that the Archangel Gabriel had managed to complete the UEWM in 23 hours, 57 minutes and 45 seconds, beating the course record handsomely and becoming the first novitiate ever to finish in less than a day. A huge firework display had been set off in Gostosa, and although Tony was on the wrong side of the White Mountain to see it, he had heard booming as it resonated through the valleys.

Fiona, who was still with Tony at this point, was delighted to hear of Gabriel's success, and explained that he would be flying around the route and stopping to give every novitiate still in the race divine encouragement. A couple of hours later, three shining white spots approached them rapidly, and as they grew in size, it became clear that they were three angels with resplendent wings. Two well-built and beautiful accompanying angels surrounded the archangel, each with a preposterously long trumpet. With great theatre, the angels stopped several metres ahead of and above the two runners, gradually descending until Gabriel hovered a metre off the ground and the two other angels landed on the ground on either side. The accompanying angels raised their trumpets diagonally to either side and played out a fanfare for about a minute. The female accompanying angel then addressed Fiona.

'Fiona! The Archangel Gabriel, all-powerful, munificent, bounteous, handsome, magnanimous, unstinting, messenger of the divine realms, interpreter of the prophet Daniel's visions, herald of the birth of the Messiah and Baptist to Zechariah and Mary, transmitter of divine words to Muhammad, patron of stamp collectors, cleric, diplomats and the nation of Portugal, portrayed by Kevin Durand, Tilda Swinton, Christopher Walker, Andy Whitfield in cinema, characterized by Nathan Alterman, Salman Rushdie and John Milton, with multiple visual representations including in the national galleries of art of the Netherlands, UK and US, Chairman of the renowned PFC, Poste Football Club, currently in contention for the Angel Cup, and UEWM record holder, wishes you every success in the UEWM.'

The fanfare then restarted, continuing for a minute more, with Fiona curtseying before Gabriel, who said nothing all the while. Fiona looked duly awed and turned to Tony with a glazed and ecstatic look. Gabriel gave a nod and the two angels began trumpeting again, but Tony had been feeling increasingly cross and was itching to move on.

'Now look here,' Tony said, 'I just want to get on. I don't want any more of this fanfare tomfoolery.'

The trumpeters stopped abruptly. Fiona looked rather shocked, and all looked at Gabriel, who nodded and made a gesture of his hand at the second male accompanying angel, who started, 'Tony, the Archangel Gabriel, all-powerful, munificent...'

Tony scowled and made to interrupt the angel, who looked up at Gabriel, but the Archangel waved his hand again. The male accompanying angel coughed and continued.

'... hopes you swing through the tunnel and, if you get beyond it, have commodious winds at the Agulha de Meio-dia.'

The Archangel nodded again at his accompanists, who played yet another melody, this time dramatically synchronizing their trumpets to point in different directions. Immediately Tony recognised the music: John Williams' 'Superman' theme tune. And, lo, angels bearing the other instruments of the orchestra zipped in around Gabriel and the two trumpeters as they joined the score, all harmonically hovering in front of the two exhausted runners. Gabriel raised his hands to his chest and dramatically pulled apart the two sides of his toga, revealing a gleaming silver 'G'. He rose slightly, with the members of the orchestra choreographing perfectly to emphasize the prominent place of the Archangel.

'Oh for goodness sake!' grumbled Tony, who had become even more irritated. However, out of respect for Fiona – who had prostrated herself on the ground in devotion – he waited for the performance to finish. Towards the end, Gabriel gave Tony a sneer and thrust his chest even further forward before leading the ensemble of angels away in a burst.

'We've wasted at least ten minutes with this nonsense when the last thing we needed to do was stop and get cold, which could cost us the UEWM,' he fumed.

Fiona stiffly picked herself up off the ground and they started again. She had been upset when he had interrupted the Archangel, but then a little shocked to hear the archangel's message to Tony.

They ran in silence until they got to the next refreshment tent, and at this point Fiona announced her blisters and said her cramp had become too much. She was very emotional and rather confused by now, insisting Tony should continue without her.

'Oh Tony, do take care of yourself,' she appealed to him, and hugged him.

By this time night had fallen for a second time and the refreshment tent was a mix of novitiates prostrate on the ground for whom, like Fiona, the UEWM was over, while a handful were ready to continue. Gustavo had just finished receiving a massage, so he and Tony left together, conscious that the White Mountain tunnel was very close.

After they had climbed for some time, lost in their own thoughts and with little dialogue between them, Gustavo grunted, 'The tunnel's coming soon'.

They were exhausted, it was the middle of the night and there was no moon, so outside it was pitch black, and the beams of their head torches were all they had to light the way. When Tony heard trumpets again he began to think he was hallucinating, but this time it was a different, familiar melody.

Suddenly, the last 500 metres of the road up to the tunnel of the White Mountain was illuminated with pulsating coloured disco lights, and Tony realised the trumpets were introducing 'The Final Countdown' which was being pumped out on speakers. All along each side of the road, crowds of novices and many of the novitiates that had already dropped out or finished were lining the side of the road. They clapped and cheered, holding up colourful banners and bright yellow smiley faces.

'Stay strong, Tony,' shouted Lara, his ski instructor, towards the front.

One after the other he saw many of the other friends and acquaintances he had made over the last year. They all encouraged Gustavo and him, and the two men held hands and surged forward, delighted to receive the boost and support.

After taking a quick break to stock up on energy and liquid, they entered the tunnel, and the world around them changed dramatically again. The hubbub behind them faded, and they found themselves in a sombre environment. An empty road stretched out ahead of them between cream walls, under a black-brown roof dotted with fluorescent lamps. They continued for a few minutes in silence, apart from the echo of their footfalls. Both knew that after 10-15 minutes they would become vulnerable. Gustavo's face was taut as he remembered the last time, five hundred years before, when he had passed through to gain his wings. Tony's anticipation was tense. He was remembering all the novitiates who had warned him of darkness and of a fate almost worse than death, or at least one that paved the way to that end. But he also wondered how there was such a fuss about running through a long, nondescript tunnel.

'Just try to keep going straight ahead,' said Gustavo out of the silence, 'and keep happy memories in mind. Remember that there is a way out.'

They continued, immersed in their own thoughts. As Tony had frustratingly still not been able to recall substantial memories of Earth, he ruminated on the various ones that he had acquired since leaving it. Singing in the Bright Hall, with joyous angels circling around. Driving with his grandfather in the countryside around Hefyn. Training and watching football with George. How different the last months would have been if he had been here, perhaps even in the tunnel now. Fiona's face had been so sad as she told him about George's death. She had been distraught when he had left her earlier in the day. He should have been running with George, so that he could have saved him. Instead he had fluffed the training, nearly falling off the cliff close to where George had lost his life. He was so weak, so dehydrated. He had fallen into the ditch and Sue had come, in her swimming costume, to tell him how he had failed. There was such a long way to go. How could he, from scratch, after a year's training, expect to be able to complete something so strenuous as the UEWM? Fiona was unhappy with him. Her face when they left had been in so much pain at the idea of a human doing the UEWM. Was there any point in continuing? He had already done so much. It would be good to take a rest now.

Gustavo's hand stretched out and gently pulled Tony back to the centre of the tunnel, but his reflections continued. *Gustavo must be so unhappy with me. He thinks I'm responsible for George's death. They all think I am. I'm so worthless. I'm so tired. Why am I doing this? I want to curl up and go to bed and sleep. It would be better if I wasn't here. I don't understand this business about the eyelash, about these angels? Are they angels or demons? I'm going to end their world, in any case. It's all catastrophic. I've been waiting so long. She will never be coming back. She must be dead. I want my cat.*

Tony flinched and felt a sharp pang of terror as a low moan broke the repetitive pad-pad of his and Gustavo's footfalls. At the side of the tunnel, a female novitiate was lying in a foetal position, shaking and crying.

'Keep going. Mustn't stop,' said Gustavo with a strained voice. They left her and continued. Ahead, they could see three or four other bodies dotted across the road ahead, whimpering and piteous.

I want to stop like them. How peaceful it would be. There are too many of these silly angel realms in this fantasy world. Perhaps we should just turn round. I don't like going underground. I'm beginning to understand what claustrophobia really means. I can imagine a terrible end. Not some stupid business with airplane toilets but one of those lorries that come at you through the traffic. It would slip and burst into flame. There would be waves of fire. Everyone would suffocate and burn. There would be peace. I want to be at peace, like those novitiates swinging by the side of the tunnel. They are very clever to have done that. Swinging, their necks taut and funny faces with tongues sticking out. With those shadows and the flames licking up the side of the tunnel. It's all black. Like me, how awful I am, how I deserve to burn, how I deserve to swing. There is a choir singing for me, I will sacrifice myself, the flames are coming, I can feel the heat, we are down, we just need to make a noose. Wait! I hear the sound of a motorbike.

Gustavo and Tony were lying on the side of the tunnel. Gustavo's noose was ready. Tony searched for something that could go around his neck and realised that there was already something hanging there; something small and metallic. He closed his hand around it, and almost completely lost, looked dully down. It was a small silver wing with the word 'HOPE' engraved on it.

CHAPTER 26

The helicopter soared through the pre-dawn clouds, its main compartment resounding to a four-part harmony performed by wingsuit-wearers.

Wie lieblicher Klang,
o Lerche, dein Sang!
er hebt sich, er schwingt sich in Wonne.
Du nimmst mich von hier,
ich singe mit dir,
wir steigen durch Wolken zur Sonne.

Tony, also in a wingsuit, looked at the singers. Gill, Pradeep and Gustavo were looking completely exhausted and, like him, would have probably gone to sleep if they sat down for more than five seconds. There was also Sue, looking extremely stressed, glancing frequently at Tony.

'I've just heard that the Archangel Gabriel will personally supervise your training, next year, if you don't complete the UEWM this year!' she had announced in terror to Tony as he and Gustavo left the tunnel of the White Mountain, before he had a chance to open his mouth.

Gustavo was barely conscious. He was leaning on Tony, who was gratefully relieved of him by Pradeep and Gill.

'It's very touch and go as to whether you'll get you through the Agulha do Meio-dia before the third crow of the cockerel. There are freak winds and we haven't got a second to spare,' said Sue after bundling them into the helicopter. 'Now get suited up and I hope you all remember your extreme weather experience wing-suiting through the Agulha.'

Tony remembered having only a couple of jumps with light winds that at the time Sue said would hopefully see him through – if he actually got this far. However, he didn't give it too much thought as everything he did still felt like he was plodding through treacle. Mercifully the helicopter had been waiting just beside the tunnel, and after they had heaved on the wingsuits, Sue went round them all one by one to give them a grey, glutinous substance which Tony recognised. He felt quite a lot better for gulping it down.

'Thank you Tony,' said Gustavo after the singing had ended. 'I don't know how you got us out of the tunnel when I thought we were both finished. I owe you a great debt.'

Above the clouds, the black, grey and white outlines of the mountains brooded splendidly under the orange horizon of the approaching dawn. The fading twinkling of the stars met the glistening peak of the White Mountain, although Tony was not really enjoying any of the scenery given the noise and buffeting of the helicopter, which was flying well beyond its safety limits. Sue had organised a jumping order for the novitiates, with Tony last. No one spoke now; each was engaged in a concentrated and strained individual meditation.

Gill was out first, then Pradeep, then Gustavo. Tony watched the grey figures plunge and diminish in size, speeding and wobbling precariously in the winds as they rushed towards the gap under the bridge of the Agulha de Meio-dia. A large crowd of figures in white lined the bridge and the two pinnacles either side. There was a white flash, then another, and then another: all three novitiates had passed under the bridge, and at that instant had gained their wings.

'Come on Tony!' screamed Sue, 'you've got to go now!'

But Tony didn't jump; he was mesmerized by the scene below him and the grim drumming and swaying of the helicopter, stinking of fuel, all which seemed to get worse all of a sudden, giving him intense vertigo. At last, with a sudden resolve, he shut his eyes and stepped out. But he did not experience the levity and the sudden rush of the expected free fall. Instead his face smashed into the undercarriage of the helicopter, breaking his nose, and he hung upside down with a strap around his ankle, swinging crazily round and round as blood spurted and dribbled into his eyes. In the stress, haste and bumpiness of the departure from the tunnel, somehow a strap had become loose, somehow his foot had got caught, and somehow it had gone unnoticed.

As he twisted round and round, he caught glimpses of the sunlight as it swept over the eastern peaks in the mountain range, the dawn inexorably galloping towards him.

Then, as unexpectedly as the bottom of the helicopter had punched into him, his ankle was free and he was falling.

What really happened during the instance of the novitiate who had the closest-ever gap (missing or passing) going under the bridge of the Agulha de Meio-dia would be the subject of intense popular speculation in Angeland for many months, as well as more detailed scrutiny by UEWM historians. Because of the very poor conditions at the time, it was impossible to obtain a coherent narrative from the several hundred angels and novice observers on and around the bridge. One of the few pieces of salvageable evidence was a knife found on the mountainside several hundred metres below the Agulha. One of the most popular theories was that either Sue or Tony had tried to kill the other after a year of difficult and fractious training in which a simmering resentment had resurged in the stressful last minutes. The narratives converge around seeing the two wing-suited figures falling from the helicopter, grappling each other and turning as they plunged towards the bridge. Just metres before the bridge, one figure separated from the other, smashing into the north part of the Agulha. There was great confusion at the time about the resulting flash, which was not, as many thought at the time, the standard explosion of light when a novitiate gains her/his wings and becomes an angel. At almost exactly the same moment as the second figure passed under the bridge, the out-of-control helicopter crashed into the mountainside and exploded, and nothing in the burnt-out remains provided any clues as to what had transpired. And at the same moment, the dawn sunlight touched the bridge of the Agulha, and all heard the crowing of the cockerel of the third morning.

The incident led to a number of calls to review the rules of the UEWM, including from A2 level, particularly with regard to the right to assistance to novitiates. Given the extreme controversy and interest in the case, for the first time UEWM regulations reached the CRAP for judgement. The Archangel Michelle advocated at this tribunal that had the novitiate and novice passed under the bridge together, it would have been a clear infraction. There was also not enough evidence, if any, that the novice had been aiding the novitiate during the time between the two falling from the helicopter and separating before the bridge. On the contrary, the blow that the novitiate had received in the face appeared to be a vicious and premeditated attempt to incapacitate or at least severely hinder him during the final descent. Furthermore, several experienced wingsuit experts concurred that there was no precedent for a similar manoeuvre with two people in perfect conditions, let alone high winds and darkness. Testimonies of angels who had been novitiates at Willkommenhaus pointed to Sue having been unusually sarcastic and hard on Tony during his training, so the theory that she had been nurturing a growing sense of jealousy and even hatred for him was the most widely accepted. Any suggestion that she had helped him, particularly at the expense of her own life, was dismissed as outlandish fantasy.

—— * ——

Sue cut the strap that held Tony, and launched herself off the flailing helicopter, grasping him and trying to get a hold to steer the two in the winds. Round and round they turned, but Tony was not only in the hands of the best wingsuit user in the history of Angeland, but also one with something hidden that no one else would have expected and which made the impossible possible.

As they approached the Agulha, Tony remembered Sue's hands gently guiding him. He looked up at the bridge and the two sides, lined by hundreds of white figures. The dawn sunlight was rushing towards them. There were two flashes, just before which Sue separated from him to his right. And at that very instant before separation, he distinctly heard, as soft as a falling feather touching the ground, the words 'I love you'.

CHAPTER 27

Yuri

He must be so very pleased with me. I've brought so much value to the table in PirogRus, where now the pleasure fits the commerce rather than the punishment the crime. There, after I was finally able to retire the Titans, I maximized the ROI and created a shopping paradise. In a win-win situation, instead of worrying about bronze anvils falling on their heads, angels can spend their wings during weeks of educational and recreational stays.

Of course Natasha has much to thank me for as I invented the *wing* currency – not to be confused with actual wings – after all, she benefits just as much as me from it in Hull. It was a fair deal for her to have the rights to entertainment and for PirogRus to keep shopping rights, although I didn't realise that the overlaps and lack of clarity in the agreement would lead to so much litigation. Still, who would have thought that so many angels would have had to get legal expertise to deal with it all, building angel skills for the future? The perfect example of positive synchronicity and creation achieved through commitment and splendid ideas.

Yes, providence has moved for me, and PirogRus, after I put my stake in the ground, has gone from good to great. How proud I've been as the circulation of *wings* multiplies as malls and hotels have expanded and, above all, as more and more angels have gained transferable skills and empathy with humans shopping as they visit and delight in PirogRus.

Naturally, the beautifully effective rebranding of the PirogRus logo – 'Yuri with the pie,' as so many customers affectionately refer to it – has helped angels to put the previous old-fashioned images of pits and fires well and truly in the past. As an idea with legs that has gone further than anyone could imagine, PirogRus still looks to the future.

He had a message for me, I remember well, at the last CRAP He attended all those millennia ago. After announcing that He was nipping out, He looked me straight in the eye and told me that what He said was just for me, to 'keep things going while I'm away.' And how they have gone! Wherever He is now, there's no doubt He's very proud of his prodigy, his heir-apparent above all the other archangels. How He would admire the way I've started the ball rolling to achieve what I have while He's been away.

Then, when I thought I had it all, like a good old explosion in a pit of fire, I realised during the CRAP that the best new commercial opportunity in millennia was on the doorstep. The perfect storm created by Gaby's wayward eyelash showed me how I could raise the bar even further. I knew the suggestions of Sandeepa, Ray and Michelle would fail pitifully – unsurprisingly, given that their levels of business acumen are so weak. With Mehi being too detached and unable to think outside the box, and Natasha always being the last resort, I saw it was my moment to run my suggestion up the flagpole and get enough of them to salute.

CHAPTER 28

'My Archangel Yuri extends a personal invitation to you to visit PirogRus,' said Gill, smiling at Tony as she cradled him in her arms. Her wings were beating gently as she flew towards Zimbro in the brightening post-dawn light.

Tony was exhausted and confused; he had black eyes and his broken nose was swollen, stinging and stuffed with cotton wool plugs. Almost immediately after passing under the bridge of the Agulha do Meio-dia, Gill, gleaming in full angelic apparition, had risen up to seize him in mid-air. She explained that there was doubt about the legality of the final moments of his UEWM attempt, with adjudication required at the highest level with the CRAP. Unfortunately, despite his state and at the insistence of one archangel, he would have to wait for treatment until the matter was resolved.

'It's terribly exciting,' Gill continued. 'In the meantime you'll be joining the most recent successful UEWM contestants who, thanks to the munificence of the Archangel Yuri, each get 500 *wings* to spend in PirogRus.'

Gill fed him water and bananas like a baby as she flew, humming a gentle lullaby which, along with the gentle swaying motion, soon induced him to sleep.

'Great to see you again Tony,' said Yuri, vigorously shaking his hand in the Zimbro airport terminal.

Tony had only woken a few minutes before and was groggy. He noted that they were surrounded by a flock of angels. The brilliant whiteness of their clothes gleamed in contrast to Tony's dirty, sweaty UEWM kit. Some angels had wings, some were without, and some were snapping away with cameras.

Yuri presented Tony with what looked like a computer tablet and a plastic stylus. 'You just need to sign here,' he said, pointing to the screen that displayed TONY PIROG'R'US AGREEMENT, with a box for a signature underneath some smaller text which read 'I agree to the terms and conditions' next to a check box.

'Just check the box and put your signature here, easy as pie,' said Yuri.

'But what's this?' said Tony. He had clicked instead on the 'terms and conditions' that opened up, with tiny hardly legible text, at the top of which it stated 'page 1 of 18,004.' He started scrolling down, but after reading the first few sentences he was completely lost in the legalese.

'Oh, you know how these things are,' said Yuri with an enormous grin. 'With all due respect it's just par for the course, and we don't want to get granular with so much to do ahead of us.'

While he was talking, Yuri had gently taken the tablet back, returned to the original page, checked the 'terms and conditions' box, and held the screen so that the box for the signature hovered a centimetre under the plastic stylus in Tony's hand.

'It's a no-brainer,' continued Yuri, his beaming face rather too close to comfort. He was nudging Tony in a way that seemed a lot more conniving than confiding.

'Erm,' started Tony, looking round at all the angels with cameras who were poised in anticipation.

'Fantastic,' cut in Yuri, bringing the screen of the tablet up to touch the tip of the stylus, then closing it and handing it to an angel behind him. He clasped his arm around Tony's shoulders and spread his other arm wide.

'Here's to thinking outside the box,' he boomed. 'We're going to resonate. Let's get disruptive!' The sustained barrage of the flashing cameras blinded Tony, who was beginning to feel quite ill.

After what seemed an age, it was over, and the group of angels disappeared en masse with Yuri, who tapped Tony's arm as he walked away from him.

'We've got so much to do together, Tony. I'll see you in PirogRus. Remember, only the lead dog sees the scenery change.'

Tony was left with Gill in the near-empty airport hall. He had noted that a lot of the common sense of the human-Gill he knew had seemed to drain away from the angel version, and to his consternation he had seen her face express the same worshipful adoration towards Yuri as Fiona had shown for Gabriel.

'Isn't he wonderful?' she said. 'And he's personally delegated me to accompany you to the special event at PirogRus. You can't imagine what a privilege this is.'

Gill, now without wings but retaining her whiter-than-white angel appearance, explained that as Tony didn't have any *wings*, he wouldn't be able to travel on Angel Air like most of the angels. Travelling on planes, in first class of course, allowed the angels to share the experience of humans as well as to start contributing to the *wing* economy. Clever Yuri had developed the *wing* through a system of ryptoffycurrency, and it had rebuilt PirogRus.

'He's an entrepreneurial genius,' Gill enthused. 'I know you'll feel at home in PirogRus, and you'll have so much to do.'

Gill explained that they would be going from Zimbro to Aornum Airport, PirogRus, with the airline Paltry Planes. 'It's just for novices. In his superfluous generosity, Archangel Yuri is giving you a free one-way ticket. I'm sure you'll feel quite comfortable,' she said.

Paltry Planes was branded in fluorescent pink, with check-in in a corner of the airport. A long queue of several hundred novices snaked back and forth, and Tony and Gill joined the tail end.

'When will I get a chance to sleep or have a wash?' enquired Tony. Gill said that the flights were usually delayed so he could sleep at the departure gate, and suggested that he should go and freshen up in the gents' toilets while she held their place in the queue.

On returning from the toilet, the white figure of Gill was easy to find among the grey-clad novices in the queue, who all looked curiously at Tony. Gill explained that the incident at the UEWM finish line was the main news across the Angeland realms.

Four out of the five check-in desks were inexplicably closed, even though there seemed to be enough Paltry Planes staff, but Tony and Gill finally got to the front. Tony was only kept awake by Gill's non-stop eulogy about the different shops in PirogRus.

'Does your rucksack fit into the 20cm by 20cm by 20cm space?' enquired the novice at the check-in. Tony took everything out of it and squashed it back in several times before it fitted. They then passed through security, which involved waiting in another lengthy, snaking queue, and further delays as Tony was instructed to put three plastic bags around every single item in his rucksack. He was also a bit miffed when they confiscated his suntan lotion.

'Remember, all this is to help us learn about the human condition,' said Gill as Tony finally emerged. As she was a full angel, she had bypassed security.

'That's all right for you to say,' responded Tony, 'but I already know the human condition, and I think I would have preferred the First Class condition.'

'I see the flight is at gate AG41,' said Gill, with a smile that flickered slightly, 'and it's slightly delayed, so you can get some sleep.'

They passed through what seemed like a never-ending series of tunnels, stairs and further checks, before finally arriving at the flight gate. A crowd of novices swarmed angrily around the entrance, as the departure time was still not clear. The plane had been held up earlier and was already three legs late in its itinerary.

'Perfect,' said a completely exhausted Tony. 'This looks like a lovely comfortable place to wait,' and with that he lay down on the dirty marble floor and immediately fell asleep.

Tony slept for nearly eight hours before being woken by Gill to tell him the plane was boarding. He was feeling extremely stiff but nevertheless somewhat refreshed, and they filed through the departure gate and crushed into three buses that took them in a long winding route around and across the airport. The bus came to a stop by their plane, which was gleaming pink with jets on either side but looking a little old-fashioned. They waited 15 minutes inside the bus, and were then driven back to the gate and herded back into the terminal without any explanation.

The novices, looking thoroughly bedraggled after the long wait, milled around or pushed irritably up to the desk, where a single attendant in an impeccable pink uniform looked very stressed as she tried to handle the riotous scenes around her.

'Don't worry, this is perfectly normal,' said Gill gaily to Tony. 'I'm sure you must be very happy to have lovely memories of Earth coming back to you.'

Finally, there was an announcement that the buses had returned. They boarded them and were put on the plane, only to find that they had to disembark once more and regain the terminal before finally boarding the plane a second time, at which point they were told there would be another two hours' wait.

Tony found that on the Paltry Plane jet, the so-called seats were thin vertical dividers designed to hold all of the passengers in a standing position.

'It increases the capacity by 20 per cent,' smiled Gill, 'and means that the tickets are 40 per cent cheaper. In fact this model, the T3 Ilyushin 76, came from Earth and is one of the originals from when production started in 1974, having already seen service in seven companies on Earth. The Archangel Yuri is a stakeholder in Paltry Planes and he selected this model himself. He has an eye for potential valuable museum pieces, you know.'

'Isn't there simply a HARP, you know, the toilet portal thing?' said Tony, remembering with something approaching fondness the rapidity of that method of transport.

'That's the beauty of this plane, it pre-dates the first HARP installation,' said Gill. 'To maximize efficiency the toilets were taken out to provide extra standing space.'

The interior of the plane had not had the same treatment as the shiny pink exterior, and Tony judged that the tatty fittings must be the original ones. Some overhead luggage flaps were missing and others didn't close, and the carpet was sticky and black. More disturbing, a distinct odour of urine pervaded the plane. The vertical dividers were crudely made of cheap-looking chipboard with splinters at the edges, and they wobbled when any pressure was put on them. But Gill was next to him, and he leant against her and asked her to hum another lullaby, and despite having to stand, he was able to get a little more sleep.

Tony was unable to estimate how long the flight took, because he was slipping in and out of sleep as the plane took off and during periods when it was being buffeted by turbulence, and red and white lightning illuminated the dark outside.

Eventually Gill roused him to say that they were about to arrive. She explained that air travel had made it a lot easier to get into PirogRus as they could simply fly over the Flogafoal, and both would shortly come into view. Looking out of the window, the inky blackness was broken by a gradually intensifying pink glow coming from the direction in which they were headed. The plane banked and Gill clapped her hands in delight, exclaiming, 'There's the Flogafoal and PirogRus! Aren't they magnificent? It's so great to be coming home after the UEWM.'

At first Tony thought it was an illuminated football stadium surrounded by a meandering stream of traffic travelling away from them, but then he blinked and realised that what he was seeing was something quite different and on another scale altogether. What had seemed to be the red tail-lights of thousands of vehicles was in fact a river of lava, ejecting occasional jets of molten rock along its length, which formed an enormous and uneven circle. In the space inside the circle, a colossal bank of orderly white lights somehow suspended in the air was not illuminating just a stadium but a whole city. Tony could make out skyscrapers in the centre of the city, including a very big square building in the heart of it, and saw a runway to one side towards which the plane turned and dipped. Throughout the entire length of the border of the city and the lava river were grey hills, illuminated red on one side and white on the other.

CHAPTER 29

'Welcome to PirogRus!' said Gill, after a somewhat bumpy landing. 'We've arrived at Aornum Airport, gateway to the shopping Xanadu of angel realms.'

The vast lights above the city gave the impression of strong sunlight, and in the distance across the runways Tony saw a modern flight terminal with many planes parked around it. Their pink plane, however, had parked on the other side of the runway and they had to wait as buses and service vehicles drove to meet them.

'I can't wait to breathe in the air of PirogRus!' announced Gill, who was positively glowing with delight. In contrast, the novices on the plane were looking completely exhausted after all the traumas of the in-flight experience. The door opened, and as Tony stepped out he was hit by a furnace-like blast of heat mixed with a whiff of sulphur.

'Oh, it's delicious,' beamed Gill, 'sunshine and a constant 55 degrees, thanks to the Flogafoal. It's like a beautiful summer day all year round.'

She was beaming with a zeal that Tony had begun to fear,

and sounding and looking more and more like a hyperactive, cheerful tour guide. While she somehow managed to retain her immaculate coiffured appearance, Tony and the other travel-weary novices were bathed in sweat moments after they left the plane. They plodded down the rickety stairs and across the runway with as much haste as feasible to reach the waiting bus.

'The air conditioning in the bus is broken today,' said Gill, 'but that gives you more chance to enjoy the local ambiance, as you won't get much opportunity to do so after reaching the terminal.'

As Tony had expected, the departure of the bus was delayed, and there was not much to do but stand still inside in order to expend as little energy as possible.

'This is the place where novices go if they have failed twice to complete the UEWM,' confided a panting novice to Tony as they waited while Gill popped outside to take in the air and do a little pirouette of delight. 'PirogRus couldn't exist without our labour.'

The plane had parked on the very edge of the runway, which Tony realised was on the very edge of PirogRus. The 'grey' hills he had seen from the plane were several hundred metres high, but now he realised that they were heaps of twisted garbage of every description, with old cars, building waste and other smaller items that sloped down towards the plane, stopping just ten metres away. Tony noticed some movement and saw that a metre-high grey robot was sweeping the garbage back with a small brush.

Gill boarded the bus and saw where Tony was looking. As the bus finally started on its way to the terminal, she explained, 'That's ACHE-E, Angel Cleaning Helper and Eradicator E-class. Created by Archangel Yuri to address waste management in PirogRus.'

'You seem to have a slight problem,' said Tony, looking up at the vast hills of rubbish they were driving away from. 'You must have a lot of these robots.'

'Actually he's the only one, a prototype, but very cute, and he does high-profile work here in the airport so he gets high visibility. Sales of ACHE-E action figures have been excellent since he was introduced. Visiting angels find the accompanying 10 per cent 'Planet PirogRus' tax very innovative and it salves their conscience no end.' She continued to babble on about the wonders of PirogRus as the bus wound its way around the runway, explaining to Tony that, in addition to ACHE-E, work groups of some lucky novices were also occasionally selected to help with waste management, although they tended to collapse from heat exhaustion, while the efforts of ACHE-E, who worked non-stop, were more consistent.

The bus finally reached the gleaming terminal buildings, whose decorative arches appeared in modern elaborate shapes. They climbed some stairs and passed through two sliding doors into what seemed like a fridge after the heat outside. The novices were channelled away through a side door, but Gill took Tony alone into a long corridor with moving walkways along each side. They stepped on and headed to the centre of the terminal, and Tony gradually got used to the air conditioning.

There were advertising screens on the walls they passed, and Tony realised with a shock that the figure moving on all of them was himself. Open-mouthed, he was face-to-face with his own facsimile, which was talking at him.

'Avoid all the trouble, avoid all the fuss, do great shopping at PirogRus,' the facsimile declared at him, with a big smile. The words 'PirogRus' appeared on the screen, and then Yuri appeared, taking a bite out of a pie. Then the advertisement looped and began again. The image of Yuri taking a bite out of a pie was transformed into a symbol: a white circle surrounded by a bright red background, with the profile of Yuri opening his mouth and holding a big pie in one hand appearing in black in the circle. Tony realised that between each of the screens, and in many other locations, this appeared in red, white and black flags.

'I may spell the end of Angeland, but shopping at PirogRus isn't half grand,' said another facsimile of Tony at the next advertising screen they passed, this time with the apparition waving an eyelash. Another simply showed the word 'DOOM?!' above Tony and then 'SHOP!'

'Hear about my amazing experiences with the UEWM and come to the exclusive book signing in the stadium in the mall within a mall within a mall,' the next Tony-double said, and this time he was joined by Yuri. They shook hands and beamed at the camera together, and once again the image of Yuri eating the pie came up and transformed into the red, white and black graphic.

'What on Earth is going on?' said Tony to Gill, who smiled innocently back at him.

On all of the advertising screens as far as the eye could see, the Tony facsimile appeared again holding a book titled 'Angel apocalypse now?' with the subtitle, 'The amazing story of how I swallowed an archangel's eyelash to spark imminent catastrophe.'

Tony gaped again at his image, which was wearing the same clothes but looking perfectly fresh. Doppelgängers of him continued to speak at the same time in synchrony on every screen, with books in hand. 'From HARP to Hefyn to UEWM to PirogRus: come to my book launch to hear my story and how I finally reached a shopping paradise.'

After this, Yuri appeared on the screen again and arm-in-arm with the Tony double they both bit into a pie, and pointed at the viewer with a knowing look. Up came the PirogRus logo with Yuri again.

'You've got an awful lot of explaining to do,' fumed Tony to Gill, as the other angels nodded and waved at him as they passed him.

'But you did sign up to it,' said Gill innocently.

'I didn't sign up, and I didn't agree to anything like this,' said Tony, grasping Gill and shaking her so vigorously that her hair became dishevelled. 'This is horrific!'

Meanwhile, the screens continued to beam images of Tony and Yuri. There was what looked like a film poster with Tony in the centre, Gabriel snarling behind him and then various other people and angels: Quentin and Fanny, Sandeepa and Ray, Albert, bodies strung up in the White Mountain tunnel, Sue dramatically flying towards Tony in a wingsuit with a knife posed just above his back....

'I don't accept any of this!' screamed Tony, who was particularly upset at seeing Sue portrayed in this way. As he raged and Gill tried to calm him, he saw that the boards were advertising DVDs, graphic novels, action figures (including Sue with a bloody knife) and the music of the Tony film. The images seemed to whirl around and around Tony and intensify and, for the first time since he had entered the realms of Angeland, he raged uncontrollably. He realised that angels with cameras had assembled on either side of him. 'Perfect, perfect,' they exclaimed, 'this live footage will be great to show ahead of the launch.'

In a frenzy, Tony ran down the moving walkway, looking left and right for some way to escape. The angels passing by continued to nod and smile as if nothing was remiss, and some even clapped. A couple of angels with cameras jogged alongside him, filming him constantly and giving him the thumbs up.

'It's wonderful to see you do an action scene,' one of them said. 'I'm looking forward so much to reading your book and hearing more about the wicked novice Sue.'

Tony lurched away towards a large atrium with a huge window that looked out onto the airport where big white planes were parked with 'Angel Air' written on their sides.

Two giant red, white and black PirogRus banners were draped down the side of the window. A fountain bubbled in the centre of the atrium and hundreds of angels in the space and the walkways around who had stopped to stare at him admiringly erupted in a collective round of applause. Around the walls, giant screens of Tony appeared, and he realised that this time they showed images of him desperately running around the airport. 'Tony can't contain his excitement to be in PirogRus,' a narrator announced.

The room seemed to spin and Tony sank to his knees, looked upwards and screamed.

Unknown to him, Gill had approached him from behind. She grasped his arm and thrust in a syringe. He looked at her open mouthed and then collapsed inert on the ground.

CHAPTER 30

Tony woke up to realise that he was clean, wearing a grey tracksuit, very groggy and in a straitjacket. He was in the back of an Ange Rover with Gill next to him, and she was grinning, with the continued unnatural sheen to her teeth and eyes. The seats had the red, white and black PirogRus logo stencilled into them.

'What's this?' Tony uttered, wriggling but not moving anywhere.

'We can't miss your book signing appointment,' smiled Gill. 'It's all just to make sure everything goes smoothly, in line with the Agreement.'

This was delivered matter-of-factly and with a hint of menace. Tony did not respond, but paused and then looked out of the window. The Ange Rover was stuck in a traffic jam, surrounded by and bumper-to-bumper with other gleaming white cars and a few dustbin vans. Hotels of various descriptions rose up on either side of the road, and from small flags on cars to giant ones on buildings, the PirogRus logo fluttered.

'Isn't this wonderful!' a contented Gill said after a few minutes, during which they had moved a few metres. 'Such modernity, such a perfect representation of human experience created by my clever archangel to help us serve all humans. And now you are here to help us reach even greater commercial heights.' She looked at Tony affectionately, and then pointed. 'Oh my, don't you look wonderful with the archangel!'

More screens showing Tony and Yuri could be seen in all directions, by the side of the road, on advertising hoardings and, even more prominently, in gigantic banners on the sides of the larger buildings. The two figures beamed, ate pies, and played with the action figures in an amalgam of the images Tony had seen at the airport. Tony realised that he could not move, let alone escape, so he decided to accept his fate for the moment and question Gill.

'So why do angels need hotels?' he enquired.

'Why, to try to get as close an experience as possible to that of humans of course, that's what PirogRus is all about,' said Gill, who was pleased at this constructive approach rather than all the wriggling. She continued, 'Angels love the brief chance to rent a place to stay, order a meal on room service, use a the minibar, open all the drawers to look inside, take away the little knick-knacks like shampoo and sewing kits, throw the towels on the floor, roll around in the nice clean sheets. You know it makes us feel so... ready to serve humans.'

'But angels don't sleep, consume food or drink, or need sewing kits,' said Tony. 'And I can't imagine you even make anything dirty.'

'No, but *wings* are paid and it all contributes to the economy of PirogRus,' said Gill. 'We provide employment to the lucky novices who clean the rooms and prepare the food – and of course who are also the mainstay of our flourishing garbage industry.'

Tony looked again out of the car window. He saw that there were cafés and restaurants at ground level with angels sitting in them with food and drinks, served by novices standing out in their grey clothes. Nothing, however, was being eaten or drunk. Across the highway, between the cars, some novices walked up and down in sunhats selling all manner of things – toys, packets of food, Tony action figures and PirogRus flags. Car windows would be lowered occasionally and an arm in white would be thrust out offering some *wings* in payment and, typically a few minutes later, the arm would emerge again and drop the item in the road. Tony was about to exclaim, but a few seconds later a grey-clothed novice with a brush and pan came and swept it up. All the while, Tony became more aware of the dustbin vans that were heading out of the city laden with waste.

'Normally angels can only afford to stay in PirogRus for two or three days, but fortunate ones like me who have gained their wings at the UEWM can stay a week or more, or splash out and stay in the grandest hotels like L'Eléphant Blanc or El Hull, which have the most luxurious offerings, including a special dispensation from Archangel Natasha for entertainments and authority for angels to engage in more bodily experiences,' she said, winking at him.

The traffic inched forward and the buildings became taller and more elaborate. Gill was almost jumping up and down with excitement at this stage. She announced, 'We're at the centre of PirogRus and approaching Temple Mall – the biggest and best mall on Earth or in all the Angeland realms.'

A huge gold temple-shaped building rose up in front of them, higher than any of the surrounding buildings, including the skyscrapers. 'Today – Tony's Testimony' appeared in enormous words across the front, with giant banner screens showing more images of the facsimile Tony and Yuri, side-by-side in front of the PirogRus flags. Smaller signs like 'Book signing!' and 'A Once in the History of Angeland Occasion' banners also shimmered on high.

'We've never reached sales like this before and it's all thanks to you,' said Gill, fondly taking off Tony's straitjacket and helping him out of the air-conditioned car into the blast of heat outside. Any thought of escaping was scotched by two tall and muscular angels who had been in the front of the car and had now emerged and put a firm hand on his shoulders as he was guided towards the entrance of Temple Mall.

The entrance was at least 50 metres high, with PirogRus banners dangling from on high. A space had been cleared and Tony walked on a red carpet. On either side, thousands of angels were waving PirogRus flags and cheering. Yuri walked up from the other end of the red carpet with open arms.

'My dear Tony,' he announced, directing his words mainly at the gathered masses of surrounding angels and the assembled media scrum that was clicking and filming away, 'it's so wonderful to see you on this great occasion for PirogRus and all the realms of Angeland. We feared you initially, but you will be the final and greatest solution for us!'

Yuri grasped Tony's arm, the two beefy angels following closely behind, and they began walking into the Mall.

'You know Tony,' said Yuri, this time jabbering excitedly to him while offering the occasional wave to the crowds lining each side of the Mall thoroughfare which was wide enough to run a motorway through it, 'We've had many things in the history of PirogRus that have boosted the economy and given pleasure and education to angels – bottled water, designer clothing, cosmetics a-plenty, exotic pets, Sinclair C5s, potties with built-in tablet holders, insurance, selfie sticks, gym subscriptions and of course fantastic money-off vouchers, to name but a few. But I never thought in my wildest dreams that you would transform PirogRus into the new centre of Angeland's realms.'

On all sides, the angels continued to cheer with sustained fervour. From the ceiling on either side, red, white and black PirogRus banners hung down. The group comprising Yuri, Tony, Gill and the two 'guardian' angels turned towards the side of the thoroughfare and climbed up to a viewing platform.

'Time for the procession,' said Yuri, clapping his hands together excitedly. 'All this is for you, Tony.'

Along the centre of the thoroughfare, regiments of what seemed like thousands of angels marched, goose-stepping along with PirogRus flags distributed evenly among them. As they passed the platform, they turned and raised their right arms in unison in salute. 'Pirog-R-us! Pirog-R-us!' they chanted, followed by 'To-ny! To-ny!'

'They adore you, Tony!' said Yuri gleefully, hugging him, to further waves of applause.

When the procession had finally passed, the small group descended and continued to enter further into the depths of Temple Mall, which on either side had splendid shops selling goods of every description, including grand cars with small silver angels on the bonnet, televisions with screens the size of walls, and elephants.

'We are approaching the Rub-a-Dub-Dub Mall,' explained Yuri, 'the most important of the multiple malls within the Temple Mall.'

Further in they went, and Yuri took time to point out an indoor ski slope, an aquarium with a blue whale in it (more notable, bizarrely, for having the largest ever acrylic panel), a zoo and a 200-storey underground car park – including a 180-hole crazy golf course.

'You see, Tony, we learn the wonderful lessons of Earth and do better, so angels can be the best at what they do,' said Yuri, pointing in the distance towards a group of buildings that seemed vaguely familiar.

'And here we have an historical perspective,' explained Yuri, 'the Roman Forum, in its original glory, and I must say any angel with a toga – which is most of them – can't resist it.'

They walked up to the mall within a mall within a mall. The buildings rose up before them and Tony forgot that he was restrained for once. He had the impression that he had walked into ancient Rome. 'Don't you just adore it?' said Yuri, responding to Tony's awe.

They walked up to a big temple fronted by tall columns. Up a few stairs to the temple entrance there was a white marble chair with a table in front of it. Around the temple, trestle tables were arranged with all manner of knick-knacks, all associated with Tony – action figures, postcards of the UEWM and Hefyn, and heaps of 'Tony's book, *Angel Apocalypse Now?* On a couple of outlying tables, piles of *wings* were neatly assembled with queues of angels taking their turn to deposit them.

'We've started a great line in gifting circles,' said Yuri to Tony, 'and soon you'll be profiting too, now that we're business partners.'

Yuri turned away and faced the crowd of thousands of angels who had assembled in front of the temple. The crowd went quiet, and the many PirogRus flags stopped waving in anticipation.

'Friends, Angels, PirogRusians, give me your *wings*,' boomed Yuri, continuing with dramatic flourishes, 'I come to save the Angeland realms, and exalt Tony. He who we feared was our greatest bane is in fact our ultimate saviour and source of profit. For Tony has agreed to take this blue pill, becoming forevermore an angel but retaining that so powerful gift, his human love, which he will channel henceforth to all of us and for eternity. Signing copies of his book for every visiting angel to buy, in multiples, costing only 50 *wings* each. We thank Tony for his agreement.'

There was a roar of applause and Tony, who had begun struggling halfway through the speech, was again pinned down by his two minders. Gill's teeth gleamed and she looked theatrically emotional.

'I'm so proud of you, Tony,' she said. She firmly placed her hands on his face to open his jaws. Yuri triumphantly held up a blue pill to the crowd, then turned and dropped it in his mouth, which Gill clasped shut along with his nostrils.

'Just a little swallow,' she said, 'all that's needed to save Angeland and its realms. To become immortal.'

Tony's eyes bulged as he tried uselessly to expel the pill. He struggled in vain, his head beginning to throb and his lungs close to bursting.

Suddenly there was a discernible thump above the noise of the cheers of the crowd, which fell silent, followed by an almighty crash.

'Mandrills! Selfie-stick sellers! Lemons! Zits! Anthropologists!' screeched a high-pitched woman's voice.

'The renegade angel!' shrieked Yuri, 'What are you waiting for? Grab her!'

All of a sudden, the pressure was released from Tony as Gill and his minders stepped away. He turned and spat the blue pill onto the ground, and took a big breath. The crowd was fixed to the spot, standing open-mouthed. There were more banging noises as tables were overturned by a diminutive woman who ducked adroitly away and around the various angels who tried to capture her. Where she had overturned the table with the wads of *wings*, they fluttered around in the air.

'Wallflowers! Jolly Rogers! Bakr al-Baghdadis! Lecherers! Algae! Cogomelos!' she shrieked, heading towards Tony. 'Religious observances, poppet,' she said with great calm as she passed him, before launching into more wild invective. It was Fifi. She passed to the other side of the chair now and continued to turn the tables over, with the pursuing angels tumbling over themselves and bumping into each other.

Gill masterfully leapt over a collapsing table and seized Fifi's shoulder. Without missing a step, Fifi turned and slapped Gill hard on the face, and said something to her that Tony couldn't catch. Gill suddenly collapsed like a sack of potatoes with her hands to her head.

'Call the Policia Estatal Secreta!' screamed Yuri in frustration.

With incredible dexterity Fifi continued to avoid the pursuing angels while tipping over yet more tables. Then Tony, from whom attention had been diverted during the rampage, saw with a start that Gill was next to him. But her complexion and demeanour had completely changed: gone was the gleaming white-teethed perfectly-toned semi-goddess who had restrained him in PirogRus thus far. Before him now was a being crumpled, careworn and sheepish and seemingly almost human.

'Oh Tony,' she wept, 'please forgive me!' Tony saw once again the Gill he remembered from the Saint Wünschenswert spa and the Realm of the White Mountain.

'You must go into the temple, Tony, hurry now!' She pointed up the stairs, where a hand emerged from the shadows and beckoned him in. Tony heard sirens in the distance, and looked up over the melee of angel chaos to see airborne black-winged angels with blue flashing lights on their heads approaching from afar.

'Freemasons! Amoeboids! Lilliputians! Feios! Grave robbers! Organ grinders! Nincompoops!' Fifi screamed, but she was now surrounded on all sides as the flying black-winged angels swooped down and landed.

Tony mounted the stairs towards the shady figure at the entrance to the temple. He turned to see Yuri pointing towards him and yelling at the other angels to intercept him. But Tony reached the outstretched hand just in time, and as he was frantically pulled inside, not for the first time in his adventures, he lost consciousness.

CHAPTER 31

Mehi

We were annihilated. Scenes of the Battle of Megiddo came to mind as Natasha leaned over and shot me a smile full of sarcasm and triumph during half time. I knew it was going to be a difficult game, but all my worst fears were realised when my Hexahedrons were five-nil down at halftime, to finish eight-nil down at the final whistle. Well, we can fairly safely expect a better result in the third place play off. I suspect only the Angeland team, with the formidable Rita, can have any chance of beating the Alles Schwartz, if they get through to the final.

I also sensed during the match that Natasha was salivating at her other game: bringing Tony to Hull. In desperation the CRAP voted four to three that she should be next after my efforts to try to extract Gabriel's eyelash. I hope Tony has sufficiently burnt his tongue from the soup to blow in yoghurt. Unsurprisingly, Yuri lived up to expectations with his approach. I was happy to be there to pull Tony to safety from the PirogRus melee.

Here I am, however, on the platform with Tony to provide a transition before Hull, but on the pretext that coming to the Cube might help to dislodge Gabriel's eyelash. Completely without hope, as I know well, but I am rather keen to spend some time with Tony before Natasha gets her way with him. I am glad he mercifully stayed unconscious all through the semifinal, as I would not wish that memory upon anyone. He looks tranquil on the bench now, not perhaps realising the full extent of disruption and fear that he has caused across Angeland and its realms. Yet I cannot hide a certain nostalgia when I see him, and am reminded of when Sandeepa first came to Angeland, joining me as the second human to become an archangel.

Alas, how I reminisce on my human achievements. Who else can claim to have held the record for constructing a building that was the tallest in the world for 3,800 years? Twenty years it took, the prime of my human life, to organize 100,000 men, whose names I came to know; the joy we shared as the 2.3 million blocks of the monument rose up from its foundations towards the sky. The white limestone cover and golden capstone are gone now, but how much more majestic it then looked compared to the ragged brown it is today. With a ratio of perimeter to height of 1760/280 royal cubits the edifice was and is a temple to geometry, astronomy and aesthetics.

As the capstone was placed, I welcomed my fate: entombed with the mummy of Pharaoh Khufu, in the centre of my great work, taking the secrets of construction and planning so that no one could ever emulate me. My wish to be sealed in the centre, in what is erroneously called the Queen's Chamber today, was granted, and I took with me enough provisions to last me several months. They provided final peace, perfect silence and a time for reflection after so many hot, crowded years of toil.

I remember clearly when Gabriel appeared, and the shock I had, with the light emanating from him and illuminating the chamber as if it were day. He was softer then, before both his great missions to Earth, and then his subsequent decline into folly and vanity.

'Mehi, the greatest architect of the world, few will have the abilities you possess and no one will achieve your greatness,' he said. 'Come, for it is your destiny to become the architect of the angels.'

The Cube was in a terrible mess when I arrived, so I got to work immediately, improving the transport and marshalling the angels working inside, many of whom were quite unskilled. As the Cube Overseer, even though I could follow all the activity of the Universe and enjoy reminiscing and learning more about everyone I had come across during my human life, I was secretly delighted when Sandeepa came to Angeland and joined the ranks of the archangels like me. And thus it is with Tony.

For I and most other angels have a great interest in Tony: this 'everyman' who in swallowing Gabriel's eyelash inexplicably erased all records of his human past, present and future in the Cube. Yes, Tony, who represents not only uncertainty and catastrophe but also hope, the unknown, and is a figure of fixation and lust for many angels. No angel has ever seen, even Him I daresay, a human with such endless possibility. Tony's adventures are like a blank book unfolding chapter by chapter into a story that no one, not even I, can foretell.

CHAPTER 32

Tony woke up. He was slumped on a green plastic chair, on the platform of an underground metro station, and there was a warm, musky and slightly rubbery smell in the air. Angels, some with wings and some without, were milling around and shooting sideways glances at him. On the seat next to him he saw the Archangel Mehi looking at him intently, in his crisp white suit and with slicked-back black hair.

'Welcome to the Cube,' Mehi said, 'the biggest realm of angels, where we monitor all activity in the universe.'

Tony looked around. He was a little distracted by the fact that many of the angels with wings were flapping them in short restrained bursts. A blue and white sign gave the name of the station: 'Close Shaves.' The station was lined with bright white tiles, and behind him there was a large and incredibly complex map of the metro system with lines of different colours. He spotted some of the names of the lines which were in larger font, Laplace, Boscovich, Heraclitus and Leibniz, and some of the station names in much smaller font; there were many – 'Births,' 'Serendipity,' 'Nose Picking' and 'Déjà Vu.'

'This is the central RATC system,' explained Mehi, gesturing to the map. 'It stands for Reticular Angel Transports for Contemplation, although most angels have forgotten that and just use the acronym. I would have liked to have shown you round the fuller network which extends beyond this and is managed by SNOF, the Seraphim Network of Omnipotent Focus, bus I'm afraid time is against us. It was all designed by me. Before that I constructed the Subsolo and many of Angeland's buildings. But let us get the next train.'

An aquamarine and white train pulled into the station. It was quite full of angels, and as it came to a halt and the doors opened a male voice and the sound of a guitar wafted out with a familiar tune about angels.

They boarded the metro, sitting on two narrow folding seats that had been vacated. The busking angel stood out from the other angels; he was unshaven with long black hair, and dressed in a worn black leather jacket and black jeans.

'You had rather a close shave in PirogRus,' said Mehi, unfazed by the singer. 'I must apologise for the discomfort you faced.'

The singer continued until he gently came to the end of the song, at which point the angels with wings, who had arranged them carefully behind their backs so as to avoid poking them into the others, flapped them lightly and nodded appreciatively at the busking angel, who finished somewhat abruptly. He picked up his guitar, and then wandered up and down with a paper cup into which several angels dropped *wings*.

'Hey man Tony, I hope to see you in Hull,' he said, tapping Tony on the shoulder with a smile. He left their carriage and headed for the next one.

There was the sound of a siren, and the doors closed.

'He's sojourning from Hull,' Mehi explained. 'They wear black, not white like other angels, and they're excellent entertainers, so I tolerate them in the Cube if they keep to the metro. But safety procedures next. It's a ritual that angels in the Cube take turns at doing in order to keep themselves amused, even though no one else watches. But as you're here for the first time, I advise that you pay careful attention.'

In each of the three open areas between the seats, an angel stood up and looked pompous. A microphone crackled. 'Angels and Tony, we request your full attention as the attendants demonstrate the safety features of this metro carriage.'

Tony felt distinctly as if he was in a plane as the attendant angels told him to fasten his seat belt (to his surprise there was one), pointed out the exits of the carriage, explained that oxygen masks would drop from the ceiling in the event of decompression, elaborated the bracing position, and indicated that a life vest was under the seat. The female angel who was giving the demonstration in front of Tony had seemingly whisked the mask-on-the-end-of-a-tube and life vest out of thin air, but more disconcertingly she had spent the whole demonstration eyeing him up, and then made rather saucy gestures with her whistle.

'Thank you Lana,' Mehi said to her. 'Beautifully demonstrated, but even more beautifully suggestive.'

Mehi turned to Tony, who had been looking for the place where the mask dropped from the ceiling and the life jacket.

'Don't worry, there aren't any,' Mehi said, 'but you will find that your seat belt comes in handy.' Tony noticed that all the angels in the carriage had buckled up, including Lana, who continued to flash her eyelashes at him from the opposite side of the carriage.

'You must forgive her as she's just come back from Hull, which has got a lot more popular recently because of you,' explained Mehi. 'But I think you already realise that the fact that you are so different and dangerous to angels makes you irresistible to many of them.'

The music of the busker struck up in the adjacent carriage as the train pulled out of the station, but Tony did not pick up any of the words or manage to put a question to Mehi about his so-called irresistibility. Instead of entering a tunnel, the train exited into what seemed like outer space; a vast inky blackness, twinkling stars and illuminated strands. Then it suddenly lurched vertically downwards at great speed like a roller coaster. Tony gripped his seat in terror, and but for his seat belt would have been thrown towards the ceiling. The train spiralled recklessly from side to side, but none of the angels in the train seemed the least perturbed, and the music from the next carriage continued uninterrupted.

'Before I built the metro, the angels had to fly from station to station,' explained Mehi. 'If they put a wing wrong they might end up diverted, late or in the wrong station. Many angels still speak quite fondly of the old days of course, although there are plenty of tales of them ending up in completely the wrong place, such as Quantum Physics rather than Newtonian Physics, Best Soccer Goals in place of Best Home Runs, or Farts instead of Belches.'

Tony had got slightly more used to the motion of the train and was also taking in the view. Mehi explained that the seeming millions of dots of lights were stations, and the thin illuminated filaments between them were the metro lines.

'But what is it with all these funny station names?' asked Tony.

'You've seen, of course, your guardian angel,' said Mehi, 'and perhaps have heard of the idea that every blade of grass is observed by angels?' Tony nodded. 'That example only became popular on Earth when an errant angel from the Grass station absconded about 2,500 Earth years ago in what you now call Israel. The point is that there are about a quindecillion angels who observe every possible combination of things in the universe.'

'Everything?'

'Every fundamental particle in the universe has been diligently observed in its pre-ordained path since the beginning of time. The Metro and its stations are in the centre of the network, where we are now, and exist to track and follow specific things related to humans.'

'Golly,' said Tony, 'So you're saying that everything is predetermined? Like, I mean, not just our lives but every grain or sand or dust, or atoms like the ones that got expelled with Queen Victoria's dying breath?'

'Yes,' said Mehi, 'exactly that. Although nothing is predetermined in the angel realms. We are the unpredictable watchers of a predictable universe.'

'So you know the future?' asked Tony, who had completely forgotten about the train's rapid lurching gait.

Mehi was pleased to have some different company to that of the quindecillion angels that he was used to. He continued, 'Time, as you know it and as we are experiencing it now, does not affect angels in the Cube in the same way. So, here we can effectively see backwards and forwards in a two-way manner, although as a human you can only exist in one dimension. Without going into a long and complicated discourse, the most accurate way of explaining this is to say that the temporal disjunction is wibbly-wobbly timey-whimey. This also captures nicely why angel activities cannot be predicted themselves. It doesn't however explain why all trace of you has disappeared from the Cube, but we are still working on trying to understand that.'

'This is all rather silly,' said Tony. 'How did you lose track of all the atoms in me, their history, and their future? Seems like a bit of a monumental cock-up somewhere down the line. And if you're just observing a predefined universe it must get rather dull.'

A brief flicker of annoyance crossed Mehi's face, but he calmly explained again that it was down to the wibbly-wobbly nature of things and they would soon get to the bottom of it.

'Aha,' Mehi said, 'we're coming into the station where we need to get off. Near Misses. I think you'll enjoy it.'

The train slowed and abruptly left the apparent infiniteness of the dots of light, filaments and darkness, to enter another metro station much like the previous one, although it was indeed named 'Near Misses.' They and a number of other angels got off, and down the platform Tony saw the busker in black leaping quickly from one carriage to another, waving at him.

Mehi stood in the station for a moment admiring the pristine white tiled blank walls. 'Yuri has been imploring me for millennia to put up his adverts in the Cube, saying it's a great waste of space,' he said, 'but I'll have none of this commercial nonsense here.' He paused for a moment, and then barked, 'Follow me,' and proceeded into a passage and up some stairs. There were lots of side tunnels with signs pointing towards curious destinations such as 'Sliding Doors,' 'Ships That Pass In The Night' and 'Football Penalty Shoot-Outs.'

'There are many sub-categories in each station which often have to deal with millions of different and unique instances in the universe, which is complex and requires more angelpower when they are happening simultaneously,' explained Mehi. 'I frequently rotate angels between stations and sub-categories to keep motivation high and build their skills.'

In the tunnel they passed a number of angels who were walking back and forth and looking very purposeful, although Tony felt like the centre of attention as they shot glances and him and murmured discreetly to each other.

'For example the sub-category 'Chat-up Lines That Only Just Failed' is one of the most sought-after in this station and the entire network, closely following the 'Birth' station and the 'Romantic Encounters' sub-category in the 'First meetings' station. Those stations, of course, are two of the biggest intersections between lines on the metro network.'

Further and further they went through the tunnels, with Mehi pointing out that 'Doors Closing And Others Opening' and 'Jokes Just Falling Flat' were also very popular, before Tony worked out from the frequency of signs where they were going.

'Insufficient Persistence?' queried Tony.

'Yes, exactly. We are going to the 'Insufficient Persistence' sub-category,' explained Mehi, 'only because it will give us the fastest route to the situation that I want to see on Earth at this time. The alternative, to go to the 'Knock On Effect' station on the Spinoza line, would have meant making a lot of changes on the metro system to get there, and I didn't want to submit you to too much corny music and undue angel attention on the way.'

With that, they arrived at the end of the passage and were met with four barriers. Mehi pulled out what looked like a credit card and swiped it over the top of one of the barriers, which opened to let him through, but not before handing Tony a small light blue rectangular ticket, which he inserted into the corner barrier.

'I know, it's old technology,' said Mehi, looking at Tony, 'but good for visiting angels, and indeed a human like you.'

Tony was curious to see what was beyond the barriers in the 'Insufficient Persistence' sub-category, and he was not disappointed as the passage curved around and upwards and then opened out at the base of a vast sphere. All round the inside of the sphere, angels with wings sat on chairs in front of giant television screens. Tony saw that Mehi had extended his wings, and after exchanging a gesture, the archangel picked him up, flying upwards through the empty centre of the sphere.

As they gained altitude, Tony looked with interest at the television screens, Mehi stopping to explain when requested.

'This man here,' said Mehi, as they looked at a man grimacing as he tried to open a champagne bottle, 'is about to stop just before the cork would have come out. This is an interesting incident, as it will subsequently be observed in the 'Unexpected Explosion' station and 'Champagne Cork' sub-category of the 'Unusual Injuries' station.'

'But he's completely motionless,' said Tony, realising that all of the screens in the sphere appeared to be presenting static images.

'To your perception, yes,' said Mehi, 'but I think you realise that angel time and human time are not the same?'

Tony nodded, remembering all the way back when he had been in the plane and met Albert and the other guardian angels, and how everything seemed completely frozen.

'In fact thirty-two hours of angel time passes in one Earth second,' Mehi explained, 'and human time is 115,200 times slower than angel time.'

This seemed to be a jolly long time to Tony, and he reflected that he had spent just over a year in Angeland already.

'That leaves you – indeed us here in Angeland – twenty-nine and a half angel days left to work out how to remove Gabriel's eyelash from your lung, otherwise Heaven or all of the other Angeland realms are doomed,' Mehi continued in the same cool tone.

Tony's estimation of Mehi grew as the archangel dispassionately explained the situation and also gave credence to what had seemed like strange ranting by Fifi earlier. They flew higher, passing screens, all with many images but with a higher frequency of people in interviews, looking at or holding food (particularly chocolate), writing, or just gazing into thin air.

'You'd be fascinated to know what goes through peoples' heads,' said Mehi. 'Maybe another day I can give you a longer tour.'

Then Mehi stopped climbing and they landed on one of the platforms supporting a chair. A prim-looking female angel was sitting on the chair and she shook hands with Tony when the Archangel presented him to her.

'This is Priscilla,' said Mehi.

All of a sudden a small alarm went off and Tony realised it was coming from a band around her wrist, which had a screen that flashed red. She blushed and reached to turn it off.

'You must forgive her,' said Mehi, 'but there is this craze now with these Ang-It devices coming from PirogRus that I find completely nonsensical. They say they encourage angels to keep active by measuring the number of times they flap their wings, but these devices also measure other things that angels don't normally do, such as the number of farts and belches, and things they say, for example, 'um' and 'you know', or think, like having lustful thoughts. And in my view it's more corporate tyranny with an ulterior motive, as you're well placed to understand.' He turned to Priscilla and continued dryly, 'No doubt you said 'um' but didn't mean to.'

Priscilla nodded and looked a little flustered. She responded, 'Archangel Mehi, you've come just at the moment when the subject, Arthura Dent, is giving up on her crossword.'

'Ah yes,' said Mehi, 'and how poetic that she's giving up on the word 'calamity', which would have allowed her to complete it. I see she's already got the 't' from getting 'fortytwo' down.'

Mehi turned to Tony and pointed at the screen. 'But of course we haven't come here to look at the crossword. Tony, do you realise where this is? Maybe if we pan out a bit you'll have a clearer idea.'

The image on the screen panned backwards and Tony saw that the woman was sitting on a seat next to someone else, in a plane.

'Why, I was on that plane!' exclaimed Tony, looking intently at the static scene in front of him, and recognising it as the very same flight that the Archangel Gabriel had visited.

'I want you to look very closely at this,' said Mehi, 'as it may help to understand your situation further and give us vital clues.'

Tony looked hard, and the moment he had left the plane came back in sharp focus.

'But something – or rather someone – is missing,' said Tony.

'That must be you,' said Priscilla, who, despite having organized herself to look serious, was having a hard time concealing her interest in him.

'No, well yes,' said Tony. 'I was in the group of three seats here, but there's no one in any of the seats.' He remembered, suddenly, with a sharp pang of nostalgia that he infuriatingly could not place, that he had been sitting next to someone on the plane. Someone special.

'Maybe they're in the toilet?' questioned Priscilla.

'No, no, there's something more,' said Tony after a moment. He pointed to some of the scattered empty seats. 'The plane was full when I left.'

Mehi, Priscilla and Tony looked at each other, and Mehi turned and scanned the screen, looking carefully at all the seats in the plane. He turned and looked at the other two, deep in thought, and then suddenly what had been up until then non-stop calm evaporated and an enormous smile crossed his face. He slapped Tony and Priscilla on the back and then boomed out a huge guffaw. Then he stepped off the platform towards the centre of the sphere, where he hovered, his wings flapping and his body shaking with convulsive giggles.

'Seven plus two! But who's the ninth then? Maybe it's Him. Why, it could be Priscilla for all I know!' He looked at Priscilla and Tony before collapsing in fits of hysterical laughter.

'The unpredictable watching the predictable,' he continued in between laughs, addressing all of the angels on the platform, who had turned away from their screens and were staring at the archangel in the centre of the sphere. Mehi landed on the base of the sphere, his wings folded away, and descended the curved passage. He was soon out of sight, with bursts of laughter and ejaculations of 'unpredictable' and 'predictable' gradually diminishing in volume until there was complete silence in the sphere. The angels were looking at each other in horror, and Tony was surprised to see Priscilla quite shaken and wiping away a few tears. A light murmur grew quickly into a cacophony of voices as the angels, ignoring their screens, started talked frenetically to each other.

'What was all that about?' said Tony to Priscilla, 'I mean this 'predictable' and 'unpredictable' stuff and the 'ninth?'

'Oh, the Archangel Mehi is the most intelligent of all angels, and says many clever and arcane things which we don't always understand,' said Priscilla. 'What is a lot more perturbing is his – well – change in mood.'

'Well he seemed to find something very funny indeed,' said Tony, 'is that all that strange?'

'It's unheard of,' said Priscilla. 'The Archangel Mehi is known very occasionally to smile, but never, never in all his time in the Angeland realms has he ever been known to laugh, even a little giggle.'

CHAPTER 33

Priscilla was clearly delighted to take over looking after Tony after it became obvious that Mehi was not going to return any time soon.

'The Archangel is a fantastic leader, and he encourages every angel to take responsibility and pride for their work,' she explained to him, 'even though it is rather dull here for most of the time.'

'Dull?'

'I think the Archangel explained that angel time goes a lot slower than human time, which means that a minute of your time is 80 days for us. That allows us to be extremely attentive but it also makes us extremely bored, as it takes us for example a week to follow a sentence in a conversation, or a day to observe a typical human thought.'

Priscilla had picked up Tony and flown him down to the entrance of the sphere where they had entered the network of tunnels to stretch their legs.

'We'll only be gone a few human microseconds, and nothing's going to happen in that time anyway,' she said.

'So how do you cope?' asked Tony, 'I mean, you're watching these screens all the time, knowing exactly what's going to happen with things unfolding at a glacial pace.'

'We're very dedicated to our work,' said Priscilla proudly, 'but it is true that a few luckier senior angels get to go to Heaven once in a while and interact with humans, as I think you've seen.'

Tony nodded, realising that they were heading back the way he had come, for the 'Near Misses' platform.

'Then there are two places where angels temporarily become human, although they are very different.'

'The Realm of the White Mountain,' said Tony, 'I lost a good friend there. Two, in fact.'

'Yes, tragic, and every loss affects us deeply,' Priscilla continued, 'but the mortality we pass through allows us to appreciate life in a way that is richer and more acute than anything we experience here. It means...' and she hesitated, 'you, Tony, are something quite unique and unusual in the Angeland realms, as well as having a terrifying potential to end everything as we know it.'

There was a pause in the conversation and Tony was more conscious of the looks from the other angels as they passed him. He had no idea where Priscilla was taking him but was pleased at her frankness, despite her awe of him.

'And the second place? I guess that must be Hull,' continued Tony.

'Yes,' said Priscilla cagily. 'Perhaps I shouldn't tell you too much about it. I hope you don't end up there. Any angel can go to Hull and become human temporarily, which allows them to have experiences that they can't find elsewhere, but on the flip side, it opens them up to dangers at the same time. Since you've been in the Angeland realms many more angels have been going to Hull, although it's not up my street. Archangel Mehi is not at all a fan and is quite discouraging, although that doesn't stop some angels from the Cube visiting. Then again, there is one important above-board and unpredictable thing that unites all of the angels.'

'What's that?' asked Tony

'While I'm terribly disappointed that the Hexahedrons lost, I am looking forward to the next semi-final of the Angel Cup, which is coming up soon. It's football, Tony, of course, with every realm aspiring to win it.'

They arrived at the platform of the station just as a train was pulling in. Priscilla turned to him with her face shining.

'Do you want to go on a little adventure? I shouldn't really, but if we're quick we won't be missed.'

Tony nodded assent and reflected that, compared to his previous experience, this well-ordered and rather sterile place seemed not a bad one to have an adventure in.

They hopped on the metro, went through the safety demonstration and then put on their seat belts, and Priscilla told Tony that she was taking him through her favourite station, 'Angel Depictions.'

'It's a fascinating place because it shows us how humans see angels,' she explained. 'Being posted there as an angel is the next best thing after being in Heaven for many angels, and there is stiff competition.'

'What about Earth itself?' asked Tony, 'I mean, it's all very well doing your stuff in the angel realms, but when do you actually interact with real-life humans rather than dead ones?'

Priscilla paused carefully and nodded. 'The archangels and the guardian angels are the main ones authorized. There are also a few renegade angels that slip in and can cause unregulated havoc. Archangel Michelle oversees teams that are charged with sorting out the mess that is sometimes created. I'm sure you're wondering how angels can straddle the two time zones.'

'It's wibbly-wobbly timey-whimey, no doubt,' interjected Tony.

The train passed through several stations and they got off at 'Déjà Vu.' We'll change here off the RATC and join the SNOF network, which is the fastest way to 'Angel Depictions,' said Priscilla.

After going through a few more passages, they arrived at a larger platform. They had to wait a few minutes and Priscilla chatted with a few other angels on the platform. There was a heightened atmosphere and the platform filled up quite quickly with many angels. Those with wings flapped them nervously and rather noisily.

'I've never seen so many angels on a platform,' said Priscilla, 'but the latest news is that Archangel Mehi has gone missing after his extraordinary outburst. I'm sure angels in the Cube will keep calm.'

A long double-decker train pulled in. They boarded it, and with difficulty found a seat on the upper level. All the angels on board looked anxious and scrutinized Tony as they got in. Priscilla and Tony sat silently and the sense of foreboding rose.

As they passed into the black ether with the speckled dots, Tony saw a few angels flying outside. 'Is that normal?' he asked

'No, it's not,' whispered Priscilla, 'it's rather worrying.'

They arrived in the next station, 'Religious Misconceptions,' where there was an almighty crowd of angels on the platform. Tony heard a collective intake of breath from the angels in the train as they took in the scene. As it pulled to a stop, Tony was aware of a huge crush as some angels tried to leave the train and others forced themselves on, filling every space, wedging into the corridors. There were shouts and exclamations coming from the doors as the siren for closing sounded several times before the doors finally snapped shut. There was a crackle from an intercom.

'Angels and Tony,' the voice said, 'due to the extraordinary crowds, we are exceptionally not able to perform the standard safety demonstration. You know it already of course, but I wish all of you not strapped in good luck.'

There was a stifled silence and the angels looked at each other and at Tony with an expression he had seen before, in the Realm of the White Mountain, and in Heaven after the catastrophes that had happened there: it was fear. The train pulled out of the station and into the ether before swinging upwards. The angels in the corridor, without seat belts, were thrown violently towards the back of the train. In the carriage and beyond, there were shrieks and screams as the train plunged on helter-skelter. The angels used their wings to buffer themselves, jerking back and forth, left and right and up and down.

'Tony, we've got to get off here,' said a panicking Priscilla as they arrived after what seemed like an age at the 'Angel Depictions' station. They were, however, completely hemmed in by the tightly-packed angel bodies and wings. A tumble of white feathers of every size floated in the air and covered every surface and every weary angel. The crush of angels in the station was worse than in 'Religious Misconceptions.' Although the doors opened, the sheer density of angels inside and outside the train made any movement to leave or enter the train impossible. Tony and Priscilla made to get up and leave, but it was impossible.

'We'll be stuck for weeks of transit until we reach either of the terminus stations at the end of the line, far beyond human and most angels' comprehension, 'Quarks' or 'Physicists',' wailed Priscilla.

Then suddenly Tony knew what he had to do. In the hubbub, he took a deep breath and announced in a booming voice,

'Listen to me angels, this is Tony.'

In the carriage, there was instant silence, and the babble of voices outside dimmed somewhat. He repeated himself, and there was complete silence.

'You must make space for me and Priscilla to leave this train,' he continued. He paused, then added for good measure, 'otherwise there may be a catastrophe.'

The result was almost instantaneous. Outside the train a space opened on the platform as angels parted like the Red Sea in front of Moses. Those in the corridor retreated in an atmosphere of hushed respect. Like a royal couple, Tony and Priscilla walked out of the carriage, over the feather-covered floor and past the astonished angels with their battered wings.

On the platform, they passed the mass of angels on either side, who had made a clear path and were looking at Tony with expressions of awe and fear.

'You have developed quite a reputation in the angel realms,' said Priscilla with pride as she escorted Tony towards a passage and out of the crush. 'Oh golly!' she stuttered as they joined the passage with panicking angels rushing to and fro on the platform. 'This is really the end. Archangel Mehi would never allow this. Things have fallen apart so quickly.'

On the shiny tiled walls of the passage, posters had been hastily pasted up. 'PirogRus' announced many in large font at the top, with a picture of Tony holding up 'Angel Apocalypse Now?' and in a speech bubble, 'Visit the mall within a mall within a mall where Archangel Yuri staged my dramatic escape.'

Tony sniffed. 'Humph. I didn't even write the book and the escape wasn't staged. Archangel Yuri wanted to turn me into a puppet signing books all day.'

Priscilla was very interested to hear the alternative version of events that Tony proffered, but she explained that since his arrival in the Angeland realms there had been an upsurge of a new phenomenon, 'incorrect information,' which meant it was difficult to believe anything. She had been upset to see the PirogRus posters but was shocked to see others for Hull, and encouraged Tony to walk swiftly pass them. 'HULL' they announced in big red letters, with pictures of funfair rides, casinos and licentious images that were far from angelic. Tony looked at the text underneath with interest.

'Take a break from halos and harps!'

'Your last chance to experience human pleasures before the Apocalypse!'

'Fall into Fun, Feasting, and Fornication!'

The posters were clearly of interest to a good number of the angels milling around in the corridors, although they looked a little ashamed as Priscilla and Tony walked past them.

'You must be very careful of Archangel Natasha, Tony,' she said with purpose as they strode on. 'Very careful. Enough said.'

They progressed into the depths of the 'Angel Depictions' station, leaving the last of the posters behind as the passages narrowed, then passing large signs for 'Music' and 'Clothing' sub-categories ('Togas' seemed to be at least as big as 'Clothing'). The flow of angels continued intermittently in both directions, mainly up towards the platform.

'It seems that every angel has had the same idea as me,' said Priscilla. 'Initially they popped out for a brief break and then, when they realised Archangel Mehi had really disappeared, they decided to go on the metro system to visit another station. The problem is that the network has nowhere near the capacity for all the angels working here, as we've never travelled all at the same time before. It's going to completely paralyse the system.'

'Misconceptions' was also a large sub-category with many sub-sub-categories, and Priscilla drew his attention to 'Fairies' and 'Weeping Angels.'

'Humans are constantly making things up about angels which either aren't true or completely twist reality,' said Priscilla. 'To be honest, it really makes us cross sometimes. I mean, do I look like a fairy to you?'

She stopped, hands on her hips, glaring and looking distinctly unfairylike. 'And then more recently we have had television series that have completely wrecked our image with poor graveyard statues of angels which have terrified children and adults alike, so they hide behind the sofa whenever they appear on the TV.'

They walked a little further and passed a big sub-category sign, 'Watchers.' Priscilla brightened up.

'However, as well as being insulted we have the compensation of being amused. I think Yuri has engineered a lot of illegal, subliminal marketing about angels which means all manner of humans address and label us with magical powers to intervene in their lives.'

'Hold on a moment,' said Tony, butting into Priscilla's monologue, 'but you *are* watching humans and many people *do* believe you have a beneficial role?'

'Things change if you know how everything is going to happen on Earth,' said Priscilla, 'but also I guess I'm a bit jealous that none of the angel manuals mention me as a specific angel who they can ask for assistance. The archangels are quite lucky to be so famous, with some, like Gabriel, letting it all get to their heads, given all the prayers and supplications directed at them.'

They passed several signs for 'YouTube' which Priscilla explained had become very popular, as it provided chances for Yuri to slip in plenty of commercial breaks.

'Naturally, most of you humans get completely fooled by all the fake angel videos out there,' Priscilla explained, 'whereas there's plenty of videos escaping from Hull of real angels, despite the adage that what happens in Hull stays in Hull. Around two thirds of all that silliness, debauchery and pornography that you humans see online is down to angels, despite our best efforts to control it.'

Tony thought he had learnt a lot about angels, but this news was a shock and hard to digest. They passed some big signs for 'Gratitude.'

'But you will be pleased to hear that we angels do appreciate all the thanks that humans send us,' Priscilla went on. 'A lot less than requests for things, but every 'thank you' warms the cockles of one's heart, you know.'

Tony wondered where they were going as they passed more passages and signs, a little smaller than the previous ones, for 'Foodstuffs' and sub-sub-categories for things like desserts, beer and fish. The passages went up and down, left and right, but there didn't seem to be any logic to the overall organization.

All of a sudden they emerged into a much bigger passage where there was a large queue of angels, pushing and shoving rather boisterously.

'Aha, I thought as much,' said Priscilla. 'I thought 'Erotica' would be popular. This is just a side tunnel,' she continued, shooting Tony a side glance that made him uneasy. 'The main tunnel is several kilometres in that direction, to give you an idea of the length of the queue.'

Priscilla and Tony continued, turning away from the throng of angels, passing sub-categories called 'Cherubs' and 'Genitals' and coming into another big sub-category, 'New Age,' which seemed to have a lot of sub-sub-categories like stones, essences and spirituality.

Priscilla led Tony towards the 'spirituality' sub-sub-category and before he knew it they had arrived at a barrier and she handed him a ticket, looking furtively back and forth. They had not passed any other angels for a while. They climbed up to the base of another huge sphere resembling the 'Insufficient persistence' one to which Mehi had led Tony. This one too had platforms with televisions and chairs all along the inner sides, albeit devoid of angels.

'I wanted to bring you here, Tony, because I knew that all of the angels on duty would be so bored that they would have left,' Priscilla announced. She scooped Tony up in her arms and flew around the inside of the sphere. He felt his arms pinned back as she held him gently but firmly in front of her, her face flushed now and breathing more rapidly.

Tony struggled slightly, but only succeeded in knocking the Ang-It around her wrist, which immediately started flashing red and emitting the alarm he had heard the first time they met. Priscilla swooped round and round the edge of the sphere.

'Oh Tony, the angel realms are coming to an end, and everything is disintegrating,' she said sadly. 'Life in the Cube is so terribly boring, watching humans in extra slow-motion and never being able to reach out and touch them. I'm not one for the vulgarity of Hull or Heaven, but you can't imagine after so many millennia what it is like for me to have you in my arms.' They were swooping at such a speed that Tony felt too disorientated to respond. 'We are counting down until the end of it all, but no one will find us here in this abandoned outpost. Come, Tony, let us kiss each other for the last 29 days before the apocalypse in a perfect romance.'

Priscilla looked tenderly at Tony, still whizzing him around on what now felt like a never-ending stomach-churning fairground ride. She grasped his head firmly, closed her eyes, opened her lips slightly and inclined her face towards his.

'Tony? Tony?' a male voice came from the passageway at the base of the sphere, causing Priscilla to look up in astonishment. She veered uncontrollably towards the side and almost hit it before landing heavily on the base and detaching herself hurriedly from Tony.

'Hello Tony,' the voice called out in a friendly way, and Albert emerged onto the base of the sphere.

'Hello Priscilla,' said Albert, 'I think you need to turn that off.' He was pointing to her Ang-It, which was flashing and beeping furiously.

CHAPTER 34

Albert courteously thanked Priscilla and suggested that she should find her own way back to 'Insufficient Persistence', as things were now being brought under control. She nodded, took a sheepish and mournful look at Tony, and headed off.

'Thankfully the Archangel Michelle, ever resourceful, was able to step in and bring some order back to the Cube soon after the mysterious disappearance of Archangel Mehi,' explained Albert to Tony. 'I knew you would be in safe hands with the angels in the Cube here, but we didn't want you to be too safe.'

'It's been a long time,' said Tony, thinking back to the last time he had seen Albert, in the bedroom of his grandparents' house in Hefyn. 'But I'm very pleased to see you. It would have been nice to see you on a few other occasions, in fact.'

They wandered out through the passages of the metro system, passing angels who seemed to be moving around in a lot more orderly way. The posters for Hull and PirogRus had gone, and when they reached the platform, many angels were waiting, though nothing like the number when they had passed through the first time. There was once again a sense of calm.

'Follow me,' said Albert, taking Tony to the end of the platform and up some stairs that he hadn't spotted before. 'We need to take the lift to get us back to Angeland.' They came to the end of the passage and pushed the lift button.

'I'm sorry for the undue attention and excitement that you've received,' said Albert, 'but you will appreciate now that the very fact of you being here' (he coughed rather embarrassedly), 'has rather shaken things up.'

The lift's arrival was announced with a ping and they got in. Inside, everything was simple unadorned metal, with a keyboard and a screen on one of the walls. Albert swiped a card and then typed 'Angeland Stadium.'

'Don't worry, this will be nice and quick and very civilized,' said Albert. 'With luck we'll arrive for the kick-off, and you and I have got seats. I'm very excited. Competition for seats in the stadium is normally intense, but Archangel Sandeepa gave me two complimentary tickets.'

The lift moved, but Tony couldn't tell in which direction. He felt his stomach moving in an odd way, but after what seemed like less than a minute, the doors opened. The noise of boisterous chanting from thousands of people wafted into the lift, and it was magnified as they stepped out into a curved passage with arches and stairs leading off it, each with a different number.

'Welcome back to Angeland,' said Albert, 'and welcome to the Waldgebiet stadium, which you'll recall we saw from the Subsolo over a year ago when you arrived.' He gestured for Tony to follow him through a nearby door, into a room where clothes, football shirts and scarves of various descriptions were hanging up.

'We need to dress up in human clothes for the match,' explained Albert. 'Take your pick. Poste are yellow and Angeland is normally white but playing in their second red kit today.'

Tony was pleased to change out of the sporting kit that he had been wearing since the Realm of the White Mountain, and picked some jeans. He wasn't keen to put on the kit of Gabriel's team Poste, but instead opted for a white Angeland shirt.

They climbed a flight of steps up from under the rim and into the stadium, and the noise of cheering from the crowd burst upon them as they came to the gate. There was a sea of yellow, red and white bobbing and cheering.

'I feel just like I'm back on Earth,' said Tony, although he was hardly audible above the raucous waves of noise.

They found their seats, and the two teams came on, Poste in yellow and Angeland in red. Tony recognised a number of players he had seen before, most notably Rita, the Angeland striker, who was shorter in the flesh than she appeared on television. Tony and Albert had very good seats in a stand in the middle of the ground, and Tony looked around and saw that many of the spectators were pointing and looking at him. Several of the archangels were in the neighbouring stand, including Sandeepa and Ray, who both looked friendly and waved. Gabriel, sporting a yellow shirt, sneered at Tony then looked away.

'So each archangel has a team,' Tony said to Albert, 'but what about the Angeland team?'

'You see that empty seat there?' Albert indicated one next to the archangels. 'That's been held for A1, I mean Him, the boss of the archangels. Although it seems all rather symbolic now.'

Tony nodded. He vaguely remembered Albert filling him in about angel grades and this mysterious and powerful angel who had disappeared in strange circumstances over a human millennium ago.

'Angeland has therefore lacked a head coach in His absence, and has never won the Angel Cup,' Albert continued in an awed tone. 'Some say that if the team wins the Cup, He will come back. So it's rather portentous that Angeland are so close now at the same time, well, as you being here. There are all sorts of rumours circulating. But I've said enough – look, the kick-off is imminent.'

The roar of the crowd grew, with 'Aain-ge-land', 'Ree-ta, Ree-ta', and 'Po-oste' being the dominant cheers. The teams shook hands. The referees were wearing black (Albert informed Tony that they were from Hull) and the game got under way. It was a shock when, after 12 minutes, favourites Angeland were behind after Hiwot from Angeland misheaded a cross to Anselma from Poste, who despatched the ball into the left-hand corner of the net. However the game was level after a free kick in the 19th minute, which Jennifer from Angeland took immediately, floating a cross into the Poste area, where Rita rose unchallenged and levelled the scores with a downward glancing header.

The scores were unchanged at half time, and Tony could not but continue to marvel at how everything seemed just as it would be on Earth. Albert was also delighted, as he said it was the first time he had seen a live match.

After 77 minutes, Angeland won a corner and Alana delivered the ball to Rita, whose deflected shot from the edge of the area found Martina, who beat the Poste keeper from eight yards.

'Angeland are just 23 minutes from the final,' enthused Albert, 'can they hang on?'

The clock ticked down, but with just a minute of regular time to go, Chantal from Angeland conceded a free kick going up from a header. Into the wall the ball went, and after a deflection Wilhelmina from Poste levelled the score at 2-2 and forced the match into extra time.

During the break between full and extra time, Albert looked a little agitated and turned around in his seat, carefully surveying the crowd.

'Whatever happens, Tony, keep close to me,' he explained nervously. 'The Archangel Natasha is going to try to take you to Hull one way or another, and despite the vote of the CRAP we must avoid that at all costs. The Archangel Sandeepa is leading the resistance and has a cunning plan to keep you safe. Just make sure that you don't follow any other angel but me.'

Albert, Tony and the rest of the stadium were in a frenzy of tension as extra time kicked off. Angeland pushed forward several times and Roberta hit the post in the 5th minute and sent another shot wide. At the 11th minute there was huge controversy as Rita put Angeland into the lead again. Alana put in a cross and Rita swivelled and shot from close range. The ball hit the underside of the crossbar, bounced down and was cleared. The referee was not sure if it was a goal, but she consulted the lineswoman, who in a moment of drama indicated that it was.

'I suspect Natasha's fixed all the referees to put their biggest rival Angeland in the final against the Alles Schwartz,' Albert informed Tony.

The replays on the screen seemed to suggest that the ball had not crossed the line, but Albert said that goal-line technology was not being introduced until the next Angel Cup. There were huge cries of protest from the Poste supporters, but to no avail. It seemed that time was up, and the Angeland supporters had started invading the pitch, but then Robertinha hit a long pass down the left side to Rita, who ran with the ball and hammered a long shot that went past the keeper and burst into the net to give her a hat-trick. Delirium ensued as the Angeland supporters were shouting with joy, and leaping up and down and hugging each other.

'Tony,' Albert hollered in his ear, 'I need to check in with Archangel Sandeepa. Don't move until I come back.'

With that, Albert left Tony surrounded by the celebrations both on and off the pitch. The Angeland team had started to do a triumphant tour around the perimeter of the pitch, holding Rita aloft for short stretches with some players breaking off to hug members of the crowd and give them autographs.

The Angeland team had almost done a tour of the pitch and was approaching the stand Tony was on. Rita was beaming and looked for a moment directly at Tony, at which point he had a funny feeling. But it vanished as she looked away, as a teammate diverted her attention and led her off to the side of the stand.

At the same time Albert had returned and gestured to Tony to follow. Tony felt that there was something not quite right. Wordlessly Albert grasped his wrist, but Tony let himself be led out of the crowd and downstairs to the level of the pitch and into the players' entrance tunnel, despite increasingly feeling that something strange was happening. With a shove, Albert suddenly thrust him into the centre of the tunnel. Shocked at this rough treatment, Tony looked quizzically at the old man. With a quick gesture Albert ripped away the mask he had been wearing, revealing the face of a younger man with greasy black hair.

'Bon voyage, Tony,' the young man said. 'They say it's nice and warm going up the rabbit hole.'

Disoriented, Tony spun around and saw that at each end of the tunnel there was a black rabbit the size of an elephant – Lapindee and Lapindum again. 'Oh my god!' said a female voice, and Tony spun round to see Rita a few metres away from him, looking as perplexed as he was.

With lightning speed, Lapindee shot towards the centre of the tunnel, snatching Rita with it and heading towards Lapindum. Tony heard Rita scream in horror. The sound was suddenly cut off as Lapindee quickly pushed her up Lapindum's backside.

The rabbits turned towards Tony, who was finding it hard to take everything in. They thumped their back paws, and the young man with the slick black hair smiled at Tony from the side of the tunnel. Like bullets, the two beasts raced towards him. With a blur of black fur, the smell of shit, a terrible schlopping noise, and a warm crushing sensation from head to toe, everything went dark.

RED

CHAPTER 35

Flat on his back, Tony opened his eyes and saw an impossibly black hole surrounded by smeared, radiant, shimmering white fluff and red patches, with a deep blue-black sky filled with twinkling stars.

'Am I dead or is that an eclipse?' he said aloud.

He angled up his head and became aware of a buzz that sounded like a mix between a giant funfair and a traffic jam. From one corner of his eye he saw two looming black elephantine shapes that he recognised as the titanic rabbits that had accosted him, and rolling to the other side he saw Rita. There was a terrible smell and he realised he was covered with a cloying stickiness which was clearly the source of it. He looked up and saw a big neon sign above him with a flashing star and lights around it. In red and blue it proclaimed 'Welcome to fabulous Hull'.

'Up you get now,' said a gruff voice as two hands with long yellow rubber gloves lifted him up.

Tony saw a figure in a black suit wearing similar gloves lift Rita up.

'Time for a shower,' the voice said.

Before Tony knew it he and Rita were hit by two high-pressure jets of water from a fire engine, which played up and down their bodies. They gasped and crumpled up at the shock, and were left dripping and bewildered.

'My dear Tony, my dear Rita,' said a smooth female voice. 'Welcome to Hull, or more accurately, fabulous Hull.' It was Natasha, wearing a black leather trench coat. She handed each of them a large white bath towel and looked at them sympathetically.

'I must apologise for the manner in which you were brought here, but it was the most expedient way to follow the mandate of the CRAP for you to come to Hull, Tony, in order to give us more time to find a solution to avoid an angel apocalypse.' She smiled at him. 'And Rita, I'm terribly sorry that you were in the wrong place at the wrong time. Lapindee and Lapindum can be rather primitive at times, and it's difficult to restrain them. In fact I think they have taken something of a – shall we say – taste to both of you, and if we hadn't intervened when we did we'd never have got you out. You should do your best to avoid them in the future as they clearly feel very affectionate towards you, but they'll just have to assuage their ardour when they don't see you.'

All the while, from a distance, Lapindee and Lapindum were thumping their back legs, snorting and emitting low growls.

'Now listen here,' said Rita, looking very pugnacious, 'I don't care if you're an archangel, you know very well that footballers have diplomatic status. You've no right to bring me to Hull against my will, and certainly no right to forcibly turn me into a human here when retaining my angelic status is crucial for the upcoming Angel Cup Final.'

'Yes, you're quite right my dear, it was a terrible mistake,' said Natasha. 'You'll be back for the Final, but in the meantime you and Tony can enjoy the pleasures of Hull. In my magnanimity, while we sort out the paperwork to get you back, I'll even let you train with the league teams here, which will give you a huge advantage for the big game.' She pointed at Tony. 'Assuming it takes place in full, given the catastrophic expectations around our friend here.'

'This is outrageous!' fumed Rita.

'The Angeland Embassy opens in the morning,' said Natasha, 'so you've no worries at all. In the meantime, a suite is ready for you at the 'Soccer', where you can freshen up. I regret that despite our best efforts, you and Tony's soccer kits still look a little tanned.'

Natasha paused and then said with a smile, 'You can always make an appeal to the CRAP of course. That would be rather poetic in the circumstances.' She hooted with laughter.

A chunky black car arrived and Rita was ushered in. 'We're not going together?' Tony asked.

'No, you and I need to have an important chat alone,' said Natasha, 'but I'm sure you'll get to see Rita again.'

Tony looked into the car, where Rita was seated in the back. After her earlier indignance, she was looking glum and washed out.

'Erm, I hope we'll meet again soon. Keep your spirits up,' he said, feeling a little awkward.

Rita turned to him and Tony suddenly felt a jolt as he looked into her brown eyes. She suddenly brightened and beamed a broad, beautiful smile. 'Don't forget that the team is always behind you,' she said. The door was closed and the car drove off.

Tony looked around and saw that the gigantic rabbits had gone, as well as the fire engine that had been used to hose him and Rita down. There was just another chunky black car remaining, and Natasha was talking with the driver. The eclipse had not changed, and he looked to where the sounds of the traffic jam and funfair were coming from. He saw two enormous illuminated buildings in front of him. The first, on the left, was shaped like a pyramid and at least twice the size of the Great Pyramid of Giza. The second, on the right, was in the form of a giant treble clef and was at least twice the size of the pyramid. A massive dome stood behind them, marked as if it was part of a giant football. Sticking out of the middle of the dome, a tower rose above everything, twice as high again as the treble clef. The ensemble lit up the sky in a myriad of colours.

Turning and walking back towards Natasha, Tony saw that they were on a road with a barrier leading away from the hubbub, and the 'fabulous Hull' sign was the only landmark in the vicinity. He made out some much more modest lights, from what seemed a much smaller scale version of the scene behind him, and some orange traffic barriers barring the way which announced 'Paving the way', 'Building a legacy', and 'Sorry for any inconvenience'.

Natasha walked up to join him. 'You're looking towards Hull Downstreet, the much smaller historic centre,' she said. 'It's only the locals that go there now.' She turned to the giant glittering conurbation. 'But inside this is the Copula.'

'The Copula?'

'The Copula is the name for the street that runs in a circle between the five ultra-mega hotels that I've developed here. Soccer – the one which looks like part of a football and has the big tower – is the sixth hotel in the middle. You'll soon get used to them. Anyway, come inside the car, I don't want you frying outside.'

Tony realised that it was very hot, and that his wet clothes had almost dried. They got into the car and she removed her trench coat.

'The coat's got in-built air conditioning,' she said when she saw his look. The back of the car seemed frigid at first, although it became more comfortable as he acclimatized.

Under the trench coat, Natasha was wearing a pair of black jeans and a casual, rather businesslike, black top. He was reminded how stunning she was, and a little bashfully he remembered some of the fantasies he had experienced during his time in the Angeland realms. But he also remembered a number of warnings about her, for example from George, Priscilla and Albert, and also Sue's protectiveness towards him when she was around, and he felt rather cautious.

She indicated to the driver to start. 'So Tony,' she said, 'don't worry, I'm not going to bite you. I'm sure you've heard a lot of things about me and about Hull, but it's only because many people don't understand and are a little old-fashioned. Hull is in the Angeland realms, but it is right on the edge of them, so it has a different resonance. Simply put, Hull is pure fun.'

The car quickly moved between the pyramid and treble clef buildings, then came to a main road with virtually stationary traffic, all beeping and honking.

'This is the Copula,' explained Natasha. They turned into the road and promptly passed all the stationary traffic. Natasha explained that they had been given priority.

'I'm sorry that I won't have much time to see you during your stay,' she said. 'Unlike some of the other archangels, I have a full schedule that requires me to attend to the smooth running of Hull, as well as my representational duties outside this realm. But I would like to offer you the opportunity to stay at any of the hotels here – Würfel or Musica,' (she indicated the pyramid and the treble clef), Soccer, Montagne Blanche, Compras or Reiss.'

'What's the signification of each?' asked Tony.

'Each of the outer ones is based on an Angel realm, and the central Soccer is based on the beautiful game that unites us all. You see, Tony, I've created a perfect playground for angels to let their hair down and relax in their time off. The Angeland realms would be very dull without Hull.'

Tony chose Montagne Blanche, as he had correctly guessed it was related to the Realm of the White Mountain, the one he knew best.

'Excellent choice,' said Natasha, 'and here it is coming into view. You'll have one of the best suites.'

As the Copula curved around, an illuminated mountain, about as high as Musica's treble clef, came into view.

'Tony, unfortunately I'm not going to be able to come into the hotel due to another engagement I have,' said Natasha, 'but I want you to be reassured that you will be able to pass relatively incognito here – you'll see why in due course – and above all I want you to have a good time.' She handed him a wad of notes in a large plastic packet. 'This should be enough *wings* to allow you to have a very good time, but please don't blow them in the casino all at once. Don't tell others I asked you as I'd completely lose my reputation if people knew I was giving wise council.' She hooted with laughter again.

'Now, dear Tony, you're still pretty stinky and dirty and I advise you to have a real shower pronto, but you need to have a secret word so I know you're the real Tony next time we meet… let me see, yes, how about "wet", as a memento of when I saw you?'

She looked at him rather impishly and chuckled seductively and laid her hand briefly on his arm, which gave him an unexpected frisson. He didn't have much time to get another word in because they had now arrived at the entrance to Montagne Blanche. Feeling confused, bewildered and swept off his feet by the bundle of energy, sensuality and humour that was Natasha, he stepped out.

Her head popped into the car one last time. 'Oh yes, by the way, there'll be someone you know who'll come and pick you up from the room in 30 minutes. Mr Bastão. Have fun, and until the next time!' She smiled and winked, and with that the car drove speedily off.

Tony turned and saw that the entrance to the hotel was a perfect replica of the entrance to the tunnel under the White Mountain. All alongside and leading to the street was an expansive and beautifully-rendered model railway set in mountainous terrain, with little trains whizzing back and forth.

Then the action before and around him sank in, and he nearly lurched over in shock. There were people, normal humans, dressed in normal clothes, all different styles and colours, in every size, fat and thin. They were milling around and walking back and forth into the hotel lobby, real people and not just angels dressed in grey who happened to be humans. Tony hadn't seen anything like this since he'd been in the plane just before he left Earth.

'Hello sir, I believe you're Tony?' a voice enquired, and Tony turned to see a woman in a black suit and tie. 'I'm Eleanor the Reception Manager, and we're honoured to welcome you to Montagne Blanche. Please follow me.'

He followed her into the tunnel entrance and they walked through an atrium with a waterfall and plants and down through several passages which had a chalet-like theme with sepia photos of mountain scenes, skis and cuckoo clocks on the walls. All of a sudden, and completely unexpectedly after the rather calming and rustic surroundings, the corridor opened out into a vast room covered by flashing and bleeping slot machines and card tables. There were hundreds of people playing, with thumping upbeat music and occasional whoops of joy coming from the crowds.

They weaved their way through the machines and Tony felt, for the first time in a while, that no one was paying him any special attention; everyone seemed focused on their gambling. They reached a lift that took them at comfortable speed to the 101st floor (of 110). Eleanor handed him the key for room 101-66, showed him around, wished him a good stay and left him.

Tony realised he did not have much time to reflect on his vast hotel suite and splendid view, given that he would have a visitor shortly. The shower room alone was bigger than any hotel room he had seen, and he gratefully dispensed of his brown football top and jeans. Drying off and luxuriating in feeling clean again after his shower, he opened the wardrobes and found rows of beautiful clothes in multiple colours and patterns to suit every occasion. He slipped on a green silk shirt, light brown chinos and brogues, which all fitted perfectly.

'I feel quite human,' he murmured to himself, admiring the view. He could see he was near the top of the mountain and was looking out onto the two other big hotels in addition to the Pyramid, the Treble Clef and the giant football. There was a collection of buildings which looked like giant shopping bags, and a giant globe which in turn had familiar buildings stemming out of it. He recognised the Eiffel Tower, the Statue of Liberty and the Taj Mahal among others.

He remembered the package that Natasha had given him. Opening it, he saw that it contained hundreds of thousands of *wings*. Locking the majority in the hotel room safe, he put a few thousand in his pocket just before he heard a knock at the door.

Looking through the spy hole, he saw a man in a black suit with black sunglasses. 'I'm Mr Bastão,' announced the man, and Tony cautiously opened the door.

'How fitting that we meet again in the Montagne Blanche! It's great to see you, Tony,' said Gustavo as he took off his sunglasses.

CHAPTER 36

'My dear Gustavo! You look a lot better than when I last saw you leaping out of that helicopter and flashing under the bridge of the Agulha do Meio-dia,' said Tony delightedly.

Gustavo had seemed a little guarded for the first few seconds, but he quickly grinned and they hugged. 'You're the real McCoy,' said Gustavo 'Who would have believed it!' He looked serious again, 'I think it's time for a little training, perhaps a 50km run around the Copula for old times' sake?' He winked at Tony, 'Only joking of course – I think for once it's time we got some beers in.'

They descended a few floors in the lift and Gustavo took Tony to the Agulha, a bar with a structure which almost perfectly recreated the Agulha do Meio-dia and overlooked the huge open space in the centre of the mountain structure. All around the interior, there were corridors with hotel room doors. An artificial ski slope began ten metres or so away from the bar, descending elegantly around and through the interior over a drop of about 500 metres in total.

'Maybe no ultramarathon today but at least we'll ski down together for a meal after the beers, hey?' said Gustavo.

Tony had seen a few impressive things in his time in the Angeland realms, but with all the people dressed as humans around him he couldn't help but feel that he was on Earth, where nothing on this scale existed. He remembered Gustavo from the UEWM, their harrowing experience in the tunnel of the White Mountain, and watching the football match with the Hull team Alles Schwartz in the Willkommenhaus chalet.

'You see Tony,' Gustavo explained, 'everything in Hull is one big party. I and all of the other Hull angels – the ones with the black suits – are charged with making everyone's stay as enjoyable as possible.'

A waitress in a short grey dress brought them their BWB (Black Wing Beer) and said 'enjoy your beer' with a smile. But she seemed to flicker momentarily as she spoke, which caused Tony to frown slightly.

'She's not from Hull?' Tony asked when she'd returned to the bar.

'Oh no, she's one of the unlucky ones who failed to get her Wings. In addition to serving in the White Mountain, there's lots of them who come here and go to PirogRus.'

'Yes, I've seen the ones in PirogRus for myself,' said Tony.

He dismissed it at that point, but there had been something disturbing that he couldn't put his finger on when he had looked into the eyes of the waitress, and it continued to haunt him.

They enjoyed a couple of beers, starting by reminiscing about Willkommenhaus and the UEWM. Gustavo didn't believe the popular theory that Sue had had it in for Tony, but Tony hesitated to relate his full experience after he had fallen from the helicopter, preferring to say that it was all a bit of a blur. He did talk about his experiences in PirogRus and the Cube. Gustavo's story of his return to Hull was rather more prosaic, as he had simply returned to his job of being a blackjack dealer at Musica.

'Most angels only get to see their archangels once every few years,' he said. 'But you've met all of them and you seem to have non-stop adventures, including getting to share a car alone with my lovely Archangel Natasha and slipping out of the hands of Archangel Yuri, and you also had this wacky effect on Archangel Mehi. They found him recently, by the way, gibbering and virtually incoherent. You can appreciate why there are so many rumours going down about you and why every angel is falling over themselves to meet you. There's even a kind of Tony cult developing.'

They skied down all the way into the Casino, to which Tony quickly realised all paths in the hotel led, and entered the Blackjack restaurant. Before they entered, a couple approached him.

'Gee, it's a Tony,' the woman said, 'Can we have your photo please?'

Gustavo nodded that Tony should accept, took their camera, and snapped a photo of the couple and Tony together. The couple thanked Tony and walked off.

Over fondue, Gustavo explained to Tony that he was in luck as the number of Tony impersonators in Hull had tripled recently because a convention was planned.

'Look, over there,' he said. He pointed, and Tony saw someone looking very like himself with a grey wingsuit, surrounded by several people and taking turns to be photographed. He now realised how, as Natasha had told him, he could pass effectively incognito. Or, rather, blend in as just another Tony.

'At the moment with that garb you're wearing, you'd lose your own look-alike contest,' said Gustavo, 'but I'd absolutely advise against any hanky-panky with any other angels around here, even though you'll get plenty of propositions. Safest to pretend that you're pretending to be yourself – and no romance or little adventures of the flesh at all. Sorry to say this amigo, as it's rather hard on you, particularly with all these angels in human form here getting a leg over.'

Looking around, Tony realised that there were a lot of canoodling couples. 'I remember now, I was told that a cardinal rule was that angels mustn't fall in love with a human,' he said, curious to see this through. 'So where does that come from?'

'They say it goes back a long time to when He, I mean the A1 boss of all the angels, disappeared,' Gustavo explained. 'Rumours quickly circulated that He had fallen in love with a human, renounced being an angel, and irreversibly become human Himself. Since then it's been the biggest possible sin for an angel to express romantic love for a human. Any angel would be cast out and bring enormous shame to their realm. Fortunately, it's never happened.'

'Not as far as anyone knows,' said Tony, making Gustavo look questioningly at him for a second. 'But it's a very strange idea. I mean, angels have such a loving reputation, and they're clearly bonking each other silly in various parts of the Angeland realms. And all these senior angels are lining up to sleep with humans in Heaven.'

'Yes,' said Gustavo, who was a little flustered now, 'but that doesn't count, because those high-ranking trained angels are simply performing their professional duty without any love involved. You must remember that cultural taboos can run deep and strong.'

Tony didn't feel that it was the right moment to push the matter any further, so they ate their meal in more-or-less companionable silence. He reflected on everything that he had seen, remembering his discussions with Gill and Pradeep in the *Saint Wünschenswert* spa, and the golf course in Hefyn when he had seen his grandmother and Geoffrey kissing, or the distraught face of the caddie angel Teetee when her human lover Henry had been hit by Tony's wayward golf ball. More than that, Sue's proclamation before her death and Priscilla's amorous advances were at the top of his mind.

'Let's go outside,' said Gustavo, who perked up after they left the restaurant, 'we can have a good look at Copula.'

Outside on the pavement, Tony saw that the eclipse still dominated the sky, creating an eerie, dusky umbrella over everything.

'It's always like that,' said Gustavo, 'it keeps Hull in permanent excitement because the night always seems to be just starting. No need for morning here!'

Tony had drunk half a bottle of excellent Chasselas in addition to the two beers he had consumed at the Agulha, and by now he was rather drunk with a slight headache, as he had not had alcohol in such a long while. He remembered that there was something in the morning, although it didn't concern him directly, but he couldn't quite pin it down, so he let it go in a haze. They passed at least five Tony impersonators in the street, including one who was female; they all gave him the thumbs up or high fives as they passed.

The traffic on the Copula was jammed, and it was as hot as a sauna, but the atmosphere was like a party. Street performers in grey clothes performed acrobatics and swallowed and spat out fire. People milled around, talking, smiling and sipping from big plastic cups. All around, particularly on the huge hotel buildings, the lights flashed all colours. Above the Copula, Tony saw monorails going between the hotels.

'Each of the hotels on the outer rim has a separate monorail going to the other four,' explained Gustavo, 'and they all pass through the rim of the Soccer. It makes for a beautiful sight from the Soccosphere, the tower in the centre of Soccer. But instead of taking the monorail, you get a lot more atmosphere on the Copula if you walk. 'Let's go to Musica – I'd love to introduce you to my mates there, but of course as *a* Tony rather than *the* Tony. They're immensely impressed and jealous that I got to do the UEWM with you.' They approached the Treble Clef hotel, which was adjacent to the Montagne Blanche. Tony saw that the giant hotel and the paths leading to it were covered with musical symbols. They passed topiary, sculptures and pools with all sorts of types of music playing.

'Hold on, it's almost time,' said Gustavo, 'you're gonna really dig this.'

Tony had noticed that crowds had gathered and were looking up at the Treble Clef in hushed anticipation. Suddenly, all the scattered pieces of music stopped and the hotel lit up in a blaze, and started to flash in rhythm to 'The Entertainer' by Scott Joplin. It was a magnificent spectacle as the ragtime switched through many styles of jazz (Gustavo explained that the 15-minute show presented samples of different types of jazz to the present day) with videos of the artists, clever changes in the illuminations, and a final firework display, which finished with the crowds clapping and whooping with joy.

When the cheers had subsided, Gustavo explained. 'Mirroring jazz itself as a style of music, and every hour the pieces are slightly different. All the pieces are played live and it's a great honour for angels to be chosen to play for the Musica display. They tend to have solo performances in venues in other parts of Hull during their stay. Let's go inside.'

They went in through the mouth of a giant saxophone. Musical instruments of every possible type were on the walls, and as Tony looked up at them he saw that every now and then one seemed to magically animate and play a little solo ditty. They went down a long corridor resembling the inside of a flute, and came out into the hotel's casino.

'Oh,' Tony said, with a hint of disappointment, 'it's big and impressive, but it looks more or less the same as the one in the Montagne Blanche.'

'Well they're all rather the same, with the same type of games,' said Gustavo, 'but you can have just as much fun wherever you are.'

Tony had never gambled in a casino before, so Gustavo pointed out the different machines and types of card tables.

'Have you got any *wings?*' asked Gustavo.

'As a matter of fact I do,' said Tony, reaching into his pocket and pulling out the few thousand he had taken from Natasha's parcel earlier.

Gustavo whistled. 'Whoa! That's several months' salary for an average dealer round here. Best to hide those carefully and maybe set aside a limit of a few hundred. You wouldn't want to lose all that at once!'

Tony didn't mention the much larger quantity of *wings* he had in his hotel room as Gustavo led him to some blackjack tables. 'Hey guys, look who I've brought with me, a Tony! And he's got loads of *wings* and wants to play blackjack!' announced Gustavo to three of the dealers. Some of the people on their tables looked up and smiled at Tony, one couple giving him high-fives.

One of the dealers turned to Tony and the other punters at the table, gesturing at Gustavo. 'Has this guy told you that he not only trained for the UEWM with the real Tony, but Tony saved his life in the White Mountain tunnel? But being a Tony, you probably know that already. But how awesome, eh? Gustavo's a minor celebrity round here. Let's get a photo of you with this Tony.'

The dealers and many of the other people crowded round and took photos. Tony recognised the oticels they were using to do this, frequently looking into them at regular intervals.

The subsequent hours for Tony were lost in a hallucinogenic haze. He remembered giant playing cards and men and women in skimpy bathing suits serving drinks, leaning over him and brushing him with their muscles or their cleavage. The women often seemed to have the face of Natasha. Round betting chips grew and shrank to all sizes, shifting back and forth and rotating, and in one case expanding to the size of the White Mountain tunnel entrance, through which he saw himself hanging, next to the woman in grey he had seen serving in Agulha. He kept on hitting giant aces and standing on the faces of picture cards, one of which had the eyes of the server in the Agulha and was dressed in grey, and one of which was Sue. He vomited all over the impeccable green baize and then little puppet figures started to sing 'So Long, Farewell' to him as he swayed back and forth on a hammock. He was travelling in a little train carriage with a drum that suddenly made two sharp beats...

Tony fell out of bed and onto the floor of the bedroom of his hotel room, which was covered with *wings* scattered all over the floor. Outside, the eclipse was still there. He had no idea what time it was.

'Tony, are you OK in there?' Gustavo's voice called from behind the door on which he had just knocked.

Tony had a fleeting moment of déjà vu but was then hit by the realisation of the immediate, long-forgotten and unwelcome experiences of a crushing headache and nausea. He staggered up towards his door and opened it.

'Gee, you look like you've just failed the UEWM,' Gustavo said. 'Mind you, we had a blast at the Musica, no? Tripling your initial stake is pretty good going. I just had to carry you home with a couple of the guys after you vomited all over the table. On the way back you kept on yelling about Sue and asking her to forgive you which was a bit weird.'

Gustavo helped Tony down to the Agulha.

'Hmmm, let me see, ice with coffee, ice with kirk, ice with tea... ah, ice with angelade is probably just the thing,' said Gustavo as he scanned down the menu.

The woman in grey who had haunted Tony's dream was not there. Instead a man in grey greeted them and asked them how they were.

'I'm fine thanks, how are you?' managed Tony, but he didn't respond as Gustavo ordered ice with angelade and some toast.

'That'll help you to rehydrate and sop up all that alcohol last night. I think they gave you a bit more than usual because of the crowd that you and I attracted.'

Tony's ice with angelade came in a large plastic cup full of ice and what seemed like a thimbleful of sweet red liquid. He realised that there was an enormous ice-making machine behind the bar with a big sign, "Ice! Ice! Ice! Ice! Lovely Ice! Lovely Ice!" which was dispensing ice into many plastic cups and being served to several other customers.

Tony sipped his ice and angelade, which numbed his mouth, and munched without much enthusiasm on his toast, although after a few minutes he started to feel slightly better.

'How do you manage to put up with this relentless non-stop music?' Tony asked Gustavo, as the upbeat background tunes continued.

'Oh, but it's great Tony,' protested Gustavo. 'It provides us with a memorable and lively listening experience which is fun, interesting and accessible to everyone. In fact one of our top-time favourites is playing now.'

Tony picked up on words like *Eclipse city gonna sell my soul... Gonna sell my soul so cool*' wafting through, but his head was hurting too much to register much more apart from the chorus, which went round and round: '*Ha-il Hull, Ha-il Hull!*' Gustavo got up and started gyrating in delight.

'Thanks for coming by, Gustavo, I feel a bit better but could do with a lie-down,' said Tony.

Gustavo was sympathetic and took Tony back to his room. 'Here.' He handed Tony an oticel. 'I've programmed my number into this. Give me a call when you're feeling better. There's a football match on at Soccer later that I want to take you to.'

Tony put the 'Do Not Disturb' sign on his door and lay down in his room, pleased to be in a relatively silent place (though the music playing in the corridors was audible in snatches). With his head still hammering, he sipped water and finally slipped into a restless but dreamless sleep whose duration he could not measure.

Upon waking, he realised that there were no clocks anywhere. The eclipse still hung over Hull, with the corona stretching out in its ghostly fashion.

Feeling a little better, Tony had a shower, put on some jeans and a T-shirt and tidied up his room. Although Gustavo had been very helpful in showing him around and explaining, he wanted to explore without him for a bit. Bracing himself for the barrage of music, he stepped out in the corridor and took the elevator to the ground floor. Passing through the casino, he got lost and was accosted for his photo a couple of times (each time he was given a *wing* or two), but then he found a map of the hotel.

'This is more like it,' he thought to himself. He saw that there were a number of theatres, including the Pinnacle and the Dive, showing cabaret and 'Inangity', produced by SCC, the Sunny Circus Circle group that he had seen; they were now playing a different show at Musica. There were wedding salons, waterfalls, a golf course, various themed restaurants and bars (including Agulha), nightclubs, a funfair and a spa and health centre. 'Aha,' thought Tony, 'just the way to shake off the cobwebs.'

He hadn't been in a gym since leaving the Realm of the White Mountain, and although his tour of PirogRus and the Cube had been brief, he was itching to get some exercise.

Returning to his room, he passed an Astroprata selling big plastic cups of ice in a similar way to the Agulha – they were clearly affiliated, as they both had the same round blue logo with an angel in a wavy suit and sporting spiky hair. He realised that he had seen Astropratas every 50 metres or so along the Copula and several times in Musica. Reaching his room and searching his wardrobes, towards the back he located a red tracksuit and trainers, which he slipped on and headed down to the health centre.

After a walk of at least a kilometre, up and down numerous escalators, he found the health centre which was tucked away at the back of the hotel, past a further five Astropratas. Many of the guests were overweight and used little cars like golf buggies to get around. The gym's reception was unmanned, but Tony signed up anyway and went in. There were at least a hundred modern cardio and weight machines, but only five people using them. They were all wearing grey tracksuits and looked a little surprised to see Tony.

Tony couldn't find a towel, so he asked a woman using one of the weights where he could get one. She indicated a cupboard. He did a warm-up and then a full tour of the weights machines and felt quite energized, although he yearned for some fresh air as the subterranean and air-conditioned gym was a little claustrophobic.

Seeing one of the men in tracksuits help himself to water from a dispenser, Tony broke off to do the same.

'Hello,' he said cheerfully, 'how long will it be before you attempt the UEWM again? I guess you didn't succeed and you're working here while you wait for another chance?'

The man looked a little fearfully at Tony. 'What's the OOOM?' he said. 'I'm one of the dancers in the cabaret in the Pinnacle here.'

The man, who was extremely well-built, did not seem keen to continue the conversation, but Tony detected the same odd expression as the server at the Agulha and pressed on with questions.

'But which angel realm do you come from?'

The man gave Tony a strange look, and became a little aggressive.

'I don't know what you're talking about,' he said, 'I live in Downstreet like most of the performers and workers around here. Not like you and the others, who just fly into Hull to have fun.'

The man had begun to raise his voice, and the other four people in tracksuits were looking awkward and uneasy.

'I'm sorry if I'm asking questions out of turn. I'm Tony,' he said, offering his hand to shake.

'We don't have names,' the man said. 'I'm afraid I have to go now as we have a show.'

He left and the four others slunk out soon after, leaving Tony alone in the gym. He finished his workout alone and walked back towards his room, past the crowds, the golf buggies, the Astropratas, the extraordinary array of shops, the exotic floral displays and the perfect gleaming marble lining the corridors. He also became aware of the staff in grey all over the place, working as shop assistants, tending the floral displays, cleaning, and of course serving in the Astropratas.

He took the lift to the Agulha, where the female waitress he had seen before was on duty. He sat down on a stool so he could speak with her.

'Hello sir, how are you? Would you like some ice?' she beamed, but somehow there seemed to be a crack in her smile.

'I'm fine,' said Tony, 'How are you?'

She seemed surprised to be asked and hesitated slightly, but then seemed to adjust herself.

'Thank you for asking. I'm fine. What can I serve you?'

The bar was relatively quiet and she had no reason to attend to anything else, so Tony continued, 'Which angel realm do you come from originally?'

Her face had the same puzzled look as the man in the gym and she didn't respond, but Tony continued. 'So I guess you live in Downstreet?'

'Yes,' was the subdued response. She gripped the counter and looked around with a lost look.

'What's your name?' asked Tony.

After a pause, the face of the woman suddenly seemed to cave in and she staggered backwards and began screaming piteously. There were about 15 people in the bar and all turned to see the scene.

All of a sudden, as if out of nowhere, Eleanor, the Reception Manager, was standing by his side in her black suit, with two men in black suits and sunglasses.

'I'm sorry for the inconvenience Mr Tony, we will deal with the situation from here,' she said as the two men in black suits led the deflated woman out towards the lifts. She led Tony to a corner of the bar and continued in a serious tone.

'You'll appreciate that failing the UEWM can be a very traumatic experience for an angel. Here in Hull we offer gainful employment to those angels who have been the most psychologically scarred. Their treatment and recuperation can be a very delicate matter. For their wellbeing, I would therefore request you not to ask personal questions of the support staff. Thank you for your understanding, and have a nice day.'

CHAPTER 37

Tony went back to his room, rather disturbed, and started flicking through the TV channels showing movies, cartoons or football. He began to get slightly mesmerized as he watched the screen, which had a strangely nostalgic effect upon him. However, he was still a little uncomfortable about the incidents that had happened in the gym and *Agulha*, and wanted to explore some more and above all talk to more people.

After changing into some smarter jeans and a blue shirt, he wandered around the hotel, quickly becoming aware that whenever he saw support staff dressed in grey undertaking a function, there was a Hull angel in a black suit and sunglasses discreetly in the background. Rather than approach someone in grey, Tony decided to try a different tack and find a Tony.

He had already seen what seemed like 50 or more other Tonys, in many different forms: typically wearing a yellow football shirt and jeans or a grey tracksuit, but of different ages and sizes. They always greeted him and each other warmly, and the ones he had seen when he was with Gustavo had asked for the angel's signature a few times. Passing an Astroprata, he saw a plump Tony with a long beard sitting down with a cup of ice. Grabbing a cup himself, he sat down opposite him.

'Hi, I'm Tony,' said Real Tony, offering his hand.

'Hey man, well that's a coincidence, as I'm Tony too,' smiled Bearded Tony, warmly taking his hand, 'you know you're a pretty fine look-alike. If you put on a grey tracksuit like me you could make a ton of *wings* daily on the street.'

'I like to take some time off once in a while,' said Real Tony. 'Are you going to the convention?'

'Of course,' said Bearded Tony, 'I've heard there'll be more than 2,000 of us. Gee, what any one of us would give to meet the real Tony. Last I heard was he's missing, last seen at the Angel Cup semi-final match between Angeland and Poste. It's all quite mysterious, but as the Apocalypse hasn't arrived yet we hope he's still with us.'

Bearded Tony was warming to his favourite subject, so Real Tony asked, 'So what does Tony mean to you?'

'Gosh, well, I'm from the Cube originally but I've enjoyed being in Hull for a while, as you can appreciate from my girth, but like all us Tonys, he became an influence on me ever since I heard about his misfortunes in Hefyn, and of course he sealed a place in my heart after he succeeded in getting his wings at the UEWM – and I sincerely believe he did, yes siree, even though those archangels are still deliberating. And before that he saved the life of an angel. I can't get enough of the great stories about him. I mean there's the one in PirogRus when he escaped Archangel Yuri's plot, and then that one where he turned Archangel Mehi bonkers in my home realm.'

'Yes, he certainly has had plenty of adventures,' said Real Tony wryly. 'What happens next?'

'If the real Tony sat down next to me I'd go down on my knees in reverence. We've never seen anything like him in the history of the Angeland realms. You know,' he continued, looking around to ensure no one nearby was listening, and leaning in close to Tony, 'I'm in with the theory that the real Tony is Him, the A1, and He's toying with the archangels who are all – Archangel Mehi being the first – in for a reckoning.' He nodded, his finger to his lips.

'It's been lovely to chat with you, and I look forward to seeing you at the convention,' said Real Tony after some final small talk.

'I do as well, Tony, but perhaps I could suggest you come in some more appropriate clothes,' Bearded Tony said, and they shook hands and parted.

As Tony was returning to his room, he suddenly spotted a woman in white Angeland football strip in the distance in the casino. She had her back to him and was putting *wings* into a slot machine.

'Rita?' he asked.

The woman turned and Tony saw it was not Rita, although she had a distinctive likeness to her. Clearly she was a Rita impersonator.

'I wish, my dear, but I see that you're clearly Tony in person. We could maybe charge triple for photos of us together.'

Tony started to return to his room, quite disturbed at the conversation with Bearded Tony. As he was wandering through the casino, his oticel rang and he saw it was Gustavo.

'Hey Tony,' said the friendly voice, 'there's a football match starting in an hour in Soccer, and I've got two tickets with a great view. Do you want to meet me at the entrance to the West Stand? Just take the monorail direction Compras and get down at Intersection 1.'

'That would be super,' said Tony.

The monorail was easy to find, and Tony found that there were three platforms in the Montagne Blanche station. The first one, the Cupola circuit, went to Musica (he had vague recollections of arriving from there after his blinder at the casino with Gustavo) on the left and Reiss on the right. Two platforms beyond this went to Compras and Würfel, and Tony took the first. The monorail glided above the traffic jams and activity of the Cupola below, and then entered Soccer as it passed through the dome that was marked like part of a giant football. Inside the dome, it was like a small city. Tony passed all sorts of elegant buildings, a golf course, and a multi-tiered set of pools linked by water slides. The monorail stopped at Intersection 2 where you could change for Reiss and Musica or Soccosphere, and then continued past nightclubs, an amusement park and a botanic garden. In the centre of the city, Tony saw the base of the tower that pierced the centre of the massive dome. The monorail arrived at Intersection 1, and there were signs to the KCUM Stadium which he and many others followed.

'Hi Tony, you're looking a lot better now than before,' said Gustavo as they met outside the West Stand. 'Have you had fun?'

They entered the W5 block, next to the tunnel, and had seats about seven rows from the front. Tony waited until they had sat down and for the rest of the crowd to come in before talking discreetly to Gustavo about his experiences. It was a good place as no one else could follow their conversation, given the noise. The crowd was soon at capacity and was chanting and roaring.

'I can confirm that what Eleanor the Reception Manager told you is everything I know,' said Gustavo. 'To be honest, I never talk much to the serving and support staff. But it's a bit odd that they don't know their names or which angel realms they come from. I guess it's because of the psychological stress they've gone through. I mean, you and I know first-hand how awful the Tunnel of the White Mountain is.'

On the question of Tony being a messiah-like figure, Gustavo nodded. 'Yes, to be honest every angel has heard all sorts of stories and rumours about you. If I hadn't lived and trained with you for the UEWM then I might have similar crazy theories. But I've always told others who ask – plenty of course – that you're an ordinary human who simply lost his memory of his previous history on Earth. All I know is that my orders from Archangel Natasha are to make you as comfortable as possible in Hull. She feels that if you have a good time here and are reminded of the best things on Earth then it will be the best way to make you recover and expunge Gabriel's eyelash. All of this while keeping your identity top secret, and the Tony look-alike epidemic provides ideal cover. There's nothing more to it than that. But hey, look, the players are coming out.'

Tony felt Gustavo was being very honest, and was very grateful for his friendship. Despite all the bad things he had heard about Natasha, Gustavo was the best possible companion here in Hull.

The game was a league match, Soccer (white with black hexagons strip) versus Downstreet (black and white chequered strip).

'As you've found out, the support staff here stay in and around Downstreet, and there's a suspicion that many of their players actually come from other Angeland realms,' explained Gustavo.

'It's Rupa and Cristiana in Downstreet,' said Tony, pointing to them. 'They play for the Alles Schwartz team, no?'

'Absolutely,' said Gustavo, 'all this is practice for them before the Angel Cup final. There's a huge buzz of anticipation and excitement in Hull about it.'

The game proceeded, and Tony found it a lot rougher than previous matches he had seen. When the referee finally showed a yellow card for a player, this drew enormous boos from the crowd, although there had been all manner of kicks, trips, charges, strikes and pushes with only occasional fouls signalled by the referee.

'This is all very rough,' said Tony, 'and extremely lenient on the ref's part.'

'Unlike intra-Angeland realm matches, in which the players are extremely well behaved, here in Hull league matches, things are a lot rougher. Actually, they say it toughens up the players no end in the Alles Schwartz team. But the crowd are booing the player who got the card, not the referee. After falling in love with a human, getting a yellow card is probably the next worst thing an angel can do.'

By half time, Cristiana had scored a hat trick and it was four goals to Downstreet and nil to Soccer.

'This is hardly a competition,' harrumphed Tony as they walked around the KCUM stadium before the second half to pick up a beer.

'Ah, wait and see, there's a rumour that the balance might be tipped soon,' said Gustavo mysteriously.

About ten minutes into the half, one of the Soccer forwards took a nasty fall (the referee seemed to have looked the other way when a shoulder charge had thrown the player to the ground) and two assistants ran on with a stretcher. The noise of the crowd mounted and suddenly burst into a huge roar as the substitute stepped onto the pitch.

'My sources were right,' Gustavo said delightedly. 'Look who it is.'

Rita walked up to the touchline and looked around edgily before jogging onto the pitch as the stretcher departed.

'There's been a lot of rumours that Rita was paying a visit to Hull, and might play in a league game. Now she's up against half the players in the Alles Schwartz team who play for Downstreet, it's going to give us a taste of how the final might play out,' said Gustavo.

'Assuming there's going to be much left of her,' said Tony, which was a fairly accurate prediction. The moment the game started the level of aggressiveness shot up, with Downstreet players homing in like guided missiles on Rita.

'But how could the referee miss that punch?' gasped Tony.

'Goodness gracious, that was a double-footed tackle!' And a few minutes later, 'That's the fifth tackle that would have got a red card and a multiple-game ban!'

Rita was literally being beaten black and blue all over, but each time she went down to a 'tackle' she got up and continued stony-faced, sometimes limping or clutching a part of her anatomy that had been bashed.

'It's unusual to see the referees being criticised, but I think most people agree a card or two was in order,' said Gustavo, looking a little subdued as the sound of the boos increased above the cheers.

Despite the onslaught, Rita nevertheless strung together some remarkable passes and runs and then, at last, in a single brilliant movement, she dribbled past half the Downstreet team from behind the halfway line and then curled in a beautiful shot that beat Rupa and went into the side of the net with centimetres to spare. The cheers in the stadium had built up and they now hit a crescendo, with all the spectators standing. There were some tall angels in front of Tony, who obscured the moment after Rita turned undemonstratively away from the goal. But there was a sudden murmur from the crowd and when the angels moved out of the way, he saw Rita lying prone and motionless on the ground and Rupa standing over her.

'Rupa head-butted Rita in full view of the referee!' said an astonished Gustavo.

Rupa was given a yellow card, followed by a cacophony of whistles, and the inert Rita was stretched off.

'This is a bit more violent than a normal game, I have to say,' admitted Gustavo, as Tony watched the crumpled form of Rita entering the tunnel. The level of violence dropped significantly for the remainder of the game and the final score was Downstreet 10, Soccer 1.

'Well, you don't get that level of excitement in an intra-realm game, do you?' said Gustavo. 'I hear that now we're in for another treat. The Alles Schwartz mascots are going to come out and entertain the crowd. Just wait – you'll love them, they're ever so cute. You'll remember them from when we saw the Poste–Alles Schwartz match at Willkommenhaus.'

As Tony feared, the two great black shapes of Lapindee and Lapindum now came out of the tunnel and walked onto to the middle of the pitch, facing away from them.

'Gustavo, I think it would be a good idea to leave now,' said Tony, but he was drowned out by the sound of 'Saturday Night' blaring out from speakers around the stadium. The rabbits mounted on their hind legs and started to dance with their paws, with the crowd mimicking them joyfully.

Tony tugged Gustavo and shouted in his ear, 'We've got to go, now!' but Gustavo shrugged, pointing at the rabbits with a thumbs up and dancing along with them. Then the thing that Tony had most feared happened. The rabbits swung round the centre of the pitch to face the crowd, and one suddenly faltered and its ears sprang up. It sniffed the air and then looked directly at Tony, crouched facing him, and thumped one of its back legs. The other rabbit did the same.

'This is interesting,' said Gustavo. 'I've never seen them do this before. It must be part of a new routine for the Angel Cup Final.'

While Gustavo was finishing his sentence, both rabbits charged directly at Tony, smashing through the hoarding surrounding the pitch and pulverizing the Soccer dugout. They scrambled up the tiers of seats in front of him, crushing the unfortunate crowd in their way. There were terrible screams as the snarling black elephantine monsters hurtled forward, trampling on and pushing aside bodies and seats in the lower tiers as if they were paper.

Tony held up his arms and ducked, in the knowledge that it was as much use as trying to stop a tsunami, but instead of the impact and expected sensation of being thrust up a big furry arse, there was a snarl, a whimper and a crash and the two great faces of the rabbits thudded unconscious down on the seats in front of the angels. The music had stopped, and Tony heard the heavy breathing of the animals along with the screams. Gustavo had lifted Tony, with his two black wings extended and poised to take off and pull Tony to safety.

'Give me a red card!' he said. 'Where in all of Angeland did that come from?'

— * —

The Lapindee and Lapindum tragedy created wide interest, and there was extensive mourning for some time afterwards for them as well as the angels they had killed. Had it not been for the quick actions of their minders, firing no fewer than five tranquilliser darts into each, the toll could have been much worse. The rabbits' inexplicable behaviour in charging at the crowd was much debated. A certain proportion of angels thought an event as extraordinary as this must, failing any other explanation, be due to Tony. This was however greatly disputed by the Tonys in Hull, who mounted a demonstration in defence of Tony, and without firm evidence it remained a mystery. Members of the Lapindee and Lapindum fan club contributed over a million *wings* for the rabbits' recuperation, and Archangel Natasha refused to completely rule out the possibility of their appearance at the Angel Cup Final.

CHAPTER 38

'Let's go to a nightclub,' said Gustavo, who had put away his wings after the disaster. 'I think a good dance will cheer us up.'

They took the monorail in the direction of Hotel Reiss, and during the ride Tony filled Gustavo in with the details of how he had arrived in Hull. The angel was open-mouthed.

'Golly, if only I'd known Lapindee and Lapindum had this crazy lust for you I'd never have brought you to the game' he said glumly. 'I feel responsible for the deaths of all of those angels.'

Tony tried to reassure Gustavo, reflecting that the head-butt that had knocked out Rita had probably saved her from a worse fate. He looked up as the monorail approached Reiss.

'As you've seen, the hotel has all sorts of landmarks from around the Earth on its dome, and you can visit the various restaurants and venues inside them,' explained Gustavo. 'For many angels like me this provides one of the best chances to 'visit' places I'd never otherwise have a chance to see.'

They came into the main entrance hall that made up the inside of a giant globe, which gave you the impression that you were looking from the core of the planet outwards, with all the physical features of the surface of Earth around. Gustavo led Tony through a door in the South Atlantic that led to the casino, and Tony politely declined his suggestion of having a few bets. 'Le Paradis club in Reiss is considered one of the best nightclubs in Hull, and I think you'll like it,' said Gustavo.

Having left the casino, they entered a long tunnel surrounded by an enormous aquarium, with fish, turtles, sharks and other sea creatures illuminated as they swam gracefully around. Tony and Gustavo came to a queue that stretched some distance down the tunnel in front of them; they walked past this, passing young-looking angels who were hip and elegantly dressed.

'I hope you've got some of those *wings* that you won in the casino with you,' said Gustavo. 'I reckon a few hundred will be enough for the jar service.'

They arrived at the front of the queue, where two tall and muscular angels in white suits and white sunglasses were self-consciously imposing themselves and surveying the crowds. Behind them were two large white iridescent gates, which were closed, with a small angel in white wearing a fake halo sitting at a desk behind them.

'Hi, I'm Gustavo, as you can see I'm a Hull angel like you and me and my friend Tony here want to enter the club,' said Gustavo to the muscular angels.

'Sorry sir, I don't believe you're on the list,' the female angel said, pushing him back without much gentleness. 'I don't care if you're an Archangel or Tony in person' – she looked at Tony – no one gets in.'

Gustavo nodded at Tony, who pulled out and waved a wad of *wings*.

'It's OK, he's on the list,' said the high-pitched voice of the small angel, and the muscular angels moved aside to let them pass.

'Call me Pedro,' said the little angel, 'and I recognise you Gustavo. You're the angel saved by Tony, and here you are rolling up on my doorstep with a Tony. Miracles still happen. So, my human friend,' he winked at Tony, 'how much you got for jar service?'

Tony pulled out 500 *wings* and placed them firmly on the desk with two hands.

'Aha,' said Pedro, 'as it happens we have a central table that's just been liberated. Enjoy your night.' He gestured to the gates, which now opened to let them pass.

Inside, everything was white, from the decor and the drinks to the waiters. The waiters all had dainty fake fluffy wings affixed to their backs, and wore tight, revealing clothes. Gustavo and Tony were taken to a table in an alcove across from the dance floor. As they approached, they saw the old occupants being rather unceremoniously shooed away, and when they reached the alcove it was clean and ready for them. Angel waiters brought a bucket of ice in what seemed like white plastic and a large version of an Astroprata cup, and Tony and Gustavo ordered beers.

'We can be seen by almost everyone in the club from here,' Gustavo said. 'It's one of the most prestigious spots in the city. Just you wait. With these spare seats on our table we'll receive lots of propositions.'

Indeed, a short time later a string of handsome and beautiful angels came up to speak and sit with them, either saying they knew Gustavo or someone who knew Gustavo, or admiring Tony's likeness to the real Tony. Gustavo liberally ordered many of them drinks as they clucked and fawned.

Then, suddenly, all the lights went out, the music stopped, and there was an eerie noise. A deep voice reverberated. 'There was a beginning... there will be an end, maybe due to Tony, but now all we want to do is party.'

At that the lights came on and played across the dance floor, with a pulsing beat which shook the room and everyone in it. From the ceiling, an imitation cloud descended, and on it in was a figure in white robes wearing an obvious fake white beard and surrounded by turntables.

'Hey party angels, I'm A-DJ-1! Let's start dancing in the present,' he said.

The evening continued, with A-DJ-1 occasionally directing some of the waiters or other angels to do special moves. He even put the spotlight on Tony and Gustavo once, and they jovially participated. The two of them got up and danced a few times and each time on returning to their table they found they had a couple of female angels wearing skimpy clothes in tow. Tony found it all a bit superficial. He was getting a bit weary of the attention, even though the angels were all pretty and trendy things, and came to feel that most of those coming up to the table were just opportunistically trying their luck to get a few free drinks, although Gustavo was in his element playing the congenial host.

When yet another female angel with a little black dress approached, Tony was about to ignore her, but then he smelt a perfume that only one other angel had worn before. It was Natasha. She leant over him and Tony saw Gustavo's astonished face. Natasha said something to Gustavo that Tony couldn't hear because of the music. Then she glanced briefly at Tony and walked onto the dance floor with Gustavo trailing behind.

Gustavo and Natasha danced for a couple of songs and then Gustavo, his face a picture of delight, sat down next to Tony again. Natasha continued to dance with an eager crowd of angels, each almost pushing over the others to be close to her.

'Wow, did you see that!' said Gustavo, almost shouting in Tony's ear to be heard. 'I've never spoken directly with Archangel Natasha and then she invites me to dance at Paradis!' He paused to savour his beer and the moment. 'She said I'm doing a great job looking after you, and she's proud of me. She even said the incident in the KCUM stadium was a tragic accident and I shouldn't feel guilty. She's got a reputation for appearing among the rank and file of the angels. A real 'woman of the people', if you'll excuse me using the human metaphor.'

While Gustavo had been expounding enthusiastically, Tony's gaze had been fixed on the dance floor. Natasha was taking turns to dance with most of the angels who approached her, dancing quite suggestively with some. Every now and then she gazed in his direction, but Tony felt peculiarly and unjustly ignored.

He and Gustavo sat in silence for a few songs. Then Gustavo looked back and forth at Tony and the dance floor and said, 'Well, what in the Archangel's name are you waiting for? I mean, how often does one get to dance with the most gorgeous angel in all of the Angeland realms?'

Tony got up and negotiated his way onto the dance floor. The crowds were packed around Natasha, but somehow – not without a few irritated exclamations and dark looks – he managed to squeeze in next to her. She was thrusting her crotch at a swarthy and very masculine-looking angel. Suddenly, the music changed and she turned in Tony's direction.

'Would you like to dance?' he shouted in her ear, and she nodded cautiously.

'I'm Tony,' he said, as they started to dance, keeping a modest distance apart.

'That's what all the Tony impersonators say,' she said. 'How do I know you're the real one?'

'How do I know you're the real Archangel Natasha?' he said.

She was obviously expecting another answer and looked a little taken aback, but she laughed sweetly.

'You know what they do with impersonators here, particularly cheeky ones?' she asked darkly. They were both sweating profusely.

'They take them to dark mysterious caves with a beautiful siren who gets very *wet*,' he said, suddenly emboldened and speaking out of character.

She looked at Tony full on, and for a millisecond he had the impression that all the dancers as well as the rest of the club had suddenly fallen away. Tony felt a sudden desire that he had not had since being on Earth, with memories of the sex and passion that had been curiously missing in the Angeland realms. It was only a brief vision, and it did not allow him to identify any of the subjects of his past Earthly desires, but he looked at Natasha and knew that he deeply, urgently wanted her.

They danced together without speaking, Natasha shooting suggestive glances and smiles at him as they got closer and closer. She placed her arms around his shoulders.

'My dear Tony, I very much regret to say that duty calls and I have to leave,' she said. 'But perhaps soon you'll have time to visit my cave.'

With that, she walked out, glancing back at him once from the other side of the club with a penetrating look, with her mouth slightly open and her tongue between her teeth.

'Wow!' said Gustavo after Tony had got back to their table. 'She danced with you a while, nice and close too.'

'Yes,' said Tony, 'she's quite something.'

CHAPTER 39

Tony woke up and leapt out of bed. The eclipse was still in the sky and his encounter with Natasha and the promised tryst gave him a spring that he hadn't experienced for a long time. Looking out of the window, a billboard caught his eye that seemed to perfectly reflect his feelings: 'We're not in Hull for a long time, but for a good time.'

Calling Gustavo, Tony took out a good quantity of his *wings* from the safe and told his friend he was ready to hit the town.

'Wow,' said Gustavo, 'You're suddenly so enthusiastic and animated. That's great! Let's get to it.'

'Show it all to me, Gustavo, I'm ready to have a wild time,' Tony said, sipping his ice with coffee in *Astroprata*. It tasted like divine nectar.

So Gustavo and Tony went into Hull and hit the town. Tony blew sums of *wings* in several casinos that were extraordinary for an average angel, but won many times, landing number 7 red and 17 black on a couple of occasions in roulette, which led them both to whoop with abandon and high-five everyone in the vicinity. He won with flushes and four-of-a-kind in poker, threw sevens in craps, and got naturals in baccarat that led to expansive and enthusiastic displays of joy. Plied with drink after drink, Gustavo and Tony became more and more boisterous and popular, drawing crowds of other punters who wanted to witness these skilful and successful players. They shifted to the wheel of fortune and slot machines, roaring with delight at the glittering animations and sounds that egged them on and rewarded them just at the moment when a suspicion of doubt or boredom might have crossed their minds. But Tony was masterfully aware that he should not get too drunk or too sucked in, and after some ice with whiskey he headed back to his room and fell into bed.

Waking up with a thumping headache, Tony realised that he had lost about three-quarters of all his *wings*. He crept sheepishly down to the Agulha to have some ice with angelade and toast.

'That was a blast,' said Gustavo on his oticel. 'I think we must have been going for 24 hours without a pause. I think you got well introduced to all the games on offer in the casino. Great fun, eh?'

Tony decided to take some time out. He felt he needed a detox and, above all, some exercise to keep him in shape in anticipation of another meeting with Natasha. He located a multiplex of swimming pools at one end of the Montagne Blanche, but they were full of punters standing around drinking and gambling at tables incorporated into the pool, with zero scope to exercise in them even if Tony had wanted to. A helpful attendant pointed out the swimming lane that weaved around the inside of the mountain, half way up. 'It's always empty,' the attendant told him.

Indeed it was, so Tony swam for a good while until finally his head felt a lot clearer.

He hooked up with Gustavo again, this time avoiding the casinos, and they did more tours of the hotels. The time passed by easily. They played golf on each of the hotel courses, dined in the exquisite multiple-themed restaurants and went to other nightclubs, although disappointingly Natasha was not to be found in any of them. They went to many of the shops in the hotels too, between gleaming, perfect walkways and many branded and exclusive products.

In Compras, Gustavo explained that Archangel Yuri owned all the shopping rights; there was a huge mall called Comprasso with recreations of some of the biggest and most prestigious department stores on Earth. Visits to Harrods and Selfridges brought back frustratingly limited snatches of memories of Earth. Angels left the stores with bags and bags of products, and Gustavo informed Tony that most of the goods would quite quickly be thrown away, but they would be recycled in PirogRus.

'Angels love shopping,' said Gustavo. 'They're so jealous of the fun you have as humans.'

Gustavo also took Tony to many of the shows, with illusionists, bands, boxing matches, comedians and all sorts of other acts. They were indeed wonderful, but all along Tony was hoping to see Natasha, and his hopes were always dashed.

On one occasion, when they were in the Würfel hotel, the big Pyramid hotel with a bright light on top shooting up like a beacon, Gustavo suggested they should go and see Wau by SCC, the Sunny Circus Circle, which happened to be in the Würfelring theatre in Würfel. 'You'll love it,' said Gustavo, 'SCC have shows all over Hull, but Wau is the first and many think still their best.

They got front-row seats at the last minute and Tony was entranced by the complex moves and beautiful costumes of the show, with many of the acrobats wearing dog masks. There were also clowns who performed short skits every now and then, pulling people in from the audience. All of a sudden for one presentation, they playfully dragged Tony onto the stage and locked him in a box. He heard the sound of a chainsaw and the audience laughing, then there was a pause and a tick-ticking sound, a flash and a lot of smoke and the sensation of the box doing a controlled fall as the sound of the audience clapping receded. The door was opened by one of the acrobats wearing a dog mask, and Tony realised that he was backstage, because other members of the cast and technical staff were waiting and moving back and forth.

The acrobat with the dog mask took him to one side and, in a voice distorted by the mask, said, 'Thank you for being such a good sport for Wau. A clown will be along shortly to take you back to your seat.'

The dog mask looked furtively back and forth as if checking that no one was looking. Then with one quick motion she leant towards Tony, gently took the back of his head with one hand and pulled back her mask with the other. It was Natasha. Rosy-faced with excitement, she kissed Tony passionately on the lips for a few seconds. But just as he opened his mouth and their tongues touched, she pulled away and slipped her mask back down.

'You can't imagine how much I've been thinking about you, but frustratingly I've been tied up with all of my responsibilities,' she panted. 'Look soon for the invitation to my cage.' With that, she turned and ambled away, joining others in dog masks going on stage.

A clown duly arrived a few minutes later and escorted Tony back onto the stage. He felt the spotlights on him and waved as the audience applauded.

'Hey, that was great,' said Gustavo, 'they were going to chop you in half and then blow you up.' He stopped when he saw the look on Tony's face.

'What on earth happened to you, did you really get blown away?' he said smiling. Tony nodded, but he did not relate his experience with Natasha. Instead, for the rest of the show, he gazed at the acrobats with dog masks on, but he was unable to identify Natasha.

'I need to get some sleep,' Tony said uncharacteristically at the end, before returning to his hotel feeling a mixture of elation and confusion.

Gustavo called Tony several times on his oticel afterwards to check on him, but Tony didn't want to go out, nor did he feel very communicative towards his friend.

'OK, no worries,' Gustavo said in the end. 'I'm worried about you, but I'm sure you'll be safe in Hull as you know the place well now. Call me anytime you need, as I'm always there to watch your back, like you did for me in the tunnel of the White Mountain.'

CHAPTER 40

Tony wandered alone, with heightening anticipation, through Hull, but ignored most of the sights, sounds and characters that drifted by. To while away the hours, he went back and did the same rigorous routine of exercise and diet that he had cultivated in the Realm of the White Mountain, and was pleased to feel his body quickly regaining the form that had slipped away since his training. Around him, he increasingly heard snatched conversation about the forthcoming Angel Cup final, and the imminent catastrophe or new order that would be announced, but it seemed very distant and unimportant as he stared longingly at the various images of Natasha. He realised that her face was everywhere, on posters, on billboards and in every possible type of literature or flyer that could be found. He smiled when he saw a serious picture of her on a postcard on 'Responsible gambling' which he found, by accident, in an obscure corner of the Compras casino.

Time passed, although you could not measure it, as clocks were non-existent. The attractions of Hull were beginning to pall for Tony. Every hotel seemed to have the same casinos, the same range of golf courses, restaurants, wedding salons, spas, and acres and acres of perfect wall-to-wall marble and chandeliers several floors high. The angels seemed to drift round and round blindly, gambling in a glazed, identikit procession in air-conditioning that felt increasingly stifling. Along with his profound desire for Natasha, Tony began longing for fresh air and reality.

'Hello Tony,' said a voice one day as he was daydreaming on the Copula, away from the air conditioning but still very torrid. It was Bearded Tony.

'Hi,' said Real Tony.

'Hey, you seem miles away,' Bearded Tony said cheerfully. Tony shook himself out of haze.

'I look forward to seeing you later at the closing of the Tony convention,' Bearded Tony said. 'Naturally they're finishing well before the Angel Cup Final tomorrow. 'I don't seem to have seen you yet, but of course it's easy to mistake your Tonys there. I really enjoyed the sessions on the White Mountain, although I thought they were going a bit over the top by burning the effigy of Sue at the end.'

Tony looked up and felt a pang, but suddenly his oticel buzzed and he saw a text message had arrived:

Free AT LAST!!! Come to the Reception of the Soccosphere as soon as you can. Kisses, N

'I need to go,' said Tony, feeling a boost of euphoria. 'I doubt if I'll make it this evening, but have fun.'

He waved curtly and headed off to his room, where he beautified himself as much as possible and as fast as possible before heading off towards the monorail station. He had not yet been to the top of the Soccosphere, but he had heard that there was a swanky restaurant and funfair rides at the top, as well as a great view.

After a few minutes, he arrived at the base of the Soccosphere, where there was a long queue to take the lift up. He walked purposefully towards Reception.

'Hello,' he said, 'I'm Tony and I've come to see Archangel Natasha.'

The black-suited angel behind the Reception looked at him and indicated the lift. 'Yes sir, the private lift to the restaurant is reserved for you, please go right ahead.'

Tony hesitated for a moment, and asked, 'How do you know I'm the right Tony?'

The angel smiled and said, 'You don't need to worry, sir. We know who you are.'

Tony was alone in the lift, which climbed rapidly and passed through the dome of Soccer. He had seen several views of Hull, but this one from the central and highest vista that the tower had to offer was the best. The five hotels were twinkling and alive with action, and Musica was in the middle of one of its hourly shows. The red and white lights of the slow traffic on the Copula formed a perfect circle, and threading between it were the lights from the illuminated monorails. He saw that together the monorail lines passing across Soccer formed a symmetrical five-pointed star.

The lift slowed to a halt, announcing its arrival with a ping. The smooth gold, red and black furnishings of the Pentacle restaurant at the top of the Soccosphere tower were impeccable, with secluded niches that ensured privacy for each couple or group. The restaurant was slowly revolving, providing a gradually changing view below. A waiter took him to a table on the rim of the restaurant, where Natasha was sitting. She wore a ravishing red dress and a black veil around her shoulders, and her hair was beautifully styled.

She turned and stood up and looked at Tony with a softness he had not seen before, and they approached each other and kissed. She was wearing deep red lipstick and he wanted to smear it over her mouth in a passionate embrace, but instead she chuckled as their tongues met and they softly nibbled each other before she gently manoeuvred him into the seat opposite him.

'Dear Tony,' she said, 'we have plenty of time to get closer later, but I thought we could get nicely into the mood over dinner. After all, I have a lot of explaining to do and you must have a lot of questions. For the first time in what feels like centuries I've been able to liberate an evening without any other responsibilities. I feel like a young woman! I also have an important proposition to make to you, but I will only speak of it after the meal.'

Tony felt rather old opposite the youthful-looking Natasha, who struck him as very young with her enticing curves. But the thought quickly faded; seated opposite her, he felt marvellously rejuvenated and very special. Two glasses of champagne were brought to the table. It tasted delicious.

'It comes from Earth itself,' Natasha said, 'almost as rare as you are in the Angeland realms.'

'But why me?' he asked. 'I mean, you're an archangel with so much power and we've fallen for each other. And so quickly.'

Fresh shrimps and oysters were brought as the first course, and Natasha ate them suggestively as she explained. 'You probably realise by now, Tony, that you are the most extraordinary and dangerous thing that has passed through the Angeland realms, perhaps ever. You will claim modestly that you are only a human, but there are very few angels that have the same ability and determination you've shown to get through the UEWM and other challenges. Of course, I was also deeply touched that you saved Gustavo in the White Mountain tunnel. Then I had a chance to talk to you and… well, shall we say it was pretty much lust at first sight. For someone like me who has a reputation which is, shall we say, chancy, I couldn't control my feelings.'

She took his hand, and the titillating laugh that burst out uncontrollably at times was infectiously attractive. Tony felt almost helpless as the deep, primeval craving to have sex with her kept on returning to the front of his mind. There had been another question stirring within him, something more engaged and committed, but he approached it carefully to hide where his intentions lay.

'But I see that you are an exquisite professional. No chance of love in your approach,' he said.

Again a laugh emerged from Natasha, who beamed with pleasure. 'If I speak in the tongues of angels,' she said, 'one realises that love is a resounding gong or a clanging symbol with which one gains nothing. In reality, love ultimately dishonours and is self-seeking. It gets angry, and keeps a record of wrongs. I don't need to tell you as a human who has seen the reality of this on Earth.'

A waiter brought caviar and Natasha continued her monologue.

'Because, in the end, love always fails – it's a childish imagining. Falling in love is like looking in a hazy mirror and forgetting your own reflection. One loses the ability to know and master oneself. So, dear Tony, you will understand why love between an angel and a human is considered the worst sin of all. I offer the opportunity in Hull for all angels to explore their baser – I might add, their best – desires, and provide a crucial service for the Angeland realms. In Heaven only the most senior angels, those able to suppress any notion of love, are permitted to service the spoilt residents.'

Tony swallowed his caviar in slightly uncomfortable silence as Natasha spoke, and was somewhat relieved to see some geographical features come into view as the restaurant rotated. He pointed. 'What's over there?'

'Oh,' said Natasha, delighted to be showing off her realm, 'we get a good view of Downstreet from here, the original Hull, which is rather a backwater now. The service staff from Hull live in the houses and tower blocks around it that you can just see.'

Just beyond Downstreet, and all round Hull, Tony made out what appeared to be a dark expanse of water. Beyond this, and visible from the height of the tower, the sun beyond the edges of the eclipse illuminated a vast open canyon. Both the water and canyon wound around Hull in a near-perfect circle.

'That's the Umbro estuary and the Comba Vasta,' Natasha indicated, 'and next to Downstreet you can see the Apple International Airport – based on the fruit you eat, in case you're wondering – where most angels come in and out of Hull.'

Tony had noticed a regular line of planes landing and taking off. They enjoyed the view together in silence for a while, holding hands. More excellent wine and the main course of lobster and truffles were brought. Natasha did not eat or drink much, partly as she was the main one talking.

'You know, it's not easy being an Archangel,' she said. 'That's one reason why I adore your human simplicity and frankness, which are sadly absent elsewhere. Take the other archangels. Gabriel, as you will have seen, is frustrated and egotistical as he hasn't had a prestigious mission for a while. He used to be much more charming. Michelle is a sweet little thing but uncontrollable at times. Mehi was clever but is now mad. Yuri is terribly jealous of the success of Hull – and indeed I must apologise for his boorish treatment of you. And Sandeepa and Ray are wet blankets who can't do more than sing or manage a costume shop.'

Natasha seemed pleased at having such a rapt listener and discussed some of the achievements and changes in Hull, and how she had grown the realm over time.

'You see, I'm well organized, a great builder, and I make things happen. I'm ready to fill a gap to do my duty,' she affirmed as they tucked into the café gourmand dessert with a range of delicious dark chocolate creations. Finally they had liqueurs, and Natasha smiled particularly seductively at Tony.

'Now's almost the moment when our lust can be consummated,' she said 'Come, Tony.'

They left the table and took the private lift up to the highest floor of the tower. It opened out onto a single large room completely encased in glass. The eclipse seemed closer and dominated the sky.

'Isn't it beautiful?' Natasha said, glancing up at it. 'I froze it there nearly a thousand of your years ago when He left us, in a tribute to His memory, heralding the beautiful modern age of angels.'

In the centre of the room, there was a metal pole from floor to ceiling. An enormous round bed, with red silk sheets, featured prominently. There were exquisitely carved stone gargoyles at various points around the room, with candles in their mouths providing a soft, sensual light.

Natasha gestured for Tony to sit on a black sofa at the foot of the big round bed. 'We're going to play a little game,' she said, doing a quick dance around the pole and then kicking off her shoes and sitting on the bed opposite him. 'I'm going to remove one piece of clothing in turn from each of us, as I tell you about my little proposition that you can't resist. Ladies first, *bien sûr*.'

She removed her gloves and then reached down and pulled off Tony's shoes. 'Nothing for a pair here,' she said. He continued to pull off his socks. 'And that goes double.' Then she removed his shirt. 'Now I think that puts us on more even terms,' she said, and teasingly removed her red dress to reveal black lingerie.

'Oh, fair's fair,' she said, removing her stockings and garters.

She pulled her black veil over herself and reclined on the bed, writhing sensually, before approaching Tony again, standing him up and removing his trousers.

'I thought you'd be a big, big boy,' she said, throwing her veil to one side and easing down his underwear so he was completely naked. She looked up at him. 'And I'm right yet again.'

She sat on the edge of the bed again, removed her brassiere and placed his hands on her breasts.

'Now, Tony, the offer you can't refuse. Fuck me with your very soul. Give me your all. You will become immortal, and every night for evermore in our lust we will take each other to greater and greater heights of ecstasy.'

She reached up around his neck and detached his silver wing necklace, casting it to one side.

'So you're completely in your birthday suit,' she said. 'Now it's my turn.' She reclined on the bed, looking up at him, and slowly drew her knickers down. But as she cast aside the wing inscribed with 'HOPE' and given to Tony by George, Tony recalled the memory of his dead friend in the wood when they had been training. 'You should be very careful around the Archangel Natasha,' George had said. Memories from Priscilla, Albert and above all the measures taken by Sue to keep him from Natasha sprung unexpectedly to Tony's mind.

'Don't give up on me, soldier,' said Natasha. She was kneading away, but the sensation had turned suddenly from stimulating to sordid.

Tony took a step back. Natasha's face quivered and, for an instant, the candles flickered and picked up her profile and slightly ruffled hair. Her eyes had a slightly more reddish tinge, and above her shadow behind the bed there appeared to be two points diagonally protruding from her head.

Suddenly, she bent forward and flipped over acrobatically, clasping her legs around Tony's neck. Then she grasped the metal pole in the centre of the room with both hands. With superhuman strength she began swinging around the pole, all the while gripping Tony and hooting with laughter.

'Oh Tony, I should have known I couldn't rely on a man. A real disappointment from you. I thought you were of different mettle.'

Tony continued to whirl round and round, hardly able to breathe and becoming more and more disorientated.

'You could have had it all,' Natasha continued, 'but for your pathetic impotence and hesitation. I was going to make you immortal and lay the foundations for a better Angeland, but now it will have to be plan B, the one I should have implemented from the start. I will simply end your mortal existence so that we can chop out dear Gabriel's eyelash.'

Round and round Tony was whirled, and all he could do was ineffectually hold onto Natasha's legs to try to stop his head being pulled out of its socket.

'I could just throw you at the plate glass window,' she said, 'but slicing you to smithereens might generate a little suspicion'.

With one hand she picked up a stone gargoyle, twirled it and released it at the window, which smashed into tiny pieces. 'In my generosity I would like to give you one more view of my beautiful Hull.'

Still cackling with laughter, she released her grip around Tony and he flew straight through the open frame of the window. The lights of the city continued to gleam below and the eclipse still shrouded the sun above.

CHAPTER 41

Tony hurtled downwards, stark naked, and saw the top part of the Soccosphere rapidly disappear into the distance before his skydiving experience kicked in and he calmly turned to face downwards and forwards. He reckoned on having around 15 seconds in total before hitting the dome of Soccer at a couple of hundred kilometres an hour. More than anything else, he felt it was a shame that he didn't have a wingsuit on.

As the dome approached, he had a pang of regret that he would not be able to say goodbye to that someone, almost lost in the depths of his memories, who he loved and remembered snuggling up to.

In the last seconds, he turned to face the sky, his arms stretched out. But then, instead of the impact he was expecting, he felt himself being plucked out of the air. An angel with black wings had scooped him upwards.

'I told you I'd be watching your back,' said Gustavo, 'but I didn't expect you to do a base jump out of the top of the Soccosphere without any clothes or a parachute.'

Tony realised he had been wrong not to tell Gustavo of his infatuation for Natasha. He shared everything with him as they soared over Hull.

'I think by picking you out of the sky I've probably condemned myself then,' Gustavo said thoughtfully, trying to come to terms with the situation. 'The non-appearance of your body will create questions very soon. You need to hide in a place where no one can recognise you. For a start, that means none of the hotels, as they've got hidden cameras all over the place. There's Downstreet, but I wouldn't recommend it.'

Tony now realised how all his movements must have been tracked, but this suddenly gave him an idea.

'Can you get me a grey tracksuit?' he said, 'and then take me to the Convention Centre?'

'Certainly.' Gustavo left Tony behind a bush and went to get a grey tracksuit of the right size.

'Excellent,' Tony said with the clothes on, 'who do I look like to you now?'

'Well, Tony of course,' said Gustavo.

'Exactly,' said Tony with a grin.

Outside the Convention Centre entrance, hundreds of Tonys were milling around. Gustavo landed in a side alley and Tony turned to his friend.

'I think you can safely drop me off here, Gustavo,' said Tony. 'You need to make yourself disappear quickly. I don't know how to thank you.'

'We're equal now that we've saved each other's lives, and I'd do the same again any day' replied Gustavo, 'but I'm going to linger around a bit here to make sure everything is OK before slipping off. Best if we're not seen together.'

The two embraced before Tony joined the crowd of Tonys who were filtering into the main conference hall, which must have had a capacity of nearly 2,500 people. He looked around and about four rows from the front saw Bearded Tony. He went over and sat down next to him.

'Hi Tony, you made it,' said Bearded Tony. 'I knew you couldn't resist this closing session. It promises to be rather revelatory.'

A tall female Tony in a yellow shirt and blue jeans sat on the other side of the real Tony, who looked around and saw that the room was nearly full. A track-suited and eloquent bald Tony took the stage.

'Dear Tonys, this is the closing session and we've saved the best until last. You thought you knew Tony, but this next speaker was in his presence, and she will completely change your preconceptions. Please welcome... Priscilla from the Cube!'

Priscilla walked onto the stage to great applause, and on the screen behind her the words, 'Ravished by Tony: the true story' came up.

Bald Tony gave an introduction. 'As you know, dear Tonys, there are thousands of eye-witnesses in the Cube who saw Tony with Priscilla in the 'Insufficient Persistence' sub-category, Near Misses station, and in the Angel Depictions station of the RATC. In the latter, Tony famously parted the angel crowds. But let us now hear what happened afterwards. Over to you, Priscilla.'

'I'm honoured to be here,' said Priscilla. 'I want to tell you a true story that will change your view of Tony.'

Real Tony was curious at the title of the talk and what would come next. The other Tonys were stirring in their seats with anticipation.

'So we came to the 'Spirituality' sub-category,' said Priscilla after an introduction, 'and Tony took my arm. We came into the sphere and there was no one there, and he said, "I knew it! No angels bothered to stay here. At last we are alone". I didn't know what to think, but before I knew it he had kissed me on the lips and said he loved me!'

A collective gasp escaped from the audience, and Priscilla looked agitated but delighted. 'I could not reject his advances due to duty and fear, and I let him kiss me all over. He said he had had an overwhelming passion for me the moment we met. He pulled off his shirt. He was panting with excitement. He ripped off my toga and exposed my trembling body. He...'

'That's all lies!' Real Tony stood up and exclaimed, 'it's a complete and utter distortion.'

There were more gasps and exclamations from the audience. Bald Tony confidently stepped forward on the stage.

'Please, we must let the speaker finish. You know stepping out of line like this could make your archangel sanction you. Which realm do you come from?'

'I don't, I'm the Real Tony. I was there with Priscilla.'

A ripple of laughter and whistling began to emerge from the audience.

'Dear angels,' Bald Tony said, 'you know in tragic cases angels do blur reality and imagination and think they really are Tony. Please be sympathetic for this angel. We will deal with him as soon as possible.'

He clicked his fingers and four burly Tonys emerged from the shadows and headed towards Real Tony.

'I am Tony,' he yelled, and a little panicked, 'I can prove it. Albert is my Guardian angel. I did the UEWM.'

But with speed and efficiency, the burly Tonys were upon him. Bearded Tony and Female Tony looked at Real Tony sympathetically as the burly Tonys whipped a straitjacket around him and started to fit a gag. Tony knew he had only a crucial second, and bellowed, 'Gustavo!' But he was silenced and marched out towards the exit.

'Normal service is resumed,' said Bald Tony, 'and without any more disturbances or upsets let's continue.'

Priscilla looked rather shaken, but she smiled and got up.

The side door opened. It was Gustavo, who walked into the auditorium and onto the stage. The auditorium started to whistle and slow handclap.

'I'm sorry sir, but this is a private session reserved for Tonys,' Bald Tony said, irritated. 'I don't know who you are, but I'm going to ask you to leave.'

'I'm Gustavo,' he said. 'I think you know who I am. Where is Real Tony?'

There was a sudden stunned silence as Gustavo was recognised. Nobody spoke.

'Gustavo, I'm over here,' said Tony. The burly Tonys had hesitantly ungagged and then quickly released him. Gustavo walked up to him and Tony whispered, 'Gustavo, you're risking yourself in here, you've got to go quickly. I can look after myself. Just prove who I am.'

'This human,' said Gustavo to the assembled Tonys, 'has the greatest courage I've ever seen in any being. He saved my life in the tunnel of the White Mountain and he's my best friend.'

They hugged, in tears, and Tony told Gustavo to go. But a pandemonium of hysterical screaming, swooning and adoration had begun in the room, the sort of thing you'd expect if the Archangel Gabriel had suddenly walked into an aeroplane of devout Christians. Tony didn't know what he was going to say, but he quickly walked back to the stage. Bald Tony was on his knees now, all composure gone, raising his arms and wailing, 'Oh Tony, forgive me, forgive me!'

'No hard feelings,' said Tony, gently lifting him up and putting his arm round him, 'do you think I could speak?'

Slick Tony brightened up, smiling, and pointed to the lectern, which Priscilla was gripping in absolute terror.

'He's right, I lied, oh I lied!' Priscilla burst out, 'I trapped him and wanted to kiss him forever and ever. He did nothing untoward. I... I... I just wanted to be famous.'

Tony approached her and took her hands, speaking to the auditorium. 'Without Priscilla's help I would have never managed to leave the Cube after the archangel Mehi vanished,' he said kindly. 'I feel a great debt of gratitude to her.'

He took her in his arms and she looked up at him with sparkling eyes, then turned and left the stage. The audience of Tonys had become less hysterical now and were all standing, clapping and looking at him adoringly. Tony bowed, clutched his heart and gestured for them to be seated. He did not know what he was going to say, but he knew he had to speak.

'I'm sorry, but I don't want to be an idol or a reason for a catastrophe. I'm very touched by your kindness and interest in me, which I find very odd, but I think I should say a few things to set the record straight. I am and always will be just a human who fell into the Angeland realms by accident, and then simply went where I was taken in these fantastic places. I just want to get back to Earth. I never asked for the adventures I found here.

'There's clearly a lot of misconceptions about me. But there is one above all on which I want to set the record straight. When I was doing the UEWM Sue was my protector, and she died saving my life, not trying to take it.'

There were more gasps at this point and Tony could see many angels bowing their heads in anguish and shame. He hesitated before continuing.

'If you permit me to say so, there are many warped and unfair things in Angeland which are just as bad as those in Earth. But I'm pleased if my actions have somehow inspired you, broken down hierarchical barriers and created a sense of camaraderie.'

He began to relate some of his adventures in the Angeland realms, the Tonys listening to with rapt attention, whooping, hissing and applauding at appropriate moments.

All of a sudden, one of the burly Tonys burst in through the side door. 'Quick, hide!' he said, looking at the real Tony. 'The Hull Secret Policy are coming, they want to arrest you!'

Bald Tony suddenly sprang into action, asking Tony to quickly descend to the empty space in the audience that he had previously occupied. He gestured for all the Tonys to calm down and quietly took the podium. Bearded Tony put his hand on real Tony's knee, saying with a smile, 'You're better in the flesh than anything I ever imagined.' An instant later, all of the doors suddenly burst open and tens of Hull's Angels in black suits and sunglasses marched through them.

'... as we review Tony's interesting ability to extricate himself...' Slick Tony was saying from the podium. He turned calmly to face the Hull Angels.

'Hello, we are in the middle of the final session of our convention, can I help you?'

'Silence!' boomed an angel that Tony recognised, though she was now in a different guise. 'I am Eleanor, Chief of Hull's Secret Police. I bring you a message from the Archangel Natasha, Ruler of Hull. You are all guilty of hiding something.'

She paused and there was murmuring, but she raised her hand and continued. 'Angels you were, humans you are now, and angels you will become again. In Archangel Natasha's great mercy, the penalty of never being allowed to pretend to be Tony again has been set aside on the single condition that you identify the body or the living person of the human called Tony.'

Smirking at the Tonys, she walked up onto the stage and faced the audience. The real Tony looked around, and decided what he must do. There was absolute silence. He stood up and prepared to announce himself.

However, before he could do so, Bearded Tony and Female Tony stood up either side of him.

'I'm Tony!' Bearded Tony said proudly.

'I'm Tony!' Female Tony said with gusto.

'I'm Tony!' another Tony yelled, and in the space of a few seconds the whole room was full of standing, defiant lookalikes all claiming that they were the real Tony.

CHAPTER 42

Eleanor, the Chief of Hull's Secret Police, stood open-mouthed at the roaring and gesticulating crowd before her, while some of the Tonys quickly discussed their next move. Female Tony turned to Real Tony. 'The secret police angels are much stronger than us, in human form, but by working in a team many of us – and most importantly you – can get past them,' she said. 'We're going to rush them all together. Stay with me, Tony!'

Bearded Tony turned to Real Tony and shook his hand. 'It's been an honour,' he said.

Suddenly and simultaneously, as if an invisible signal had been given, the Tonys rushed at the doors in all four corners of the room. Some of the secret police were initially knocked over, but they quickly spread their wings and began hurling the Tonys back and to the side like rag dolls. But Female Tony, holding Real Tony, was right; although the secret police were laying into the Tonys, their sheer numbers and determination ensured that a steady flow were escaping out of the room.

Female Tony skilfully guided the real Tony through a door past the melee. Outside in the corridors, Tonys were running in all directions and yelling to create confusion. Female Tony steered Real Tony into a service corridor, where they passed some startled catering staff with grey clothes wheeling trays with coffee and biscuits. She took him through a kitchen where they further astonished staff labouring away with huge industrial dishwashers.

'Tony,' Female Tony said, 'you mustn't put a foot inside the Copula because they'll easily find you there. I'm a Hull angel myself, but like Gustavo I'm ready to sacrifice all for you. I used to work in the Convention Centre and I know a way out.'

They rushed along dingy, undecorated corridors and came to a lift that indicated it only went down. Female Tony pushed the button to call it and they stepped inside.

'This is dangerous, but it's the only path open to you, and crucially there are no cameras,' Female Tony said, keeping the door open. 'The main underfloor corridor will take you to Downstreet, where you can try to make your way to the airport. Keep hidden, and whatever you do don't go into any rooms or go down any lower than level minus one. Good luck Tony, you're better than any angel or archangel to me.'

They hugged, and she pushed the 'minus one' button and stepped out of the lift, watching him wistfully. The doors closed.

The lift, which had buttons going down to minus nine, seemed to descend for some time before it pinged and the doors opened into a similar dingy undecorated corridor at floor minus one. It led away from the lift doors, with occasional doors dotted along or corridors going off perpendicularly. Tony started to run down the main corridor, memories of the UEWM coming back to him. There were no mountain vistas here, just mustiness and oppression. Tony saw that the doors each had a larger number at the top, all beginning with '1' followed by nine numbers or letters. Underneath each, in much smaller numbers, there were anything from one to several hundred nine-figure codes.

Tony had been running for about 10 minutes when he heard a voice approaching from a side corridor ahead. He stopped to turn back, but from behind him in another side corridor he heard another voice approaching. He was trapped, and the only alternative to discovery was a double door to his right, which had 1.NZ195845D followed by hundreds of other numbers on it. Taking a deep breath, he opened the door, stepped in and gently closed it behind him.

The room was the size of a football pitch, but filled with rows and rows of small cubicles, each with a person in grey sitting and speaking, which created waves of babbling. Everyone had a nine-figure code on his or her back. Tony had the impression that it was a call centre, but realised that there were no telephones. No one had noticed him, and as he approached he saw that most of the people were elderly and that each was fixated in a world of his or her own.

'I shouldn't have said that,' one woman was saying. 'Oh goodness, how it gnaws at me that I never apologised to Jean.'

'I hit him. How could I do that to my own son?' a man next door to her was saying.

Tony realised that all the people in the room were expressing regret for something that they had done, mostly in a circular and very anguished way. He tried approaching and even lightly shaking or pulling people away from their cubicles, but they all ignored him, quickly returning to their monologue.

Then the door by which he had entered opened and two angels in black suits entered, each driving what looked like a big golf buggy. One had six people in grey sitting on it, and the other was empty.

The angel who was driving the empty buggy checked a list and then guided a person from a cubicle into his buggy. 'So,

Fuscus,' he said, 'what chance do you think we've got in the Angel Cup Final? Rupa and Cristiana were pretty strong in the Downstreet–Soccer match. And given that Rita is going to be absent, it'll be a walkover, don't you think?'

'You know me, Arun,' Fuscus replied, 'I just do my job. I'm content moving my chariots around on level one and I'm not too bothered about the football or these fantastic stories about this human called Tony. I think angels get far too fanatical and excited these days. I mean, as long as I come to work every day and there's an eclipse over Hull, that's all I need.'

As he talked, Fuscus led one of the people in his buggy to the vacant spot that Arun had created. They worked together, methodically removing one person from each cubicle and replacing them with another. However, they were now approaching the spot where Tony had hidden himself. He looked around and saw there was another door, also with hundreds of nine-figure codes. Timing his moves carefully, Tony waited for Arun and Fuscus to turn the other way and then opened the door and slipped behind it.

A blast of noise and the smell of stale sweat hit Tony as he entered the new room, which was full of hundreds more people in grey tracksuits vigorously training on a variety of cycling, running, rowing and other exercise machines. 'Water, water!' some were panting. All looked worn-down and zombie like. As in the previous room, none acknowledged Tony. He spoke to some of them and even pulled a couple who seemed in a particularly bad state off their machines, but they all stumbled back to their machines and restarted without seeming to see him.

Trying to keep his sense of direction, Tony passed right through the room and saw three more doors at the other end, each with just one nine-figure code on it. He entered the middle one, and found himself in a small steam room in which there was a man with long hair holding a wet towel.

'Must dry my hair,' the man said, 'it'll be fine soon.'

The man continued to murmur and rub his wet hair ineffectually with the towel. Like all the other people in grey Tony had met, the man did not appear to realise he was there. Tony even took the towel from the man and went outside and shut the door, but the man followed him, wrestled the towel back as if Tony was a disobedient towel rack, and returned to his room.

Tony found all this very creepy. He tried the left-hand door and found a woman facing a washing machine the height of a building. Inside the massive open drum, there were thousands and thousands of damp socks.

'Got to get them into pairs,' the woman was saying. She was wading through socks of all sorts of patterns and colours. Tony stepped back and closed the door. The people on the gym machines were still exercising, furiously and exhaustedly.

Then Tony entered the right-hand door. The tick-tock of thousands of clocks greeted him as he entered, and he realised he was in a large circular room with cuckoo clocks lined up around the edge. A man was hurrying round the room, attending to each clock in turn by pulling up its weights or moving its hands forward. He cursed as he turned the minute hand of one of the clocks round and round almost twelve times, gasping, 'Not another fast one!'

He stopped the pendulum, removed a weight and then adjusted the wooden leaf on the base of the pendulum before replacing the weight and starting the clock again. Suddenly, one of the clocks chimed 'cuckoo' and then others followed, one at a time at first before building to a crescendo and then slowly dying away. 'Six minutes difference!' the man cried in anguish, and continued desperately on his circuit.

Tony gently retreated into the exercise machine room, only to find Fuscus and Arun waiting for him. 'Cuckoo, sunshine!' said Fuscus. He and Arun handcuffed and grasped Tony perfunctorily, taping his mouth and covering his head with a hood.

'He's not one of ours,' said Arun examining his back. 'He must have taken a wrong turn in Downstreet or perhaps, by the look of him, he's a Tony impersonator.'

'Well, whoever he is, it never rains but it pours,' said Fuscus. 'I don't have to put anyone in jail for years and then three turn up almost all at the same time.'

Tony was led to one of the golf buggies and driven for some time. Then he was led down a short flight of stairs; there was a jingle of keys and a clank as a door was opened. The hood and tape were removed and he was thrust into a cell. Fuscus waved goodbye to him as he wandered up the stairs.

'Now be good,' he said, 'I need to go and do some real work.' The door slammed and the key was turned.

Tony saw he was in one of two grim jail cells separated by iron bars. He turned to see a female figure in the shadows and was shocked to realise it was Rita. She was so bloody and beaten that she was almost unrecognisable.

'Hello poppet,' said Fifi's voice gaily from the other cell. 'So glad you could join the party.'

CHAPTER 43

'Goodness, Rita, what's happened to you?' Tony asked, but she put her face in her hands and her body began to heave with sobs.

'What's going on?' Tony said, turning to look at Fifi in the other cell. Fifi's cream garments were in a filthy state, and the veil she wore over her face was covered with cobwebs so Tony could only make out her face. She gently lifted it off and grasped his hand between the bars. The familiar body odours wafted through the bars.

'I've had too many adventures, poppet, and seen too many prisons,' she said. 'But now I've seen too much. One moment the best footballer in the Angeland realms arrives beaten up and only hours before the Angel Cup Final, and then the next moment in comes the human who's just about to create a catastrophe. I mean, you haven't come up with a solution to any of this, have you?'

'Erm, no.'

'Well, I'm going to have a nap then. I'll let the two of you formulate the miracle we all need in the meantime.'

'Wait!' Tony cried. But Fifi had retreated onto the bed in the corner of her cell, where she lay down and very quickly started to snore.

Rita had followed the conversation, and she stopped sobbing. She looked up at Tony.

'I never realised how hard it was to be a human, to be so fragile and feel such a sense of despair,' she said. 'I'm sorry for everything you must have had to endure during your time here. I mean I've done the UEWM several times of course, but I've never received physical and mental abuse like this.'

Tony reached for a nearby bucket of water and ripped off a corner of his tracksuit top, which seemed to be the cleanest thing around. Then he sat down next to her and started to gently wash her face.

'I saw you at the Soccer–Downstreet match,' he said. 'You were fearless and brilliant. I would be inspired if I was on your team.'

Rita winced slightly as Tony dabbed at her face, taking away the blood and revealing a slightly cleaner face which gradually lit up as she smiled at him, battered but defiant.

'Tell me about yourself,' Rita asked. 'I want to hear about the real Tony, not the one in all the made-up stories.'

'Well, you know I don't have memories of Earth,' said Tony, bowing his head. 'They begin with me sitting on the aeroplane next to someone I think I was in love with. My biggest regret is that I don't remember her.'

'I'm so sorry, Tony,' Rita said.

Tony told her about his adventures in Angeland. When he finally paused, she began telling him about herself, about the intensive training and selection that angel footballers were subjected to, and how she had admired great footballers before her, like Ruth. As a resident of Angeland, she remembered when it was smaller, and how the great architect Archangel Mehi had overseen the construction of the modern buildings.

Their conversation weaved in and out and back and forth in a comfortable, complementary fashion. Tony found it was easy to tell her everything, even revealing his unusual tryst with Natasha, which horrified Rita.

'You're ready for the Angeland Cup Final,' said Tony when Rita had finished attending to her wounds. This was far from the truth, but she did look a lot more presentable. She laughed.

Tony realised that what must have been an hour and a half had seemed to pass in a matter of minutes. 'I really enjoy talking to you, Rita,' he said.

'Me too, Tony,' said Rita. 'Despite learning about all the bad things you've experienced. You've cheered me up no end.'

The sound of keys turning broke their conversation. With a clunk the door opened and Fuscus walked in. 'Eleanor, the Chief of the Secret Police herself, is interested in you, sunshine, and she's sending some agents down to check up on you,' he said to Tony. 'They'll be along in ten minutes. It's a rare treat for Fuscus to receive so much attention.'

Fifi had woken up and wandered into the centre of her cell. 'Poppet, I need you to do something,' she said to Tony.

'Quiet now, the rest of you,' Fuscus said. 'No talking!'

'Just repeat after me but address the nice man,' Fifi said, looking rather bored.

'I'm going to have to sanction you if you say anything more,' said Fuscus, reaching towards a menacing-looking spear in the corner of the cell.

Fifi nodded at Tony. 'I'm going to open the cell door,' she said.

Tony paused and looked at Rita, who looked as perplexed as he felt, but he turned to Fuscus and repeated, 'I'm going to open the cell door.'

Fuscus put the spear down, sat on a chair and burst out laughing. 'I'm going to open the cell door!' he chortled. 'I'm going to open the cell door!' Then he reached for his keys, unlocked Tony and Rita's cell and opened the door, all the while continuing to laugh to himself.

Fifi looked at Tony again. 'The prisoners will leave the cell, I am going to take their place, lock the cell, hand the keys to the nice lady in the other cell, and then forget everything that has happened,' said Fifi.

It was a bit of a mouthful, but Tony managed to repeat it to Fuscus, who all the while had his arms folded and was looking bombastically at him.

'The prisoners will leave the cell, I am going to take their place, lock the cell, hand the keys to the nice lady in the other cell, and then forget everything that has happened,' Fuscus repeated. Then he started to do exactly as Fifi had bidden. Before they knew what had happened, Tony, Rita and Fifi had left their cells and Fifi had locked Fuscus up. He was still hooting with laughter.

'You'll have to teach me that trick one day,' said Tony to Fifi.

'It's just copying what happens in movie franchises if they get too long,' she said, 'in general, uninspiring recycling playing on overhyped nostalgia, something that Angeland could have done without.'

She went to the corner of the room, where there were some lockers, and retrieved a rucksack.

'Why, that's my rucksack!' said Tony with a start. 'From the UEWM.'

'Yes, you lost it in PirogRus and I picked it up. It's got vital things like spare socks and sports tape. Unfortunately no suntan lotion, which I think it's always useful to have, just in case.'

Tony looked in it and saw some energy snacks and a torch at the top. 'Perfect, Fifi!' he said, handing round the snacks.

'Much as I know this will sadden you, here is not the place to have our picnic,' said Fifi. 'I'm heading Hullward and I think

you need to go in the opposite direction, towards Downstreet.'
With a cursory wave, she mounted the golf caddy outside the
room and headed away down the corridor.

'Yum,' said Rita, munching on the energy snack. 'I must
say, I'm starting to enjoy being in your strange adventures Tony.
Did you know that Fifi is a renegade angel from Angeland? She
said she was a big fan of mine.'

'We'd best not disappoint her and make sure you get to the
match,' said Tony, and they jogged down the corridor. They
didn't come across anyone else in the corridor, which began to
slope upwards until soon they could smell the sea. They came
to a large, rather rusty door and pushed it open.

'We're in an aquarium!' Tony exclaimed.

The room they had entered contained modest, dully-
illuminated tanks with rather grey-looking fish and a mournful-
looking dolphin as well as a seal. There was a clanking noise,
and they looked behind them to see that the door they had
come had closed, leaving an almost invisible joint on the white
wall as the only evidence it was there.

'Well, I'm not sure if we want to go back,' said Tony, but
he carefully got his bearings in case they needed to return.
'Let's see what we find outside.'

They crept out of a back door of the aquarium onto a jetty
and found themselves outside in the torrid heat. Above there
was the eclipse; dark, salty water lapped below.

'I'm so pleased to be outside at last,' said Rita, 'although
you said we need to get across town and then to the airport.'

Tony nodded. 'This must be the Umbro estuary which I
saw from the top of the Soccosphere. Look, I think that's dawn
over there, the sun is breaking through on the Comba Vasta.'

They looked for a moment and then turned away from
the jetty towards the centre of Downstreet. It was rather an
unassuming place, with brick buildings generally three or four
storeys high. They turned and saw the sign which read 'The

Abyss Aquarium, Closed until Further Notice'. Scatterings of people in grey were furtively moving around the streets and there was an intangible oppressiveness.

They saw an illuminated shop in the distance and approached it. It was called 'SlowSilver' and the shiny front with glittering signs read 'Join our loyalty club', 'The home of great tournaments' and 'The VIP experience'. A slow but steady stream of people in grey was going in and out.

'Let's take a look,' said Tony. Inside, there were arrays of slot machines chiming and flashing away, with the odd chunka-chunka noise of coins dropping. There was a depressing, stifling air and the people played soullessly, without any interaction between them.

'What a horrible place,' said Rita, and Tony nodded. They left, continuing through the dimly-lit streets. They passed an old woman sweeping the road, and unlike the other people they had seen, she looked up and spoke to them.

'Hello my dears. Looking for somewhere to stay the night? I've got a couple of beds free – only three *wings* each.'

'Let's have a peek,' said Tony, taking Rita's hand and indicating that they should stay close.

'I had to stop working in the kitchens in Hull because of my bad knees,' the old woman said, 'so I've kept everything spick and span here in Hope House.'

'Hope House' was indeed written on the entrance to the house, which had nothing but a few blackened tree stumps in the front garden. They entered the hall and looked into the front room, which had about ten triple-level bunk beds crammed in, some occupied by sleeping figures and others coughing or snoring. A man was sitting on his bed shooting up.

'That's the luxury room,' she said. 'The other ones at the back have smaller beds and no windows, and there's fifty people per toilet rather than thirty down here. Two *wings*, if that interests you.'

'No,' said Tony, 'actually, I think we'll be on our way.'

'OK love, well good luck,' the old lady said. 'Most of the others don't rent the beds for the full four hours, mind, so you're missing a good deal here. The clientele also tend to be a bit more upmarket, you know, the ones who work in Astroprata.'

'Tell me,' Tony said with sudden interest, 'What's your name and where do you come from?'

'It's been a very long time since someone asked me that. But I've had a bit more time to reflect since my knees gave way. My name begins with an E, I think it was Edwina. I think I came from a place beginning with 'Lon', but it seems so far away.'

'London?' enquired Tony.

'Yes, that's it,' Edwina said, 'London. West Ham, I remember now. I recall I came down somewhere or other to get to Hull but I can't remember the route. Anyhow,' she wheezed, 'my asthma is playing up so you'll have to excuse me if you're not interested in a bed. The best place for good clean fun in town is The Fug, in the direction you're going, but you might be a bit young for that.'

'OK, we'll be off then. Thank you, Edwina.'

Rita and Tony were quickly on their way through the streets again. 'What was all that about?' Rita asked.

'You know they say that angels that fail the UEWM get sent here, or PirogRus, to work in human form as 'support workers' while they wait to re-take the event at the White Mountain' said Tony.

'Yes of course,' said Rita, 'every angel knows that.'

'It seems many of them were not angels in the first place.'

CHAPTER 44

They continued in silence until they came across a more imposing building, with two towers and a statue of a headless woman on the top of the facade. A sign read 'The fug'; it had clearly once been 'The Refuge' but the 'R' and two 'e's had long since fallen off. A poster, looking fresh compared to everything else, announced, 'One night only: Frederica Arder'.

'I've seen her before,' said Tony, 'come on, let's go in.'

Memories of the Hefyn Shangri-La dancehall, animated with twirling and swinging energetic young people, came flooding back to Tony. Inside the Fug, the dancehall was fusty and unadorned, and there were four very elderly couples dancing. On the stage, there was a band of four musicians in shiny clothes. Frederica Arder was in the spotlight. If she recognised Tony, she did not make any sign of doing so.

'Ladies and gentlemen, it always gives me and my band great pleasure to play a few numbers in Downstreet before heading into Hull. This first song is one of my favourites.'

Tony had positioned Rita and himself in an open part of the dance floor and she was looking quizzically at him. 'But

I've never danced,' she pleaded, looking completely out of place.

The music started and Tony reassured her, 'I'm no good either, but just follow my steps and we'll be as bad as each other.'

Hefyn, I'm in Hefyn
And I have a fervour such that I can't sleep
But I reach the ecstasy I want to keep

Tony and Rita danced, slowly at first but with every-increasing confidence in their own performance, and soon Rita found herself cheek to cheek with Tony.

And the worries seeming close along my way
Disappear like chances taken through the day

Round and round they went, until suddenly, unable to help themselves, they burst out laughing and beamed with pleasure as everything around them seemed to fall away into insignificance.

Oh I love to take a challenge
Climbing up so very high
But it's so much more of a delight
When it's in your arms I fly

The music stopped and they looked at each other in a strange kind of wonder. Tony leant towards her and whispered in her ear.

'That was wonderful, Rita,' he said, and kissed her neck.

They both looked up and saw the dilapidated interior of the building with the other couples still tottering around. Tony caught Frederica's eye and she winked at him.

'We've got to go, Rita,' he said, suddenly remembering the direction in which they had been heading. 'I'm very sorry, but we can't dance any more. Not tonight at least'.

They left the Fug and were hardly aware of how perfectly naturally they held hands as they walked together. 'There's where we need to go,' Tony said, pointing to the airport.

They came to the outskirts of Downstreet and saw the lights of the airport neatly arranged in the distance. There did not appear to be any road there from Downstreet, so Tony retrieved his torch and they began to wander towards the airport through the desert landscape with nothing but sand, gravel and stunted scrub to show the way. It was quite hard going, and without the torch they would have fallen into one of the many deep gulleys and thorny patches that dotted the landscape.

'Tony,' Rita said, 'I think there's something out there, some animal. Did you hear panting and rustling? I think there's two of them.'

Tony turned his torch in the direction of the movement and a hundred metres distant saw two pairs of dark oval eyes, twitching whiskers and big long black ears.

'My goodness,' he said, 'It's Lapindee and Lapindum.'

The giant black rabbits reared up, thumping their black legs, snorting triumphantly and shaking the ground like a mini earthquake as they approached the objects of their anal desire. Tony wondered desperately what could save them, and in an instinctive reaction slipped off his rucksack and reached inside. Down past his spare socks and batteries, he touched the bottom and found something smooth and fluffy.

'Tony go go with bunny!' Michelle's instruction came to him as if from nowhere. He remembered the moment when he had been on the White Mountain and stopped to receive something from the Archangel. He pulled out her floppy bunny and held it aloft.

With ear-splitting squeals the giant black rabbits reared up to avoid the fluffy toy, creating a cloud of dust that enveloped both Tony and Rita. There was the sound of awful crunching. It was impossible to see what had happened, but split seconds afterwards Lapindee and Lapindum were fleeing in terror towards the Umbro estuary. There were two splashes in quick succession, followed by sounds of irregular but desperate efforts to swim and shrill cries of pain. Gradually the sounds diminished into the background.

'Tony, Tony, are you OK?' said a concerned Rita, as the dust cleared.

'All here in one piece, but we've lost our torch I'm afraid,' Tony responded.

'Oh Tony, I was so worried that I'd lose you. I've never met anyone like you, anyone who makes me feel the way I do,' she said, her words breaking with emotion. They were sitting opposite each other and she put her face close to his. 'It's against all angel taboos but I just can't help myself,' she said tenderly, his face in her hands. 'Everything in my soul is forcing me to proclaim this. Tony, I lo…'

There was a clap of thunder, as if something had broken the sound barrier. Rita was silenced, and they leant back and looked up. The robes and majestic wings of the Archangel Gabriel were perfectly silhouetted against the eclipse in the sky. He landed slowly and deliberately in front of them.

'Well, well, well. I expect a routine mission to retrieve the lost artefact of the Archangel Michelle, and lo and behold I find not only Angeland's missing striker but the missing human of the moment.' Tony and Rita looked at him, astonished.

'I think I need some heroic music to match my mood,' he continued. He put his thumb and forefinger in his mouth and gave a penetrating whistle. Almost immediately, there was a further series of sound-barrier thumps and an orchestra of angels surrounded Gabriel, hovering around him with their instruments in anticipation.

'The theme tune to *Indiana Jones*,' he said, 'one of my favourites, and nice and rousing,' and the orchestra began to play.

'Let's see,' he said, picking up the floppy bunny, 'this artefact is dusty. Absolute sacrilege! What in the name of A1 were you doing with it?'

Tony opened his mouth to speak, but like lightning Gabriel's hand popped out and grabbed his tongue. 'Ungh ungh!' gasped Tony, unable to do anything against Gabriel's strength, although for a surreal moment he recognised a pattern in the Archangel's musical taste; everything began with dramatic horn playing.

'Archangel Gabriel, we are forever in your debt for finding us,' Rita said falteringly, looking at Tony with concern.

'How dare you speak to an archangel without permission!' roared Gabriel. With the dexterity of a conjurer, using the hand not attached to Tony's tongue, he seemed to magic some white duct tape out of thin air. He tore off a piece and pasted it over Rita's mouth, then used several more pieces to bind her arms and legs. She wriggled helplessly on the ground.

'As you do not have an archangel, it falls to me to discipline you, and in my benevolence I am treating you kindly,' Gabriel said to Rita, as the music bounced along. 'Now, I think finally my luck has turned. After months of ignominy while you, Tony, had the temerity to be more popular than me, I find myself in the fortunate situation of being in Hull with you.'

Gabriel lifted Tony up by his tongue with one hand, suspending him off the ground. A knife appeared in the other, and with a quick movement Gabriel sliced off Tony's tongue at the root.

Rita's eyes bulged in horror and filled with tears. She struggled and rolled around ineffectually.

'Now, now,' Gabriel said, addressing the orchestra, 'I picked up at least five wrong notes then. Whoever plays the next one gets demoted. You all know how many Poste angels are on the waiting list.' He turned to Rita, who was whimpering piteously, and said patronizingly, 'Of course I'm going to cauterize it.'

He whipped out a tool which looked like a fat pen, and again with great skill held Tony's bloody mouth open. With surgical precision he thrust the instrument inside, and Tony screamed in agony a second time.

'Now keep quiet please,' said Gabriel to Tony, producing more white duct tape to paste over his mouth and bind him up in the same way as Rita. 'There we are, the same class of travel for everyone. Then reflectively he added, 'Of course I can count on you to keep mum Tony, but let's work together to ensure your silence. Trust me, I'm the foremost expert in communication.'

Gabriel then grasped each of Tony's hands and systematically broke all the bones, including those in his wrists. 'Righto,' Gabriel said, 'I'm sure that feels a lot better.'

With the music still playing, he picked up Tony's ankle in one hand and Rita's in the other, and they flew at great speed over the Umbro and out into the sunshine over the Comba Vasta. Down in the distance on the floor of the canyon, two black shapes could be seen running desperately away from Hull.

Tony was conscious of very little during the time he was being carried by Gabriel, because he was experiencing physical pain that he had never imagined possible. Every now and then as his body twirled upside down he caught a glimpse of Rita, or during a romantic moment of the music he found that he was being bashed against her.

They passed through what seemed like dense clouds for a long time, and then suddenly the clouds parted to reveal far below a football stadium spanned by an enormous arc.

Gabriel announced in jolly tones, 'Here we are angel and gentleman, the first port of call.'

When he turned them both the right way up, Tony saw that Rita had suddenly returned to perfect form. Her previously blood-stained and torn grey football strip was now unblemished and shining white.

'Now, my dear Rita,' Gabriel said menacingly, 'you're going to play as every dutiful angel should and say nothing about this, because if you do, our human friend might have an accident. Unfortunately they are quite common at this height.'

Gabriel ripped off the duct tape from both of them and then descended towards the centre of the Waldgebiet Stadium. It was filling up, about half full, and there were thousands of angels outside. Some of those on the ground caught sight of Gabriel descending with Rita and Tony gently propped up in his arms and pointed up, so that very soon the whole crowd was transfixed by the sight of the archangel's elegant descent, to the accompaniment of rousing music from his orchestra. There were shrieks and cheers of delight, and a chorus of cries of 'Gabriel, Gabriel!' resonated up to them.

By the time Gabriel landed, the entire Angeland team had run out to receive Rita, greeting her with tears and yells of delight. But as they took her away on their shoulders with Gabriel smiling and waving munificently, she could only stare back at Tony, her face a picture of desolation.

Gabriel raised Tony's arm so it looked as if they were both saluting in triumph, and then flew them round and round the stadium, waving and nodding graciously at the adoring angels below. Tony, completely exhausted, did not have the energy to do anything. He could only think of Rita's face as they had left.

CHAPTER 45

Natasha

I was pleased that they recovered my gargoyle, which I thought might have smashed on the way down. However I was not a happy bunny. Never again will I have a Tony in Hull. For their own benefit, of course – I'll throw the next one I see out of a high building, just like last time. My entire secret police force was kept busy for hours trying to round up all the wayward Tonys. Then to cap it all I heard that Fuscus had lost selective parts of his memory. First he was looking after our sporting guest, and then a Tony who Fuscus said he'd captured for the secret police an hour before. Worst of all Lapindee and Lapindum, who'd I'd let recuperate nicely by the airport, were last seen running directly away from Hull and not responding to any entreaties to return. The Hull supporters will be mortified not to see their favourite mascots for the final.

So I had to send a message to the other archangels ahead of the extraordinary CRAP that Tony should be added to the missing list, in addition to Rita, who had been up there for a week. So humiliating, as he was in my care.

I attended the extraordinary CRAP with the sole issue of addressing what we should do with Tony. Of course I'd had my plan A and plan B dashed, and either would have solved everything perfectly, but like everyone I knew that a missing Tony with Gaby's eyelash in him would lead to the catastrophic end of all of the Angeland realms 24 minutes into the Angel Cup final. If we'd had Tony in the same state in our hands, we would have thrown him into Heaven and locked the key and watch that implode. It makes me wonder what He would have done.

Then as I'm passing through the reception of the D-F on my way up to the Jardim do Ceu, who do I see on the TV screens showing breaking news but Gaby, like a smug cockerel ready to say cock-a-doodle-bloody-do, with Tony in one arm and Rita in the other. The vain bastard was lapping up all the adulation and as I took the lift up I steeled myself.

'Fellow archangels,' said Gaby, flying in through the side entrance of the Jardim, 'we thought all was lost without Tony when he went missing in Hull.' He sat him down on a seat at the back of the room. 'Behold! The barbarity that we suspected takes place in Hull is horrifically demonstrated!' he said. Then Gaby opened Tony's mouth and showed us his battered hands. Tony was trying ineffectually to say something, but he was so pathetically weak that he just sat there like a rag doll. All eyes turned on me and I was caught out for a second. I agreed it was absolutely terrible, but I couldn't really deny it had happened in Hull, and said I would expend every effort to root out the culprit. And, as a note to self, congratulate that genius who did such a good piece of work.

Naturally Sandeepa started weeping away, pawing, stroking and cooing at Tony. Michelle got down from her baby chair and wordlessly crawled to Tony and stood up and hugged his leg. Gaby gamely gave her floppy bunny to her – it looked a bit brown, which is maybe why she threw it across the room. Mehi, in his straitjacket, was looking as unperturbed as he had been since his breakdown.

'We are so sorry for everything you've suffered, Tony,' Ray chimed up, and then indicated to all of us to assemble around the table. 'By some miracle, we have Tony with us and so now at least we can find a concrete solution, but one which is likely to test our principles like nothing else before,' Ray continued. I picked up Michelle and put her on my knee.

'We have Tony with us,' Ray said, and addressed him. 'It is right and proper that you should hear us and give us your choice.'

Then Ray talked about the two options open to us. The first was making him immortal, but at a terrible price as he hadn't been in the Angeland realms long enough to transform properly, meaning he would effectively lose his mind and be able to focus on only one thing. Ray shot a glance at Yuri, who had said nothing all along and was scowling. None of them, apart from our mute chum Tony, knew about my clever plan A, which I thought was far more humane and utilitarian than Yuri's botched idea. I mean, given the choice between having an immortal who's good for nothing else but signing books, compared to an immortal dream lover who can fulfil all your sexual wishes on demand, after whom every angel lusts after, I feel there's hardly any competition. Furthermore he would have had more or less the same single-minded desire as most men on Earth, so it would have all have been hunky-dory.

It was all very melodramatic, particularly when Ray talked about the option to end Tony's life, which no angel could ever imagine doing voluntarily. He went on about the ethics of it all and what He, A1, would have said, and then made as if to ask Tony to indicate what he'd prefer (although even I wouldn't want to be made immortal in the state he was in).

But I saw it was the moment and seized the floor and persuaded them all to come quickly to a vote, before we kept on talking until the Angeland realms came to a catastrophic end. I knew that Sandeepa and Michelle wouldn't vote to end Tony's life but I could see Ray was teetering with the idea. That would have given us a 4-2 majority in the absence of Mehi, who was smiling detachedly at all of this. I spoke about the needs of the one having to be sacrificed to the needs of the many, said we needed to make difficult and painful decisions sometimes, and we could build new, better realms of Angeland. I could see Yuri and particularly Gaby looking jealously at me, but I knew that if I managed to swing this vote I'd be in a good position to make a much bolder move to head the archangels. When Ray began nodding sombrely at my suggestions I knew I had it in the bag, I just needed to propose the vote.

Then I felt something warm on me and realised that Michelle's nappy had leaked, and I was covered with toddler piss. Michelle screamed and then Gaby stood up to continue my line of argument, but Ray suddenly seemed to have a change of mood. He tried to say something but got drowned out as Sandeepa insisted on speaking, and then we were all speaking or screaming or shouting, and we went round and round for minutes at a time. Mehi continued to smile his little smile and I turned for a moment to His empty chair, remembering things were always a lot more ordered when He was around.

Then from nowhere Tony got up from his chair and walked up to the table. He had a little black hair covered in mucus in his hand, which he placed on the round table.

'It's your eyelash, Gaby,' said Ray, breaking the silence.

Sandeepa held Tony and we all looked at him. Tears were rolling down his cheeks and there was terrible sadness in his eyes.

'Thank goodness,' said Gaby, gently picking it up and wiping it carefully before removing his false eyelash and pinning the real one on. 'Quindecillions of angels will be grateful to be able to see the entirety of the Angel Cup Final and not just part of the first half. Which I'm off to see. I think the meeting is adjourned.'

'So,' said Yuri, 'Tony's now got an hour or two before he reverts to human time. I suspect it's still too much of a risk to send him to Heaven, and he won't have much fun in the state he's in anyway. So we just need to push him through the HARP and then we'll be done with things. But we don't know if he'll end up on Earth in this state, given there's no precedent. It's a shame Mehi's not compos mentis enough to tell us.'

Then Yuri left and I asked the question I'd been waiting to put to Sandeepa. 'What finally shifted the eyelash when no archangel or any other effort could do it?'

'It is a force that is greater than all of us,' Sandeepa said, stroking Tony's head, 'It must be love.'

'OK, I'm off for the game then,' I said calmly. Of course I was hiding my whoopie-doopie internal celebration.

Albert, Tony's guardian angel, looked pretty upset as I passed him coming out of the lift. When the doors closed, I yelped with joy. I knew it was a long shot, but I'm not an archangel for nothing, and I'd have the full proof before me as the game unfolded. I mean, who else, when plan A and plan B have failed, has a great plan C?

CHAPTER 46

Sandeepa, Albert and Tony remained in the Jardim do Céu.

'I'm so sorry, Tony,' Sandeepa said, 'at the end of this we've failed you. And you've saved us and you can't tell us why. When you are back on Earth, you'll forget all this. But you've touched many hearts here in Angeland. Albert will take you to the HARP, and then continue to watch over you. Goodbye Tony.'

They embraced and Albert and Tony left together, taking the same path in reverse that they had when Tony had arrived, a taxi to Angelgate station, then the Subsolo towards Angelham. The Subsolo was virtually empty, and as the train rattled along Tony and Albert sat in silence.

Albert pulled out his oticel and tried ineffectually to get a signal to see the live stream of the Final, but as they passed the station Estrada Padeiro, the old angel noted that they would soon be out of the tunnel.

'Aha, it's the end of the opening ceremony,' said Albert as he got a signal. There was a blonde angel singing the end of an aria that was instantly evocative. 'It's been a favourite in

Angeland for a long time,' Albert said, 'but the words are a bit mysterious, and no one knows what they mean.'

Then the game kicked off, and Tony could see Rita, just a centimetre high on the screen. It soon became clear that she was playing very poorly, and moving lethargically around the pitch. She made a few errors and then made a terrible pass that was intercepted by Cristiana and despatched into the Angeland net.

'It's very one-sided,' said Albert, 'but there are all sorts of rumours about Rita's disappearance. She must be out of training.'

Tony also saw Natasha at the side of the pitch, egging on her Hull players. Dotted around the sides of the pitch were 'GO HULL' placards with the head and shoulders of a life-size Natasha on each.

As they approached Waldgebietpark station Rita once again made an error that let in a goal, and it was two-nil.

'They'll take Rita off at this rate,' said Albert. 'Unthinkable!'

The siren for the doors to close sounded and Tony looked up. He could see the Waldgebiet Stadium in the distance, and it was possible to pick up the roars of the crowd. He suddenly fell back into his seat, as for a second the train seemed to lurch forward.

'It's happening sooner than expected,' said Albert. 'You're adjusting to human time now that you are no longer part-angel. You'll get the sensation that time is fast-forwarding more and more. I doubt at this rate we'll get to the HARP before you fall into a stasis.'

The train was about to leave the station when Tony stood up again, went to the emergency stop button and not having the use of his hands, somehow managed to push it with his nose. The train slammed to a stop and Tony gesticulated wildly that he wanted to go to the Stadium.

The voice of the train driver came over the intercom. 'What's the matter?'

There was a pause, and Albert responded, 'This is Albert, I'm here with Tony. Please let us out so we can go to the Stadium.'

'Well bless my lucky stars for having Tony on my train. Can I get an autograph?' the driver said, and the doors opened.

'This is completely against protocol,' said Albert, who had certainly not stopped just to allow Tony to sign an autograph and was now flying towards the Stadium with Tony in his arms. 'Only archangels or choirs have the right to fly over Angeland. But I'm sure Sandeepa will support me. After all, I already brought you to Angeland when I shouldn't have done, and I don't see anything more that could go wrong at this stage.'

Albert paused and looked at Tony, whose eyes were occasionally blank as he began to slip into human time. 'After all,' said Albert, suddenly very emotional, 'there's not much time left before you leave us.'

To avoid attention, Albert came in carefully over the top edge of the Stadium and then slipped behind the crowds so they were behind the top row of seats. The stadium was full and the roar of the crowd was intense. Albert landed and gently held up Tony so he wouldn't fall, and they looked down at the game.

'Hello poppet, I knew you'd make it,' called Fifi, who had suddenly appeared from the shadows behind. Ignoring his physical state, she pointed at Rita on the pitch. 'Look, my favourite player,' she said. 'Let's wave and show our support.' She signalled for Albert and Tony to wave all together.

Down on the pitch, Rita turned in their direction as she plodded mechanically over the pitch after yet another ineffectual move. Her teammates were looking at her in despair, and the Angeland assistant coach seemed to be preparing a substitution. Then she looked up at the crowd, high, high in the corner of the Stadium.

'She saw us,' said Fifi, and started gabbling away to Albert about the fact that she had shared a jail cell with her. Her voice faded, as his attention was elsewhere. Tony looked down at Rita, and Rita looked up at Tony. Suddenly the aria he had heard at the start of the match came back to him. The words were different from the version he knew, and in a different language, but he suddenly understood.

Nobody shall rest!
Nobody shall rest!

Rita straightened up.

Even he, mortal,
Watches the moon

She turned back towards her goal, where Hull were mounting an attack on the edge of the area, stealing the ball from an unsuspecting Cristiana.

Which hides ardour and hope
And love within,

Returning towards the opposition goal, she tackled her way past three Hull players, flicked up the ball, and with an exquisite volley smashed the ball past Rupa into the net.

And the void will be illuminated
Secrets immortals will never know, no, no
And lips one day
Will cast shadow and silence

Running away from the goal, the faces of her teammates and the Angeland crowd turned from joy to incredulity as she emotionlessly pulled off her shirt and the referee gave her a yellow card.

Aside and bring forth the sun
With full desire

Hull kicked off and within seconds Rita had stolen the ball away. From behind the halfway line, she kicked it in a high arc that beat Rupa and went into the corner of the net. She stared up at Tony for a moment.

Everyone will know his name
He must, alas, fade and slow

She pulled off her shirt again, as if she was doing so at the end of the game, and most of the players stood motionless as the referee approached and gave her a second yellow card, followed by a red card.

Vanish, gloom!
Move on, moon!
Move on, moon!

As Rita left the pitch she picked up one of the advertising hoardings with 'GO HULL' on it, and as she passed Natasha she smashed it over the archangel's head. Natasha slumped to the floor, and her dazed head popped through exactly where the photograph of her head had been.

At dawn, love!

Rita moved away the side of the pitch and ascended the stairs in front of Tony.

Love!

Love!

'A red card, assault on an archangel and doing that to a human, in plain view of the whole of the Angeland realms,' Fifi was saying. 'That makes her even more renegade than me.'

'I think we've lost him,' said Albert gently. Tony's eyes flickered and went into a permanent glaze, as angel time turned into an unseeable blur and he returned irreversibly to human time.

—— * ——

As Albert heaved Tony into the HARP a little later, the guardian angel reflected that whatever state Tony was in when he arrived on Earth, his loss of memory of the angel realms would at least save him from monumental jet lag. However, the quindecillions of angels from all the realms of Angeland who were watching at the same time would have plenty to discuss after the match. When the missing striker Rita returned just before the end of the match, the excitement had reached an intensity that quite overwhelmed a good proportion of the audience after her poor initial showing in the game, her subsequent exquisite goals, and the unheard-of red card. Topping this, her assault on the Archangel Natasha as she strode off the pitch shocked the viewing angels even further, dragging them from the equivalent of the Coronation of Queen Elizabeth II to the most excruciating and violent of talk shows in one fell swoop.

Naturally enough, when Rita reached the top of the stand where Tony was, the Angel Cup final had become a mere distraction. The roaming cameras meant every angel eye was hanging on her every move and every word. There was eager and horrified expectation that Rita would perhaps go the extra mile and commit the last taboo possible (all this more unusual, maybe, than an archangel's eyelash detaching and lodging itself in a human's lung).

In any case Rita did not disappoint as the quindecillions looked on. She told Tony she loved him and then kissed him passionately.

There were some angels who said Tony made no discernible response, so there was no proof that he loved her. There were rumours of the couple having been seen hand-in-hand in downtown Hull, but there had been at least ten sightings of Tony and Rita impersonators together in Hull at other times.

There were an awful lot of angels who felt terribly jealous of Rita and wished they could be in her place, but never dared let on. There were a few who knew that love, however fleeting and in whatever form, brings us closer to infinity.

Archangel Natasha was somewhat disabled after the assault and did not have much time to reflect on the further sensational images of Rita. Someone was frantically telling her about Baily's beads in Hull, which didn't mean anything to her, nor did the talk of the diamond ring effect, which served to confuse her even further.

CHAPTER 47

A1

Perhaps we all should have spent more time with Plato. All the singing, the ultra-sports and the larking around Heaven and Hull is fairly harmless, but it doesn't provide the same time for reflection or self-improvement as a good read. When I consider it all, I think making a human live among angels, compared to my experiment 2,000 years ago to make an angel live among humans, went quite well. Seems like there are a lot fewer differences between the two in the end. I mean, you turn your back for an instant of geological time and not only the furniture but the beliefs flip upside down.

But I think it is definitely time to pull the beard back on. Or maybe not. Whatever, these capitalised gender pronouns really get on my wick. One thing is clear – it's about time I changed the executive committee. Although many are still performing well, it's time for a new broom.

I knew Mehi would understand one day. I mean, it seems a bit naive really to think that only human and not angel affairs are completely predictable. Except of course for angel football. If absolutely everything went like clockwork, things would be far too boring.

Now, where were we with the Final?

EPILOGUE

Tony had been quite constipated, but he was very satisfied when he did finally crap. When he came out of the aircraft toilet the captain was announcing that they would be landing in São Paulo shortly, and she turned on the fasten seat belt signs. The man outside the toilet was furious. He was not very attractive: obese and sweaty, with a spotty face, a stupid look and terrible scraggy hair, and wearing a T-shirt with a poodle on the front.

The plane was full. Tony passed a Middle Eastern guy in the front row who was playing with a gigantic Rubik's cube. 'Seventeen by seventeen by seventeen,' the man said to Tony, and continued twisting the cube back and forth with delight.

An Indian lady was singing gently to a toddler on one of the seats by the window, and she smiled at Tony. The toddler looked up and gurgled and said something like 'unny, unny', and waved her cuddly toy at him.

Further down, a ginger-haired teenager was cowed between two dominant-looking parents, who were reaching over him and scolding. They were pulling a duty-free catalogue back and forth and taking it in turns to whack the boy with it.

A gentle-looking elderly man sitting in the aisle opposite was reading a book, *Punting with Happy Ending*, and he nodded at Tony good-naturedly.

Opposite Tony's own seat, there was a woman who seemed to be deaf, blind and dumb. She had a neck brace, and Tony felt sorry for her. She was blonde and young and pretty. She suddenly lurched towards him for a second before her minder, a pleasant-looking young guy with a T-shirt announcing, 'J'ai fait l'UTMB' gently steered her back to her seat.

Tony sat in his aisle seat and cuddled the blanketed bundle with brown hair poking out of the top which was sitting in the adjacent window seat. The bundle moved towards him and exposed its lips for a kiss, then indicated to him to look out of the window. 'Dawn,' it said in a sleepy, muffled tone and snuggled closer to him.

Tony saw a beautiful blue sky, dotted with wispy white clouds, above a broad red band on the horizon, out of which the sun suddenly glinted like a diamond ring as it rose. Tony's imagination flew, caught for a moment by the idea of an angel landing on the wing.

ACKNOWLEDGEMENTS

Angeland was born fitfully after a long gestation period, with a good deal of early angst and self-doubt. Thanks are due to many people for their thoughts, advice and contributions. If I have inadvertently not mentioned anyone I hope they do not mind, knowing that they have mattered. The Cairo Write Stuff group commented on the first chapters as the book began to take shape. Kirsty Griffths and Gildas Bokonon-Ganta provided musical inspiration. Peter Koopmans and Sarah Hess shared visceral details about ultramarathons. Winifred van Gool, Fiona Hamilton and Geneva book club members (Julie Archer, Peter Godfrey-Faussett, Chantal Migone and Hiwot Haile-Selassie) read drafts of the book and provided valuable feedback and encouragement. Mary Ahern and Mary Ungoed-Thomas did fine copyediting and proof reading. Irwin Law's creative genius and patience gave birth to the cover. Gary Humphreys, Susan Tiberghien and other members of the Geneva Writers' Group provided perspectives on production. Chris Newton did a thorough and thoughtful edit. My wife Liza provided support throughout.